IN THE
BLACK

TOR BOOKS BY PATRICK S. TOMLINSON

THE BREACH

Gate Crashers

Starship Repo

INTERSECTION SPACE

In the Black

IN THE
BLACK

PATRICK S. TOMLINSON

TOR

A TOM DOHERTY ASSOCIATES BOOK
NEW YORK

IN THE BLACK

Copyright © 2020 by Patrick S. Tomlinson

A Tor Book
Published by Tom Doherty Associates
120 Broadway
New York, NY 10271

www.tor-forge.com

Tor® is a registered trademark of Macmillan Publishing Group, LLC.

The Library of Congress Cataloging-in-Publication Data is available upon request.

ISBN 978-1-250-30275-5 (trade paperback)
ISBN 978-1-250-30276-2 (ebook)

Our books may be purchased in bulk for promotional, educational, or business use. Please contact your local bookseller or the Macmillan Corporate and Premium Sales Department at 1-800-221-7945, extension 5442, or by email at MacmillanSpecialMarkets@macmillan.com.

First Edition: October 2020

Printed in the United States of America

0 9 8 7 6 5 4 3 2 1

My thanks go out to David Weber, Walter John Williams, Marko Kloos, and James S. A. Corey (both of them) for showing me how mil-spec sci-fi should be done and lighting a fusion torch under my ass to do it.

IN THE
BLACK

PROLOGUE

Hovering in the dark silence, it waited, and watched. It had neither ears to hear, nor a mouth to speak, because there was nothing to hear, and nothing to say.

It waited, and watched. That's what it was good at. Best at. Its endurance was measured in years, and its eyes could see everything from the infrared straight through to gamma rays. It never tired. It never grew bored or distracted. It could differentiate units of time down to picoseconds, or distances in parsecs. It was vigilance given form in metal and polymer.

And it wasn't alone.

It was the thirteenth of fourteen identical siblings, down from fifteen when the deployment began. One sibling had been lost to a micrometeoroid impact that had been below its detection threshold until it was too close to maneuver against, but the rest continued to function optimally. They floated within a sphere more than three AU in radius, each tasked with monitoring their own sectors of that volume, as well as providing overlapping coverage for one another. Whisker lasers kept them connected to each other and with Mother across the yawning chasm of space. It took two thousand, eight hundred and eighty-seven seconds for its data stream to reach its furthest sibling, and the same time again for a reply to arrive.

Since arriving at its assigned station two thousand, one hundred and forty-seven hours ago, it had tracked, identified, and catalogued more than seventy-three thousand objects inside its sphere of responsibility, eighty-six percent of which had been cross-checked and independently verified by a minimum of two other siblings. From protoplanetary dust grains only a few millimeters across, all the way up to comets and asteroids many thousands of meters wide, it tracked them all, assigned them log numbers, projected their trajectories, and assessed the threat level they presented to Mother's navigation.

But insofar as it could experience satisfaction, tagging specks of dirt and balls of ice did nothing to fill that requirement. It was a machine of war. Its sensors were meant for spotting and tracking missile plumes, warship emissions, and intercepting clandestine signals. Its adaptive camouflage and meta-material skin, identical to Mother's, was designed to fool or absorb enemy scans that went poking around looking for it.

It was intended to find targets for Mother's weapons, resolve firing solutions, guide missiles into armor belts, and warn Mother of incoming threat vectors. It was not built to chart billion-year-old planetary rubble. That sort of task was supposed to be left to astronomical survey drones. If it had lungs and air to breathe, it would've sighed.

An encroaching object set off its proximity alert, drawing its full attention. It reviewed the last six milliseconds of collision-avoidance radar data. The threat object was cylindrical, eleven-point-two millimeters across, moving at fifteen thousand meters per second on a direct intercept course. Projected impact in seven-tenths of a second. A full emergency chemical thruster burn would be necessary to avoid a collision. Blackout protocols stepped in to stop the burn, projecting such an action would mean an unacceptable risk of detection.

After a fraction of a millisecond's consideration, it overrode the protocols. Six hydrazine thrusters on its ventral surface erupted at once, expelling rapidly dispersing clouds of scorching hot gasses that would light up like torches for any passive IR scanners within ten light-minutes in every direction. The thrusters pushed hard to overcome the inertial momentum of its seven metric tons of mass to move it out of the threat envelope.

They were very nearly successful.

Its chassis shuddered under the glancing blow, sending shrapnel, electrical surges, and jarring vibrations throughout its internal structures. Fuses snapped open to protect delicate electronic components from burning out as its gyroscopes barked instructions to the thruster array to calm its chaotic spin and maintain station-keeping.

The violent gyrations came to heel with only seventeen percent of its hydrazine stores left in reserve. It could still maneuver under ion thrusters, or warm up its fusion rocket plant, but neither was capable of the short-duration, multi-g acceleration of its chemical rockets necessary for collision avoidance.

Nor was that the end of the bad news.

Diagnostic reports streamed in from its peripherals. Six panels of adaptive camouflage were damaged. Two were still drawing power, but had been cut off from the data network. Two burst capacitors were off-line. The portside gamma ray detector was out of calibration. Structural frame members three, four, five, seven, and eight had been compromised. But most importantly, its primary omnidirectional whisker laser gimbal mount was frozen and unable to remain locked on its mother.

It had survived, but would need a major overhaul to return to optimum functionality. It began the procedure to bring its secondary whisker laser mount online so it could inform its siblings of the impact and its diminished capabilities. At the same time, it turned an eye toward inspecting the debris cloud left over from the impact. Something about the incident nagged at its logic and pattern-recognition software.

It knew exactly what it had lost in mass down to the gram, and knew the chemical makeup of its missing constituents. Armed with this information, it turned a spectrograph toward the expanding junk cloud and scanned the particulates. After accounting for all its own damage and removing it from the analysis, all that remained was approximately twenty-nine grams of an unknown tungsten alloy refined orders of magnitude beyond the purity of any naturally occurring meteorite.

A bullet.

Its proximity alert tripped again. Three more threat objects approached, arranged in a perfect triangle, tracking from an identical vector and velocity as the first.

It had been boxed in. Any evasive course it could have taken away from the first projectile had led it inexorably into the path of one of the other three, and with such a paltry volume of chemical propellant left to burn, it couldn't escape a second time.

In that nanosecond, it knew what had happened to its lost sibling, and knew it was fated to fall to the same unseen enemy. It had failed to spot the intruder, but there might still be time to get word to Mother and its siblings. With the tenths of a second that remained, it warmed up its high-gain radio transmitter, overrode half a dozen communications blackout and security protocols, dumped all the data and telemetry it had collected in the last few seconds into an encrypted burst packet, and maxed out the transmitter's power output. In a last, desperate act, it relit its emergency thrusters and burned what little reactant it had left.

It managed to broadcast two and a half kilobytes of data before being obliterated.

"Hmm," Ensign Mattu said from her drone stream aggregation station on the CCDF *Ansari*'s virtual bridge. "That's weird."

Officer-on-Deck Esposito's avatar turned to face her wearing a quizzical look. "Define 'weird,' Scopes," she said, using the fleet's term of endearment for their sensor data interpreters.

"We just lost feed from a second recon drone, ma'am."

"Which one?"

Sitting at the VR chair in her quarters, Mattu pulled up a relative-time situ-map of the 82 G Eridani system, their home for the last three months on this impossibly boring tour of duty. Mattu highlighted the nonresponsive unit and kicked the map showing the assigned positions of the ship's web of Mk XXVI platforms over to the OoD.

"Platform Thirteen just went black."

"Lucky Thirteen, huh? Is that one of the birds NorKel serviced? They've been having integration problems ever since we pulled out of Proxima. Useless Nork contractors."

Mattu smirked. The competency of civilian technicians hired and trained by the NorKel Corporation was of no small controversy among fleet personnel, but a quick search of Thirteen's maintenance records disproved everyone's favorite scapegoat as a possible culprit. "No, ma'am. Last maintenance overhaul was done right here by our own deck monkeys on the return leg from the Tau Ceti deployment. And it gets stranger." Esposito's avatar held out an upturned hand in the VR environment of the bridge in a "Go on" gesture. "Well, Thirteen sent out a burst transmission just before it went off-line, on high-gain radio, not whisker laser."

"What did it say?"

"It's only a partial burst. The packet is tiny, not even a megabyte. We only got random shreds of the total file it was trying to send."

"Error codes? Letting us know what broke?"

"I thought so, too, at first. But if it was just error codes, why did it break radio silence protocols to send it over high-gain instead of the laser? I've never seen one of them make that call before. And there's more . . ."

"Well? Don't make me drag it out of you, Petty Officer."

"I just turned an eye over to Thirteen's last reported position. There's a cluster of IR contacts, lots of them cooling off quickly, but none of them big enough to be an entire Mk XXVI."

"You think that's what's left of Thirteen?"

"Probably."

"Didn't Eight go out like that, too?"

"Yes'm, three weeks ago. We put it down to a micrometeoroid hit. It's been known to happen."

Esposito's eyes narrowed. "But to two platforms in less than a month?"

Mattu shook her head. "I wouldn't bet a cup of square dog on that being a natural rate of occurrence, ma'am," referencing the ship's coffee supply, which came in square containers and tasted like dog shit.

"That *is* weird. I want you to pull archive data from the rest of the recon constellation, see if any of them had an eye turned toward their sibling in the final moments."

"Pull archives from the constellation eye, ma'am. What are you going to do?"

"Wake up the XO and pass the buck to him, God help me."

ONE

Captain Susan Kamala woke up in stages. After her first drill-filled training deployment in the Combined Corporate Defense Fleet as a lowly E2 banger's mate, she'd picked up the trick of waking up in the span between resting heartbeats. Twenty-four years later, after going mustang to become an officer and eventually captain, she'd mastered the art of recognizing when that trick wasn't necessary.

Instead of a blaring klaxon portending some unfolding calamity, the noise that had roused her from a rather pleasant dream about swimming in the Melville Ocean on Osiris was a gentle repetition of the door chime to her quarters.

Susan waved a dangling arm over the side of her bunk to trip the ceiling lights, which came to life and cast their harsh, bluish-white glow. They said the output gave the ideal balance of energy conservation while still delivering the wavelengths necessary to synthesize vitamin D, but nothing beat the sensation of soaking up real sunlight, melanoma be damned.

She unbuckled the straps over her chest and thighs that would hold her to the bunk in the event of gravity loss. She'd been lax about it as a younger officer, as were many other crewmen who'd entered the service after artificial gravity had been perfected. But her first CO came from the old school. He'd run a surprise drill in the middle of third shift where he ordered the gravity cut while a third of the crew dozed, then flipped it back on again. Susan had gotten a concussion, a reprimand, and a newfound appreciation for the importance of anchoring straps. She'd even run the drill herself once attaining command of her own boat, and broke an ensign's arm.

Susan swung her feet out into space and hopped down from her bunk. "Who is it?" she called to the hatch.

"Azevedo, mum," her Brazilian XO answered.

"Miguel, you do know it's . . ." Susan glanced at the chrono in her augmented reality retinal display. ". . . 0350, right?"

"Yes, mum. It's important."

Susan sighed. "Isn't it always? Just a minute. Unless you insist on seeing your captain in her undies?"

"Not if you paid me a bonus, mum."

"I'm not actually sure how to take that, Miguel."

"Anytime there's a question, default to respect, mum."

Susan smiled. "You're a smart kid; I'll just be a moment." She moved from the bed to her closet, which took all of two and a half steps. Compared to any other ship's quarters she'd ever occupied, the captain's suite aboard *Ansari* was palatial. But compared to any dirtside apartment she'd ever rented, it didn't even rank as a studio.

But it was hers alone: she had a bathroom with a door, a genuine water shower, and a kitchenette with the only supply of genuine Darjeeling tea to be found within four light-years of their current position. A gift from Miguel, as it happened.

And a steward for my laundry. She smiled as she pulled an immaculately cleaned and pressed duty uniform off the rack. She fell into the clothes from muscle memory alone, then went to the vanity in her bathroom to straighten her hair. It was longer now than strictly permitted by regulations, but seeing as she was the ranking officer for at least two parsecs in any direction, there really wasn't anyone to call her on it until the tour was over. Besides, Susan felt she'd earned the silver in her hair just as much as she'd earned the gold on her shoulder patches, and displayed both with equal pride. She donned the gold beret top cover with black trim of a warship commander in the commission of the Combined Corporate Defense Fleet, gave it the five-degree tilt to the left she fancied would draw attention to her good side, then touched her forehead and chest in offering to the two small statues of Durga and Shiva in the cubby above her bed she'd long set aside as a shrine. They were hollow porcelain instead of traditional solid marble, owing to personal mass allotment aboard a warship, but Susan assumed the Gods understood the sacrifices of military service.

Susan took the three steps to the hatch, spun the wheel until the toothed bolts hit the end of their tracks, then pulled the handle toward her. Her XO stood across the threshold, waiting patiently.

"Commander," she said playfully. "What brings you to my door at this hour?"

"We lost another recon drone, mum."

"Another?" Her mind recoiled at the thought. "A *second* meteoroid strike?"

"Scopes doesn't think so, mum."

"We're going to the CIC," she said firmly. "Warm it up."

"Yes, mum."

"And call everyone out of those stupid VR chairs. We have real work to do." Susan pushed past him across the hallway and called the lift. The captain's quarters sat deep inside the *Ansari*'s forward hull, safely behind many meters of armor, structural material, and other compartments, and directly adjacent to the main elevators to give her ready and rapid access to the rest of the ship. The Command Information Center was only two decks above, but the elevator was still the quickest way to get there.

The decks, all thirty-five of them in the forward hull, were stacked vertically along the ship's keel like the floors of a skyscraper turned on its side, instead of layered horizontally like the decks of an oceangoing vessel.

The *Ansari* was a class ship, the first and namesake of the CCDF's new generation of long-endurance, system-defense cruisers, and Susan was a plank-owner. Not as captain, but as a greenhorn ensign on her first assignment as a commissioned officer after her snotty cruise aboard the fast frigate *Halcyon*. The *Ansari* was seventeen years old now, and the paint had worn off her sharper edges, but the edges themselves hadn't been rounded down yet, and she was fresh out of the first of three planned midlife refits. It had been during that stretch in drydock that Susan had been reunited with her old ship.

The elevator stopped and slid open onto deck twelve and the home of the CIC, possibly the only spot on the ship buried underneath more armor and composite than the captain's quarters. Save for the antimatter confinement tanks, of course. One of the ship's marines stood watch just outside the main hatch to the CIC, polished, resolute, and bright blue in the face.

Susan buried a smile as she approached the young man. "Private Culligan, have you been holding your breath?"

His shoulders squared to parade-ground attention. "No, mum."

"Then why is your face blue?"

"Someone put microfracture test dye in my shampoo, mum."

"As revenge for?"

He began to blush, turning his cheeks purple. "I'm sure I wouldn't know, mum."

"Mmhmm. I hope it's not a permanent lesson?"

"Doc says a week for the skin to grow out."

"I see. Permission to enter the CIC?"

"Of course, mum." The azure private spun open the hatch

and, standing on tradition, leaned inside to announce "Captain on deck!" to an empty compartment.

"Thank you, as you were." Susan stepped over the lip of the hatch into the *Ansari*'s heart. Or more accurately, its brain. The compartment was still cool, but Susan could feel the air processors working overtime to warm it up to a more comfortable level. No one had been inside for weeks except to run system integrity tests and a drill or two.

Most of the bridge preferred to pull their shifts in the VR environment, as had become customary across much of the fleet over the last fifteen years. It held several advantages, not the least of which was that during a live combat situation, no single shot or internal failure could take out the entire command staff.

Still, Susan had been around long enough to have some of her own old-school opinions of the-way-things-are-done.

"XO on deck!" the private standing watch announced as Azevedo crossed the threshold followed closely by two junior officers and a noncom. The rest of third watch would be along in another few seconds or they'd be running crash assembly drills for a week.

"Stations, people," Susan said as she sank into the command chair, her chair, and thumbed it to her presets. "What do we know?"

Ensign Mattu, seated at the Drone Data Integration Station with a mop of hair that looked a little worse for the early hour, turned to face her captain. "We lost another Mk XXVI platform, mum. Number Thirteen. It wasn't an accident."

"And you can prove that?"

"Yes, mum, I believe I can."

Susan nodded. "Show me."

"It'll take a couple of minutes to compile all the data, mum."

"Take your time, Petty Officer."

Miguel took his usual position hovering behind Susan's left

shoulder, far enough not to intrude on her personal space, but close enough for his presence and support to be felt. He was, at present, the only man in the CIC, the rest of the stations filled by women and whatever Ensign Broadchurch settled on, if they cared to.

This wasn't unusual. Indeed, the *Ansari*'s crew complement was sixty-four percent female, which was right in line with crew breakdowns in the rest of the fleet. The demands of long-duration deep-space operations favored female recruits in a myriad of ways. Psychologically, women trended more toward cooperation and conflict resolution, while men tended to be more confrontational and competitive, which could cause friction and personality conflicts on long voyages. Women's bodies had been found long ago to have a slight edge when it came to tolerating high-g maneuvering. And most importantly, the average woman's daily caloric requirements were just sixty percent that of the average male, making their onboard food stores and aeroponics capacity last that much longer.

Indeed, the men who did manage to overcome these selection biases had to be very good to earn a slot. Of course, they had a very strong incentive to study hard and get a billet. If they did, they guaranteed themselves a place aboard a sealed metal tube where they were outnumbered two-to-one by young, physically fit women for eight to sixteen months at a time.

Needless to say, everyone was on birth control, and a lot of unauthorized "hot-bunking" went overlooked by the section heads.

"I'm ready, mum," Mattu said.

"Proceed."

The round plot table sunk into the deck at the center of the CIC glowed to life and traced a three-dimensional tactical map of the 82 G Eridani system in the air where everyone could see it. The *Ansari* sat at the center of the display orbiting Grendel, the fourth planet out from the star and the target of this round of surveys. Three different companies had joined up to tackle the claim in a rare display of solidarity. Ageless Corp. held a majority stake, but had partnered up with NeoSun and Praxis Inc. in smaller supporting roles. Usually, the only thing three or more transtellar boardrooms could agree on was the importance of the CCDF budget. "Fleet First" had become a mantra among the various corporations.

Much further out, between about two and four AU distance, icons representing the *Ansari*'s constellation of recon drones orbited the outskirts of the inner solar system in a shell. At these distances, the heavily stealthed platforms would be nigh invisible, even to the cruiser's powerful suite of active sensors. The real-time locations of the red icons were best-approximations based on data streamed in from the platforms themselves, adjusted for the light-speed com delay.

The plot skipped, almost imperceptibly at the scale of the display. The time/date stamp had moved back forty-three minutes. Mattu zoomed in on the coordinates of their missing drone until a red silhouette hovered in the air.

"We're about ten seconds before Platform Thirteen went offline. It's fully functional, just ran a surface diagnostic on itself three hours earlier. Network to its siblings and back to Mother is five by five. Then . . ." The drone suddenly jumped to life, sprinting away on six pillars of flame. But less than a second later, the feed cut out. ". . . it detects something and tries to evade, but doesn't have time. It takes one in the teeth and we lose telemetry. Still, we know Thirteen survives the first hit."

"First hit?" Susan asked. "There was a second?"

"CL on deck!" the marine on watch announced from the hatch. A middle-aged man, soft around the middle by military standards and busy tucking a button-up shirt into his slacks, stepped into the compartment. The only nominally civilian person aboard, Javier Nesbit was serving as the *Ansari*'s Corporate Liaison for the deployment. Every boat bigger than a skip courier had one. He served strictly in an advisory role, but as the designated representative of the interests of the shareholders or private owners of the consortium of the nine transtellars and their subsidiaries that contributed to the CCDF, his voice carried outsized weight.

Perhaps even more than his body did.

"Mr. Nesbit," Susan said warmly. "I'm glad you could join us."

Nesbit straightened his collar. "Yes, damnedest thing, but I didn't get notification we were having a powwow. I wouldn't have known it was going on if I hadn't heard the frantic shuffling of feet in the hallway outside my quarters."

"An unfortunate oversight, Mr. Nesbit, I'm sure."

"Uh-huh."

"You've only just missed the beginning of the briefing. We're trying to tease out what happened to another of our recon platforms. Ensign Mattu was just about to tell us what she's learned. Scopes, please continue."

"Yes, mum." The plot zoomed back out again. "We were lucky, because Twelve's wide-angle IR camera just happened to have Thirteen in its field of view at the time of the impact." The first hit replayed from the new vantage point. The image resolution was poor, but clear enough to make out the cloud of superheated gas coming from the drone as it strained against Newton. The exhaust cut off. "That's when we lost the feed from the whisker laser; I assume it was damaged. However . . ." Less than two seconds later, the thrusters lit off again. An eyeblink later, the drone exploded into an expanding field of dozens of heat point sources.

"Thirteen sent out the beginning of a burst transmission just before it died, encrypted, but over high-gain radio, breaking protocol, which is why I think its whisker laser was dead. It also tried to move a second time, but had already burned up most of its hydrazine. I think it saw the threat and was trying to tell us what killed it. That's why the onboard AI overrode its orders and switched to radio."

"But it was already damaged. How can you be sure its AI wasn't malfunctioning?" Nesbit asked.

"Virtual neural networks are firewalled like crazy to keep that from happening. They're also incredibly fragile. Any damage to the physical components and they just collapse. It's pretty much an all-or-nothing deal," Mattu answered confidently.

"And how do we know the explosion wasn't the result of an internal failure?" Susan asked. "The platform was already damaged; maybe there was a leak in the hydrazine tanks, or a deformation of one of the engine bells that caused the explosion."

Mattu nodded. "I can't rule that out, mum. But it doesn't explain why Thirteen tried to move again. It saw something else coming and tried to get out of the way. Maybe it blew itself up in the attempt, maybe it was hit. Either way, it was reacting to something."

Susan found herself nodding along. The ensign's argument was sound, even if she wished it wasn't. "So, what was it trying to avoid, micrometeoroids?"

"Two of them traveling in nearly perfect parallel courses less than five seconds apart? The odds against that are—"

"Astronomical," Miguel finished for her.

"Yessir," Mattu said. "Losing Eight two weeks ago was remarkable enough. But twice? With a follow-up shot? No way."

Susan took a deep breath, then let it out through her nose. "Well argued, Scopes. So, someone is not only finding our recon drones, but picking them off."

"I think we can consider our cage appropriately rattled, mum," Miguel said.

"How are they doing it?" Nesbit asked.

Susan turned to the head of her Weapons Department. "Warner?"

The stout, short-haired lieutenant looked like she could muscle a three-hundred-kilo guided missile onto the pylon of a dropship wing by hand if the situation called for it. She held up three fingers.

"Well, there's three possibilities: beamers, boomers, or bangers. We can rule out beamers, because you can't see a laser coming in order to dodge it in the first place. Boomers are out, too, 'cause even if you sent a missile in ballistic and set for kinetic kill only, the energies are too big. Even a glancing blow from a fusion-drive missile is like a low-yield nuke going off. There wouldn't be anything left." One finger remained up. "So that leaves bangers. A railgun round fits the circumstances. But that opens up its own questions."

"Like what?" Nesbit said. "We're not all tacticians, Lieutenant."

"Obviously."

"Lieutenant," Susan interjected. "No need to be rude. Mr. Nesbit's specialties inhabit a . . . different axis from ours. Please, give him a rundown."

"Sorry, mum. Mr. Nesbit. Just got yanked out of my rack, is all. Mattu, can you pull the projection out to the Red Line?"

The ensign nodded. "Yes'm." A moment later, the display zoomed out in scale once more, until it encompassed not just the inner system, but all the way out to twelve AU from the primary. At the twelve-AU boundary, a bright red dividing line encircled the system. This was the treaty line negotiated after the Intersection War. This was where company claims to a given star system ended, and free space began. It was the dividing line the Xre dare not cross, unless they wanted to find themselves on the receiving end of megatons or gigawatts.

"Thank you, Scopes. Now, the problem is twofold. One is detection. Our Mk XXVI recon birds are absolutely state of the art. Fresh off the assembly line for this deployment. They have the radar return of a peppercorn and the IR signature of a squirrel fart. We have trouble tracking them even when they're shining a damned whisker laser at us. I simply don't believe anybody could spot them from, what's the closest approach? Nine AU out? No way, I don't care how good their passive sensors have gotten."

"Fine, fine," Nesbit said tersely. "And the second problem?"

"If we're talking about railgun rounds, which we pretty much have to be, there's an issue of time-to-target. Our guns are a little slower than the Xre, but they're limited by the same physics and material science we are, so their projectiles cap out at a hair over fifteen kilometers per second. To cover nine AU at that speed, the projectile would've had to be fired . . . um . . ."

"Two years and nine months ago," Susan answered for her.

"Yes, Cap, that's right," Warner said after finishing the number crunching in her head, clearly impressed.

"I started out as a banger's mate." Susan smiled. "We worked out ridiculous shots in our spare time. So, Mr. Nesbit, the inescapable conclusion is someone fired a railgun almost three years ago at an invisible target that hadn't even arrived yet. . . ."

"Or?"

"Or, someone snuck their own armed drones into the inner system to kill ours."

"Why are you so sure it's just a drone and not an entire warship?"

Susan smoothed out a wrinkle on her tunic's sleeve. "Because, Mr. Nesbit, if they had the technological edge to hide an entire warship from one of our Mk XXVI platforms until it was inside banger range, there would be nothing preventing the same ship from killing every last one of us before we even saw the shot."

For a long moment, the only sounds to be heard in the CIC were the fans circulating warm air into the compartment. Nesbit cleared his throat to break the uncomfortable silence.

"Why are we sure this is the Xre and not, I don't know, commerce raiders, or claim jumpers?"

"Because . . ." It was Warner's turn, apparently. ". . . they know attacking our drones would be suicide. Corsairs are like cockroaches. They'll prey on the odd civilian transport, but they scatter at the sight of even a five-kiloton orbital defense cutter. The *Ansari* draws a quarter million tons. The dead-last thing any corsair operation wants to do is start poking us in the eye."

"I agree," Miguel said. "Someone is making a statement. They're demonstrating this new capability in a way we can't overlook or ignore. That someone believes they can match or beat a system defense cruiser in a stand-up fight, or they wouldn't be poking the bear."

"But how do we know it's a Xre incursion and not, I don't know, a CCDF ship?"

"A rogue crew?" Susan held an exasperated hand to her chest. "With the stalwart defender of the interests of fleet's stakeholders on the bridge to thwart them? Impossible."

Nesbit frowned. "There's no need to be disrespectful, Captain. We both have a job to do."

"You're right, of course, Mr. Nesbit. In short, no, I don't think it's a mutinous CCDF warship. We keep pretty good track of our inventory, and they'd have the same problems as a corsair, which they would effectively be the moment they stole fleet property. Why risk drawing our attention?"

"Okay, so it's a Xre incursion. What do they want?"

"Probe our defenses, gauge our new capabilities, observe our responses. It's been almost seventy years since the treaty, and almost thirty since the last skirmish. They're as intelligence-starved as we are. This is probably just a fishing expedition."

"So what do we do?"

Susan smirked. "Grab the rod and yank the fisherman out of their boat. Mr. Azevedo . . ."

"Mum?"

"Sound general quarters. Warm up our rings and make calculations to pop our bubble one thousand klicks sunward from the platform's debris field."

"Yes'm." The XO keyed the 1MC to bring his voice to the entire crew. A whistle chime sounded throughout the ship. "All hands, general quarters. General quarters. Prepare for Alcubierre transition. This is not a drill. Repeat, this is not a drill." He cut the circuit. "Helm, what's the status of our rings?"

"Alpha and gamma rings are in the rotation for our next jump, sir," Ensign Broadchurch answered. "Engineering board's green."

"Bring them online and make calculations to pop the bubble at one thousand kilometers sunward and zero velocity relative to plot marker six-two-seven-dash-three-eight."

"Zero relative velocity one kiloklick sunward of marker six-two-seven-dash-three-eight, roger, sir."

Susan casually removed a piece of lint from her trouser leg. "Manual calculations, Charts."

"Mum?" Broadchurch said, sounding quite a bit less confident.

"Make your calculations without the flight computer. You do remember your astrogation certifications, yes?"

"Yes'm. Just, um, haven't used them since the Academy. I might be a little rusty."

"A warship is no place for rust, wouldn't you agree, XO?"

"Absolutely, mum," Miguel agreed.

Broadchurch swallowed. "Of course, mum. I'll just . . . um." They turned back to their station and started digging through menus.

Miguel leaned in close and whispered in Susan's ear. "That's a pretty tight window to calculate by hand. What's that have to be accurate to—nine decimals?"

"Eleven," Susan said. "Don't worry, the closest planet is more than twenty light-minutes away. We're not going to pop our bubble in a molten core. I just want to see what Broadchurch's got."

"Your ship, mum."

"Captain, I recommend we bring CiWS and our active targeting array on line. If there's an armed drone out there, we should be ready to deal with it in case it takes a shot at us," Warner added.

Susan nodded. "Do it."

A few tense minutes of frenzied math equations later, Broadchurch looked up from their station. "Okay, I think that's got it."

"You *think*, Ensign?" Miguel inquired sternly. "I'd rather not go into Alcubierre on a hunch."

"No, sir. I mean, I have it sorted."

Susan smiled. She sympathized with Broadchurch, she did. But she also needed to know her helmsperson wasn't going to beach them on a proverbial sandbar if the ship started taking damage and had to get gone in a hurry. The ship's mainframe was at least thirty years out of the state-of-the-art compared to consumer electronics, but for good reason. It was a time-tested and dead-stable system. Still, every computer, no matter how many built-in redundancies, could malfunction. And when that happened, if you couldn't break out an abacus and do the maths, you were dead in the water.

She knew from experience.

"Okay, Charts, lock it in. Scopes, do we have a clear sky for transition?"

Mattu pulled up a display of the local airspace around the *Ansari*. "We have a weather satellite inside the gooey zone moving away at seventeen kps relative. It will reach minimum safe distance in . . . twenty-seven seconds."

"Charge rings. Bring us to one-two-six-point-eight-seven-one by zero-zero-one-point-three."

"Charge rings. Bring us to one-two-six-point-eight-seven-one by zero-zero-one-point-three," Miguel repeated.

"Come about to one-two-six-point-eight-seven-one by zero-zero-one-point-three, aye sir. Charging rings," Broadchurch echoed back.

A slight tremor ran through the deck plating as reaction control thrusters at the bow and stern lit off and gently aligned the grand ship with its destination, then counterburned to cancel their momentum.

"On trajectory, mum," Broadchurch said.

"Sat has cleared the gooey zone. Sky is clear," Mattu reported. "We're green to blow the bubble."

"Thank you, Scopes. XO, at your pleasure."

Miguel nodded. "Helm, blow the bubble."

"Blowing the bubble, aye sir." Broadchurch reached up a finger to their holographic display, touched a floating icon and, with very little fanfare, bent the known laws of physics to within a micrometer of their breaking point.

Behind the *Ansari*'s forward hull, where all the perishable organisms resided much of the time, lay the engineering hull. Inside it were most of the ship's mechanicals, long-term stores, drone launch tubes, and of course, negative matter condensers. Mounted to the outside of the engineering hull were three enormous rings stacked one after the other like hula hoops. These were the Alcubierre rings, the innovation that had made FTL travel possible. Like poles on a magnet, a ship needed two rings to create the stressed spacetime field bubble that allowed them to skirt Einstein's speed limit. Like all warships in the CCDF larger than a corvette, the *Ansari* held one ring in reserve in case of malfunction or battle damage. In a civilian ship, this would be an unjustifiable extravagance in both tonnage and cost, but in the harsh math of military preparedness, two was one and one was none, so it only followed that three was two. The largest assault carriers went so far as to mount four rings for a fully redundant set.

At the push of the virtual icon at the helmsperson station, banks of capacitors inside the engineering hull released a torrent of energy through three structural pylons into the stream of negative-matter plasma channels and radial gravity-well accelerators inside the rings themselves. Outside the rings in a rough sphere reaching out to five hundred kilometers and change, spacetime had a little fit as it tried to sort out exactly how it was supposed to be shaped. This was, in centuries-old naval parlance, the "gooey zone," so named because the effect this warping of spacetime had on anything or anyone unfortunate enough to be trapped within it were not conducive to continued mechanical or biological functioning as they tended to end up the consistency of chunky peanut butter.

However, *inside* the gooey zone, the *Ansari* pinched off a perfect little bubble of universe of its own. Several things happened then that maybe six living people actually understood. The *Ansari* stood perfectly, absolutely still inside its little bubble universe, while powerful gravitational eddies stretched spacetime at the bow, and compressed it at the stern. Twisting the very fabric of the universe in such a violent and unnatural way came at a price. Nearly an entire recon platform's worth of antimatter fuel had to be annihilated just to charge the rings to create the bubble in the first place.

Pulled from ahead and pushed from behind, the bubble universe took off like a scalded cat. At its center, the *Ansari* sat, perfectly serene and immobile. It was impossible for anything to travel through space faster than light, and would remain so until the death of the universe. But space didn't actually care what it did inside itself. A simple-enough idea that had regardless taken centuries to take from bar napkin, to blueprints, to hardware.

Trapped inside its bubble, the *Ansari* was completely cut off from the outside. The inside surface of the bubble reflected any light or other active energy emissions. If the ship had portals, a crewmember could wave and see a funhouse mirror image of themselves waving back. Anything inside the bubble was nigh-invulnerable to anything in the universe outside, except against sufficiently intense gravitational shearing, such as the forces found inside a star or black hole, which could collapse the bubble prematurely, then collapse everything inside it permanently.

The downside was, as long as they remained inside it, the *Ansari* and her crew were completely blind. They couldn't see out to know if they were on course or to see approaching dangers. They couldn't make any midcourse corrections. They just had to trust in their astrogation and hope for the best until it was time to pop the bubble and see where they ended up.

In the case of this jump, they didn't have long to wait. The *Ansari* covered the twenty-six light-minutes of the journey in less than four seconds. The precision necessary to drop them exactly where they wanted to go was beyond human reflexes. A preset countdown that ran out to eleven decimal places reached zero, and the same sequence that created and sustained the bubble ran in reverse, collapsing it in an instant almost too short to measure. The ship reappeared in the "real" universe at a dead stop.

A small bow shock of gamma rays burst out and continued on in the *Ansari*'s direction of travel at the speed of light, the remains of the handful of dust grains and stray high-energy particles that had gotten trapped on the outer surface of the bubble during the jump. Over such a "short" distance, the effect was minimal. But it compounded the longer one traveled in Alcubierre. After a few light-years, the burst of gamma rays was powerful enough to destroy ships or punch holes in atmospheres. You *really* had to be careful where you pointed an Alcubierre bubble when it popped.

"Jump complete," Broadchurch reported.

Susan worked her suddenly sore jaw. Something about Alcubierre transitions always made it clench involuntarily. A succession of ship's doctors had told her that was impossible and it was psychosomatic, but it stubbornly kept happening anyway. "Stand down alpha and gamma rings," she said while working her mandible.

"Stand down alpha and gamma rings," Miguel echoed.

"Standing down alpha and gamma rings."

"What's our position?" Susan asked.

"Coming in now, Captain. We are . . . nine hundred forty-seven kilometers sunward of grid marker six-two-seven-dash-three-eight at zero-point-one-nine-meters-per-second closing rate."

"Not bad, Charts," Susan said with satisfaction. "You're a few dozen klicks past the line. Do you think you can beat that on the next jump?"

"I will certainly try, mum."

"Weapons, where are we?"

"CiWS is hot and streaming data from the active array," Warner answered crisply. "Decoys and countermeasures on standby. Missiles on standby. Ready to bring up the laser and rail-gun systems."

"I think a ship-killer missile half again as big as a combat drone might be a little overkill, Guns."

"Overkill is my job, mum."

Susan shook her head. Some things were universal among weapons officers. "Scopes, bang away with the active sensors. Damn our EM signature. If there's something hiding out here, flush it out."

"Yes'm."

"Also, launch four armed drone platforms and establish a perimeter of a half million klicks at bearings zero, ninety, one-eighty, and two-seventy relative to the eclectic. Don't bother stealthing them, go full active sensors."

"Bait, mum?" Mattu asked.

"Something like that."

"Yes'm. Armed drones at compass points flat to the eclectic. Should be ready to launch in t-minus ninety seconds."

"Good. XO, alert Flight Ops to get a shuttle and an EVA team ready. I want them in vacuum in fifteen minutes."

"Mission profile?"

"Retrieval. Bring back the biggest piece of Thirteen they can find for inspection."

"We're in an unsecured combat zone. Marines'll probably ask for combat air patrol to run cover for their bird."

Susan considered this for a moment. "That's fair. Scopes, launch another armed drone and hand it off to Flight Ops."

"Launch CAP drone for the recovery bird, yes'm," Mattu answered.

Satisfied, Miguel moved away to get on a com line to the small craft bay.

"Okay people, we've cut the hole in the ice and dropped our line in. Now it's time to lean back and wait for a nibble."

"I thought we were the fish," CL Nesbit said dryly.

"Yeah." Susan allowed him the point. "I guess I lost track of the metaphor."

TWO

It was Tyson Abington's favorite part of the day: when a hush came over the office tower as its occupants filed out from another day's labors for a night of well-earned relaxation with their friends and loved ones.

For Tyson, it was one of the few moments of calm during the day when he could reflect and appreciate everything he and long generations of his family had built. His two-meter frame stood up against the transparent aluminum observation window of his penthouse office, close enough he almost left a nose print on the cool metal.

The transparent metal was ten centimeters thick, yet clear as a still pond. It was seamless, and required no structural bracing, being more than strong enough to carry unaided the weight of the dozen engineering floors and communications antennas above it. Both electrical power and data passed through it wirelessly. The optical clarity and lack of framing made the illusion that the ceiling was simply floating overhead incredibly convincing. It was easy to forget the "glass" was there at all. An expensive illusion to create, but on nights like this, Tyson knew the extravagance had been worth every nudollar.

The space took up the entire two hundred and eighty-eighth floor of the Immortal Tower in the heart of downtown Methuselah, capital of the entire planet of Lazarus. The nomenclature sounded ominous, but its history was quite innocent, bordering on cheeky. At the dawn of the company, Tyson's forbearer, the legendary Reginald Abington, had been a brilliant engineer and savvy businessman. He'd been the first to perfect and patent an industrial-scale method to condense negative matter using over-lapping gravity wave interference. The resulting company was named Abington Gravitonic Engineering, or AGE for short. Over the generations, AGE became Ageless Corp., and once Ageless set up shop on its very own colony world, well, the names sort of picked themselves.

For reasons of pride and exclusivity, the Immortal Tower was the tallest building in Methuselah. It would remain so in per-petuity, on account the Abington family owned all of the air-space above seven hundred and fifty meters inside the city limits, and anyone that wanted to build above that height had to pay a monthly licensing fee that increased logarithmically with each additional floor.

Technically, Ageless owned the airspace, as all the transtel-lars were publicly traded companies by law. But the Abingtons had managed to maintain a controlling interest over the centuries through clever maneuvering and more than one "incentivized" marriage proposal. Ageless wasn't the largest transtellar, or the wealthiest, but it was one of the oldest, and the most stable. It had provided for its customers, shareholders, and employees in equal measure for centuries. Tyson took immense pride in his family legacy, and felt the weight of his responsibilities as its newest stew-ard every day.

He inhaled deeply, the native air laced with the slight cop-per smell that somehow survived even the best HEPA filtration. Between the shield mountain ranges that protected Methuselah from the gale winds of the rest of the planet's equatorial regions, the pulsing heart of the city spread out before him. It was electric with trains of transport pods, buzzing drones, and blinking pedestrian crossings. The lower commercial and residential districts mingled with green patches of parks, and blue rivers cut through the entertainment district both to provide recreation and cooler temperatures in the city's hot summers. Thin, needlelike towers raced up to the seven-hundred-fifty-meter "ceiling," many connected by a latticework of aerial walkways that let the people working inside save the trouble of going all the way down to street level and up again just to attend a meeting.

Stretching down Shensing Boulevard directly in front of him, "Embassy Row" played host to the Lazarus headquarters of the other major transtellars, as well as two towers jointly owned by half a dozen of the smaller consortiums. It also had the only two legitimate embassies on the entire planet: the UN embassy representing the interests of the governments of Earth, and the Xre embassy, which had stood empty since the day it had been built more than seventy years earlier. Tyson considered them both equally egregious wastes of high-value real estate, even if he never voiced the thought publicly.

Methuselah was a thriving company town of almost six million people and nearly as many AIs. A blooming city in the desert.

His city.

Tyson often fancied himself a gardener in concrete and steel, tending to a forest of commerce. Things grew tall on Lazarus. With only three-fifths of Earth's gravity, everything from plants to people to buildings to rockets had an easier time reaching for the sky.

Which made it all the more surprising when things came crashing back down again. An alert in a search algorithm he'd programmed into the office during the first hour of his occupancy flashed in the window. The trading day was over, but overnight trades were projecting a sudden drop in Ageless's stock price of sixty-three nudollars, well outside the typical background variation.

At that exact moment, a camera drone flying the colors and symbol of the Interstellar News Network dropped down from somewhere above his floor and hovered at eye level, recording his facial expression with its binocular cameras in gloriously unflattering UHD.

"Sir, there's a problem," the voice of his personal assistant, Paris, said almost simultaneously.

"Yes, there's an INN drone violating the airspace outside my office, for starters."

"Of course, sir. Let me just . . ."

A second later, a micro missile little bigger than a pen came screeching down from a Triple-A battery on the roof, struck the camera drone dead center, and blew it into four spinning pieces. Tyson watched them tumble toward the ground for a moment, then returned his attention to the matter at hand.

"Thank you, Paris," Tyson said, the warm feeling in his stomach instantly replaced with ice in his veins. "Bring yourself on screen, please."

Paris's false-depth image assembled itself from wire frame to full rendering in less than a second, her svelte body, tailored business suit, horn-rimmed glasses, and pinned-back hair hovering on the other side of the clear aluminum window like a particularly alluring ghost.

"What's happened?" he asked. "Why are we down sixty points an hour after the bell?"

"Sixty-three," she corrected. She was very precise. AIs always were. "A bulk freighter, the *Preakness,* just arrived from our colony in Teegarden's Star. There's been a bacterial outbreak among the colonists. So far, the strain has proven resistant to all available antibiotic treatments."

Teegarden's Star hardly ranked as a proper colony. None of

the little red dwarf's four planets were candidates for terraforming, nor their moons. But the night side of the tidally locked innermost planet was a veritable gold mine of rare earths and precious metals. Body-for-body, the mining operation there was one of the more lucrative operations Ageless had going in human-controlled space, even if it was only a small percentage of the company's total revenue stream.

"How many employees are infected?"

"Well, all of them, sir," Paris said with uncharacteristic hesitation. "There have already been three fatalities."

"Fatalities?" Tyson barked uncomprehendingly. "From a *bacteria*?"

"It appears to be quite virulent. And it's proven difficult to isolate, due to an airborne vector."

"How many employees in situ?"

"Three hundred and six, not including the three fatalities."

"Shit! How are we only hearing about this now?"

"Shipments to and from Teegarden occur quarterly, sir. This was the first ship to come from there in two and a half months."

"Why wasn't a skip courier sent immediately?" Tyson raged.

" . . . "

"Well?"

"The board of directors decided a permanently attached skip boat was an 'unnecessary extravagance' for a stable, low-priority outpost, sir. You signed the recall yourself."

"I did?"

"Yes, sir. Last year."

Tyson blushed. "Fine, rescind that order immediately. How did someone else hear this report from my ship before I did?"

"Are we sure that happened?"

"Your software has a better explanation for the sixty-three-point drop in our overnights?"

"No, sir. I suppose not."

"Well then? Who read this first and how?"

"I don't know, Mr. Abington," Paris said. She only used "Mr. Abington" when he was pushing her too hard. Tyson tried to calm himself.

"I'm sorry, Paris. It's not your fault, of course. Just . . . dig into the network and see what you can find out. Bribe some of the other AIs if you have to. I'm releasing five hundred thousand to your discretionary account."

"Thank you, sir. I will do my best."

"I know." He rubbed a temple. "Call up a dozen of our best infectologists and epidemiologists and get them on a fast courier boat back to Teegarden. Full hazard pay for the duration and a five-thousand-share bonus when they fix this thing. Get them all the gear they ask for. And make sure it's all in the press release. We need to be proactive about this thing and make sure everyone sees us doing it."

"Of course, sir. That's an excellent response. There's just one item you're overlooking."

"And that is?"

"The bulk freighter, sir."

"Yes? What about it?"

"It needs to be quarantined, both the cargo and the crew."

"But we'll lose an entire quarter's worth of revenue from the mines!"

"And if we don't, we risk losing Methuselah, maybe all of Lazarus. Well, you squishy meat puppets at the least."

"Was that a joke, Paris?"

"I've been practicing. Was it good?"

"It was morbid." Tyson rubbed a fresh knot at the back of his neck. "The cargo modules aren't pressurized on an ore freighter. There's no need to waste the air or energy keeping the cargo warm. Can't we at least off-load the haul?"

"There are currently six thousand, three hundred and forty-seven different bacterial spores known to medical science that can survive in the hard vacuum and radiation environment of

interstellar space for extended durations. Without having catalogued this strain, we can't know if it shares that capabili—"

"Yes, yes, all right." Tyson swore under his breath. The value
of the ore in orbit was a paltry sum compared to the quarter's
bottom line, but it was the *appearance* of the thing. Just letting an
entire megaton shipment languish in a parking orbit over his own
capital was like tying an albatross around his own neck. He'd be
hearing about it at lunches and whispered at charity events until
it was sorted. But, there was nothing for it. Paris was right, damn
her software. The downsides would be catastrophic if the dice
didn't land in his favor.

"Quarantine the crew and the shipment. Make sure that's in
the press release, too. Along with hazard pay for the duration and
thousand-share bonuses for the crew. Make sure they want for
nothing while they're locked up in that flea-trap."

"Very good, sir."

"And Paris?"

"Sir?"

"There's a memory upgrade in it for you if you find whoever
leaked this before it reached me."

"And an android carapace?"

"Are you *negotiating* with me, Paris?"

"I would never, sir. But, my Download Day is coming up in
two months, and . . ."

Tyson smiled, despite himself. "And an android carapace."

Paris nodded her perfectly sculpted virtual chin. "Thank you,
sir. I won't fail you."

"I know." Tyson turned his attention back to his city, and
marveled at how quickly night fell in the valley.

THREE

"There!" Mattu jabbed a finger at the floating holographic display. If it had been a pane of glass, it would've shattered. "There you are, you *beti chod.*"

"Language, Scopes!" Weapons Officer Warner chastised.

"You speak Hindi, LT?"

"No, but I know a fucking swear word when I hear one."

Miguel stepped over to the Drone Integration Station, blinking away sleep as he did so. They'd been searching for the armed drone everyone assumed was responsible for the death of Thirteen for a double rotation already. Everyone was exhausted, but no one wanted to be the first to admit defeat and crash out in their quarters. "You have something to share with the class, Mattu?"

"Yessir," she beamed. "I've spotted our interloper." She transferred the feed from her station to the CIC main plot. A red sphere hovered at the center of the plot less than a light-second from the *Ansari*'s current position, slowly pulling away from the debris field of their ill-fated recon drone.

"Visual acquisition?" Miguel asked, but Mattu shook her head.

"Their adaptives are just as good as ours. This thing could be sitting on the far side of our boat bay and you wouldn't see it."

"Then how did you?"

"Simple; it's trying to slink off under ion drive, keeping its ion trails pointed far enough away from us so we can't pick them up."

"But?"

"But we've got it surrounded by enough recon birds now that I was able to work out an emissions triangulation. I don't think it spotted any of them or it would've been smart enough to just go cold and drift."

"They must not know we held back a reserve of recon platforms," Miguel mused.

"Thank Shiva for the extra capacity we got out of the last refit," Mattu said.

A recent technical briefing floated to the top of Miguel's mental queue and triggered a smile. "That's not all we got from the yards. Get the captain up here, double time. And Warner, it might do you good to warm up one of our new fog machines."

"Captain on the deck!" the sentry announced as Susan put boot to floor of her CIC. The staffing situation hadn't changed since she'd pinched off for a little rack time four hours earlier.

"Didn't any of you get relieved?" she asked incredulously.

"We were offered relief, mum," Miguel said.

"I see." She pointed at the big red ball hovering at the center of the plot. "What's that?"

"That's our phantom drone killer, mum."

Susan grinned the sort of grin that serves only to reveal teeth. "I was hoping you'd say that. We have confirmation? Scopes?"

"As certain as I can get without a directed X-ray ping, mum. It still doesn't know it's been spotted, didn't think it would be prudent to tell it."

"Good thinking. How long have we been tracking it?"

"Less than five minutes," Miguel answered. "I thought this might be a good time to test one of our new toys."

Susan arched an eyebrow. "The fog machine?"

"The fog machine."

"Risky. Probably ill-advised. The suits will be angry we rushed it into deployment."

"So, warm one up?" her XO said.

"Would be an awful waste not to."

"Already in the tube, mum," Warner announced.

"It's like I don't even need to be here," Susan announced with mock indignation.

"CL on deck!"

"God dammit!" Nesbit bellowed from underneath a bird's nest of mangled hair, his lapel-less suit jacket forgotten in his cabin. "Twice in one day, Kamala? That's a formal protest."

"I only just arrived myself, Mr. Nesbit, I assure you. Now, I'll have to ask you to control your temper on my bridge. We're still in an active combat zone, and . . ." She pointed a slender finger at the plot. ". . . we've got something on the hook."

Nesbit's eyes flitted over to the red icon and locked on. "Is that—Is that the hunter/killer?"

"No other reason for it to be hanging around the crime scene," Miguel said.

"It's not, you know . . ." Nesbit adjusted his shirt collar. "We're not at risk, right?"

"Not at all. It can hurt our drones, but it's a mosquito to the *Ansari*'s elephant."

"And I was just about to swat it," Susan said. "So, Mr. Nesbit, if you could observe from over to the side, please."

"Hmm? Oh, right. Yes, of course." Nesbit stepped into the hatchway, as if poised to make a quick escape if things didn't go as smoothly as Susan's quiet confidence promised they would. "I'll just . . . be right here."

"Excellent. Lieutenant Warner, isn't there supposed to be a fog rolling in?"

"Ready and waiting, mum."

"Excellent. XO, live fire is authorized. We're going for a hot-zone field test of the CLVL Mk . . . what was this damned thing, Mk II, III?"

"III, mum," Miguel said.

"Mk III. Fire when ready."

"Weapons officer, fire the CLVL," Miguel shouted.

"Firing CLVL, sir."

Somewhere deep within *Ansari*'s quarter-million-ton mass, a single, five-meter-long missile accelerated along electromagnetic rails to three hundred meters per second and was thrown clear into the harsh vacuum, cold, and radiation of space. In accordance with Newton, the great ship lurched sideways almost imperceptibly in response to the toss. Station-keeping thrusters fired automatically to cancel the movement.

"CLVL away," Warner announced. "Internal tracking has acquired the target. Clearing safe minimum distance. Fusion rocket coming online. Missile is burning hot. Man, look at the bitch go. . . ."

The Communications Laser Vector Locator Mk III was a weapon tailored for a singular, limited purpose. Indeed, it would be difficult to categorize it as a weapon at all if it weren't for modifications added to the Mk III model after trials of the Mk I and II units. It was the sort of military appropriations project that only ever made it from drunken symposium "what if" conversation to deployment if you had a lot of bored engineers with absurd budgets looking for something to do with their time.

Fired from a standard counter-missile launcher, and encapsulated inside a standard CM casing, guidance system, and fusion-drive rocket, the CLVL deviated from its defensive brethren only in its warhead and purpose. Instead of tracking incoming ship-killer missiles and blowing them out of space before they could harm Mother, the CLVL tracked hostile recon drones and illuminated the way to *their* mother.

Seven seconds after launch, and the CLVL was already accelerating at nine gravities, piling on velocity with every passing moment. Its internal radar and external telemetry feed from Mother both pointed it in the general direction of the target a few tens of thousands of kilometers ahead. An ablative conical shield acting as the mounting plate for its fusion rocket served double-duty deflecting high-energy particles that were a waste product of its fusion reaction at obtuse angles away from its sensitive internal electronics and sensors, as well as the sensors of its prey. So long as it kept its target inside this null cone, its approach could go unnoticed.

An eternity later, the CLVL reached its effective threshold. It separated into two halves. A powerful explosive charge in the front quarter of its forward section detonated, dispersing a cloud of trillions of microscopic reflective grains. For less than a millisecond, the cloud enveloped the hostile drone, while full-spectrum cameras In the remainder of its forward half watched intently.

Spaceborne drones under stealth, regardless of who'd built them, used laser coms to communicate. The reason was simple. Unless an observer was in a direct line of sight between the drone and their mother, the signal couldn't be intercepted, jammed, or altered. It had been the standard for encrypted tactical communications for centuries. And with quantum encryption, there was really no chance of decoding any messages even if one were sitting in direct line of the beam.

But that wasn't the point.

Out of trillions of nano-scale particles, six managed to blunder into the pulse of laser energy the enemy drone directed toward its mother. A small portion of that energy reflected off of their crystalline surfaces and found its way back to the cameras in the back half of the CLVL, which then took those six geometric points in space and used them to draw a line twelve meters long.

A line that gave a direct bearing back to the drone's mother. In the end, less than a hundred photons was all it took to tell the tale.

Distance couldn't be ascertained, but direction would be enough. The CLVL took two final steps to fulfill every demand that had been placed on its existence. It sent the data back through its telemetry link to its own mother, then ordered its fusion rocket in its aft section a few dozen meters behind to detonate.

Both it and the enemy drone winked out of the universe in the fires of a short-lived star.

"Got it!" Warner shouted triumphantly. "Solid bearing captured, and enemy drone splashed."

"Scopes, confirm that," Susan said.

"Fusion detonation confirmed." Mattu's hands danced in the air as she manipulated her display. "Both missile and drone destroyed."

"Bearing to target?"

"Three-two-nine by zero-zero-four," Warner said. "And change."

"Release the telemetry to the Nav station. Charts, please put that bearing up on the main plot."

"Yes'm. Getting telemetry now."

In the tactical display, a bright streak of crimson started at the point where the CLVL just detonated and receded off into infinity just a sliver above the system's eclectic plane.

"Scopes, are we sure the drone didn't get a message off about the fog machine?" Susan asked after Mattu.

"The whole process from cloud deployment to fusion detonation took less than a hundred milliseconds, and the CLVLs throw out a riot of EM jamming. I can't be *absolutely* certain, but I don't think even one of our AIs could take in all that sensor data, analyze it through all the white noise, come to the correct conclusion, and encrypt it for transmission in that time frame. I think it's safe to assume the secret of our new toy is safe for the moment."

"That's good enough for me." Susan smiled. "Good work,

everyone. We've successfully deployed a brand-new weapons system in live fire without a single hiccup. That might be a record all by itself. Double ration of pudding tonight. And Mr. Nesbit, I think a letter of commendation for its development team might be in order back at corporate."

"I agree wholeheartedly, Captain."

"Maybe even a bonus?"

Nesbit straightened a cufflink. "That's really not for me to decide, but I'll pass it along with my report."

"Of course. Charts. How long before our rings are ready for another jump?"

"Alpha and gamma still going through cooldown and negmat recycling. Five minutes to reset," Broadchurch replied.

"Let alpha ring take a break and bring beta online."

"Yes'm."

"Wait," Nesbit wavered. "You're not actually thinking about going after that thing?"

"That's kind of the point of finding its bearing, Mr. Nesbit," Susan responded frostily. "I'm tasked with patrolling this system. Someone has just committed a treaty violation. This is a warship, if my memory serves. Weapons Officer, we do have weapons onboard, yes?"

"Oodles, mum," Warner said without containing her glee.

"Well, there you have it. Scopes, how long to get our birds back in the barn?"

"They're pretty far out, mum. Even at full burn it'll take the better part of two hours to get them to turn around, and another two hours to bring them into recovery range."

Susan paused to consider this. The *Ansari* was powerful enough as a combatant in her own right, but her real strength lay in the data-gathering and situational awareness afforded by her flock of embarked drone platforms. They were the web to the ship's spider, sending invisible signals through the silk wherever a wayward fly stumbled into one. That's how she'd earned her nickname of "Orb Weaver." A black spider with a leg resting on each of the eight planets of mankind's home system emblazoned the ship's mission patches and challenge coins.

Personally, Susan hated spiders. Something about ambush predators that didn't work for their dinner bothered her. But, it wasn't her call. The nickname had already been in the books for years before she took command, and you just didn't mess with a ship's history like that. Even dozens of light-years from their home, sailors were still a superstitious lot. And even she had to admit the metaphor was appropriate.

Leaving her drones behind wouldn't blind her, not really. The ship had an envious suite of both passive and active sensors, as well as a towed array in the aft that spooled out on twenty kilometers of space elevator ribbon that was almost as powerful as the sensor clusters mounted on the *Ansari* herself. But it was a far cry from the multiple redundancies and overlapping perspectives of a proper flight of recon drones.

Still . . .

"Leave them with instructions to rendezvous at these coordinates, Scopes," Susan decided. "We'll pick them up on the way back."

"Yes'm."

"You're leaving our recon and combat drones behind?" Nesbit asked. "Doesn't that strike you as particularly reckless when we're going into, you know, combat?"

Susan laced her fingers and leaned forward in her command chair. "Mr. Nesbit. I understand the importance of good relations between the fleet and our sponsors. Indeed, I encourage them. But I will remind you that your role in my CIC is in an advisory capacity for the financial interests of the stakeholders we're tasked with protecting, not to question my orders or undermine my reasoning in front of my crew. So, if you have *specific advice* to give, I'm open to hearing it."

The rest of the bridge crew froze amidst the sudden drop in temperature. Nesbit fidgeted.

"I just . . ."

"Yes?"

"I just wonder if we aren't rushing into this confrontation without first maximizing our chances of success." He pointed at the red line on the main plot. "If I understand correctly, and please correct me if my limited tactical experience is failing me, but the mothership that sent the drone we just destroyed could be anywhere along that line from here to the Small Magellanic Cloud. It would seem to me that abandoning a significant portion of our sensor capacity while we go looking for this interloper puts us at a disadvantage."

Susan let him finish. In truth, she didn't have much choice. Corporate liaisons were almost universally despised by command crews throughout the fleet. It was rare to get a sympathetic one, and they were deliberately drawn from well outside naval ranks to maintain "professional dispassion." Nesbit wasn't the worst she'd seen, but he was the first she'd had to answer to as ship's captain.

And you never forgot your first.

"I can see why that would concern you," Susan said with a voice like soft butter. "However, there's two things you're overlooking. First, while you're technically right that our quarry could be anywhere along the bearing we captured, or at least was expected to be at some point along the bearing at the time the drone's light-speed transmission arrived, we can narrow that window down considerably. Indeed, I can narrow it down to a single point in space."

"And where's that?"

"Simple. If I'm commanding that mother, I won't cross the treaty line. That puts me and my crew in jeopardy for little gain. But, I'm going to put the paint of my bow plates right on the line so I'm getting as close to realtime data from my HK drone as physically possible. She's there, I'll put a bag of real coffee on it."

"All right," Nesbit allowed. "But that doesn't explain why you want to engage them before we recover our drones."

"I was coming to that. The drone we just destroyed was in the middle of sending a light-speed transmission. In less than two hours, that transmission will cut off suddenly, probably right in the middle of screaming that there's a missile coming at it. Our guest will know that we've destroyed their drone and probably relocate or leave the system entirely. But, as of right now, we can blow a bubble, jump ahead of the drone's light cone, and catch them totally by surprise."

"If your hunch about their location is correct."

Susan held out her hands, palms up. "There is always a degree of uncertainty in any operation. But this is well worth the risk, in my opinion."

"But . . ." Nesbit wrung his hands. ". . . won't that reveal our new capability? I mean, if we pop our bubble right off their bow, they're going to know we've developed a way to trace their laser coms. Do we really want to give them that intel?"

Miguel sucked air through his teeth. "He's got a point, mum. All they'll know in a couple hours is we jumped in to investigate our missing drone and stumbled onto theirs. But if we show up and ring their doorbell, they'll know something's up, even if they can't figure out how we did it straightaway."

"It won't matter if we get the drop on them and capture or kill their ship," Susan responded.

"That *assumes* they're where you expect them to be, and *assumes* it's a single raider we can defeat easily and not a task group that will hammer us into scrap," Nesbit blurted out, anxiety singing in his voice like a too-taut violin string.

But, just because he was a coward didn't mean he was wrong. Existential terror had a way of focusing the mind. Susan took in a deep, meditative breath, then let it out through her nostrils. He was here to advise, and only a fool turned away good advice on account of its source.

"That's a fair point. Options?"

For a long moment, everyone went silent as they churned through the possibilities.

"C'mon kids, open forum," Susan chided.

Ensign Mattu was the first to speak. Or at least ask permission to. She actually raised her hand.

"Just talk, Mattu. It's the CIC, not primary school."

She put her hand down. "Yes, mum. Sorry, mum. We could fake ignorance. The bogey's bearing is twenty-three degrees off the shortest distance from the drone we just destroyed to the Red Line. We could wait until our platforms are back aboard, then jump out to that point."

Susan bobbed her head. "Make it look like we're taking a stab in the dark."

"Exactly. Then we launch drones at full burn banging active sensors in both directions along the perimeter. Let them see us doing it."

"It would be hard to miss," Miguel contributed.

"Wait, this gets better." Mattu's excitement was infectious. "We wait to move, but we don't wait for our drones to get inside sensor range of the bogey. Instead, we—"

"Jump the gun," Susan interrupted. "We jump in, and if their mother is still there, and even if they manage to escape, they go back home believing our drones' threat detection range is far wider than it actually is. They report back to Xre Central that the little humans have leapfrogged them in sensor tech, and they're boatloads more cautious the next time they try to pull a stunt like this, and never guess about the fog machine. Oh, Scopes, that is *properly* devious."

"Thank you, mum."

"That's our action plan, people," Susan announced. "Make it happen. Time is money."

FOUR

"Derstu, you are needed in the mind cavern."

The cool, artificial voice repeated twice before Thuk finally stirred in his den. His body was cold, owing in no small measure to the fact his skin was still too tender from molting for clothing or blankets. He'd turned the den's heat setting up as high as it went before his fugue cycle, but it was never enough.

"Derstu . . ."

"I take the path," Thuk said to the ceiling. And he would, but first he needed to stretch and align his limbs. As soon as he stood, Thuk could feel he'd lain on one of his legs wrong. With effort, he managed to straighten it out using the surface of his den's waste receptacle. Another day of this and his new shell would be rigid enough that he wouldn't need to worry until his next molt. He'd gone an entire cycle once with a misaligned plate on his left mid-arm. It was a maddening experience every Xre had a maximum of once, because they were certain never to repeat it.

Thuk took a moment to regard himself in the stillwater mounted to the wall of his den. His shell was still pale and soft. He looked like an oversized larva, which matched the way he felt.

Assigned as derstu, on his first expedition. Of all the rotten luck . . .

Thuk stretched all six of his limbs, trying to pull the wrinkles out of his new shell and set his joints properly, but something hadn't felt right since his last fugue. An itch in the middle of his back, down near his thorax junction. He contorted his abdomen, trying to get an angle on his back in the stillwater. Sure enough, right at the bottom of his abdominal segment, one of his old plates hadn't come free during the molt.

"*Cru*," he swore as he grabbed a scratch pole with a midarm. Trying to guide the scratch pole in the reversed image of the stillwater threw him off, but after three attempts, he got a claw under the slightly curled lip of the errant plate and pulled it free with a *Slurpt*.

He held the last vestige of his old shell in his primehands, turning it over several times as if inspecting a forgotten toy from his larvahood, then dropped it unceremoniously in the waste receptacle and flushed it into the ship's reclamation system.

"New molt, new me," Thuk said, trying hard to believe it. He grabbed a couple of cozzi out of their tank and popped the heads off and into the waste receptacle. Even decapitated, the little snacks wriggled until he crunched them between his mandibles and ground them up between his saw plates.

The small meal sated Thuk's hunger for the moment, but it wouldn't last. Xre were always ravenous in the aftermath of a molt as their bodies rushed to replace lost nutrients and minerals drained away by building a new shell.

"Den," he called to the ceiling.

"Yes, Derstu?"

"Please have a plate sent to the mind cavern. I'm famished."

"Do you have a preference of dish?"

"Something hot and crunchy."

"It will be waiting for you when you arrive, Derstu."

"Thank you." Normally, eating in the mind cavern was against decorum, but allowances were made for a derstu coming out of molt. He needed to be sharp of thought to understand and properly implement the orders of the rest of the ship's harmony, after all. His shell was still tender, but less so than it had been before the night's fugue. He decided the discomfort of a uniform was worth it to hold back the chills.

The garments, especially the seams, rubbed against the soft folds of his elbow and shoulder joints, and the sensory cilia on his arms and back. He would endure. He still looked like a larva, or a sun-bleached corpse, but at least some warmth returned to his core. The ascender was just down the hall, just fourteen paces. It felt good to stretch all of his leg segments. It was important to maintain a full range of motion while the new plates hardened.

A short ascent later and the mind cavern doors opened before him. Several members of the harmony sat in their alcoves, busy with their assignments, monitoring the grand ship's myriad of systems.

"Derstu." Dulac Kivits stood from his seat at the husk-monitoring alcove. Or as much as a member of his caste ever stood. The morphology of the different Xre castes was significant. Where Thuk's body was slim, featured four arms and two legs, and was optimized for moving through the tight confines and labyrinthine tunnels of a mound, Kivits's body was stout, had four legs and two arms, and a flattened upper thorax. His body plan was ideal for gathering food and materials on the rolling plains on the surface and carrying them long distances back to feed and expand the mounds. Before the time of the Grand Symphony, Kivits's caste was considered laborers at best, beasts of burden at worst.

Of course, those days were centuries in the past. But old prejudices were a hard thing for any people to shake completely.

"Dulac," Thuk answered with the formal title, as Kivits had done. He looked around the mind chamber. "Where's Garesh?"

"She has begun her molt."

"Naturally," Thuk said. It was inevitable; the longer members of a harmony spent in close proximity, the more their molt cycles aligned. It was a problem that remained unsolved even after centuries spent in the dark ocean. "The harmony needs my assistance? Is it about our husk in the inner system?"

"Indeed, yes. Come . . ." Kivits beckoned for the derstu to join him in the husk alcove. Before he'd gone into fugue, the harmony had taken up position at the bright line across the dark ocean and launched an armed husk toward the inner planets to hunt. Of course, it wasn't the only husk they'd launched. It had taken weeks, but the harmony had arranged their own sphere of sniffer husks at the treaty line looking inward at everything that moved inside the system.

Long-range scans had already confirmed the presence of a CCDF cruiser in orbit of the third planet, an *Ansari* type if their eyes were any good. The Grand Symphony had sent their harmony here to scout out the system and test the human's capabilities against Xre's newest generation of husks, sensors, and their newest warship itself.

It was a bold, unusually aggressive move. The treaty between Xre and the human infesters had been stable for decades. It had kept the peace along their spinward border, allowing the Grand Symphony to continue their expansion hubward and counter-spinward without wasteful expenditure on making war against an enemy that proved itself shockingly resilient and resourceful.

Thuk questioned the Symphony's wisdom of sticking a claw back in the human's mound, but only within the confines of his skullplates. It wasn't a derstu's or a harmony's duty to second-guess the Symphony's pronouncements, only to bring them to life.

The husk they'd launched more than a moon ago had already gone beyond expectations, having detected, stalked, and killed two of the human's most advanced "recon drones." But now, looking at the readouts in Kivits's alcove, Thuk knew their brave little husk had run out of luck.

"When did we lose it?"

"A quarter dayslice ago, while you were in fugue," Kivits said.

"Why wasn't I called then?"

"You needed rest, and we always assumed we'd lose the husk eventually. We were fortunate to take down two drones in the first place. It was on loaned time as it was."

"What changed?"

"The human ship, we're almost certain it is the *Ansari* itself. Not just type, but the launch. There's enough sniffer recordings in the core to be very confident of that."

"So we've named the ship. What else?"

"It's acting . . . strangely," Kivits said.

"Continue."

Kivits expanded the display to the surrounding walls of the mind cavern until a panoramic surround of the sensor environment filled the space.

"Within an eighth dayslice of their second drone falling, the humans entered a seedpod and jumped in. They quickly launched more husks to search out—"

"More?" Thuk interrupted. "How many more?"

"Twelve."

"How did they recover husks so quickly?"

Kivits wiggled his midarms. "They didn't. These were still in their nests onboard."

Thuk clicked his mandibles once. The *Ansari* wasn't exactly a new type. Other harmonies on other ships had managed to get good, reliable scans of them over the years. Its capacities and capabilities were well-established with a high degree of confidence.

"Then it's carrying too many husks. A new subtype, or a rebuild?"

"Possibly. Or newer, smaller husks doubling up in the nests."

Thuk thought through the implications. Double the husks meant double the sniffer density, fewer gaps, more overlap, or control of a greater effective volume of dark ocean for each of the human cruisers in service. Sneaking around on the edge of what they'd anticipated was outside the cruiser's detection threshold as they were, it wasn't a pleasant thought.

"This merits closer inspection. We'll want to get confirmation of this new capacity for the Symphony."

"Yes, Derstu, but that's not the strange part. After a quarter dayslice, the humans sniffed out our husk as it tried to sulk away silently. They destroyed it with a javelin shortly thereafter, but then . . ." Kivits focused in on a part of the treaty line closest to the fallen drone. ". . . they entered a seedpod again and jumped right up to the treaty line at this location. They've been there ever since, and have launched even *four more* drones traveling down the line in either direction along the eclectic."

"Smart," Thuk said admiringly.

"But they're nowhere near our true location?"

"There's no way for them to know that." He pointed at the human ship and drew a line back to the dead husk. "This is the shortest distance between where they knew our husk to be and the treaty line. Where is the ideal place to be controlling a husk from? Where you get the least lightlag, right? The humans know this as well as we do, so they jumped to the most likely place we might be hiding, then started their search. Run it backward for a moment." Kivits obliged. "Stop there. Good, now resume. Take notice of the timeflow when our husk falls. Now, look at the time it takes them to jump. If we really had been there, the *Ansari* would've jumped inside light-spear range before we'd even known our husk had fallen."

"Ah, yes. I see now."

Thuk itched at a seam in his uniform. "I'm impressed. These humans are clever, aggressive, and willing to take risks."

"A gamble that wouldn't have turned out in their favor even if they had been right," Kivits said dismissively. "A cruiser is no match for the *Chusexx,* no matter how many extra drones it carries."

"Yes, yes, our proud new warship and its clever new weapon has never lost a *simulated* battle. But they would have had a free hand to open the fight, and we've underestimated human ships before to our doom," Thuk chided. "Besides, we're not here to fight, just stir their mound a little and see what happens. That's what the Symphony requested."

"I have not forgotten, Derstu," Kivits said. "But I hope you will not forget that our first duty is to protect our harmony."

Thuk wiggled his primehands. "It won't come to that, not this time at least. Their drones are shouting out into the dark ocean, their echoes are bouncing off each other. We'll remain a while longer and learn as much as we can, but as soon as *Chusexx* is within double the detection range of those drones, we're seed-podding out of here. There's no sense risking becoming the hunted. And speaking of hunting, where's my plate?" As he said it, one of the mind cavern's doors irised open and disgorged a young runner holding a crescent-shaped tray wriggling with food. "Ah, just as I was about to eat a midarm."

"Sorry, Derstu," the runner said as he, she, er . . . *they* panted with exertion. They were very young, five, maybe six molts. It would be another molt at least before their gender became apparent, even to them. All four of their arms strained under the weight of the tray. A whole nest of gims crawled through a pile of purple and red jewel fronds. The little eight-legged creatures bulged at the seams of their shells, yet still munched away, oblivious to their impending fate.

"Mmm. Thank you, runner. Return to your duties."

"The harmony sings." They bowed and retreated as suddenly as they'd appeared. Holding the crescent with his midarms, Thuk picked out a particularly fat gim with a primehand and popped it into his mandibles. It made a very satisfying crunch in its death throes as the nutty protein of its shell and pollen-fed flavor of its flesh mixed in his mouth. As much trouble as being selected derstu could be, Thuk had to admit the food was quite a perk.

"Delicious," he said as he sunk into his chair and picked another gim. "Would you care for one, Kivits? They're perfectly ripened."

"It would be rude to refuse, wouldn't it?" Kivits snatched up a modestly sized gim from the tray and bit it in half. "Mm. Yes, the farm has churned out a good batch today."

"Did you know, Kivits, that humans prefer their meat dead?" Kivits shuffled his mandibles in disgust. "Yes, they store it cold, then warm it back up to simulate life. Revolting practice."

"Yes," Thuk agreed. "That's what I thought as well. Indeed, when we first learned about their culinary habits before the Intersection War, many of our wisest scholars preached that since humans were unwilling to kill their food themselves, it naturally followed that they would be too squeamish to take lives in battle." Thuk crunched down on another gim. "That prediction proved overly optimistic."

"Is there a lesson you're trying to share in this, Derstu?"

"A musing only. A curious bit of history I've always found . . . 'humorous' is the wrong word. 'Paradoxical,' perhaps."

"Well, if our scholars were as omniscient as they seem to believe, we wouldn't need the Grand Symphony. We could just go back to the infallible leadership of divine queens."

"That is true enough," Thuk said. "But the prejudice was hardly limited to scholars. Indeed, as silly as it seems today, the belief was common throughout the Symphony that—" Something nagging at the back of Thuk's skullplates jumped and waved its arms for attention.

"Is something wrong, Derstu?" Kivits asked, concern playing across his face and limbs.

"No, it's just . . . Are our rings warm? How much lead time do we need to spin a seedpod?"

"Our rings have been on standby since we took up position, you know that. And their drones are still more than an eighth dayslice away from having any chance of—"

The shriek of proximity alarms cut through their conversation like a blood-claw. All around them, the mind cavern blossomed with light. Sniffer readouts, tactical assessments, warnings, all sprang to life and competed for attention. The other members of the harmony who had been listening to the back-and-forth between their derstu and dulac with practiced indifference suddenly came to life in their alcoves and began barking updates.

"Situation!" Thuk shouted above the din as his forgotten tray clattered against the floor. Liberated gim scurried for cover in every direction.

"It's the *Ansari,* Derstu," someone shouted back. "They've peeled their seedpod."

"How far?" Thuk demanded.

The sniffer-reader blanched, frozen in place. Kivits pushed the hesitating member to the side of their alcove to read the sniffer data for himself. His face turned to Thuk, the bravado suffusing their earlier conversation forgotten. "Twenty-three hundred markers. Derstu, we're already in range of their light-spears. Their claws are around our throats!"

Thuk grinned. Bold humans. Foolhardy humans. They had no idea what kind of predator's den they'd just jumped into. But that was the thing about them. Even if they did, they'd probably jump in anyway.

"Well, the humans would never—" was the first half of a sentence that had gotten a lot of very experienced, very capable harmonies killed in the last war.

"How did they see us?" Kivits shrieked. "We're hundreds of thousands of markers outside their husk's eyes."

"Obviously we need to revisit our estimates," Thuk said dryly. "Or did you think the humans were in a fugue since the war?"

Kivits stared at him. "You asked about our rings. How did you know?"

"I didn't. Just—had a strange itch was all."

"They're singing to us!" the recorder alcove's attendant shouted.

"Put it to the mouths," Thuk ordered.

"Unidentified [Xre] warship," a human voice crackled over the mind cavern's mouths—female, if his ear was attuned. A translation played out in text on the panoramic displays. "This [Derstu] Susan Kamala CCDF cruiser *Ansari*. We corner and destroy one your [predator husks]. You violation treaty. Surrender instant and we will—"

Thuk cut the connection from his seat's controls. "Eject three decoys. Now. Burn them hard to our sides and vent."

"And us, Derstu?" Kivits asked.

"Forward, Dulac," Thuk said with as much calm as he could force. "We burn straight forward."

FIVE

"Xre warship, sixteen thousand klicks dead ahead, mum!" Warner shouted. "Class unknown, but it's big."

The right corner of Susan's lips curled up into a crescent that creased her cheek. "That'll be a hundred nudollars, Mr. Nesbit," she said.

"I don't recall wagering on it, Captain."

"It was implied in your tone, Mr. Nesbit," Susan said. "Coms, hail the vessel."

"Mic's hot, mum."

Susan leaned forward in her chair and turned her shoulders as if she was on camera, which she wasn't.

"Unidentified Xre warship. This is Susan Kamala of the CCDF cruiser *Ansari*. We have intercepted and destroyed one of your armed drones. You are in violation of the treaty. Surrender immediately and we will hold fire. Refuse to surrender and we will be forced to—"

"Link's been cut at their end, mum. They're no longer receiving."

"Sounds like an answer to me," Warner said from the weapons station.

"Agreed."

"Do we really want to fire first?" Nesbit asked.

"We didn't," Susan snapped back. "They did. Naval law is clear. A shot fired from a drone is a shot fired from its mother. We're on defense here."

"I think they've already made the call," Mattu said. "They're rigging for silent running. Detecting three fusion plumes, designating bogeys Alpha, Bravo, Charlie. Wait one . . . I'm seeing back scatter and particle wake interference off Bravo contact moving away. Possible fourth contact."

"Boomers?" Susan asked.

"No, accel is too low. Probably decoys." Mattu's fingers moved in a flurry across her display. "Confirmed, now showing four mirrored contacts of identical radar signatures moving apart at two-point-three gs at ninety-degree intervals. Bogey four designated Delta. Delta's headed straight for us, mum."

"Ignore it," Susan said. "And ignore the one moving dead astern, that's too obvious. This one's sneaky. Focus your active scans on the contacts moving to port and starboard."

"Yes'm."

"And kick out a decoy of our own. Send one straight at contact Delta. Make it loud, like we fell for their feint. Then switch to passive sensors and make like a hole."

"Decoy running hot and loud for contact Delta. Switch to passives, aye mum." Mattu hit no more than a half dozen points on her display before something deep inside the *Ansari*'s bones groaned. "Decoy away. Clearing minimum safe distance in three, two, one . . . deploying."

In the open space a few hundred meters from the *Ansari*'s outer hull, three tons of sodium azide and potassium nitrate reacted in the blink of an eye to inflate the decoy's ballute. In seconds, the Kevlar-reinforced mylar film expanded into a one-to-one scale, seven-hundred-meter-long, parade-float copy of the *Ansari*'s silhouette.

Its surface reflectivity across the EM spectrum was calibrated to be identical to its mother to all but the most powerfully invasive active scans above the X-ray range. It would even hold up to a cursory pass by visual telescopes if they were more than a couple thousand clicks away. Robust transmitters in its drive module mimicked its mother's active EM emissions for a limited duration. On the beat of zero in an internal countdown, the decoy's fusion rocket lit off and piled on acceleration toward its designated target.

"Fusion plant's burning," Mattu reported. "Plume looks good."

"Good." Susan took a breath to consider her options. "Move or die" had been drilled into her from the first day of naval combat tactics during officer candidate school. "Ships at rest rest in peace," her favorite instructor had been fond of saying. But moving in the wrong direction, piling on delta-v that Newton didn't let you just wish away, could be just as deadly.

The two most likely candidates for her quarry were moving away from each other on opposing bearings. The parabolic radiation shield mounted ahead of her ships' fusion drive section not only kept her crew from being microwaved to death, but also provided a thirty-five-degree cone in the *Ansari*'s frontal aspect where an opposing warship couldn't detect the gamma ray emissions from her hybrid antimatter/fusion rockets.

It was the same reason why Mattu could only deduce the existence of contact Delta from the interference patterns its rockets had on the plume of the decoy moving in the opposite direction. The trouble was, with the two most likely contacts moving away from each other on mirror headings, if Susan ordered pursuit of one, it would give the game away to the other one. Even if she picked the warship, the decoy would have to be completely blind not to see her drive plume and alert its mother.

Her own decoys mounted only a rudimentary sensor and coms suite, but they weren't blind, and Susan couldn't imagine the Xre would be so incompetent.

She couldn't afford to reveal herself now that her decoy was in the sky. So, going against years of training, she settled on the least-worst option.

"Maintain position. XO, I need spreads of six cold boomers port and six starboard in the vac and ready to track. Laser array on standby."

Miguel nodded. "Yes'm. Weapons, prep VLS cells A1-S and A1-P. Launch six Mk IXs from each, cold drives. Designate flights Alpha and Bravo and link their telemetry into our passive sensor stream. Await orders to fire once target is resolved."

Warner sat up straight in her chair. She didn't say it, but Susan knew it was the first time the young lieutenant had put ship-killer missiles in space in anger. Indeed, the first time anyone had since before anyone aboard had been born.

Shooting down a drone was one thing. Firing on another proper warship filled with other sentient beings, no matter what naval law said, was quite another.

"Launch flights of six Mk IXs port and starboard, cold drives, awaiting target acquisition for order to fire. Yessir."

Unlike the drone and decoy launch bays in the engineering section, the *Ansari*'s complement of offensive missiles were located in the four outer faces of the forward hull in four Vertical Launch System modules divided into ten cells of six missiles each, for a total of two hundred and forty missiles. The deck swayed under her feet as twelve of the seventy-ton monsters ripple-launched into space on electromagnetic rails, one from each side at one second intervals to make sure they didn't collide.

"Flights Alpha and Bravo in the black and cleared for maneuvering. Data links established, telemetry looks good. Drives on standby."

Susan considered the plot. They were within laser range, if only just, but the two bogeys were inching out of it with each passing moment and there wasn't time to get monocle drones in place. Besides, no matter what she'd said to Nesbit, she wasn't sure she wanted to draw first blood on a Xre mother out here when she was on one side of the treaty line and they were on the other. Lasers were functionally instantaneous; there was no way to know they were coming until the transfer energy was already boiling away armor.

But missiles, they not only had the legs to reach both bogeys, but the Xre captain would know they were coming and would have time to reconsider her order to surrender. She could call off the attack at anything but the last fraction of a second. Susan had half a mind to light them off and see which target started firing point defense. That would answer the question simply enough.

"Aspect change on contact Delta," Mattu shouted. "Angling twenty-three degrees away from our decoy, I think they fell for it, mum."

"Or they're just going through the motions," Susan said. "Any tells on bogeys Alpha or Charlie?"

"Nothing yet. They're . . . wait one."

Automatic alarms sprang to screeching life through the CIC. "Bubble blowing!" Broadchurch shouted over the wails.

"Alpha or Charlie?" Susan barked.

"Neither mum, it's Delta. Repeat, Delta!"

An electric shock of panic ran from Susan's scalp to her tailbone. The one she'd ignored, because it was too obvious. They'd hid right in the middle of her assumptions. "How far?! Are we in the gooey zone?"

"Negative," Broadchurch replied. "We're safe, barely."

Susan relaxed the death grip on her chair's armrests. "Are they inside the treaty line?"

"By twelve kliks, mum."

"XO, laser free, target their rings."

Miguel turned his head toward Warner. "Weapons, laser free. Full power. Target rings for a mobility kill. Repeat. Mobility kill only."

"Lasers hot. Mobility kill, aye sir." Warner tapped a few icons, refined her targeting lock, and pressed the button.

For an almost imperceptibly short moment, the lights and displays in the CIC dimmed as the ship's power system adjusted to the sudden, violent depletion of bank after bank of capacitors as the laser array gobbled up every spare electron.

A beam of coherent light energy only forty-five centimeters across, yet powerful enough to supply electricity for an entire continent, raced out into the night at Einstein's speed limit, covering the fourteen-hundred-and-seventy-kilometer distance between the *Ansari* and the raider in a span of time scarcely worth mentioning.

And it was still too late.

"Do we have a hit?" Susan pleaded, almost leaning out of her chair.

"Negative," Warner said, dejected. "The beam bent. Their bubble closed before we got the shot off."

"Shit!" Susan pounded her armrest with a fist.

"And now they've jumped," Broadchurch reported. "They're gone, mum."

"If we had a window, we could've stuck an arm out and waved at them," Miguel said before thinking. Susan shot a glare his way. "Sorry, mum."

"And," Mattu tagged in, "our decoy was caught in the gooey zone. I'm sorry, mum, but it's slag."

Susan's teeth ground against each other. She felt a migraine coming on. "All right, it could have been worse. Another few hundred klicks and we would've been the decoy, and there's still three enemy decoys out there we can recover for the lab rat to tear apart for intel. Charts, set course to—"

As she said it, three fusion bottles let go simultaneously, adding a trio of incredibly short-lived stars to the history of the universe.

"Er, sorry, mum," Mattu said, "but the Xre decoys have all self-destructed."

"Of course they have." Susan stood up from her chair. "XO, you have the Com. Recover our missiles, then jump back and grab our drones. Let me know when you're done."

Miguel nodded. "Understood, mum. Where will you be?"

"In the pool. And the rest of you, take your relief already. You all look like hammered dog shit."

Susan stalked out of the CIC, her head filling with proper butterfly stroke form and lap counts, anything to push the thumping she'd just taken to the background. She shoulder-checked Nesbit as she passed him to get to the hatch.

In a rare moment of self-awareness, Nesbit had the presence of mind not to say a word.

SIX

"Tyson!" called out the matronly voice from near the back of the restaurant. He locked eyes with Valeria Sokolov as she waved from a small booth in the left corner by the wall. The CEO of NeoSun beckoned for him to join her.

Paris had only received her lunch invitation fifteen minutes earlier. Tyson had to reschedule two calls and cancel a crisis response meeting to accommodate the impromptu rendezvous, but not even he could afford to decline a meeting with the leader of the second largest transtellar in human-controlled space. Especially when he was running a joint project with her company.

Tyson nodded to her and moved toward the booth, grabbing a napkin from an empty table as he passed to wipe a bead of sweat from his brow. He'd had to run from the pod to arrive in time. He'd not exercised in ages. Muscle-toning retro-virals made it unnecessary. Of all the improbable sights people on the sidewalk could have seen that afternoon . . . Actually, watching him duck into a casual-dining chain restaurant might be even more ridiculous.

Tyson slid into the booth opposite from Sokolov, the imitation leather of the bench seat feeling strange under the silk of his trousers.

"Thank you for coming, Tyson. I realize it was short notice."

"A trifle." Tyson waved away her concern. "Just juggled some things around, you know how it is. But, Valeria, I have to ask . . ." He waved an arm to encompass their surroundings. "Really?"

Sokolov chuckled. "Don't be rude, Tyson. It's quaint; besides, it's good to remind ourselves how the other half lives now and then. There's joy to be found in simple pleasures."

"Like the joy of two-for-one appetizers that made a fifteen-light-year trip a few degrees above absolute zero only to get re-heated in a microwave?"

"Salt and saturated fat taste delicious no matter how far they've traveled."

A young woman, wearing a uniform, wholesome in a not overly attractive way, slid up to their table with a small data pad on the back of her right wrist. Her left wrist and hand were decorated in a delicate lattice of traditional henna designs that she probably thought made her seem exotic or cultured.

"Hello, folks. My name's Cassidy and I'll be taking . . ." A flicker of recognition passed over her features as she glanced at Tyson, but it passed in an instant. ". . . care of you. Can I get you anything to drink besides water?"

"Just green tea for me, please," Tyson said. "Hot."

"I'll have a vodka press with a twist of limon. Make it a double," Sokolov said.

"Okay." Cassidy entered their drinks into her pad. "I'll be right back with your drinks and to take your order."

"Oh, and dearie, could we get an order of those exquisite southwest egg rolls? Two cups of dip."

"Of course. Comin' right up."

As their waitress skittered away, Tyson folded his hands in his lap. "Southwest egg rolls? Southwest relative to what?"

"The old American Southwest, I believe," Sokolov answered.

"Although the last franchise on Earth closed almost thirty years ago. Still, they do great business among nostalgic expats out in the colonies."

"How do you know so much about a chain? Do you have one on New Vladivostok?"

"What, this place? Heavens no. I denied the permit myself. We have to maintain our exclusivity."

Tyson almost took the bait. He almost rose up to defend the presence of a Chili's in his capital city when a moment ago he was ready to order it torn down. Sokolov was notorious for twisting her opponents into emotional pretzels during negotiations, causing them to lose sight of their own interests and endgames to go chasing after some rabbit that had inexplicably been laced up to their pride. As a result, NeoSun had jumped three ranks in the transtellar hierarchy under her twenty-seven standard years of leadership.

Tyson had experienced it himself during the talks over NeoSun's involvement in their recent joint venture. He'd assumed it was an artfully crafted performance, like a carefully choreographed dance where only one partner knew the steps. But now, sitting in a Chili's booth during lunch rush, Tyson wondered if it wasn't something that came naturally to her.

"Well, we're a frontier town here in Methuselah, and our cowpokes need a watering hole," he said instead. "Speaking of my city, I didn't know you were in it. Not until twenty minutes ago, that is."

"That's because I'm not in it."

Tyson's left eyebrow inched up ever so slightly. "Ah, my mistake. Because I could have sworn I was sitting across from you in this booth on an unannounced lunch meeting."

"That's also not happening."

"Mmm," Tyson purred. "A conspiracy."

"Nothing so grandiose, I assure you. We're just here for a friendly chat between colleagues." She quieted down again as Cassidy reappeared with their drinks.

"Are we ready to order?" the waitress asked in a hopeful tone.

"I think the appetizer will be enough, thank you dear."

"Sounds good, it'll be up in just a couple minutes." Cassidy disappeared into the lunch crowd again.

"So . . ." Tyson refocused his guest. "What brings you—and don't say you traveled thirty light-years for egg rolls, because I won't believe you."

"A courtesy," Sokolov answered back. "You, and by extension I, have a small problem brewing in the black."

Tyson's heart fell two rungs down the ladder. So, word of their difficulties at Teegarden's Star had made it all the way to New Vladivostok, despite his best efforts at spin control and containment.

"We're on top of it."

It was Sokolov's turn to raise an eyebrow. "You know?"

"Of course, we've known for two weeks already. We've had a team of immunologists on-site under level-five quarantine protocols for a week. They've isolated the strain and—"

Sokolov waved him off. "I'm not talking about that flu your Teegarden colony caught. Everyone knows about that. Some even before you did, as I hear it."

Tyson paused. The barb, intended or not, stung. "We're looking into who leaked the story as well. We'll find them."

"See that you do. The markets turn on news. Either you control it, or it controls you."

Tyson held his hands out, palms up. "And what news do you have to share, Valeria?"

Sokolov fell silent and took a long pull from her vodka as Cassidy reappeared to drop off their appetizer. "Here you go. Careful, they're pretty hot still."

"Thank you, dear. But we can handle the heat," Sokolov said with a smile that didn't reach her eyes. The waitress took the hint and withdrew. Sokolov set her drink back down on the table and carefully turned it.

"I have news from our mutual interests in 82 G Eridani," she said at last.

Tyson leaned back and inhaled a shallow breath through his nostrils. "Go on."

Sokolov picked up one of the diagonally cut wonton wraps and took care dipping it in what Tyson assumed was some sort of ranch sauce, then took a tentative bite off the sharp edge.

She swallowed her bite and looked him in the eyes. "There's been an intersection."

Tyson swallowed involuntarily, despite not having eaten anything yet. "An intersection? You mean a Xr—"

She held up a hand. "Not here, Tyson. The universe itself has ears these days. But, yes. As you know, there's a fleet element watching over our little project. A cruiser, I'm told. Two weeks ago, it had an unexpected guest. The first such guest in . . ."

"Seventy years," Tyson finished for her.

"Officially, at least, but yes."

"What did we lose?"

"Nothing important. The cruiser lost a couple of drones. Their captain believes it was just a probing expedition. Testing our capabilities and procedures. That sort of thing. No different from the sorts of games we play trying to hack into each other's computer networks, Tyson."

"I would never dream of it, Valeria," he said soothingly.

"You wouldn't dirty your hands," she countered. "You hire people to do the dreaming, just as I do. It's expected, I take no offense. Ours is just a friendly competition, after all."

Tyson took a sip of tea and smiled agreement, the names of at least a half dozen operatives who had gone missing during their "friendly competition" over the years floating to the foreground of his consciousness.

"But," Sokolov continued, "our 'friends' on the other side of the Red Line don't see it that way. They play for keeps, and for whatever reason, Grendel has piqued their interest. That exposes both of our investments in the system to risks that neither of our analysts can model."

"If this is two weeks old, why haven't I heard about it?" Tyson asked. "Not even the networks have to deal with that much delay."

"Because fleet intel is keeping it under wraps. Tightly. I heard a rumor, but it still took a six-figure bribe to pry confirmation loose."

"That's a valuable piece of information." Tyson grabbed a wedge of reheated whatever-the-hell and took a bite. It was every bit as disappointing as the news he'd just heard. "Why share it with me?"

"Because we're partners in the project, Tyson. If—*When* word gets out, we need to be prepared to present a united front and coherent messaging."

"And Praxis? Are you visiting Daryl next?"

Sokolov waved a hand dismissively. "That space trucker? Daryl's a good old boy and a gossip. He's useful for spilling secrets, not keeping them. We only roped him in because neither you nor NeoSun had enough spare shipping capacity from our other commitments to get the standard infrastructure in place."

Which was true enough, Tyson had to admit. His merchant fleet was stretched thin moving around the cargo and trade Ageless had already brought to market. Trade that was making them money with each jump. They just didn't have the tonnage lying around to divert into a new project that might not bear fruit for ten, perhaps twenty years. His thoughts drifted for a moment to the million-ton ore freighter trapped in a parking orbit not five hundred kilometers above his head, even now draining company resources as it waited to end quarantine instead of making him money.

New hulls were under construction, but the first of them was still another ten to fifteen months away from completion and another half a year for space-worthiness certification.

So, they'd gone to Daryl Cooper and Praxis, the "You-Buy-We-Fly" overflow fleet of human space. Daryl's ships were castoffs bought up at auction once the larger transtellars thought them to be worth little more than scrap.

Which, honestly, they were. But Daryl's people spent countless man-hours refurbishing the old heaps into something that would pass inspection, if only with a few greased palms. Which weren't hard to find among the Praxis ranks, considering how many of his employees were grease monkeys in the first place. He then waited patiently, hauling low-grade materials for fees that barely covered his overhead until the giants like NeoSun, Extra, or even Ageless bit off more than they could chew in their quest to conquer the known universe. Then, if you needed something shipped, Praxis was there to do it quickly and more-or-less competently.

For a price. In the case of Grendel, the price wasn't a fee, but a seven-percent cut of future revenue, negotiated down from ten.

Daryl wasn't smart, by any stretch. But he was hardworking, looked out for his people, and had a certain cunning about him that kept Praxis alive through the lean times, and fattened it up when opportunity knocked. Even if that opportunity was firmly in the gray area of transtellar regulations. Tyson himself had signed off on fines against Praxis half a dozen times for infractions on Lazarus that any court of law would call smuggling. But somehow, he still liked the man.

"So," Tyson said after choking down the rest of his soggy wedge of wonton, shredded vat chicken, and corn, "what do we do about it?"

"Nothing we can do, at the moment." Sokolov sipped up the dregs of her drink. "Do anything, and we give away that we knew before the CCDF made the information public, and that would jeopardize my back channels."

Tyson nodded. "I understand the need for discretion."

"But be ready for the press. You're the majority stakeholder in Grendel, you have the most exposure to the downside risks of bad optics. Especially in light of your misadventure in Teegarden."

"It's a damned bacteria. We're handling it," he said tersely.

"You'd better. Because I wouldn't want to be putting out multiple publicity fires simultaneously. Makes stakeholders nervous. Makes the Earth governments take notice. And the last thing any of us wants is for those know-nothings to start sending fucking fact-finding missions out here to play in our sandboxes. That's never good for the quarterly reports, for any of us."

"Agreed."

"Good, that's settled, then. Speaking of settled . . ."

"I'll take care of the bill. My treat. It's the least I can do for your help."

Sokolov smiled her broad, wrinkled smile. It was warm, and felt as genuine as a grandmother doting over a precocious grandson. "I like you, Tyson. You have a stout heart and broad shoulders. But I'm helping me, just as much as I'm helping you. Our little side project is a marriage of convenience, after all."

"A mutually beneficial relationship, I hope."

"Time will tell. In the short term, make sure your house is tidy, in case we have unexpected guests. *Da?*"

"*Ya ponimayu,*" Tyson answered without missing a beat.

"Hmm." Sokolov's smile persisted. "Excellent diction, Tyson. Hardly any of that atrocious Lazarus accent at all. But I really must be catching a shuttle back to my yacht."

"So soon? You've only just arrived. Surely you could spare an hour for the sandstone gardens. The native rock coral are in bloom."

"Thank you, Tyson, but if I want to breathe air clogged with gametes, I'll . . . well, let's just say that such places are readily available on New Vladivostok as well. Although I don't frequent them as much as I once did."

"A pity," Tyson teased. "Safe travels, Ms. Sokolov."

"Calm seas, Mr. Abington." Sokolov stood up from the booth and disappeared into the bustling crowd eager to leave and return to their offices and work stations. Tyson remained, chewing on his thoughts if not his lunch.

What the hell did the Xre want with Grendel? And why did they have to pick just then, out of the last seven decades, to start poking around in human-occupied space again right on the heels of the Teegarden fiasco? Of course, there was no way to answer those questions, because there were never any Xre around to ask, not that their answers ever made much sense in the first place.

Sokolov was right about one thing, though. Crisis had a way of increasing exponentially in apparent importance among public perception the more of them you stacked atop one another. Even several relatively small, unrelated setbacks posed a danger of being misinterpreted as a larger, systemic problem by the press and among market watchers.

This unwelcome bit of news put even greater emphasis and pressure on him to resolve the Teegarden situation quickly and publicly. Tyson was busy pondering vectors for accomplishing that when he looked around and realized most of the lunch crowd had thinned out. He hadn't seen their waitress in quite some time, either. Impatiently, he flagged down one of the other members of the serving staff, a young man with a cowlick even industrial epoxy would have difficulty managing.

"Son, yes. I'm in a bit of a rush. Could you grab my server so I can settle the bill?"

"Sure, mister. Who was waiting on you?"

"Cassidy."

The youth wrinkled his brow in consideration. "Like, a boy, or . . ."

"A girl. Early twenties, shoulder-length brown hair. Caucasian features. Henna tattoo on her left hand."

"Mmm, sorry mister, but we don't have a Cassidy working here."

A chill spread down Tyson's back. They'd been under

observation. But by whom? One of the other transtellars? An Earthgov? Sokovol herself, or one of her enemies? Who?

Tyson held up his wrist to speak into the audio pickup built into his cufflink. "Paris," he whispered.

"Yes, sir?" his AI assistant answered.

"I'm sending you a section of video capture from my retinal implant. I need you to ID the waitress and flag her for surveillance."

"Tyson Abington?" Paris scoffed. "Afraid to ask a Chili's waitress for her link avatar? How far the mighty have fallen."

"Not exactly, dear. You're not playing matchmaker this time. She's a spy."

"For whom?"

"That's an excellent question."

"Understood. I have it. I'm feeding her face into our recognition matrix. If she shows up on a surveillance camera or a mobile device, we'll know."

"Thank you, Paris. I'll see you at the office in twenty."

"Is something wrong, mister?" the young man asked with a tone that made it clear he was only asking to avoid blame.

Tyson stood up and wiped his mouth before dropping his napkin onto the table. "There's always something wrong."

SEVEN

Susan's hand cut a slash through the cool water, propelling her forward another half meter as her other arm broke the surface and shot out ahead. The far wall approached quickly. Susan anticipated it, tucked her chin to her chest and spun in place. The soles of her feet slapped onto the rough-textured surface of the wall exactly where she'd anticipated it would be. She pushed off, hard, and let her body glide through the water for several meters without moving a muscle before breaking the surface again to take a breath and fall back into the rhythm of her strokes.

She'd lost count at fiftyish laps, which in the twenty-five-meter pool put her well over two kilometers already, but her body could go further. And so she would.

The "pool" was actually a freshwater cistern, part of the *Ansari*'s water reclamation and purification system. It was a holding tank where water waited between steps in the filtration process. It wasn't yet safe to drink in any quantity, but the chemicals were benign enough that it posed no danger to swim in, provided you didn't swallow more than about a liter.

A couple of ship classes ago, some bright spark in Naval Development decided to throw a retractable, watertight, rolling lid onto the cistern to let it pull double-duty as a recreation pool for the crew in calm times, an innovation for which Susan and thousands of other sailors were eternally grateful. It gave her a space to work out, to meditate, and to think.

It had been almost three weeks since their encounter with the unknown Xre warship. Three weeks since the first incursion of an enemy vessel into a human-owned system in three generations, and the first time the CCDF had fired on an alien ship in just as long.

Three weeks since they'd been ghosted by that same damned ship. On her watch.

She'd replayed the engagement a hundred times since, in her quarters, in the pool, as she slept, each time turning over every aspect of the encounter, trying to spot anything she might have missed. Any clue she overlooked that could've allowed her to anticipate the Xre commander's feint that had let them escape in such spectacular fashion.

But she kept coming up empty. The simple truth was she'd never faced a Xre before, not really. Like all CCDF commanders, she'd studied their tactics from the Intersection War exhaustively at Academy. Every battle and skirmish, from large-scale fleet engagements, to commerce raids, to orbital insertions and attacks on infrastructure, right down to stray ship ambushes. They'd poured over them all, interpreting patterns, extrapolating doctrine, and even burrowing into the psychology of their foe in an effort to gain understanding and advantage in any future conflict.

Of course, the Xre had been doing the exact same thing for just as long, adapting their own tactics to compensate for what they'd learned about their human adversaries. Guessing how humans would adapt to those changes. Shadowboxing. After seventy years of such second-guessing and head-fakes, who was to say that anyone's assumptions, on either side, held water at all?

Susan shook the thought loose. She'd just been outplayed,

simple as that. But, she took some small measure of satisfaction knowing she'd managed to catch them completely by surprise and force them into such a reckless gambit in the first place.

She completed five more laps before her right shoulder started to complain too much and she had to stop. As she hung off the far wall catching her breath, someone tapped her on the crown of her head.

Susan looked up into Miguel's waiting green eyes. He stood next to one of the diving platforms, holding a towel. She pulled out her earplugs and lifted her swimming goggles. "Yes?"

"I was just wondering if you were finished or if you were bent on becoming the first person to drown in outer space."

"I couldn't be the first. Surely someone's managed it by now."

Miguel shook his head. "I looked it up. Couple of close calls, but you would get the honor."

Susan swung her shoulder around a couple of times trying to work the knot out. "I might have a few more laps in me."

"Not to be too direct, mum, but the rest of the crew would like their pool back."

"There's five other lanes!"

"Nobody wants to interrupt your 'anger swims.'"

"You wimps." Susan splashed his trousers. "Fine, I'm done. But if I catch anyone fucking in the sauna again, it's getting ripped out."

"Yes, mum."

"Honestly, we put privacy walls in the showers, for Christ's sake. Use them."

"I understand."

Susan grimaced as she pulled herself out of the water. Her rotator cup complaint couldn't be linked to any war story or heroic deed, unless one counted the battle against Father Time as an act of heroism. It had just appeared a few years earlier of its own accord, unannounced and uninvited, but it had doggedly settled in for the long haul regardless. Regular exercise, especially in the pool, helped to keep it in check, but it was the first to let her know when she'd overexerted herself.

Miguel held the towel open for her, which she took with thanks.

"Anything new stumble into our web?" she asked as she wrapped herself in the genuine cotton towel and tucked a corner of it by her armpit.

"Nothing." Miguel shook his head.

Susan sighed hard, on the verge of a growl. Since the incursion, they'd redeployed back to low orbit around Grendel and linked up with the system's spaceborne antimatter factory to top off their tanks. Once UnRep was complete, they'd deployed the rest of their complement of recon platforms and pushed them all the way out to their maximum effective range, hoping to catch a glimpse of their ghost.

With their drone constellation pushed all the way out to the twelve-AU border, the platforms' observational spheres had virtually no overlap. Each drone was effectively on its own and couldn't rely on any of its siblings to double-check and confirm their observations. There were periodic gaps in coverage that had to be covered through a preset search pattern. Further, the light-speed delay so far out was more than an hour and a half.

It was far from ideal, but with any luck, Mattu's little sleight of hand would have the enemy believing their web was a lot tighter than the threadbare, moth-eaten lacework it actually presented.

"Has that skip courier come back from fleet HQ yet?" Susan said as she slipped her feet into sandals and pointed herself toward the showers.

"Just did," Miguel replied. "Packers won the Super Bowl. Again."

Susan shrugged. "No surprise there. The Dervishes were good, but no expansion team has any business being in the big game their first year in the league. Anything else?"

"No change in our orders. We're to remain on station and monitor the system for a follow-up incursion."

"And our reinforcements?"

Miguel shook his head. "No such luck."

"God dammit. Admiralty House couldn't shake a frigate loose—really?"

"They're tightening defense and increasing patrols of the core systems. Grendel is too underdeveloped to be a priority."

"Well, the Xre consider it enough of a priority to *actually come here*. Did anyone consider that?"

"I'm sure it came up."

"Uh-huh. Do you have any good news for me, or did you just come down here to ruin my endorphin-enhanced mood?"

"They strapped a couple of replacement recon drones and a decoy onto the courier to cover our losses. It's matching orbit with us right now. Another hour and we can start the transfer."

"I'll take it," Susan said. "Maybe we can even plug a couple of holes in our web once we get them through engineering inspection and worked up."

"Frankly, mum, I'd feel better if we kept them in the barn to give us some reserve capacity."

Susan pursed her lips. "Yeah, okay. Get them onboard and integrated with our network, but leave them in the tubes."

"Yes'm."

The chime for the 1MC sounded from the ceiling. "Captain Kamala, please call the bridge."

Susan looked up. "The hell? They know I have a com implant, too, right?"

"You were in the pool, mum," Miguel chided with a smirk.

Susan slapped her forehead with the heel of her palm. "Right, excuse me." She padded over to the nearest bulkhead and grabbed a hardline handset from behind a small panel. "Go for *Ansari* Actual."

"Captain," a hurried voice said through the handset. One of

the com officers that usually worked an opposite shift from her whose name she could never remember. "The Governor of Grendel is demanding a meeting."

"She's calling herself 'Governor' now? That's adorable. Tell her we're preparing for a material transfer. She'll have to call back."

"That's just it, mum. Her shuttle is already inbound."

Susan's eyes rolled so fast and hard, for a bright moment she thought she could see the future. "You're kidding."

"Sorry, mum."

"How long?"

"They're already out of the gravity well and burning for our altitude. It'll take three orbits to match our velocity."

Two hours, Susan thought. "Understood. Thanks for the heads-up, Com."

"Yes'm."

"Oh, and Com—find Mr. Nesbit. He'll want to sit in on this."

"Understood."

"Actual out." Susan hung up the handset and closed the panel.

"XO," she called over to Miguel. "How long to cut those drones loose from the courier and secure them once it gets here?"

"An hour after it matches velocity, ninety minutes, tops."

"Put a rush order on it. Tell the boat bay we're expecting company in two hours. We'll need something to eat. And tell the galley to break out the good china."

Her hair still damp under its top cover, Susan watched through the boat bay's observation gallery windows as the small civilian shuttle maneuvered through the opening in the *Ansari*'s hull. There was space for it among a small fleet of auxiliary vehicles, maintenance and inspection drones, and marine assault shuttles, but only just.

The approach hadn't been without drama. Susan's boat bay supervisor had insisted the governor's shuttle slave its controls over to the *Ansari*'s traffic control computers, as was standard procedure for any small craft operating within a warship's gooey zone. The governor's pilot had refused, insisting that he ". . . learned to parallel park a shuttle on Proxima Centauri, you [redacted]."

This led immediately to a dick-measuring contest between the two of them that only ended when Susan herself stepped in and reminded everyone involved that indeed, *she* had the biggest dick, and politely requested the pilot turn over control to his shuttle for terminal maneuvers, on account that, while he was certainly very talented, he was not accustomed to parking next to high temp fusion plants and thermonuclear warheads.

The pilot complied, finally, but ended up with the last laugh anyway, as his shuttle's navigation system was so far out of date that it couldn't integrate with the *Ansari*'s software.

Which is how Susan and half of her senior staff found themselves standing around the observation gallery crossing fingers and mouthing silent prayers that they weren't about to bear witness to their ship getting blown in half.

"How thick is this glass?" Broadchurch asked.

"They don't make glass thick enough," Warner answered.

"Thanks."

Little puffs of steam shot out of the shuttle's nose like a snorting bull in the vacuum and micrograv of the boat bay, slowing it to a crawl as it approached the capture cradle. Fortunately, the shuttle's hotheaded pilot proved to be a cool hand at the stick, and it nestled gently into the waiting arms of the cradle without incident.

"Somebody punch that guy and then buy him a drink," Susan said idly.

"Is that an order, Captain?" Miguel asked.

"I said it out loud, didn't I?"

The assembled officers and senior enlisted chuckled, releasing the tension in the gallery even as the universal docking collar extended from the boat bay's bulkhead like an esophagus to suck onto the shuttle.

Once all the lights turned green to signal a solid lock and a good seal, the hatch popped and three people crawled out into the accordioned sections of the transfer tube. Governor Honshu led the procession, trying to look as dignified as one could while hunched over in a meter-and-a-half-tall transfer tube.

They reached the airlock leading into the observation gallery and cycled through the double sets of doors. Nesbit straightened his spine and applied his most polished corporate smile. Honshu had the slight build of her Asian ancestry exacerbated by the extra height of a youth spent on a low-g world. Which, Susan wasn't sure. The woman's hair was cropped short and angular in the style of the core systems these days.

"Margo," Nesbit said as the governor set foot in the compartment.

"Javier," she replied. They leaned in and kissed cheeks in the French tradition that had survived the centuries among a certain set of the faux-cultured before she turned and nodded to Susan. "Commander Kamala."

"It's *captain*, Administrator Honshu."

"It's actually *governor*, Captain."

"Of course. Forgive me."

A flicker of irritation passed over Nesbit's face, which gave Susan no small amount of satisfaction.

"I suppose this is the part where I'm supposed to say, 'Permission to come aboard?'" Honshu said.

"Yes," Susan answered. "To both."

Honshu giggled. "I've always thought it was funny that we ask to board after we've already boarded. What a strange tradition."

"Well, you can go back outside and try to shout for permission, Governor. I don't think you'll have much luck, though."

Honshu stared at her. "I don't think that's very funny."

Nesbit cleared his throat. "You'll have to forgive my colleagues, Margo. Military life breeds a more . . . biting sense of humor than we're used to in the civilian world."

"Of course." Honshu gave herself a little shake, then held her hand out to the two people standing behind her. "These are my assistants: Kaleb Daily, who, appropriately enough, handles the day-to-day operations down the well, and my niece, Patricia, who manages our orbital installations."

"Welcome, and obviously the permission to board applies to all three of you. Will your shuttle need replenishment?"

"Ah, sorry?" Honshu asked.

"She's asking if the shuttle needs to be serviced, Auntie," Patricia interjected. "And yes, we should probably top off on reactant mass for our maneuvering thrusters at the very least."

Susan nodded. "I'll have my boat bay supervisor coordinate with your pilot during the meeting. I'm sure he'll have you squared away by the time we've finished . . . whatever it is we're doing."

Honshu put a hand on Patricia's shoulder. "Ah, my darling niece, always talking in vectors and velocities. Obviously got all that nerdy stuff from her mother's side."

"Obviously," Broadchurch muttered. Miguel elbowed them in the ribs, but Susan would have to have a word with them later. But really, she needed to have a word with herself. Susan hadn't signed on to be a diplomat. She had a constitutional dislike for answering to anyone outside of her chain of command that had been beaten into her since basic. But that wasn't an excuse. A captain set the tone for her crew, and she'd let her personal animosity for this pushy politician leak over into her professional conduct. And that just wasn't kosher.

"We've set up refreshments in the officers' mess," Susan said. "We can have a little privacy there." She held a hand out to the elevator.

"Yes. Let's," Honshu said.

EIGHT

"What in the chasm is this?" Thuk asked, shaking the rolling scroll with the latest encoded dispatches from home.

"Our song for the rest of this expedition," the recording alcove attendant said uneasily.

"We're to remain in system, without resupply, and test the limits of the eyes of the humans' new husks and, if possible, antagonize the human cruiser into crossing into free water?" Thuk passed the rolling scroll back to the attendant as if it was covered in something unmentionable. "If they want a war, why not just sing us into attacking the mound on their new world? It would save us all time."

"I'm n-not . . . q-qualified . . . to . . ."

Thuk ignored their stammering. "We're down three decoys, a predator husk, and a third of our annihilation fuel reserves. If the Chorus is making a joke, I'll have to dig deeper to find the humor in it."

"Yes, Derstu."

"Has anyone else seen this dispatch?"

"No, Derstu. Only the two of us."

"So if I threw you out a doubled-portal . . ."

The attendant stiffened. "If you're making a joke, I'll have to dig deeper to find the humor in it."

Thuk sighed, then put a primehand on the attendant's skull-plates. "Forgive me, it's not you. I'm just reminded of an old fable, and it gives me pause."

"Which fable, Derstu?"

It was late in the day's timeflow, and the *Chusexx* was many millions of markers away from immediate danger. The mind cavern was nearly empty as all nonessential attendants had retired to their fugues. Which is where Thuk would have been had he not been called up to read the Chorus's song. They were alone in the compartment. The recording attendant was young, but sported the vestigial wing covers along the back of their thorax that spoke of lines of nobility that had been left behind with the death of the queens. Most Xre that still carried the trait plucked them off with each successive molt in a sign of contrition. It was rare to encounter one of the fallen nobles. It was rarer still to find one who didn't hide from what they were. Thuk found himself approving of their choice. He sat down in his chair.

"Your name is Hurg, isn't it?" The attendant nodded. "Which mound are you from?"

"None, actually. I was clutched on the trade spinner above Ukuol. Spent my first half dozen molts there before volunteering to serve in the Dark Ocean Chorus."

"Not a big leap, then, going from a spinner to a ship."

"There are certainly similarities," the attendant agreed. "The structure of things is quite different, though. New routines to learn."

"Indeed. Did your clutch-mates above Ukuol learn the Parable of the Seven Sacrifices?"

"I'm afraid that one didn't make the journey from the home-world, Derstu."

Thuk clicked his mandibles, excited at the chance to tell the story.

"It's an old story, from before the Fall of Queens. It's changed much as it's floated down the timeflow. But the plates of it are this. Once, when mounds still made war against each other, there was a river valley. One side of the banks held seven mounds in an almost constant state of conflict. On the other bank, there was but a single small mound, half the size of the others. The rock there was close to the surface, so they couldn't dig very deep. The soil along their bank was also poor, as the river moved too quickly there to bless the land with sediment during the floods.

"But their queen was wise and far-seeing, and her chorus endured despite their challenges, and the fact no one across the river coveted their patch of land kept them free of the conflicts that frequently erupted between the other mounds. That was, until one summer. The queen had traded with a mound far upriver for new hammers and chisels of an incredibly hard stone that would finally let them dig tunnels into the rock below their mound. But only a moon into their excavations, they struck sun-tears."

"Ack," Hurg said. "And suddenly the other mounds were very interested in their little patch of land."

"Not right away. The queen kept the mouths of her people quiet for a year, then two. But eventually rumors from other mounds they traded with up- and downriver reached the other bank. The mounds launched raids individually, but the river was treacherous near their banks and all the raids failed before they set foot in the queen's mound.

"The seven mounds eventually reached a truce and agreed to pool their resources to build a bridge across the river, kill the queen, enslave her people, and strip their sun-tears. They began immediately, and the bridge grew with each passing day, along with her people's despair. They sent boats to set it on fire, floated logs from upriver to break its pylons, but nothing worked.

"Desperate, the queen hatched a plan. She picked seven of her best traders with her midhands—not for their strength, but for their familiarity with the mounds across the river. She told each to dress up as a warrior from each of the seven mounds, then ordered them to sneak into a different mound on the same night and attempt to assassinate the queen."

Hurg's eyes lit up. "Did they succeed?"

Thuk waved his primehands balefully. "No. They failed, to the last one. They all fell, and fell short . . . just as their queen had sang." Thuk's face brightened and his tone soared.

"Enraged at the attempted betrayals, each of the seven queens launched attacks against the mound they believed had tried to kill them even before the sun rose the next morning. By midday, the seven mounds on the other side of the river were engaged in the largest, most bloody war anyone could remember. The bridge forgotten, they wasted themselves against each other until none remained strong enough to carry on. In the end, the queen finished the bridge herself and used her modest army to sweep up the remnants of the seven mounds and claim them for her own. With each passing year, her people grew to fill the new mounds one by one until they were the strongest network anyone had ever seen. The queen decreed the seven mounds renamed, each after the loyal trader that had sacrificed themselves for their people."

"That is a lovely story, Derstu. Is it true?"

"Who knows? Who cares? The best stories contain their own truth, Hurg. Whether they happened or not is the least interesting thing about them."

"I understand. But why this story? Are you afraid our harmony and the *Chusexx* are like one of the traders? That we're meant to be sacrificed?"

"I don't know, Hurg. My mind wanders from the path sometimes. Maybe it's nothing. But I can't help but wonder why the Chorus is pushing us so hard. We've been at peace with the humans for so long. Why now to antagonize them? And why here, in a system they've only begun to excavate? There's nothing here for us to easily take. It's not even one of the worlds we dually claimed. I struggle to see the sense in it."

"Our legs know not where they carry us," Hurg said mechanically, unconvincingly. But Thuk would play along.

"Yes, of course you're right." Thuk held out a primehand and pointed at the rolling scroll. "We should wake our harmony and get to work carrying out the Chorus's song, don't you think?"

As the mind cavern filled with attendants and the familiar buzz of activity, anticipation, and anxiety that always preceded action, Thuk's mind wandered to another expression. A human expression he'd heard as a part of a joke once.

"Don't poke the bear."

He'd never seen a bear. But he had an awful feeling he and the rest of his harmony had already met one and were gearing up to poke it again.

NINE

"Thanks for joining us on the show this evening, Mr. Abington."

"It's my pleasure, Ji-eun," Tyson said to the hostess of *Methuselah After the Bell*. After his rushed lunch meeting with Sokolov, he'd had half a mind to cancel the appearance, or at least move it to a call-in from his penthouse. He still felt off-balance from not only the conversation, but the discovery of the spy posing as their server, whom Paris had yet to ID or reacquire on the city's security net.

Tyson was the unchallenged master of his domain. He wasn't used to playing catch-up, or feeling like some nebulous, unseen force had gotten something over on him. It left him feeling anxious, a little paranoid, and more than a little vulnerable. None of which were the sorts of things he should be feeling under the hot lights of the local INN studio, especially when sitting across from an interviewer like Ji-eun Park.

But neither could he afford the questions a last-minute cancellation would raise. So, here he was, caked in stage makeup and trying to game out where the conversation was going to go so he could avoid the more devious booby traps. All while practically willing himself not to sweat in the heat.

The sensation was oddly invigorating.

"I know we're cutting into your busy schedule, Mr. Abington, so—"

"Please." Tyson waved a hand as it rested on his knee. "Tyson will do."

"Of course. I know you're busy, Tyson, so let's dive right into today's action, shall we?"

"By all means."

Ji-eun shifted ever-so-slightly in her chair, angling her shoulders toward the main camera to give her viewers a better look at her without breaking eye contact with him. "Ageless has had a rough couple of weeks in the markets, down over a hundred nudollars a share, another fifteen just today. What do you think is driving this sudden crisis in investor confidence, Tyson?"

So, it was going to be one of those interviews, Tyson thought as he mounted a smile. *Don't forget the eyes,* he reminded himself.

"Well, for starters, I think calling it a 'crisis' is a bit hyperbolic. The fact is, Ageless has been on quite a tear over the last three quarters, returning nearly seventeen percent over that period."

"Excluding your stock's stumble over the last two weeks, you mean," Ji-eun jumped in. "You're talking about your market high point, which came on the seventh."

Tyson opened his palms, conceding the point. "Yes, of course. But since then, we've only given back five percent of our high. There had been talk on this very program three days earlier of a two-to-three split if we'd gone much higher. Although I will admit speculation about that possibility has cooled slightly." He gave her a sly smile, as if he was letting her in on a private joke.

"So you're saying the recent contraction is the result of overvaluation?"

"Not at all, and again I think you're being a trifle contrarian. With the Grendel partnership between our friends at NeoSun and Praxis spooling up, there was quite a bit of investor enthusiasm for all three companies. Some market adjustment when excitement runs high is perfectly normal, even healthy."

"But NeoSun, and even Praxis, haven't experienced the drop Ageless has. NeoSun has actually gained a couple of points."

Tyson waved away the objection. "We share a partnership on one project. We're hardly conjoined triplets. Each company must be judged on its own merits and business concerns."

The word tumbled out before Tyson could catch it. The slight uptick of Ji-eun's left eyebrow confirmed that it hadn't gone unnoticed.

"Let's talk about one of those *concerns,* if I may. Two weeks ago, a bulk cargo carrier inbound from Ageless's mining operation in Teegarden arrived in orbit with word of an outbreak. We tried to get a statement from you personally at the time, but . . ."

She held a hand up to a nearby holoscreen. A perfect 3D-UHD of Tyson standing at the window of his penthouse office looking out into the city at sunset appeared, hands held behind his back. It hovered there for a moment as he mouthed some words blurred out in the window itself by automated security features designed to prevent eavesdropping. An instant later, the image shook violently as if struck by an earthquake, then tumbled toward the ground before cutting out entirely.

". . . our camera-drone was shot down by some sort of missile. That seems a bit extreme, doesn't it?"

Tyson's teeth clenched so hard that he had to take a moment to force his jaw muscles to relax. He distracted from his fury at the ambush by switching the cross of his legs, but the moment of silence dragged on awkwardly.

"That was an unfortunate incident, to be sure. But you must understand, Ji-eun, information security is critically important to any transtellar. We have automated systems in place to preserve the integrity of our airspace, especially around the Immortal Tower where even a brief glance could compromise the private information of any of our tens of thousands of employees." Tyson smiled warmly. The defense even had the benefit of being true, theoretically. "I didn't realize at the time it was an INN drone, but even if I had, I doubt I could have intervened quickly enough to stop the peregrine array on the roof from reacting to the perceived breach."

"You mean to tell me you have AI operating on shoot-to-kill orders on your own office building?" she said with mock indignation.

"Now, Ji-eun, you're being hyperbolic again," he said, trying to thread the needle between confronting her incendiary accusation without coming off as condescending or sexist. "Their automated protocols only apply to unmanned drones. Any action against manned aircraft requires a human command in the decision loop, as is required by intercorporate law, and even our treaty with the Xre. And I think you'll find that Ageless filed a formal apology for the incident and paid INN full restitution for your losses. Is that not true?"

"It is," she allowed, only because she had to. "But we're veering off topic."

"Only because you dragged us there," Tyson shot back, irritating her. He probably should've let it go, but it felt good to land a hit, even if it was only a jab. "Please, what was the topic?"

"Your Teegarden facility," she said icily. "How many fatalities are you up to now? A dozen?"

"Fourteen." Tyson nodded along for a moment after correcting her. She'd expected him to try and minimize the human toll with clever wordplay. She hadn't been ready for him to hit her with an even more stark assessment. It threw her off-balance for a moment and afforded him a rare opportunity to continue without a probing follow-up question. "We received a report from our medical team on station via skip courier not even an hour ago. I can't release the names of the deceased at this time, not until their families have been notified. But know that their names are on my lips even now.

I feel these losses as if they were my own. Because in a very real sense, they are. Which is why we've poured whatever resources are necessary into finding a cure for our miners on Teegarden and our spacers in orbit. We're already making progress on that front. The bacteria responsible has been isolated and sequenced. I'm cautiously optimistic we'll have appropriate antibodies synthesized in the coming days before any additional lives are lost."

"That was a carefully calculated answer free of guarantees, Tyson."

"I'm not an immunologist by trade. I can only trust what my people tell me. And I do. They are just as motivated to solve this as anyone."

"But in the meantime you have a million-ton shipment of rare-earth ores doing lazy circles in orbit, just chewing up cash flow. Doesn't that bother you?"

"The rocks they hauled here from Teegarden waited billions of years to be excavated. I think they'll keep over the next few days or weeks it takes to sort this out. Honestly, Ji-eun, I'm more bothered by the situation faced by the *Preakness*'s crew than I am about the paltry sum we're spending on their upkeep. Cargo haulers aren't known for luxury accommodations, and every man and woman aboard has already missed two weeks' worth of recitals and birthdays with their families."

"Forgive me, Tyson, but you seem mighty nonchalant about losing billions in revenue from the quarter's balance sheet. Do you really expect stakeholders to share your calm?"

"I trust that our stakeholders are intelligent enough to recognize revenue hasn't been lost at all, merely delayed until the next quarterly report. Further, it's important to remember that while our mining operations on Teegarden carry some of our healthiest margins, they still represent only a fraction of Ageless's diverse revenue stream. Indeed, just this month we're breaking ground on five new projects that are expected to start turning profit by the end of the fiscal year."

"I'm sure there are a lot of nervous investors in our audience who will be relieved to hear that. You've been very generous with your time this evening, I don't want to keep you. I have just one final question, if I may."

Tyson held out his hands invitingly. "By all means."

"You mentioned your partnership on the planet Grendel, of which Ageless holds a controlling stake. Is that so?"

A knot tightened in Tyson's stomach. This was not a direction he wanted to go. "Yes. We partnered with Praxis for logistical support and NeoSun for their orbital manufacturing expertise to help set up the initial spaceborne infrastructure, but the operations dirtside are almost entirely run by Ageless. We're nearing completion of the first phase of construction, in fact."

"Yes, I've read all the press releases," Ji-eun said dismissively. "What I didn't find in them, however, was any mention of a Xre incursion two weeks ago."

Tyson stared at her. He'd only heard the news himself a few hours earlier, in a very confidential conversation with Sokolov, who had every incentive to keep the news as quiet as he did. The spy, Cassidy. She must have bugged their table and leaked their conversation. It was the only explanation.

"Tyson?"

Ji-eun's voice shook him back to the here-and-now. "Hmm? Yes, sorry. Did you say an incursion?"

Ji-eun leaned in. "Yes. A Xre warship operating at the edge of treaty space sent drones into the system and ended up in an engagement with the system's picket cruiser, the CCDF *Ansari*. Are you telling me this is the first you've heard of it, Tyson?"

Tyson's mind raced. He had to choose his next words very carefully. If he flatly denied it and Ji-eun had acquired a recording of his lunch conversation from the spy, he'd be caught in a lie, live. It was a trap.

"I have no knowledge of such an incident," he started. "If the incident you describe occurred, it would fall under fleet jurisdiction. And would almost certainly be considered classified until a determination was made that a public announcement was appropriate."

"That's hardly a denial, Tyson," she pressed, leaning forward in her chair. "Surely you know what's going on in the skies above your own projects?"

Oh, she was a clever one. Confirm and he was caught with intel he had no legal right to possess, deny and be caught in a lie, feign ignorance and appear weak and disconnected.

"I have no special privileges where it comes to military intelligence compared to any other private citizen, Ji-eun. If something happened on Grendel, I'll learn about it with everyone else when the fleet makes any such information public. In the meantime, I think it would be irresponsible of me to speculate on unconfirmed rumors of such an . . . outlandish nature."

"I have my sources," Ji-eun said confidently.

"I'm sure they're impeccable, and also willing to come on stage with us right now to face espionage charges."

Ji-eun clapped her hands. "And that's all the time we have for tonight. I want to thank CEO of Ageless Corp., Tyson Abington, for joining us for a . . . memorable . . . visit. Next up is Gill and Li-ho with an exciting recap of today's baseball highlights, so stay tuned."

As soon as the green light on the holocapture equipment switched to red, Tyson shot up from his chair and turned for the door. "Have a lovely evening, Ji-eun," he said over his shoulder, without so much as offering his hand to shake.

"Tyson, wait!"

He turned. "What? You have another pit-trap ready we didn't have time for and you don't want it to go to waste?"

"I'm just doing my job. This is a big story and you know it, maybe the biggest in seventy years. It's not my fault it fell right on the heels of your other misfortunes."

"Who told you? Who's the source?"

"So it's true, then. Off the record?"

"I can neither confirm, nor deny the—"

Ji-eun sighed with disgust. "Yes, yes. I know the drill. And you know I can't reveal sources."

The two of them stared at each other for a heartbeat. "Well, here we are, then. Stalemated," Tyson said finally.

"I guess so."

"Good night, Ms. Park."

"Good night, Mr. Abington. Can I call a grip to—"

"I know my way out." Tyson spun around on a heel and stalked out of the studio. Savvy investors and AI trade platforms had watched the stream live. Within an hour, the interview will have been seen by half the people on Lazarus. Within a week, it will have been carried by drone skip couriers to six dozen colonies, moons, and planets across human-controlled space and seen by uncountable millions.

Tyson connected with Paris as soon as his feet hit the sidewalk. "How bad is it?"

"The overnights just lost another twenty-three points," she replied without emotion. Not that she lacked them. She just knew when best to deploy them.

"Increase INN's rent on their studio by twenty-three percent."

"That won't *quite* cover the shortfall," she said, adding a slight stress of sarcasm.

"No, but it will send a message. And more importantly, it will make me feel better. Also, their utilities."

"For how long?"

"Until I'm not mad anymore."

"So in perpetuity. Understood. I should tell you, there's several people waiting in v-space to connect with you at the office, sir."

"At this hour? Who?"

"The board."

Tyson sighed. "Understood. Be there shortly." He pressed a

chime in the nearest streetlamp to call for a transit pod, but before one came a woman stepped out from the flow of the crowd on the sidewalk and walked toward him with purpose. He didn't recognize her, and considering the rest of the day's events, he wasn't taking anything at face value. Tyson's legs and shoulders tensed, ready to take flight or stand his ground, depending on what happened in the next second or two.

"Mr. Abington!" she called with a wave to gain his attention. Well, at least she wasn't trying to sneak up on him. She came to a stop a step away and held out her hand.

Tyson took it, hesitantly. "I'm . . . sorry, but are we acquainted?"

"We are now. Dr. Elsa Spaulding. I'm—"

"Supposed to be in space," Tyson said as recognition dawned. She'd been on the short list for the team of immunologists and geneticists he'd picked to fight his bacterial adversary. "Yes, Doctor. I know who you are now. Sorry we haven't met before. But, didn't I send you to Teegarden two weeks ago?"

"You did, sir. But I'd punctured a lung in a rock-climbing accident the day before and the flight surgeon wouldn't clear me for departure."

"Goodness! Are you all right?"

Elsa rubbed absently at her side for a moment. "Perfectly. My ego is more bruised than my body at this point. Kwiknit is some amazing stuff."

"Indeed." A pod pulled up along the sidewalk. "Well, good evening, Dr. Spaulding."

"No, sir." She reached out and grabbed his arm before he could turn away. His eyes shot down and looked in surprise and affront at her fingers gripping his jacket sleeve, but she didn't relent. "I've been coordinating with my colleagues from the ground. And I *really* need to talk to you." She *really* needed to talk to him badly enough that she didn't even register the pair of Wasp bodyguard drones hovering overhead that went from passive to target-acquisition the instant she reached for his arm. Not sensing any immediate threat, Tyson waved them off with his free hand.

"I'm on my way to a board meeting."

"This can't wait."

Tyson's eyes narrowed. "How did you know where to find me?"

"I saw you on that INN interview. My flat is only a few blocks away. I ran down here as quickly as I could to catch you."

Tyson was still reticent, but he knew that when a woman wouldn't take no for an answer, it was usually best to just let things happen. "All right, Doctor. You have my attention for the span of the podride back to the Immortal Tower. That will have to suffice."

"That's all I need."

"In that case, get in."

The ride back to the tower was significantly less entertaining, yet considerably more illuminating than he'd anticipated.

"And you can prove all of this?" Tyson asked as he took Elsa's hand to help her out of the pod.

"'Prove' is a loaded term in science, but, I have substantial support for the hypothesis, yes."

"Can you access your data remotely?"

"Of course."

"Good, because you're giving a presentation to the board about everything you've just told me."

"Me." She stopped in midstride. "When? Where?"

"As soon as we reach my office. And in my office."

"But, I'm not prepared," she stammered. "I don't have any visuals ready."

"You convinced me in three and a half minutes. You're prepared. This isn't a symposium, Doctor. You're not presenting at a scientific conference where you have to defend yourself from other vultures in your field. This is a board meeting. They're an entirely different kind of vulture."

"But—"

"But nothing. Just be confident. You're the expert. They aren't going to have the background or wherewithal to challenge your contentions. Ninety percent of any C-level exec's success comes from listening to people smarter than they are and then taking credit for doing whatever they were told in the first place."

"Trade secret, huh?" she asked.

"Is it? I thought it was common knowledge. This way." An expertly cut pane of glass at the base of the Immortal Tower pivoted on its center as they approached to grant them entry to the soaring seven-story atrium that greeted visitors to Ageless's headquarters. A pair of security androids flanked the entrance, ready to deal with any unwelcome guests—politely, but firmly. A refurbished marine anti-vehicular mecha was hidden inside a false structural pylon on the far side of the lobby should polite-but-firm fail to be a sufficient deterrent, but this was not widely acknowledged.

The lobby was dim and nearly empty as they made their way to the lifts. It was already past sundown, and most of the building's workers had gone home for the day. Tyson nodded to the nightshift front desk attendant as they passed.

"Reggie."

"Good evening, Mr. Abington. Working late?"

"Story of our lives, hey Reg?"

He laughed. "I heard that, sir."

Tyson came to rest in front of his private high-speed lift with Dr. Spaulding close behind. Three different biometric systems confirmed his identity before the doors opened to grant them entrance.

"Plus one," he said as they passed through the doors.

"Plus one, what?" Elsa asked.

"Plus you. That's how the guns in the elevator know I'm not being coerced and they don't need to shoot you when we reach the tenth floor."

"I thought you said in the interview that a human is involved in the decision loop by law!"

"And one is. In this case, I decided *not* to kill you. The imprecision of language can be such fun."

The press of acceleration pushed down on the soles of their feet. Tyson's private lift only had one destination, and it got there quickly.

"How did you remember the guard?" Elsa asked.

"Hmm? Reggie?"

"Yeah, do you have an alert in your augmented reality whenever an employee is in your field of vision. Their file, maybe?"

Tyson snorted. "Reginald Sojourner Birmingham took a knife for me twenty-seven years ago when I was just a dumb kid and he was my bodyguard. Some tweaker outside a nightclub got lucky and stuck it between the base of Reggie's helmet and the top of his backplate while I was in the alley trying to jack into the tweaker's girl. I promised Reg that night in the hospital his family would never want for anything again. He spent three months on a ventilator while the docs regrew his spinal cord below the C-7 vertebrae. Took him a year to learn how to walk again. He has two daughters and a lovely wife who bakes me an entirely inedible fruitcake every Christmas, every one of which I've saved as building material for a winter home on the southern continent when I finally retire. So no, I don't need any tricks to remember his name. Anything else?"

Elsa shrunk back into herself. "I'm . . . sorry."

"It's all right," Tyson assured her. "I know what people think of me. It's even useful, sometimes. But in private like this it can be a bit . . . jarring."

The lift reached it apex with a gentle *Ding*. The doors opened onto Tyson's familiar territory. His first home, really.

"Holy shit," Elsa said behind him, just above a whisper. She physically backed into the elevator car.

"What's wrong?"

"What's—" She swallowed. "What's holding up the ceiling?"

"Ah. I see." Tyson strode over to the window and wrapped a knuckle against it with a *tunk tunk tunk*. "Several tons of space-grade transparent aluminum. It's quite solid, I assure you. It's just tricking your eyes. Don't worry. I work in here every day." He held out a reassuring hand.

Gingerly, Elsa took it and inched her way out of the lift. As soon as she'd exited, the doors closed and the capsule retreated back into the floor, the contours of its top disappearing into the swirling patterns of the carpet.

"That's a hell of a trick," Elsa said once she'd collected herself.

"You know, I haven't had anyone new up here in a couple of years who could appreciate it that much. Thanks for reminding me what that looks like. Paris?"

"I'm here," his assistant's voice called from everywhere and nowhere.

"Ghost protocol, please."

"Of course."

All around them, the once transparent window that separated the floor from the ceiling frosted over as if an impenetrable fog had suddenly fallen over the city.

"Don't be alarmed," Tyson said. "This just keeps prying eyes from lipreading while we hold our meeting."

Elsa nodded. "I understand."

"Paris, can you join us, please?"

Paris's familiar shape appeared in the opaque window. "Hello, Dr. Spaulding. It's good to meet you in, well, *person*."

"You two know each other?" Tyson asked.

"She, ah, recruited me for the Teegarden expedition," Elsa said. "I didn't know you were an AI."

"Ah." Paris fluttered her shoulders and smiled. "Passed another Turing test."

"Sorry, I meant no offense. We use AI in the lab every day. They're invaluable. Just not quite so . . . sophisticated."

"None taken, Doctor. I'm a special case."

"That she is," Tyson said. "Dr. Spaulding, if you would be so good as to give Paris permission to access your files, she'll be more than capable of throwing together the visuals and cites for your presentation on the fly. Isn't that right, Paris?"

"I'll be happy to," the AI said reassuringly.

"The data sets are pretty dense," Elsa said uncertainly.

"I'm a quick study."

"What the hell." Elsa shrugged. "You're the ones paying for all of it anyway." She pulled a small tablet from her purse, thumbed it, then typed an incomprehensibly complex string of characters into the passcode field. Tyson couldn't have remembered it even if he'd wanted to steal access later.

"That's your password?" Tyson said. "How can you remember it?"

"It's just five sets of seven characters. Anyone can do that." She opened a couple of different fields and keyed a few command prompts. "Okay, Paris. You should have full access now."

The projections of Paris's eyes closed. For a moment, she concentrated. "Yes, I can see your data. Thank you. I'll try not to leave a mess."

"You can't be any worse than my first graduate student."

The two of them shared a laugh, as if Paris had ever been a graduate student.

"Okay, are we ready then?" Tyson asked, but continued before getting an answer, "Good, let's get this dog and pony show over with. Paris, put the board members onscreen, please."

The overhead lights dimmed. One at a time, six ghostly figures materialized from the fog of the window until they resolved into something with the appearance of substance spaced equidistantly around the circular office window, theater-in-the-round style.

Tyson didn't like the idea of addressing people he couldn't see, so he held his arms out wide, toggled his forefingers, then scrunched everyone together in a neat row where he could engage with all of them at once.

The Chief Operations Officer, Chief Information Officer, Chief Financial Officer, Chief Logistical Officer, Chief Humanities Officer, and Chief Benefits Officer, sitting in lavishly appointed home offices, dens, and living rooms in penthouses atop the most exclusive residential towers in downtown Methuselah, collectively and expectantly stared back at him. Everyone except CHO Meadows, who preferred to live in a five-room hovel on the outskirts of the burber ring inherited from her parents some fifteen years ago. Foz always had been a bit of an odd one.

A spotlight cast a glow over Tyson's head and shoulders for theatrical effect. He held his arms up in welcome. "Ladies and gentlemen. Thank you for joining me tonight."

"Cut the crap, Tyson," COO Nakamura said without preamble. "We all saw that interview. What the hell were you—" He stopped midsentence as soon as he noticed Elsa standing behind Tyson's right shoulder. "Who is that?"

"This . . ." Tyson moved aside and motioned for Elsa to step forward. ". . . is Doctor Elsa Spaulding. She's one of the immunologists leading the effort to find a cure for our Teegarden plague, and she's the reason I called this meeting."

"But you didn't call this meeting!" Nakamura complained.

"I have now, Takeshi. I cede the floor to Dr. Spaulding. And trust me, you're all going to want to listen very carefully to what she has to say." He turned around and leaned in to whisper in Elsa's ear. "Remember, you're the expert here. Try not to overwhelm them with detail. And don't take any of their shit. Think teaching class at a primary school."

"I haven't been in a primary school in twenty years."

"You'll be great." He hooked an arm around her waist and gently maneuvered her under the light, then stepped away.

Momentarily startled, Elsa straightened her blouse and cleared her throat. "Ladies and gentlemen, good evening. I apologize in advance for the somewhat disjointed nature of this presentation. I didn't know I was giving it until five minutes ago." She shot Tyson a sour look, but continued. "As Mr. Abington said, for the last two weeks I've been working diligently with my colleagues both in orbit on the *Preakness* and in situ on Teegarden to develop a cure for the mystery bacteria infecting our people."

"And how goes that fight, Doctor?" Foz asked. Her gentle tones stood in such stark contrast to nearly everyone else Tyson came in regular contact with.

"To be frank, slowly. We've managed to contain the outbreak and identify its vectors. We've even managed to start sterilizing the outer structures on Teegarden and set up labs and a treatment center on-site. But as far as working toward a cure, that's been slower going. So far, the strain has proven resilient to all known phases of antibiotics, retro-viral therapies, even the bacterial phages we've thrown at it. Its mutation rate is higher than anything I've seen in more than a decade of work in the field. It's almost like the strain knows our playbook and is anticipating our next move against it."

"Are you saying this bug is intelligent, Doctor?" Nakamura said. "Because you have to know how crazy that sounds."

"No. I'm saying it gives the illusion of intelligent action because, and here's the big one, it's been programmed to."

"Walk us through that."

Elsa ran a hand through her hair. "After sequencing its genome at several stages of its development, I retroactively isolated a series of snippets laying dormant, waiting to be triggered by environmental conditions or other outside stimulus. Further, these alleles were hidden among junk DNA after being lifted from wildly divergent orders of prokaryotes that—"

"Doc. English, please," Nakamura pleaded.

"She was speaking English, Takeshi," Foz said.

"Could've fooled me."

"Regardless. Dr. Spaulding, biology wasn't a primary focus

of study for most of us in the corporate world. Could you shave it down for my associates, please?"

"Yes, of course. Alleles are just a science-y word for traits. We can track these traits backward through time by following their development and comparing it to known mutation rates and see points of divergence and speciation. But these alleles don't fit into any single catalogued lineage. It would be like seeing a person walking down the street with an elephant trunk and dragonfly wings. Evolutionarily, those traits didn't evolve together, so you'd instantly know they'd acquired them through gene-splicing, not any natural process. And even that metaphor doesn't really do the job, because the genetic diversity of prokaryotes spans many hundreds of millions of years longer than the history of the vertebrate lineage."

Foz held up a hand. "I think your point is made, Doctor. Thank you. You said the bacteria's program is anticipating your steps to attack it. Have you tried something so unscientific as going out of order?"

"We have, but it's less about the order and more just that the specimen has counters waiting for everything already in our toolkit. We need to develop a new tool from scratch, which we will, but it's going to take some time."

"We've already lost fourteen people, Dr. Spaulding," Nakamura jumped in. "We can't afford much more time."

"We've just received a shipment of cryogenic capsules for the most advance-stage cases in Teegarden. They're being set up in situ now. As we all know, cryo-sleep has its own risks and only buys us a few months, but I'm confident that anyone we have to put on ice now will keep long enough for us to crack this thing."

"That's encouraging to hear." Durant, the Chief Benefits Officer, finally broke his silence. "One final question, Doctor. Is this a weapon?"

Elsa coughed into her fist. "I'm afraid I'm not able to speak to that hypothesis, sir."

"I can." Tyson stepped back into the spotlight, gently crowding Elsa back to the side. "Ageless is the victim of a coordinated, sophisticated attack, Teegarden being only one prong of it. I assume you've all read my memo about our efforts to identify the source of the leak about the Teegarden outbreak even before I was notified. But what I haven't had time to tell you yet is I had lunch today with Ms. Sokolov. She confirmed with me in confidentiality that the rumor about a Xre incursion on Grendel is true. We really did have a Xre warship cross the Red Line in our backyard two weeks ago."

A pall fell over the board. Foz was the first to relocate her voice. "What were our losses?"

"Negligible. Our cruiser lost a pair of drones and a few decoys driving the enemy off. They didn't get anywhere near our investment."

"That's not very comforting," Durant said.

"You haven't heard everything." Tyson realigned one of his cufflinks. "I discovered later that our server during lunch wasn't a server at all, but an operative eavesdropping on our conversation. For whom, I have no idea, but I'm almost certain she was the one to share the intel with INN. Methuselah, indeed probably Lazarus itself, is compromised until we find the source of these leaks and plug it."

"In the plumbing sense, or the bullet sense?" Nakamura asked.

"I'm flexible."

"I have a question," Foz said. "If this is such a high-level conspiracy, why did they allow the genetic modification of the bacteria to be so easily uncovered?"

"It wasn't easy," Elsa jumped in defensively. "It was a bitch of a process that took me a week of sequencing and sample runs. I just happen to be really good at my job. Better than my salary, if we're being honest."

"How much better?" Tyson asked.

The question threw Elsa off-balance. "I—I don't know," she stammered. "Thirty percent?"

"Done." Tyson typed a note into his wrist display. "Now, do you mind? I'm in the middle of a thing."

"Right, sorry."

"Should've said fifty."

"What?"

Tyson held a finger up to his lips. "Anyway, now that we know these leaks and saboteurs exist, the only question is what to do about them."

"Lock down the spaceports," Nakamura said. "Tell air traffic control to freeze travel into or out of the system until we can do a complete sweep of the population and isolate the operatives."

"And start rumors that containment has broken on the *Preakness,* start a public health panic?" Lassalle, the CFO, said, finally joining the conversation. "If you want to see our overnights drop a hundred points by morning, that's how to do it."

"Rene is right." Tyson took back the initiative. "Besides, such a drastic action would tip off our foes that we've discovered their scheme and give them time to erase evidence and bury bodies. Time we can't afford to give if we're going to make these charges stick at a full corporate tribunal."

"What about the Xre incursion?" Foz asked.

"An instance of terribly unfortunate timing."

"For us. Awfully convenient timing for whoever's behind this."

"I recognize that," Tyson conceded. "But the Xre see humans as a monolithic block; they don't differentiate between corporate entities. That's why we had to create the fleet in the first place. Besides, how would you bribe a Xre? With a crate of live bugs? They don't even have a concept of money."

"Point taken."

"I know it looks suspicious, but I just don't see how it comes to pass. It took almost three years of incessant negotiation after

112 • PATRICK S. TOMLINSON

the Intersection War just to figure out what the hell they wanted to negotiate over. Besides, if the Xre Grand Symphony really did decide to conspire against Ageless individually, there isn't a good goddamn we could do about it. So I'd prefer to stick to the wild-fires we have a hope of putting out."

"That's fair."

"To that end, we have to proceed quietly to avoid the panic Rene mentioned, and to keep our quarry from realizing they're being hunted in turn. We have three different lines of inquiry to follow: the communications leak between the *Preakness* and the Immortal Tower, the server-turned-spy, and now whoever engineered the bacteria. I'm already pursuing all of them as aggressively as discretion allows. We need to be patient until something turns up in our nets."

The room fell silent while each board member considered what they'd just heard. Finally, Nakamura spoke. "Motion to approve Tyson's approach. Is there a second?"

"Seconded," Foz said.

"It's to a vote, then."

Everyone thumbed at their consoles to register their secret ballot. Three in favor, two opposed, one abstention. *Good,* Tyson thought. He wouldn't have to be the official tiebreaker for his own proposal. Still, the twin "nay" votes irked him. For a moment, he considered letting Paris loose into the system to see who'd cast them, but decided against it. For the time being.

"Thank you, friends. We will continue on the course, and I will make sure to keep you all abreast of any developments. But I must reiterate the importance of confidentiality. Until we catch the perpetrators here on Lazarus, we have no idea who's listening. That said, I won't keep you from the evening's pleasures any longer. Good night."

With a goodbye wave of Tyson's hand, the ghosts returned to the fog. Then, the room's lights returned to normal levels to reveal Elsa leaning on Tyson's desk.

"Are board meetings always like that?"

"No, no. Not at all. There's usually more cursing. Are you all right? You look a little flush."

"I just gave a presentation to the seven most powerful people on the entire planet without any notice. It took me most of grad school to get over a crippling fear of public speaking. You could say I'm a little distressed."

Tyson looked over to the image of his assistant floating in the air just outside the window. "Paris, could you leave us for a moment, please?"

"Of course, sir." She faded away. Naturally, she hadn't actually gone anywhere, and would continue to see and hear everything that happened in the penthouse office, but it would make Elsa more comfortable.

Tyson gently grabbed Elsa by the elbow and locked with her eyes. "You did marvelously. They heard exactly what they needed to hear, and took your competence and integrity as a given. That's never assured at this level of play."

"If you say so."

"I do. I also have one other question before you go. What can you tell me about the people who engineered the bacteria?"

"Well, nothing. I have no idea who they are. I'm not even ready to say it was engineered as a bioweapon without more evidence. That's not how science works."

"Extrapolate. Give me an educated guess. Let's try this another way. How many people in your field could have uncovered the tampering? Not realize something was weird, but actually find fingerprints of the programming?"

"I don't know."

"Don't be modest. The woman who demanded the attention of a transtellar CEO on the sidewalk isn't modest."

"Fine, a few dozen, probably."

"And how many people could have done the programming?"

"The same few dozen."

"At how many labs?"

Elsa started to nod along. "Maybe ten universities on Earth have the necessary equipment and experience. A few military black labs I know nothing about. Maybe another half dozen out in the colonies."

"And the heads of these programs. How many of them did you study under, or go to school with? Work with once you graduated?"

"A lot of them. Maybe even most."

It was Tyson's turn to lean on the desk. "I've heard enough. You're working directly for me, now. You'll continue with your other duties, but you're going to start making discreet inquiries among your colleagues about these bacteria and try to narrow down the point of origin. Can you do that?"

"I don't have any idea. I'm a scientist, I'm not trained for espionage."

"That's no problem at all, because this is counter-espionage. Totally different thing. You'll start tomorrow, first thing. But tonight, I want you to go home and rest. Or go home and get drunk. Whatever your coping mechanism of choice happens to be."

"Am I really getting a raise?"

"Yes."

"A fifty-percent raise?" Elsa asked hopefully.

"Thirty. You had your chance. Come on, I'll walk you out."

"Thanks, but I think I can find the way."

"There's still guns in the elevator."

"Right."

TEN

As the meeting stretched into its third hour with no relief from the endless droning of Grendel's governor in sight, Susan's eyes threatened to go cross. A half-drunk pot of square dog took up space on the mess hall table among a flotilla of half-nibbled sandwiches. If she had to spend another five minutes sealed off in the compartment listening to Honshu's prattling, she would either scream or start shooting.

". . . which is not to say that our sensors or telescopes are nearly as sensitive as those on a military vessel, but my astronomers nonetheless have assured me that they detected three distinct gamma bursts consistent with fusion plant detonations in the vicinity of the Red Line. So I have to ask again, Captain, what was the source of those explosions? Who were you engaged with? Corsairs? The Xre, heaven forbid?"

Susan stretched her arms across the table like a cat, trying to keep them from cramping up after the aggressive pace she'd set during her endurance swim a few hours earlier. "Margo. May I call you Margo?"

"Of course, Susan."

"Great. Here's what I've learned from the last one hundred

and eighty-three minutes locked in this room with you. You have a nearly limitless capacity for rephrasing the same question and presenting it in new ways. But what you haven't deduced yet is I have a finite number of responses. Indeed, only one response. Which is 'I can neither confirm nor deny the specifics of our mission.' We could've saved each other a lot of time if I'd just recorded that sentence and let you replay it whenever you stopped talking long enough to take a breath."

Honshu's eyes narrowed. "I don't think I care for your tone, Susan. I'd remind you that I'm the ranking official in this system and I must insist on your respect."

"You are the ranking *civilian* official in this system. I do not dispute that, and I'm glad, even eager to be of whatever help to your efforts here that I can, so long as it's within my authority to do so. And believe it or not, I do recognize the challenging position I'm putting you in, here. I'm sorry for that, but I'm the ranking military officer on station, and I can't break operational security on just your say-so. This is a military matter, and I couldn't tell you jack shit even if I wanted to. When Fleet Com gives you clearance, then I'll be only too happy to open the logs to you. But until that happens, you'll just have to wait."

Honshu slapped her hands down on the table and shot to her feet. "It's my duty to defend the lives of every man, woman, and child on Grendel's surface and in orbit, Captain."

Susan remained seated, but her voice inched up and her tone sharpened. "Oh, my apologies, Governor. I was running under the impression that was why I was here with my giant warship. What with the hundreds of megatons of nukes in our silos and all, I must have gotten confused." She took off her top cover and handed it up to the fuming woman. "Here, do you want to make the transfer of command official right now? Otherwise, you've wasted a trip, and you're officially wasting my time."

Honshu spun around to face Nesbit. "Javier, you're her corporate liaison, surely you can talk some sense into our friends here?"

Nesbit adjusted his shirt collar. "That's an uphill battle at the best of times, Margo, but I'm afraid in this case, Captain Kamala is in the right. I haven't seen the communications between herself and Fleet Com, but if she's been placed under orders to preserve OpSec, then there's nothing either of us can say to get her or the rest of her crew to spill the beans. She would face a court-martial if she did."

"Well, then how about you? You're a civilian and not bound by the UCMJ. What have you seen?"

"I am a civilian. But as a CL, I'm at even less liberty to talk about what I see during my time onboard than Captain Kamala is. I'm under a strict nondisclosure agreement to keep nearly everything I see and hear during my tour confidential. If I tell you anything, my career would be over and I'd be facing incredibly steep civil penalties. It's the only way to ensure enough trust between a crew and their CL to make this . . . challenging relationship work." Nesbit shook his head mournfully. "I'm sorry, Margo, but I can't help you, either."

The awkward silence that followed was broken by the sound of a spinning hatch lock. The door swung inward to reveal the drawn face of Ensign Mattu.

"Excuse me for a moment," Susan said, not caring what anyone thought of it as she pushed away from the table and walked to the hatch and greeted her drone integration officer.

"Sorry to interrupt, mum."

"Oh, believe me, you aren't interrupting anything," Susan reassured her. "What's up, Scopes?"

"We've had a hit. Platform Twenty-three made a positive contact. Twenty-four was close enough for a tentative overlap confirmation."

"Another armed drone?"

"No, mum. The whole bean burrito. It matches the emissions of the Xre ship we engaged two weeks ago, right down to the IR signature. The bastards aren't even bothering to run EM silent. It's like they wanted to be found."

"Where are they?"

"Forty-thousand klicks outside the Red Line on a bearing of one-five-seven-seven."

"Shit." Susan scratched behind her ear. "Well, nothing for it. They want to play, we'll play. Mark them Bandit One on the plot. Go to the CIC. Tell the XO we're going to battle stations as soon as our guests are on their shuttle. Tell Charts to be ready to blow their bubble for a zero-zero intercept fifty-thousand klicks sunward of Bandit One the second the governor's shuttle is clear of our gooey zone. And tell Guns to get all her toys ready. You copy all that?"

"Battle stations. Blow a bubble for zero-zero fifty kiloklicks from Bandit One. Flood the tubes and warm up the cat toys. And don't turn the governor into soup."

Susan clapped the younger woman on the shoulder. "That's it, Scopes. Go on. I won't be long."

Mattu nodded. "Mum."

Susan smiled warmly as Mattu receded down the hallway, then steeled herself once more and closed the hatch, despite the fact she'd be opening it again in approximately sixty seconds. Some habits weren't meant to be broken.

She turned back to the mess hall and the trio of foreign dignitaries taking up space on her deck. "Well, as much as I'd love to say I hate cutting this meeting short, it really should've been cut 'short' two hours ago. We've all got better things to do, and we all have . . ." Susan feigned looking at a nonexistent wristwatch. ". . . five minutes to start doing them."

"You can't be serious," Honshu objected. "You have no authority."

"Lady," Susan finally snapped, "you're on *my* ship. Here, in this place, the *Ansari* is all of creation, and I am her maker. My voice is the word of God. The cranky, Old Testament God who dabbled in smiting. And that voice just said you have four minutes and forty-seven seconds to exit the premises."

"For what?!"

"Training drill."

"You expect us to believe you had a training exercise scheduled for this very moment that you forgot about? Don't be absurd."

"Slipped my mind." Susan spun the wheel open and let the hatch swing inward. "Your shuttle is refueled and standing by for launch. In your own time, Governor."

Honshu gathered herself up and stalked toward the hatch with her paired attendants in her wake. "I'll be sending a report about this meeting to my supervising vice president. It will be *sternly* worded."

"That is truly a terrifying prospect, Margo. I don't know how I'll sleep at night with that hanging over my head."

Susan and Nesbit escorted them back to the boat bay and watched Honshu walk the short distance down the gangway until she disappeared inside her shuttle and the hatch buttoned up. The small craft cut loose from the docking tube in the silence of vacuum.

"Thank you, Javier," Susan said quietly.

"For what?"

"Backing me up in there."

"I told the truth, Captain, nothing more or less. She was out of line, even if I sympathized with her position."

"Still. Thank you."

"We're not conducting a drill, are we?"

Susan shook her head. "Nope."

Two jets of steam erupted from reaction control thrusters on the nose and gently pushed the shuttle backward out of the bay and into open space. As soon as it was clear and the doors began to close, Susan spun about and headed for the lift that would take her to the CIC.

"What's our status, XO?" she asked Miguel through her internal com.

"Mattu just arrived and relayed your orders, mum. Charts

is plotting our bubble now. Guns says she's ready to overkill something."

"Good. Take us to battle stations. Tell Charts to blow our bubble the millisecond the governor's shuttle is clear of our gooey zone. I'm on my way up."

Susan reached the bridge less than a minute later with Nesbit in tow. The marine guard, whose face was no longer blue, saluted and opened the hatch, forgoing the formality of granting her permission to enter.

"Captain on deck! CL on deck!"

"At ease." Susan swept into her chair. "Where are we at?"

"The governor's shuttle is twelve seconds from minimum safe distance," Broadchurch reported.

"Bandit One status unchanged. Looks like they're waiting for us," Mattu said.

"All weapons charged and loaded. CiWS is hot. Decoys and AMMs charged in their tubes," Warner barked a little too eagerly.

Susan looked to each member of her bridge shift in turn, taking a moment to consider their expressions. There was the anxiety everyone felt before combat, even the captain herself. But, lurking just below the apprehension was a hunger, an eagerness, even excitement. They were predators, after all. Patiently waiting at the center of a web spanning hundreds of millions of kilometers, ready to pounce. Their prey had become entangled once, only to slip free of the trap. And that just wouldn't do.

Scared as they were, everyone present was thirsty for the rematch.

"Governor Honshu's shuttle has reached minimum safe, mum," Broadchurch announced. "We're clear for maneuvering. Beta and Gamma rings queued up and ready."

"Send the navigation alert, then blow our bubble."

"Yes'm."

"Lieutenant Warner." Susan leaned forward in her chair just a hair. "Don't be too itchy on that trigger finger."

"Just put some cream on it before my shift, mum."

"Uh-huh. Charts, if you please, blow me."

Broadchurch smirked. "As you wish, mum." They twisted a virtual icon, and Susan's jaw started to hurt in the old familiar way. This time, honestly, she didn't even mind.

If my jaw must hurt, let it be because I've tired it chewing on their bones, she thought with venom. *Or is it their shells?*

The tiny universe the *Ansari* created for itself popped before she could even finish the thought as they reemerged into the real cosmos almost thirteen AU from where they'd just been. The Xre ship had taken up position on the far side of the system from Grendel this time, so their drone data at the moment the bubble burst was a hundred and six minutes behind. Anything could have happened during the interim. Susan's stomach did backflips while she stared intently at Ensign Mattu as she rushed to collect updated sensor data.

"Bandit One reacquired. They haven't budged an inch. Wait one . . ." Everyone turned to face the Drone Integration Station. "They're on the move. Drive plume just lit off and they're changing their bearing to match our position. Heading for the Red Line."

"Have they deployed drones?"

"Nothing on the scopes, mum. If they're present, the Xre have them running passive."

Susan rubbed the side of her jaw where the ache from the bubble lingered. They'd been here for the better part of two hours. It would be criminally incompetent not to have used at least some of that time getting recon platforms in place, and whoever was skippering the other boat had already proven themselves to be anything but.

"Well, it would be rude to keep them waiting. Helm, all ahead full. Reciprocal bearing to Bandit One."

"Helm, all ahead full, reciprocal bearing to Bandit One," Miguel echoed just below a shout.

"All ahead full, reciprocal bearing, aye!" Broadchurch completed the cycle. At the *Ansari*'s aft, an array of five radially mounted fusion rockets lit off simultaneously and throttled up from idle to their full capacity in less than a second. The ship's artificial gravity adjusted automatically to compensate for the sudden acceleration so that the crew never felt more than the preprogrammed eight-tenths gravity, but it wasn't instantaneous. For just a moment, Susan felt her ship pushing against the soles of her feet like a spurned beast.

At her fingertips was more combined combat capability and firepower than all but the most powerful nations of Earth at the turn of the last century. Her home could bring entire star systems to heel by itself if she so ordered it. And it was on the move, doing what it had been built to do, charging toward the enemy it had been designed to fight.

Despite the tension on the bridge, it made her smile.

"Aspect change!" Mattu shouted. "Bandit One's acceleration just spiked. Gamma emissions indicate a full emergency military burn. Repeat, full emergency burn."

That raised eyebrows. Susan looked up at Miguel's face hovering as it always did just over her shoulder. Concern traced in lines across his forehead, but somehow managed not to reach his eyes.

Both human and Xre technology were close to evenly matched. Of course, if it had been otherwise at the moment of their intersection, one would have lost quickly and definitively to the other. Both species moved about the galaxy at FTL speeds using equivalent Alcubierre drive systems. And both moved about in normal space using antimatter/fusion hybrid rockets that under normal circumstances used small quantities of antiprotons as a catalyst to trigger a fusion reaction burning traditional deuterium or helium-3 fuels.

But, under extreme circumstances, a captain had the option to bypass the fusion reaction and move to direct matter/antimatter annihilation in their rocket plume by dumping raw antimatter into the reaction chamber. This provided half again as much thrust by converting nearly the entire volume of reactant mass directly into high-energy gamma radiation and allowed for higher acceleration rates than any fusion process. It was analogous to fighter jets of the twentieth and twenty-first centuries and their afterburners. However, it also chewed through precious antimatter reserves at a simply scandalous rate, and bathed a ship's vital components aft of the rad shielding in corrosive amounts of hard radiation, to say nothing of the inevitable seepage into the habitable compartments.

There was a reason it was called an *emergency burn*.

"Someone's in an awful big hurry," Miguel mused.

"Did we agree to a second date I'm not aware of?" Susan asked.

"Must have. Glad I shaved today."

"You shave every day."

"Not talking about my face, mum."

Susan looked up and smacked him on the shoulder. "A time like this and you're putting that image in my head? Seriously?"

"Just lightening the mood. What do you think they're up to?"

"I think . . ." Susan paused, acutely aware of getting burned the last time she'd tried and failed to anticipate her opponent's move. ". . . I think they're trying to draw us past the Red Line. I think they're baiting us, trying to get us to rush out to intercept them in free space. Things get murky out there, legally speaking. Why else would they gobble up antimatter in an emergency burn? Just to move up the engagement a handful of minutes? Who's that eager to die? No, this isn't about rushing in to meet us with their tanks half-depleted. This is about choosing the place of the encounter."

"Swing set, or the warehouse," Miguel said.

"Pardon?"

"Sorry, mum. When I was a kid in Recife, we had rules for

different kinds of fights. If you needed to defend your honor, you did it by the swing set during recess where the teachers would break it up before anything got out of hand. If you demanded blood, you met behind the old warehouse after school let out."

"Did you meet behind the warehouse a lot, Miguel?"

"Only once," he said solemnly. "No one wanted to meet me there after that."

Susan realized in that moment that her reserved, polite XO probably had tattoos under his uniform that would break all sorts of fleet regs. "So what's your advice for our upstart friends here? Swing set, or the warehouse?"

"Swing set should do. No blood has been spilled. This is all still for the sake of appearances."

"So it is. Helm, reduce our acceleration to intercept Bandit One on *our* side of the Red Line."

"By how far, mum?" Broadchurch inquired.

"Whatever distance you think long enough to hold up under a board of inquiry."

"One hundred klicks it is, mum."

Susan smirked as she felt the acceleration change as a slight easing of pressure on the balls of her feet. At this distance, the Xre would be aware of any changes they made in course or speed in less than half a second. Susan watched the plot carefully to see if cutting her accel prompted any change or adjustment on the part of her opponent, but they just kept barreling forward, throwing antimatter into the furnaces at their tail.

It wasn't just dangerous, it was wasteful as hell. Susan got nervous whenever her antimatter stores dropped below eighty percent and either started looking around for a place to top off her tanks, or call in a fleet oiler for an UnRep. Fortunately, she had a ready supply of both in orbit around Grendel. But the Xre ship didn't exactly have docking privileges at a CCDF antimatter factory, and the nearest Xre-controlled system was almost three dozen light-years away.

Either their new supercruiser was built with simply ridiculous endurance in mind, which might explain some of its size, or they had their own refueling ship or even a forward operating depot hiding deeper in the system.

Or, they didn't expect to be coming home. . . .

Susan swallowed hard. Watching Bandit One's blinking red icon barreling toward her position, it was a disquieting thought, but it didn't fit the facts. They'd been hiding at the edges of the system for a month already, at least since the *Ansari* had lost its first drone. They needed to be thoughtful and meticulous to stay in the shadows. Indeed, if it hadn't been for the fog machine giving Susan the edge, they'd probably still be prowling the system with hunter/killer drones slowly and methodically eroding her recon platform fleet. And they'd been downright devious in the ensuing escape. That wasn't the modus operandi of a kamikaze mission.

But then why the hell were they on an emergency burn *now*? It just didn't make any sort of tactical sense. She was missing some important part of their thinking. Or someone else's thinking. Lord knew ship captains sometimes had to make the best out of bullshit orders from on high. That was probably universal.

"Why are they still under emergency burn?" Susan finally asked aloud. "It's obvious now we're not rising to the bait. Why keep burning A/M?"

"Maybe they're holding it a little longer, hoping to call our bluff," Miguel suggested. "They burn up another couple minutes of A/M pretending to be serious, we second-guess ourselves enough to change our minds and run out there."

"Maybe . . ." Susan crossed her legs and leaned an elbow on her knee. "Or maybe they have a resupply floating around out there and don't care about the fuel burn. They're only trying to look desperate." Her hands absently rubbed at the top of her legs as she chewed on the multidimensional chess moves lying before her. "Cut our accel to zero. Go on the drift. Quick Quiet. We're passive in five."

"Charts, blow out our candles! Scopes, Quick Quiet!" Miguel repeated her orders, then keyed into the 1MC. "All hands, Quick Quiet, Quick Quiet. This is not a drill."

Everyone grabbed the crash-webbing built into their chairs and buckled up in anticipation of the disappearance of gravity. Overhead lights shut down, replaced by the green glow of phosphorescent lights. EM dark was only the first level of emissions dampening. It meant shutting down all active sensor arrays and radio communications. Quick Quiet was the next level, and meant cutting power to all noncombat systems to reduce the ship's electromagnetic signature further still.

There was a third level. Blackout. Which was exactly what it sounded like. All electrical activity onboard ceased except for minimal life support. The ship became a hole in space, utterly defenseless, its survival dependent entirely on avoiding discovery.

Nobody ever wanted to go into blackout.

"Accel zeroed out, fusion rockets at idle," Broadchurch echoed even as the sensation of weightlessness washed over everyone present. The great nuclear fires at the tail end of the ship died away, leaving her to coast on what momentum she'd already built.

"Quick Quiet," Mattu answered. "Active radar and lidar arrays powered down and on standby. Telescopes and receivers only."

"Give me a burn to starboard minus five degrees," Susan said conversationally, "Cold thrusters only, twenty-percent capacity. Just enough to get us out of the way of any railgun rounds they might have just fired against our last known course and heading."

"Charts, cold thruster burn to starboard minus five. Twenty percent for thirty seconds."

"Cold thrust starboard minus five for thirty ticks at one-fifth, aye sir."

At eight points on the outside of the *Ansari*'s hull, highly pressurized puffs of water atomized into nearly molecule-scale droplets shot into space at many thousands of meters per second, freezing instantaneously before cooling to the ambient temperature surrounding them. Working as they did against the immense mass of the ship, the cold thrusters imparted very little momentum compared to the ship's arrays of vasimr reaction control thrusters. Indeed, even with artificial gravity compensation switched off, it was difficult to tell they'd adjusted course at all.

However, what the cold thrusters lacked in horsepower, they made up for in stealth. They neither required much in the way of electrical power, nor left a telltale trail of ionized, million-degree gas for enemy sensors to spot like a shooting star. After thirty seconds of "burn," the *Ansari* was several widths away from where she'd been relative to the last course anyone should have seen her on, which would be enough to keep her from getting cored by a railgun projectile, or roasted by a laser beam fired at them in frustration.

"Warm up a decoy and have it ready to kick out. Just in case," Susan said without taking her eyes off the plot.

Miguel cracked his knuckles. "Scopes, ready a decoy. Hold launch until ordered."

"Prep and hold decoy bird, aye. Standing by."

Susan stared at the plot, half expecting the bandit to bubble out at any moment, but instead it just kept plowing ahead at emergency flank speed, shining like a torch for the whole system to see. Even Grendel's telescopes would be in on the show.

"Looks like the governor's getting her confirmation after all," she said.

"Not even half-blind civvy scopes could miss that plume," Miguel agreed. "They'll know in a couple of hours that we're playing chicken with something big and nasty out here."

"That might come in handy, actually."

"What are you thinking?"

"I'm thinking they wouldn't be burning through A/M like a paycheck on shore leave if they didn't have an oiler hiding in the black somewhere. Grendel can use its telescopes to look for it while we're out here playing chicken."

"With civilian scopes, that's going to be the proverbial needle in a haystack."

She shrugged. "It's a long shot anyway, and it lightens our workload."

Miguel leaned down to Susan's right shoulder and pitched his voice lower. "Getting a little ahead of ourselves, aren't we? We still have to survive the next ten minutes. What's *our* next move?"

"Nothing," Susan whispered. "We wait until they make one, then respond appropriately. Just wish I had a better idea what in the hell they're thinking over there."

ELEVEN

"What in the Abyss are they thinking over there?" Thuk said to the mind cavern at large as he stared, slack-mandibles, into the tactical display. The *Ansari,* which had been there only a moment before, had suddenly disappeared from their eyes entirely.

"What do our husks see? Anything?"

"Nothing, Derstu," Kivits said from the husk-monitoring alcove. "They cut their fires and slipped beneath the dark ocean."

"There has to be *something*. They didn't spin a seedpod. We would've seen it."

"There's a slight . . . fuzziness, Derstu, but it's dissipating."

"What do you mean, 'fuzziness'?" Thuk took two long steps to where Kivits sat and pushed him out of the way. He'd trained on husks and sniffers before he'd been assigned to the *Chusexx* and didn't want to waste the time waiting for a straight answer. One of their husks, unit seven, tracked a small cloud of, judging from its rainbow hashes, what must have been frozen water vapor. Thuk ran the data time-stream backward to the moment the cloud appeared. On the exact course the *Ansari* had been on before it disappeared.

"It's propellant," he said. "They've moved off course."

"But there's no ionization trail," Dulac Kivits said.

"Because they aren't using full-powered thrusters," Thuk said as if to a child fresh out of their third molting. "They're using steam rockets."

"That's ridiculous," Kivits said. "They'd have no thrust."

"That's not the point!" The fingers on Thuk's primehands frantically danced across the interface, trying to extrapolate an approximation of the *Ansari*'s location by estimating the mass and speed of the vapor cloud and working backward, but there were just too many variables. Getting an accurate read of the mass of the cloud was impossible without multiple husks providing enough vantage points to model it in three dimensions. The closest he could narrow the sphere of possibility down to was more than a hundred markers. Useless for plotting an attack vector for anything but javelins. By the time they actually reached the treaty line, that uncertainty would have grown exponentially.

Thuk clapped his midarms in frustration and pushed away from the panel. "Am I the only one who's read scrolls since the last war?" he demanded. "The humans have had these steam rockets in place for thirty years. They're not meant to be powerful. They're meant to be silent."

"So they can run and hide," Kivits preened triumphantly. "We've scared them into silence!"

Thuk stared at the dulac for a long, uncomfortable quiet before speaking again. The eyes of the mind cavern all turned instinctively to see what came next. Xre were very patient, but the one thing they couldn't stand was silence in the company of others.

"Did the kunji beasts in the rivers outside your mound slip beneath the water because they were scared, Kivits?"

"You give these humans too much credit."

"And you give them far too little. They fought us to a draw for three years using modified transports and bulk freighters." Thuk pointed a primehand blood-claw at the tactical display running around the circumference of the mind cavern. "And *that* human has already thrown a light-spear at us. They're not out here to, what do they say? Fuck around? Their derstu is patient, cautious, persistent, cunning, and eager to fight. What about everything you've seen since we arrived leads you to believe they're hiding out of fear instead of seeking advantage?"

Kivits clicked his mandibles together twice in annoyed deference. "We will share a song when this is over, Derstu," he said with a chill. "What are your instructions?"

"Cut the burn and spin up a seedpod for the far side of the system and try again in a few days. They haven't taken our lure and they're not going to. We're just wasting annihilation fuel continuing this pointless charge."

"And our husks?"

"We don't have time to fly them back into their nests. Mark them and put them in hibernation. We'll recover them later."

Kivits looked around the mind cavern. "Well? Your derstu has sung. Execute his instructions." The attendants turned back to their alcoves and busied themselves with the work.

Kivits leaned close and whispered at Thuk's sound bristles. "Derstu, I would sing with you. In a duet."

"Before the seedpod is sewn?"

Kivits glanced around the chamber and tapped his abdomen plates with the claws on his midhands. "I think our brave attendants can handle a withdrawal. Harmonize?"

"As you say."

Kivits left the cavern, expecting Thuk to trail behind him, which he did, eventually. In his own flow. Long enough that he had to ask the ship for the dulac's present location.

"The dulac is in the clutching chamber."

"Alone?"

"Yes, Derstu."

"Thank you."

By long tradition, every Xre ship had a clutching chamber,

because every Xre ship might be called upon someday to participate in a migration to a new colony many stars away. And new colonies would need new builders when they arrived. Ships of conquest like the *Chusexx* were not intended to be colony ships, but they needed to be equipped to fill the role if the need was desperate enough. A species that had lost its original homeworld never forgot the lesson.

And although it was prohibited, it wasn't completely unknown for select members of a harmony on a long-duration campaign such as this to, inadvertently, clutch a brood during the dull periods. Those responsible would be dismissed from the Dark Ocean Chorus at the end of the campaign, of course, but their children should hardly be punished for the sins of their parents. That tradition had died with the queens. Or, more accurately, been killed along with them.

So *Chusexx* had in its belly a small, rudimentary, completely unadorned clutching chamber which, naturally, was most often used for secret rendezvous among the adventurously amorous.

This would not be such a meeting.

"You walk the path slowly," Kivits said as Thuk entered.

"Forgive the delay, Dulac. I wanted to see my instructions carried out."

"*Your* instructions." The words dribbled past Kivit's mandibles as if he'd expelled them for tasting sour. "You're fresh out of a molt, and yet your head has already grown too big for its new skullplates." Kivits picked at an excess bit of sealant that had been pressed out from between a joint during the chamber's construction. "I've served over other derstus, you know. You are my fifth, my third who was on their first assignment to the honor."

Thuk sniffed at his choice of words. Of all the words used to describe a selection as derstu, "honor" was seldom near the top of the list.

Kivits continued. "It's not unusual for a first-time selection to forget their purpose and develop quite an ego in a short amount of time. But your transformation has been especially rapid. Which is why I must remind you, Thuk, that you have been picked to facilitate and implement the decisions of this harmony, our chorus, and ultimately the Symphony itself in the most expedient way. Your judgment is only valued for doing that job quickly and efficiently. You're not here to lead us. You're not here to lecture us. The time of tyrants died with the queens in their mounds on the Old World. You're not going to be the one to resurrect it, no matter how many scrolls you've read about the humans or the last war.

"I've come to you because other members of the harmony have begun humming their discontent, and I wanted you to hear it from me privately while there was still time to adjust your path. No one needs to know what we've discussed here. A dulac may give any sort of console. Just . . . just return to your duty, humbled, and maybe you won't be selected derstu for the next half dozen assignments, or expelled from the Chorus entirely. Do you understand?"

Thuk understood, all right. He'd pushed Kivits too hard in front of the mind cavern attendants and embarrassed him. In a moment of frustration, he'd forgotten Kivits was labor caste, and held all the old prejudices that came with that heritage. His ancestors had been the ones to unify across the mounds and finally break the back of the queens' rule as their original homeworld died around them. They were the hands and claws that built the first colony ships, under the guidance of the scholar and administrative sects. Their descendants, like Kivits, carried that history with no small amount of pride.

It was possible, even probable, that the only member of the harmony who'd objected to Thuk's . . . guidance, was Kivits himself. But, that didn't mean that he was wrong, necessarily. Or that Thuk wouldn't benefit from an adjustment in his approach.

"I've disrespected you," Thuk said remorsefully. "You've done nothing but try to steer me down the path laid out for me, and I've resisted. Out of pride, or arrogance. It's too easy for us four-hands to fall into the old patterns that . . . well, you know better than most." Thuk hinted with a midhand at Kivits's quadfeet. It was a small gesture. Pointing with midhands instead of primehands was a submissive gesture, because the midhands sheathed no blood-claws.

But it was enough.

"It's in your line's nature to yearn to govern, Derstu," Kivits said. "The very best of you recognize it and work to suppress it. I'm encouraged to see you accessible to reason."

"I walk the path."

"Indeed." Kivits took a lap around the clutching chamber, letting the fall of each of his four feet echo around the space. "What do we do about the human cruiser?"

"It would be easier to answer that question if I knew what the Symphony really hoped to achieve with our assignment here."

"I've read the same dispatches you have."

"That's what worries me, Kivits. They're instructions, but that's all. They lack context to help us determine the intentions and motivations behind the instructions. You've been dulac over six derstus. Have you ever seen a song from the Chorus with so few layers? Such amateurish composition?"

"Not for an entire assignment. For simple things like 'Proceed to Adrolor for resupply,' but not for something of this . . . delicacy."

"Exactly!" Thuk said, unable to contain himself. "We're out here perched on top of the most powerful weapon our race has ever conceived of, facing the only mound that has ever fought us to a standstill, and the Dark Ocean Chorus has left us spinning like a felled leaf caught in a river curl. Spinning, no direction." Thuk moved in for the rhetorical kill. "Even the Seven Sacrifices were trusted enough by their queens to be told their true purpose, but our harmony can't be? Tell me that doesn't bother you. I will trust your judgment and say no more of it."

"*Chasm below,*" Kivits swore. "That's not exactly fair."

"It's a simple enough question."

"The hardest questions usually are." Kivits clicked his man-dibles, then grew quiet, contemplative. It stretched long. So long even Thuk felt the ancestral urge to fill the silence with something. Clicking, humming, rubbing the signalers of his midarms together. Anything.

"Yes, it bothers me," he said at last. "But what are we supposed to do about it? We have their song."

"It's enough for now that we've given voice to our concerns. I'm glad to know we're reading from the same scroll on this. As for what we do about it, maybe nothing. Maybe the rest of the assignment goes off free of rain and wind and we never have to speak of this again."

"And if the rain falls and the wind scours our plates?"

"I don't know, Kivits," Thuk said honestly. "But we should be thinking about an answer. This human ship and its . . . *cop-tan* are clever and dangerous enough. I'd rather have reassurance that I only need to worry about the enemy in front of me. Maybe request clarification of our instructions from the Chorus?"

Kivits pondered this. "We risk appearing disrespectful, and there's no assurance we'll learn anything new. They could just repeat the song, or refuse to answer altogether."

"That itself would teach us something, wouldn't it?"

"I suppose so." Kivits scratched at one of his elbow joints. "All right, we're in harmony. We'll send another singing husk back to the Chorus."

"Good, I'll return to the mind cavern and get it sent off immediately."

"I assume I don't have to tell you not to poison the minds of the rest of the harmony with your paranoia?"

"That you share?"

"*Our* paranoia," Kivits corrected. "They're bearing enough weight already and don't need two fools adding to the burden."

"I agree," Thuk said. "Although I think our recording atten-dant harbors her own suspicions."

"Hurg?" Kivits said, imitating the sound one makes before regurgitating. "I don't care for that one."

"Her performance appraisals have been exemplary," Thuk answered back.

"It's not her competence I dislike. It's her arrogance. Carrying her wing sheaths between molts, rubbing her nobility in our faces."

Ah, of course that was it. "Come now, Kivits. How would you react if everyone expected you to walk on your hindlegs and pretend your forelegs were midhands?"

Kivits exhaled, a long, slow sound. "Not well, I expect."

"Nor I, if you demanded I walk around on my midhands as if I had quadlegs. The queens were deposed centuries ago. Let her be what she is. If she tries to mutiny, I'll hold the double-door open for you to throw her into the dark ocean."

"I'll hold you to that."

"Something tells me it won't come to that. Our young royal is eager to gratify and quite a bright spark."

Kivits ran a hand gently down the wall of the clutching chamber, almost wistfully. A wisp of shame danced over the dulac's features and it all came into focus. Gently, so as not to raise attention, Thuk grazed a few nearby surfaces with the finger pads of his primehands, sampling the oily residue coating the material as he did so. The pheromones told the story the dulac dared not. Thuk swirled the tips of his finger pads together absently, tasting the past.

Kivits and Hurg had been in this very spot, no more than three or four days ago. And they'd been aroused. So, the dulac had a secret tryst with a royal. Quite the scandal, but hardly unique. After the Fall of the Queens, many among the former laborer caste succumbed to the temptation to, quite literally, stick it to a royal bloodline. As perversions went, it bordered on the mundane, but Thuk tucked the knowledge away in the back of his memory regardless.

You never knew when a little gossip could come in handy.

"I should return to the mind cavern. We're on the far side of the system by now and the attendants will be trying to get our bearings. Decisions will need to be made."

"Yes, of course." Kivits moved aside to open the path out of the clutching chamber. "But don't forget what we've discussed here."

"Oh, I won't forget what I've learned today," Thuk said, his meaning deliberately ambiguous as he left Kivits behind.

TWELVE

The bartender poured two fingers of junmai daiginjo sake from a chilled carafe into Tyson's cup. The clear, floral liquid filled his nose as quickly as it filled the cup. Chilled to a perfect two degrees, the imported sake was a welcome distraction after a brutal day.

The Nakamura family's craft brewery on the outskirts made an excellent range of sakes from locally cultivated rice, but this wasn't one of those. Instead, Tyson had come across the intoxicating brew during an extended business trip to Kyoto several years ago and had a case shipped home. It was genuine Japanese sake, brewed by the Asahi Shuzo brewery in the Yamaguchi Prefecture.

It was probably the most embarrassingly expensive liquor on the entire planet. And Tyson was the only person besides the bartenders in Klub Kryptonite that knew it was even here. A fact that at least one of them had taken advantage of, as half a bottle had been lost to "spillage" over the last several months, but Tyson didn't mind. Let them live a little, he thought.

"Thank you, James," he said, then lifted the small porcelain cup and sipped its contents. Crisp notes of apple and strawberry played across his tongue. Amazing what could be accomplished with nothing more than rice, water, time, and skill.

Kryptonite was located on the sixty-ninth floor of the Immortal Tower. Its imported marble countertops and barstools floated above the floor, trapped in electromagnetic eddy currents strong enough to hold up many hundreds of kilos thanks to steel strips imbued into their undersides. After a little idle digging, Tyson had learned the name was a clever joke referring to the one weakness of an immortal hero from twentieth-century Earth mythology. If anything fit that bill for the majority of the tower's residents and employees, alcohol was it.

During the work week, Kryptonite was an exclusive bar patronized by executives and the ladder-climbers eager to impress their superiors. Friday and Saturday nights, it was a velvet-rope, invite-only music and dance club for Methuselah's beautiful people and trust-fund babies, and the lecherous men and women who preyed upon them with promises of jobs or paid-for leisure and comfort.

But, being as it was a Tuesday evening, it was just Tyson and James.

Tyson glanced down at his tablet. The display was encrypted to the implants in his eyes. Anyone else casually glancing at the screen would see only static. He could read the reports within his augmented reality environment just as easily, of course. But Tyson, for some indelible reason, had always preferred to keep whatever he was reading out of his head and in his hands. It was a strange quirk, but harmless. Today, he wanted to keep the news at arm's length.

The two-headed monster of the Teegarden bacteria and the Xre incursion near Grendel had, in forty-eight short hours, wiped out almost seven years of Ageless Corp. stock growth. It was now the biggest drop in company history over such a short span at a time the rest of the market was running with the bulls. Despite furious attempts by his PR department at spin control, the fallout from the INN interview had been decimating. No one had any idea how to stop the hemorrhaging. The board was verging on panic as many tens of billions of nudollars' worth of market cap disappeared. For his part, Tyson was steeling himself to weather the storm and find out where the new bottom was while he pressed ahead with his investigation. There really didn't seem to be anything else to do.

"Long day?" the bartender asked.

"Longest on record." Tyson swirled his cup, then took another sip.

"I'd heard about the incursion. That was some bad luck."

Tyson waved it off. "That's the least of my problems."

"An alien invasion is the least of your problems? Wow, that *is* a long day," James said with a wink.

"It's hardly an invasion, just saber-rattling."

"If you say so. Then again, I just pour the booze. The big-ticket stuff is a little beyond the purview of people who live off tips."

"We're all living off tips, James. That's all profit is. The tip customers are willing to pay for making their lives a little easier, or longer, or more entertaining. You just earn yours on a person-by-person basis."

"Hmm, I hadn't thought of it like that. These other problems, anything you want to talk about?"

"Want to? Sure. Able to? No, not really."

James nodded as he loaded the small glass-washer at his waist. "That's fine. There's a lot of nervous people around is all. We have some mutated space super-plague in orbit, bug-eating aliens knocking at our back door—it's a lot for folks to take in."

"It's a lot for me to take in, James, believe that."

"I do. Haven't seen you in a state like this since . . . what was her name? Rachel, Rochelle?"

"Really? You're going to bring her up? I thought bartenders were supposed to help their customers forget."

"Well, which one would you rather be thinking about right now?"

"You've got me there." Tyson pulled a bit of fluff off his sleeve. "You're trying to get me to say something reassuring, aren't you?"

James shrugged. "Lot of people are looking for reassurance. It's to be expected. We haven't had any trouble with the Xre since most of our grandparents were kids. People come to me for comfort, just as you did. If I can give them some that I got right from the source, well, it would go a long way to easing their minds. And fattening my tips up a bit."

Tyson chuckled at that. "All about the bottom line, hey?"

"I'm providing a service."

"Indeed you are." Tyson drained the rest of the contents of his cup, which had begun to warm. "A fresh chilled cup and another shot, James. And pour yourself one."

"That's very kind of you, sir."

"I know you're sneaking them anyway. May as well make it legitimate."

James's normally smooth, flowing movement from one task into the next faltered for the briefest of moments, but quickly recovered. If he hadn't been looking closely, Tyson wouldn't have picked up on it at all. But he had been, and he knew the message had been received louder than if he'd shouted it. His private store of genuine junmai sake would once again be there for his pleasure alone.

His father had taught him many indirect lessons, but the most important had been the value of a subtle application of power. James set two cups down on the bar and emptied the rest of the carafe. They clinked cups, dipped to tap the bar, then drank together.

"Oh, that *is* lovely." James set the cup down on the floating marble.

"The finest." Tyson leaned back from the bar. Maybe it wouldn't hurt to give James something to spread around. He was well-liked and well-connected among the bar's influential patrons, and most people trusted the word of their favorite bartender a hell of a lot more than any newscaster or CEO. There was no sense keeping secrets that had already gotten out.

"You want some good news to spread around? I'll oblige. I've got a whipcrack smart lady coordinating the mission to eradicate this bacteria, and she's confident her team is on the verge of a treatment breakthrough. As far as the Xre are concerned, the fleet has already bumped up to full alert status. It's not a threat to Ageless, it's a danger to every transtellar in human-controlled space. Fleet is treating it accordingly. And you didn't hear this from me . . ." Tyson held the man's gaze until he got a nod to continue. ". . . but the ship stationed over Grendel is the *Ansari,* an endurance cruiser straight out of drydock with a fresh coat of paint and bristling with upgrades. Her captain has already sent the Xre running once and destroyed several of their drones and decoys. The situation is in good hands."

"That's good to hear," James said. "I'm sure more than a few people will be glad to hear it."

"Now, now, James." Tyson touched his nose. "Our secret."

"Of course. Another, Mr. Abington?"

"One more, then perhaps an appetizer menu?"

"Coming right up, sir."

Tyson laced his fingers behind his head and savored the small victory for exactly three seconds before the next fresh hell greeted him like a jilted lover.

"Sir, I have news," Paris said into his auditory implants.

"I'm trying to enjoy a quiet drink and a bite to eat, Paris."

"Apologies, but I wouldn't interrupt if it could wait."

Tyson's right fist balled up. "No, I suppose you wouldn't. What do you have for me?"

"Two items, actually. First, I've discovered the source of the leak from the freighter, sir. It wasn't a person, it was a limited

AI program. Buried deep in a communications subroutine. The worm tapped into the ship's comm records, then broadcast the information through tiny manipulations of the output of the freighter's fusion drive plume once it started decelerating toward Lazarus. Anyone listening on standard radio channels wouldn't hear a thing, but anyone who knew what to look for with a sufficiently powerful telescope and a modified fiber-optic cable repeater could read it clear as day."

"So there's no fingerprints on the local net, either?"

"I'm afraid not."

Tyson swore under his breath. It was a very clever plan, he had to acknowledge that much.

"I still get my carapace, yes?" Paris asked coyly.

"If you can trace the worm backward to where and when it was uploaded to the ship."

"I'm already working on it. And I've already ordered the carapace. I didn't think you'd mind that much."

Tyson let his assistant's indiscretion slide. "And the second item?"

"I have your spy."

That grabbed Tyson's attention. The annoyance he felt at the interruption melted away in an instant as his back went rigid. "When?"

"A few minutes ago. Methuselah PD wheeled her into Xanadu Hospital."

"I want to speak with her at once."

"That . . . will be a one-sided conversation."

"She's *dead*?"

"About as dead as one of you can be, if the initial report is to be believed. You've been formally requested to identify the body, in fact. Or what remains of it."

Tyson's stomach lurched at the implication. "Understood. Have a pod waiting for me downstairs."

"It's already parked. And sir, I would really feel better if you'd let me assign a security detachment to your person."

"I haven't had bodyguards since I took the job, Paris. Being seen with even one now sends entirely the wrong message. The CEO of Ageless needs to project calm and normalcy to his planet. Especially now."

"I understand, sir. I just disagree."

"You're free to."

"At least a hornet drone, sir. I'll keep it at a respectful altitude. It'll blend in with the media drones that follow you around below the airspace ceiling anyway."

"You want to stick an armed drone in the middle of a swarm of UHD cameras? Did you skip an update?" Tyson asked with annoyance mixed with genuine concern.

"I've taken the liberty to have one camouflaged to look like a common delivery drone in the unlikely event you were swayed by reason."

"What, you spray painted 'UPS' on its micro-rocket box launchers?"

"Something like that, except competently executed. Really, Tyson . . ."

"I'm sorry." Tyson held up his hands in mock surrender, knowing she would be watching the CCD camera feed. "Fine, launch your cross-dressing hornet. But I don't want it buzzing my head like a lost puppy, understood?"

"Completely," his AI assistant said with more than a little sass leaking into her tone. "Pod's waiting. I'll tell the MPD you're en route."

"Something wrong, sir?" James asked, stress lines reaching across his forehead.

"Nothing, James. It's fine. Please run my tab against my expense account. And give yourself a generous tip."

"An appetizer to go?"

Tyson thought again about the scene that awaited him at the

morgue in Xanadu Hospital as he pushed away from the floating bar top.

"No, thank you. Afraid I've rather lost my appetite."

Tyson kept himself from scanning the skies above for the hornet Paris had inserted among the bumblebees always buzzing overhead. The pod had dumped him out right at the Emergency Room doors to the Xanadu Hospital. There were four hospitals in Methuselah, just for the sake of redundancy in case of a natural disaster. The city had at least two of every major component of its infrastructure for exactly that reason, often more. That was the beauty of living in a city with a three-century-long central development plan. But everyone knew Xanadu was where you wanted the med-flight to land if it was your ass in the stretcher.

Tyson adjusted his jacket, cut without lapel and with a high collar as was the current fashion. Several reporters had been tipped off by their camera drones and managed to beat him to the scene even before his pod had slid to a stop. Tyson consoled himself in the knowledge the service fees for their air taxis on such short notice had been ridiculous.

Ji-eun Park stood out among them.

Tyson grimaced, but quickly put on his best poker face as the camera drones overhead descended to capture the scene in glorious UHD close-ups.

"Mr. Abington!" one of the reporters barked. "Are you here to see the body?"

"Body?" Tyson echoed. "I'm here to see to my body, if that's what you mean."

"You know it isn't," Ji-eun said. "Are you here to identify the body MPD brought in less than an hour ago?"

"I don't know anything about a body, Ms. Park, no matter who brought it in. I'm here for my tri-annual colonoscopy."

The rest of the press pool recoiled a bit at that, but Ji-eun remained undeterred. "You mean to tell me that you're here to have a camera stuck up your . . . nether-regions?" she said, catching herself before committing a faux pas that would have earned INN a significant broadcasting fine.

"Yes. And as much as I'm sure you'd love the honor, I'm afraid I must leave my prostate health in the hands of trained medical professionals. Now, if you'll excuse me." Tyson politely, but firmly, pushed past the knot of journalists trying to block his way, most of them wearing faces of discomfort or outright disgust. Indeed the only one not looking at him like he was covered in shit was Ji-eun, who wore a small smirk on her gently shaking head. Tyson gave her a breezy, two-fingered salute with his right hand as he passed through the automatic ER doors.

Once inside, he was met by a middle-aged sergeant of the MPD whom he didn't recognize, not that it meant anything. Tyson had experienced very little contact with the MPD since he'd graduated from primary school. Its independence as a police force was a polite fiction maintained by their labor union and the city's public council. In reality, the police, like all civil servants on Lazarus, had their checks cut by Ageless Corp.

"Mr. Abington." The sergeant stuck out a hand. Tyson took it. "I'm Officer Berg. Sorry to have to call you out for this. Messy business. But your, ah, assistant messaged the precinct to say you might be able to help us ID the, um, deceased."

"It's all right, Officer. But if we can move somewhere more private before we continue this conversation?"

"Doesn't get much more private than a morgue, sir."

"I suppose that's true."

"This way." The sergeant led him toward a set of elevators. Once inside, he keyed for a subbasement that required code verification. "Can't be too careful who comes and goes down here," Berg said. "The dead have a way of bringing out the worst in folks, you know?"

"No," Tyson said. "But I can imagine."

"Better you don't have to. Believe you me."

"How long have you been on the force, Sergeant?" Tyson very consciously didn't say "my" force.

"Seven years next month. Best decision I ever made."

"Oh yes?"

"No doubt. I wasn't exactly a model citizen as a youth. If the Academy hadn't straightened me out, mum would've been visiting me down here by now."

"Well, Lazarus is the place for second chances. We're proud to have you, Officer Berg." The lift came to a stop as Tyson said it. The doors opened, and the most disturbing smell Tyson had ever experienced washed into his nose. It wasn't a disgusting smell, exactly. It was too sterile for that. Instead, the lingering undertones of rot and death had been chopped up and overpowered by cleaning solvents and preservative agents. It smelled like a butcher shop run out of the back of a dentist's office.

And it was cold. Unseasonably cold.

Tyson braced himself against the chill, unwilling to let it harm the air of calm competence he maintained at all times and all costs. He wasn't entirely unprepared. Lazarus had been a largely desert world when the first terraforming rigs were set up. Unlike Earth, the problem here had been too much heat and not enough atmospheric humidity. Even after a century of solar-radiation-reflecting sulfates being injected into the upper atmosphere, the days on Lazarus still hit the high fifties C during summer. But like any desert, the lack of cloud cover at night meant temperatures plunged into single digits or worse. Everyone had gone on "nature" excursions in primary school, if only to drive the dangers of the open desert into the children at an early age.

Still, Tyson was a few decades removed from those miserable, windblown nights in a paper-thin Mylar tent out on the Aldrin Plateau. It took concentration not to shiver.

"The morgue's just up here." Berg held a hand out down the corridor toward a set of stainless-steel double doors, scratched and dented from a thousand gurneys, with copper handles polished to a bright shine in the middle. Round windows offered a very narrow view of whatever lay beyond. The whole thing looked like it had been stolen straight from an old movie set.

"You should know, sir. The coroner here is a little . . ." He wiggled his palm.

Oh, great, Tyson thought quietly, without letting it reach his features. The last week had already been strange and stressful enough. The last thing he wanted to be doing right now was to be led around in a subbasement labyrinth by a juvenile delinquent turned cop on a pilgrimage to some sort of antisocial crypt-keeper with the only prize being a dead body.

But some things one just had to endure.

"Be kind, Officer Berg," Tyson said instead. "I'm sure we would all be a little . . ." Tyson wiggled his own hand. ". . . in their position."

"Too true."

The doors swung open with a *clack* that made Tyson wonder what exactly was holding them fast to their hinges. Half a dozen exam tables arranged in rows of three lay under harsh, unnaturally white light streaming down from the ceiling. Probably all the better for inspection and photography, but it cast the entire room in an unsettling hue. Four of the tables already had customers lying in repose beneath thin green sheets stained brown in places by blood, or worse.

"Who's this?" a gruff female voice called out from around a corner of the room over the sound of a running sink.

"This is Mr. Abington," Berg said. "He's here to identify the halfsie, remember?"

"Halfsie?" Tyson asked, suddenly very aware of everything he'd eaten up to that point throughout the day.

"Er, yeah," Berg said. "Didn't they tell you? It's not going to be an open-casket funeral."

"As dead as one of you can be," is what Paris had said. Tyson swallowed. "They may have mentioned it."

The sound of running water ceased abruptly. A moment later, a squat woman settling comfortably into her sixties walked into the main room toweling off her hands. A vaporizer hung pinched at the corner of her mouth like an outgrowth of her lips, while a haze of smoke rose from her mouth and nostrils as if she was preparing to breathe fire.

The coroner looked Tyson up and down like she was mentally fitting him for a coffin. "Well, aren't you a fancy-looking one?"

"I'm not sure I approve of your tone," Tyson said, unaccustomed to open insolence.

"Heh, strap in, honey. I'm not one for diplomacy. Why'd you think they keep me down here?"

"Should you really be vaping?" Tyson asked with an unplanned edge to his voice. "I thought hospitals were supposed to be sterile."

The woman squeezed the vaporizer straw between two fingers. The tip lit up purple as she took a long pull before blowing the smoke out through her nose. She waved an arm at the bodies lying dead on the tables. Her tables.

"Haven't had any customer complaints yet." She smirked.

"I suppose not," Tyson allowed. "But I'm complaining, and I'm alive and standing in front of you. So, do you mind?"

The coroner made a display of removing the pen from her mouth and powering it down with her middle finger.

"Thank you," Tyson said.

"Bein' a health nut never saved anyone, Mr. Abington. Everyone ends up on the slab sooner or later. All you're doing is making the time before your appointment boring. So, you're here to ID my Jane Doe?"

"Yes."

"Okay, I hope you have a strong stomach for this sort of thing."

"I guess we're about to find out."

The coroner, who still had not shared her name, knelt and grabbed a small recycling bin from next to a cabinet and pushed it into Tyson's stomach. "I'm not cleaning it up if you pop. I have to deal with enough bodily fluids as it is."

Tyson took the bucket, offended, but also not entirely confident he wouldn't be in need of it. "Fair enough."

"Mr. Abington," Berg said. "If you don't mind, I'll just be guarding the door. I'll escort you back up when you're ready to leave."

So, even the seasoned cop didn't want to stick around for the messy part. It must've been bad. "That's just fine, Officer Berg."

"Thank you, sir."

"She's just over here." The coroner pointed to the far table as she walked. Tyson realized he was avoiding looking down at the green sheet with the prominent brown stain slashing diagonally across its middle. He forced himself to do so. Whatever lay beneath it ended about halfway down the examination table.

The coroner grabbed the top corners of the sheet. "Are you ready? I'm not going to sugarcoat it. What's under here isn't pretty."

Tyson steeled his nerve, promising himself he wouldn't flinch. "I am."

She grunted a nod and pulled back the sheet.

He flinched.

"Jesus . . ." For a moment, Tyson's stomach felt like it was going to implode. An unexpected wave of panic washed over his consciousness as long-buried instincts fought for attention.

"Yeah," the older woman said knowingly. If there was any mockery in her tone, he couldn't hear it.

Through a force of will, Tyson tamped down both his sudden urge to take flight and the nausea. He took a breath, then made himself look down at the table again. The body, or what remained of it, was nude, because that's how it . . . *she* had been found, or because the clothes had been removed prior to examination, he couldn't say. Deep lacerations gouged out valleys in the dead woman's flesh. Everything below the rib cage, as well as her left arm below the elbow was missing, the flesh at the edge torn and shredded as if by a shark or another such monstrous predator. But there were none native to Lazarus, at least none that had survived to the present day. The Methuselah City Zoo held a number of big cats from Earth, but he'd have heard immediately if one had escaped.

"What the hell did this?" Tyson asked in a hushed tone.

"Organics reprocessor. One of the maintenance techs down at the central recycling plant found the body half chewed up by the second-stage shredder. It's basically a big wood chipper that breaks organic waste down into pieces small enough to be composted easily. But it wasn't meant for things this big. It got through her legs all right, but bogged down by the time it reached the pelvis. Someone didn't do their homework."

A perfectly horrible thought crossed Tyson's mind. "Was she, you know . . ." he trailed off, afraid of the answer.

"Alive? No, no. Thank God. The meat grinder was post-mortem. Cause of death was a nail from one of those pneumatic drivers through the base of the skull, up into the brain stem and cerebellum. Doubtful she even felt it."

"A small mercy." Tyson was relieved. He'd been furious with the mystery woman, of course. But no matter how angry he was, wishing that kind of death on *anyone* was beyond him. The nail driver was a makeshift weapon. Guns were illegal for private ownership on the planet and had been from the earliest days of the colony. Only the police were allowed them, and even then only among the Critical Response Team, which had a great deal of additional specialized training for dealing with hostage rescue, active attacker situations, and the like. Guns were occasionally smuggled in and used in crimes, but customs and security at the spaceport were highly competent and made sure such occurrences were exceedingly rare. Murderers had to be a bit more creative as a result, but this was the first time Tyson had heard of a nail driver being used.

He inspected the woman's face. Her eyes were closed, fortunately. The hair was different than he remembered, shorter, darker. Probably she'd either been wearing a wig or she'd cut and dyed it immediately after his lunch meeting with Sokolov so she would be harder to recognize. But the young woman he'd known as Cassidy was still there in the chin and cheekbones. And more tellingly, there were still traces, barely noticeable, of the henna tattoo on her right hand and wrist. Tyson probably wouldn't have spotted them if he hadn't known to look. Cassidy had tried to wash them off, and had mostly succeeded, but a slight discoloration in the lines of her skin remained from the dye.

"Yes, this is her," he said.

"You're sure?" the coroner said with a strong, commanding undertone.

"Yes, I'm certain of it."

"Great, who is she?"

"You mean you don't know?" Tyson asked.

"No, that's why we brought you down here in the first place. What's your relationship to the deceased?"

"None. She was a waitress, or at least pretended to be."

"Pretended?"

"Yes. I'm fairly certain she was acting as a corporate spy."

The coroner shrugged. "Play stupid games, win stupid prizes."

"You don't have any ID on her? Not facial recognition, DNA profile, fingerprints?"

"Ran them all. Nada. Do you at least have a name I can give her other than 'Jane Doe'?"

"She said her name was Cassidy. But that was almost certainly an alias."

The coroner smirked and scribbled on her pad. "Well, it's her real name now. Any guess at a last name?" Tyson shook his head. "Okay, Cassidy Castalia it is. Mmm, that's not bad. Almost sounds like a real name."

"Why *Castalia*?"

"I give all my unclaimed stiffs the surname Castalia. Figure if they can't find their way back to their families, they may as well join a new one."

"How sentimental of you."

"Don't push it."

"How many?" Tyson asked.

"Hmm?"

"How many people in this postmortem family of yours?"

"Seventeen." The coroner retrieved the vape pen from her pocket and took a drag. Tyson didn't object.

"Sorry. I'm sure the family reunions are . . . lively."

"Har har."

"What's your name?" Tyson said. "Seriously?"

"You really think we want to know each other?"

Tyson touched his ear. "No, I suppose not. Is there anything you can tell me about her? Anything at all? It's important."

"Already done the standard autopsy. Deeper dive costs money." She rubbed her thumb and forefingers together.

"Isn't that part of your budget?"

"Was, until someone suffering from altitude sickness way up there in the top of Immortal Tower cut 'unnecessary procedures' from the budget. Been having to charge the families for, oh, four years now for anything beyond a cursory exam. Or the life insurance companies when they want to fight a payout."

"So, you recognize me after all," Tyson said. It wasn't a question. The coroner just smirked. "Then you know money won't be a problem."

She pointed at the incomplete cadaver on the cool, stainless-steel table. "For her, no. But it'll be a problem for the next unlucky soul that gets wheeled in here tonight, tomorrow morning, whenever."

Tyson's brow furrowed. "Are you holding me hostage, madam?"

She folded her arms. "Can you blame me?"

"A little, yes." Tyson frowned. "Seems like everyone's shaking me down lately. Show me what you're worth, then we'll talk. That's my offer."

The coroner took a bonus drag from her pen, but blew the smoke down and to the side. A courtesy? She moved with surprising speed to a cabinet at the far corner of the room, presumably by her desk, to retrieve a pair of implements that wouldn't look at all out of place at an inquisitor's table.

"You don't want to watch this part," she said. "I'm not questioning your manliness, or whatever. It's just *really* not going to be pleasant."

Tyson waved a hand over the gore on the table. "And this was?"

"Suit yourself, suit. Snap on a pair of gloves and give me a hand if you're just going to stand around."

Tyson pulled a pair of blue latex gloves from a box on the counter and slipped into them. The coroner hefted a pair of pliers.

"What are those for?" Tyson asked with a rapidly souring stomach.

"Oh, you'll see. Hold her mouth open."

Tyson obeyed before really thinking through the order. He pulled down on Cassidy's lower jaw, gently at first, but rigor mortis had set in and fought back against the attempt. With some strain, he managed to leverage the mouth open a few centimeters.

"That's good. Just hold it there while I . . ." The coroner stuck the pliers into Cassidy's mouth and gripped one of her incisors. Then, she put a foot on the table and cranked back, aggressively wrenching at the tooth trying to loosen it in its socket.

With a final wet snapping sound, the root of the tooth gave way, sending the coroner tumbling back almost a meter before catching herself. Between the clammy feeling of dead flesh under his fingers and the sound of the extraction ringing in his ears,

Tyson's stomach finally rolled over. He just made it to the waste-basket before throwing up everything he'd eaten and drank in the last several hours.

"Well, that's a pity," he said between spitting bile from his mouth.

"What is?" the coroner asked.

"Wasting perfectly good sake like that."

"Don't think of it as a waste. Think of it as enjoying it twice. Thanks for hitting the basket."

"You're welcome." Tyson picked up a paper towel to wipe the spittle from his mouth. "Are you going to tell me why you yanked out her tooth?"

"No, I'm going to show you." She walked back to her desk and cleaned the tooth of coagulated blood and hanging tissue, then dropped it into a clear cylinder with a robust-looking black top that looked for all the world like a coffeemaker. She pressed power and the room was suddenly filled with a small, but discern-able high-pitched whine right at the edge of Tyson's hearing. A second later, the tooth simply vanished into a puff of fine powder.

"Acoustic pulverizer. Neat little gimmick, huh?"

"We're a little beyond a stone and pestle, I see."

"Quite." She took up the glass cylinder with its tooth dust and fed it into an adjacent machine. "Our teeth are formed in the womb. They're all there from the moment we're born, and they're fixed for life. Unlike the rest of our skeleton, they don't heal or regenerate. The minerals that went into them in the beginning are there straight through to the end. So, they're like a little time capsule of the environment we were in while our mothers were busy throwing us together."

"Isotope ratios," Tyson said as the woman's words sunk in. "You're using a spectrograph to pin down the isotope ratios of the minerals in her birth environment to tell us where she was originally from."

"Very good, Mr. Abington. Got it in one."

"How sensitive is it? I mean, can you narrow it down to a particular system, or planet?"

"Honey, we have enough profiles in the databank to narrow it down to a particular country or colony city in most cases. But then I'm going to do you one better. Do the same with a bone cross section and I can tell you where she's been over the last seven to ten years. A lock of hair and I can tell you where she's been and what she's been eating, drinking, or snorting for the last eighteen months. Is that worth something to you, Mr. Abington?"

"How long will the results take?"

"Twelve hours, tomorrow for sure."

"I assume you don't need assistance collecting the bone cross section?"

The coroner laughed. "No, tough guy, I'll spare you *that* sight."

"Send the results to my office under encryption as soon as they're ready. Do not include them in her police file."

"That's a pretty big breach of protocol."

"I *am* the protocol in this city," Tyson said firmly.

"Hey, you're paying for the tests. I'll send the bill along, too."

"Do that." Tyson pulled the blue gloves off his hands and dumped them into the wastebasket with his sake, then headed for the door to meet up with Officer Berg, relieved to be leaving the morbid sights, sounds, and smells behind him. Once he was back to ground level, he connected with Paris.

"Sir, where were you? I lost contact for almost an hour."

"In Hell, Paris. Thankfully, I was just visiting."

"I'm grateful for that."

"You should be receiving an encrypted file from the coroner at Xanadu Hospital sometime tomorrow. I want to know the moment you have it."

"Of course."

"And Paris, make a note to double the coroner's office budget."

"Yes, sir."

"And make a donation to the hospital of a half-million nudollars in the name of the Castalia Family."

"Okay . . ."

"And Paris?"

"Yes, Tyson?"

"Tell the hospital to enforce its no-vaping policy in the basement levels as well."

THIRTEEN

"Captain, you're needed in the CIC," OoD Esposito said through the com in the officers' mess.

Susan looked down at the peanut butter and jelly sandwich hovering dangerously close to her open mouth and sighed. She was famished, and the sandwich represented the first shot of carbs and protein she'd had in twelve hours. This late, the kitchen was closed. Third-shift cooks were busy working, of course, but they were tied up cleaning sinks, ovens, dishes, and doing prep for the six meals they'd be serving over the next eighteen hours. PB&J was the only option at 0330.

"Can it wait five minutes?" she asked, even as she knew the question was rhetorical.

"Don't think so, mum."

"Fine, I'm on my way. Make sure to drag Mr. Nesbit out of bed, too."

"I called him first, mum. You know how long he takes to powder his nose."

"Play nice, Esposito." She slammed the mug of square dog sitting on the table in front of her, nearly scalding her palate in the process, then topped it off with a long pour from the pot. Susan kept the sandwich and scarfed it down on the hoof.

"Captain on deck!" the marine guard shouted less than a minute later.

"Yeah, yeah. At ease," Susan said as she took her seat. "Okay, OoD, hit me."

Esposito looked back from the plot, smiling like the Cheshire cat. "You're not going to believe this, mum."

"The last time someone said that to me, my sister got a divorce three months later. This had better knock that memory out of position or you're in trouble."

"We've just heard from Grendel's astronomy department, mum. They've found it."

"Found what?" Susan's sleep and nutrient-deficient brain asked before the answer floated to the surface. There was only one thing they could've found that would put such a ridiculous grin on the OoD's face.

The Xre's fleet oiler.

"Oh," Susan said. "Ooooh! Where is it?"

"We're calculating drift now, mum. They've only had intermittent contact, but it's in a parking orbit, not under power. Should know in a minute or so."

Susan looked up at the main plot hologram with invigorated eyes. Three tentative sightings had been pinned in the volume with yellow pyramids flanked by bearing and velocity data. The variables narrowed with each sighting until the cone of space the oiler could possibly occupy shrank to a tunnel in space.

"Where's Miguel?" Susan shook alertness into her head. The caffeine had yet to catch her up. "I mean, where's the XO?"

"In his rack, I hope. I only relieved him two hours ago."

"Okay, let him sleep for now. How sure are they this bogey is the oiler?"

"Greater than ninety-five percent, mum."

"That seems awfully confident."

"There's actually good reason for that." Esposito zoomed the plot in to the space immediately surrounding the projected path of the bogey. A small constellation of Kuiper-belt objects shadowed its course. "Apparently, this cluster of asteroids sits on a damned elliptical orbit and makes a deep dive for the inner system every hundred and twenty local years or so. They were catalogued a couple decades ago by the first survey crew to come through here, both because they posed a potential impact threat to the inner planets, and because their spectrographics were interesting enough to warrant a closer look for a future mining claim. This cluster is well-known by the locals as a result."

"And all of a sudden, there was an extra asteroid," Susan finished the thought.

"Exactly."

"What are the odds the cluster just happened to capture a stray asteroid?"

"With less than a percent standard gravity between the lot of them?" Esposito shook her head. "Not worth mentioning. Any captured object would've had to be moving in a nearly identical orbit at a relative velocity you could measure in meters per second, otherwise it would've just sailed right on by or pulverized one of the members of the cluster. The locals would've spotted it years ago. This was placed recently. That's why the locals are so sure. We just got really, *extremely* lucky the bugs picked a pile of rubble Grendel had already mapped to park their tender in."

"But why could Grendel see it at all?" Susan asked, but the answer presented itself before the OoD could correct her. "Because it's not stealthed. We don't coat our oilers in expensive adaptive camo, why would the Xre? They're logistics ships, not frontline combatants."

"That was my thought as well, mum. They probably figured bringing it in cold and setting it on a wide orbit would be stealth enough. There's no way we would've spotted it if they'd picked almost any other place to put it. Just bad luck on their part."

Susan's thoughts came to an abrupt halt as the marine at the hatch announced Mr. Nesbit's arrival.

"CL on deck!"

"Jesus, son, people are trying to sleep," Nesbit said as he stepped through the hatch. For once, Susan sympathized with him.

"Good to see you, Mr. Nesbit," she said.

"Wish I could say it was good to be seen. What's going on?"

Susan beamed. "Grendel's astrogation department believes with a high degree of confidence that they've located the fleet oiler the Xre cruiser has been using for UnRep for its ongoing operations in system. We're in the process of confirming their findings."

Nesbit rubbed at his left eye. "English, Cap."

"We found the bug's gas can." Susan bared her teeth. "And I'm going to blow it up."

"You're what?"

"It's where they're storing their antimatter and reactant mass. Take it out, and they have to schlep all the way to Blumenthal and back to refuel and refit. That's a three-week round trip. Damn inconvenient."

"Where is this 'oiler' now?"

Susan pointed at the shrinking yellow cone on the main plot. "We've marked it as Bogey Six."

"I thought confirmed enemy targets were called 'Bandits.'"

"They are. The astrogators on the surface have only had intermittent sightings, but there's nothing else it could or should be. We're still resolving its drift course, but it's definitely somewhere inside that cone. Scopes will have a precise location for us shortly, won't you, Mattu?"

Her drone integration officer pumped a fist in the air. "Yes mum!"

"See?"

"Where is it in relation to the treaty line?" Nesbit pressed.

"Charts?"

Broadchurch toggled an icon at their station and a red line representing the treaty boundary appeared nearly an AU *behind* the bogey.

"It's in open space," Nesbit barked.

"Yeah? And?"

"Aaaand blowing up a ship in fair trade space is a treaty violation and an act of war, Captain."

"So is sending armed drones past the treaty line to destroy our remote platforms, Mr. Nesbit. We didn't ask for this dance, but it's time we took the lead."

"Can't we wait until it swings back over the treaty line?" Nesbit asked.

"That would be impractical, as its elliptical orbit won't bring it back across the line for . . . Charts?"

"Ninety-two years," Broadchurch said.

"Ninety-two years," Susan repeated. "Which is a bit longer than I'm willing to commit to this enterprise."

"I can't advise this course of action, Captain. It's exactly the sort of thing that could spark an interstellar incident."

"We already have an interstellar incident, Javier." Susan took off her top cover and ran a hand through her hair to scratch a sudden itch. "What if *we* don't blow it up? Would that make you happy?"

"That's exactly what would make me . . . wait a minute. Why did you stress 'we'?"

"What if something else destroys the oiler?" Susan asked, thinking out loud.

"What, you expect to convince them to obligingly blow themselves up?"

"Not at all. But the outer system is a dangerous place. Lots of uncharted meteors and asteroids tumbling around out there."

"You're not seriously suggesting we—" Nesbit started, but Susan's brain was already moving under its own power.

"Lieutenant Warner," she called into the com.

"Go for Warner," came her weapons officer's sleepy voice.

"Get up to the CIC. I need a rock."

"Are you proposing to me, mum?"

Susan smirked. "If you manage to pull *this* bullshit off, my dear, I just might."

It took them the rest of a duty shift working with their civilian counterparts on Grendel to locate an appropriate meteor for the task. It was harder than Susan had first assumed. Despite a decade of constant human occupation, and many years of intermittent survey missions prior, they still didn't have anything like a complete catalogue of all the rocks in Grendel's outer system. Normally, this wouldn't pose a huge problem because any asteroid or comet that did wander into the inner system could be intercepted and safely diverted or destroyed, so long as it was spotted with a few weeks' notice.

For Susan's purposes, they needed a rock in a specific orbit, at a specific period in that orbit, moving within a specific velocity range, that wasn't so small that the oiler's automated defenses could take it out, but not so big the booster packs *Ansari* had in inventory couldn't overcome its momentum enough to adequately alter its trajectory.

But, in the second miracle of the day, find one they did.

It took a week for a three-person engineering detail to sneak out to the rock on a marine recon shuttle crammed with equipment, and another day and a half on the surface setting everything up for the attack. They were still making their way back to the barn.

"I almost feel bad," Warner said as the rock they'd appropriated entered its terminal approach and the booster packs bolted to its surface used what was left of their propellant to self-destruct. There couldn't be any trace left of their involvement when the rock struck the oiler. Naturally, the thruster packs had been arranged on the far side of the rock, which massed fully three-quarters as much as the *Ansari* itself, to shield their exhaust and eventual destruction from the oiler's sensors. They'd taken the further precaution of keeping one of the other asteroids in the cluster between the target and their hot rock until it was too late.

"All boosters have detonated," Mattu said quietly. They were committed, now. With the boosters gone, there was no way to alter the meteor's course. In truth, they'd been past the point of no return for four minutes already, as they were almost half an AU away from the scene of the crime. Mattu had expertly maneu-vered a recon drone running passive under stealth into a parallel course with the rock so they could get light-speed updates on the proceedings. Everything had already played out, they were just watching the rerun.

"The covering asteroid has drifted out of line of sight. Our rock has entered the tender's threat envelope. Active scans have acquired. Countermeasures deploying."

Despite years of active warfare and decades of an uneasy armi-stice, mankind had never been able to pin down the Xre's home-world. There was no single nexus point to their deployments or logistics. But war strategists had inferred from reams of tactical data, after-action reports, and capture hardware some of the un-derlying psychology of the enemy. They fought defensively, with more resources and equipment dedicated to repelling counterat-tack than offensive operations. They were cautious and calculating, which early in the Intersection War had been mistaken by over-eager human commanders for cowardice or a lack of commitment. Many of them had paid for the miscalculation with their lives.

What it meant in practical terms was Xre ships were, without fail, tough nuts to crack. Not even this lowly fleet replenishment ship broke *that* mold. The sheer volume of point-defense fire that swarmed out of it like amorous fireflies on a hot summer night was testament to the aliens' design philosophy.

"Are their resupply ships drones like ours?" Nesbit asked.

"I expect their oilers are, too, yes."

"Why do you keep calling it an 'oiler'?"

"It's an old, old nautical term from just after the days of sail, back when ships burned heavy fuel oil. Their UnRep ships carried the oil, so, oilers. My military history instructor back in Academy used it and I guess it stuck with me."

"Why doesn't it just bubble away?"

"Charts? Would you like to answer the CL's question?"

"Sure, mum," Broadchurch said. "Not enough time to charge their rings unless they keep them on hot standby. Which not only puts unnecessary hours and wear on the components, but gives off IR and makes it harder to hide their little secret."

"I see. Same goes with their fusion rockets, I take it?"

"Yep. Not as much lead time, but still too much if you're starting cold."

"Will the Xre cruiser know when it happens?" Nesbit asked.

"Are you kidding?" Miguel said. "When that much antimatter loses containment? They'll see it in the next system in five and a half years."

On the "live" feed, the front of the meteor boiled and hissed as the oiler's version of CiWS lasers and mass-drivers desperately clawed at the newcomer in a bid to save their ship, but they'd been designed to swat down railgun slugs massing a few dozen kilograms up to anti-ship missiles of a few dozen tons. They were not meant to destroy a solid iron/nickel asteroid of over two hundred thousand tons. A well-placed salvo of ship-killers *might* have enough punch to nudge it out of the way. But then, tenders didn't have missile tubes.

"What's the closing rate?" Susan asked.

"Leveled off at three and a half klicks per second," Mattu said.

Warner whistled low. "That's going to leave a mark."

"Ten seconds. Nine. Eight. Drone entering safe mode. Seven . . ."

The air in the CIC froze everyone in place, immobilized by the cadence of Mattu's countdown. Susan had to remind herself to breathe.

"Three. Two. One. Impact."

Even from its position some ten thousand kilometers away from the carnage, the camera feed from the drone platform they'd sent to shepherd the rock on its death plunge flashed brilliant white, then cut out entirely as the EM pulse and hard gamma radiation hit and forced the onboard AI into shutdown to protect itself. The main plot flipped automatically to a feed from the *Ansari*'s own onboard telescopes, each one several times more powerful than the original Hubble Observatory. The unbridled savagery of the explosion they'd unleashed left even Lieutenant Warner hushed in awe. The death of the Xre tender had pulverized not only the ship itself and the rock they'd thrown at it, but the two closest asteroids in the cluster, while breaking one of the larger ones further out into three pieces. The cluster had been reduced to a cloud.

"Holy shit," was all Nesbit could muster.

"Do I need to bother with kill confirmation, Captain?" Warner asked.

"No, I think we got it in one," Susan said. "Good work, everyone. That was . . . for once calling it *awesome* isn't an overstatement, I think. How long until our drone reboots, Scopes?"

"Twenty seconds."

"Good, get it up and burning away from there as soon as possible. That cruiser will be along soon enough to try and figure out what happened and I don't want it giving the game away."

FOURTEEN

"Impossible," Dulac Kivits said. While the rest of the attendants in the mind cavern were silent, everyone's expressions and posture conveyed a similar sentiment of stunned disbelief at the last few moments of timestream from the eyes of their now-destroyed annihilation fuel reservoir.

Everyone, that is, except Thuk.

"Hurg," he said, drawing the attention of the recording alcove attendant. "Could you replay the . . ." He almost said "attack," but caught himself before the word escaped. ". . . impact? Move back up the timestream to the moment the reservoir's eyes spotted the meteor and begin, please?"

The fallen royal stared at the static playing out in the display surrounding the cavern, transfixed.

"Hurg?" Thuk prodded gently.

She gave herself a shake. "Yes, Derstu. Apologies." Hurg's claws fritted and danced over her alcove, peeling back time until the threat first came into focus.

"There," Thuk said. "Begin again from there." The timestream resumed. The meteor took up only a claw-tip at this point, but its considerable velocity meant it grew quickly in the display. The reservoir spotted it and reached out its meager talons to try and divert or destroy the threat, but it was like trying to turn back a kunji with a fishing spear. As spectacular as the firepower pouring out of the reservoir and into the front of the meteor was, Thuk's eyes scanned everywhere but, looking for . . . he wasn't sure what. Something that didn't belong.

The front of the meteor glowed from the heat of light spears and the impacts of hundreds of sling bullets, but advanced without pause or mercy until it filled the screen. Then, the feed fell to the familiar chaos of background static as the reservoir's song abruptly ended.

"Dulac?" Thuk said cheerfully, hoping to break the tension.

"Derstu?" Kivits said after a moment.

"Do you remember a few moons ago when we were planning this expedition and I said to the Chorus that we should seed the asteroids around the reservoir with eyespots in case an uncharted rock blundered into its path?"

"I . . . seem to recollect that, in passing."

"And they said it was a waste of resources because the odds were so long?"

"Yes . . ."

"We should've placed a friendly wager with them. We could've retired early."

"Heh, yes. Truly a missed opportunity," Kivits said stiffly, but he could be forgiven for that.

"Bad luck, everyone. Take a break while your dulac and I decide what to do next. Go grab a hot plate. The crop is fresh."

The rest of the room filed out quietly, still a bit dazed, but not nearly as frightened as they'd looked moments ago. Thuk caught the recording attendant by her arm. "Hurg, wait a moment, if you can spare the time?"

"As you need, Derstu."

The door irised shut as the last attendant exited, leaving the three of them alone for the first time. Thuk looked long into each of their faces in turn: first Hurg, then Kivits. Only then did he speak.

"Are we all in agreement that what happened to our reservoir was not a random meteor impact?" They both clicked their affirmation. "Then we also agree that the humans just found and destroyed our source of annihilation fuel and reactant mass. The first Xre ship lost to enemy action since the last war, I believe."

"Officially," Kivits said.

"Officially," Thuk granted.

"But . . ." Hurg said, then faltered as her superiors turned their heads toward her voice.

"Go on, Hurg," Thuk said encouragingly. "We're alone, no one to hear this triplet. I didn't ask you to stay just to be a mute witness."

". . . I was going to say this still isn't 'Official.' They hit it with a well-aimed rock, not a javelin or a light-spear. They can still feign innocence, because no matter how long the odds, we can't conclusively prove it wasn't a genuine accident."

"Not sitting out here polishing our plates, we can't," Kivits said. "We need to get to the scene of the attack as quickly as possible, before any evidence drifts too far away. We should spin a seedpod immediately."

"And jump right where the *Ansari* and that sharp-clawed captain of theirs is expecting us to show up? Even if we could win in the end, I'd rather not put my hand *directly* in their mouth to start the fight, thank you. Besides, we started this game when their husks fell to 'accidents' inside their territory. I'm sure their captain delighted at the opportunity to return the gesture on our reservoir."

"How in the Abyss did they find the reservoir in the first place?" Hurg asked.

"*That* is an excellent question, Attendant," Kivits said, pacing now.

"I concur. Although they have been awfully good at sniffing out the *Chusexx* twice already, they had some idea where to start looking. Are we sure they didn't stick some sort of tracker on our hull in that first engagement? It would explain much."

"We've been over the hull with a mandible brush, Derstu, you know that."

"Yes, wishful thinking on my part. Because the alternative looks too much like someone told them where to look for our reservoir."

"Surely you're not saying someone in the *Chorus* is helping the humans? You must know how unhinged that sounds."

Thuk wiggled a midarm to convey ambiguity. "I'm not making any specific accusations, I'm merely noting patterns and possibilities. I've felt, we both have, that we're being pushed into a confrontation with this ship by the Dark Ocean Chorus. If that's true, then it's not the humans they would be helping by whispering the location of our reservoir, but their own plan."

"Explain."

"We're out of time now. Without our reserves, we have to either go against their song and return home, or force the issue here and now."

"That is an . . . unsettling thought, Derstu," Kivits said.

"I join the dulac in that," Hurg said.

"No other theory presents itself at the moment," Thuk said. "I would simply love for one of you to come up with one better sewn for the facts."

Neither could.

"So, here we are, what do we do about it?" Thuk said quietly.

"It was clever of you to make a show of good humors for the rest of our harmony, Derstu," Kivits said. "But then why bring the two of us into your paranoia?"

"Because I know the two of you have shared it, as well as each other," Thuk said lightly. The revelation of his knowledge hit the floor like a heavy sack of milled gim shells.

"I would never—" Kivits started, but Thuk cut him off with a wave of a primehand.

"Oh don't insult my senses, Kivits. I tasted your union in the clutching chamber. And I don't care, not one grain. It was not an accusation, merely an observation. The point is we all have good reasons for our suspicions, and good reason to trust one another, yes?"

"And good leverage to assure our silence with the rest of the harmony," Hurg said firmly, if quietly.

"It was not meant as leverage, or a threat, Hurg. What you do in your leisure time, and who you spend that time with, is not my concern, or that of the Chorus as far as I'm concerned."

"Then what is it about?" Kivits demanded.

"Honestly? Because as you made clear in that conversation, Dulac, I'm to serve the interests of the *Chusexx*'s harmony, not lead it. Not make decisions for it. Which is why I need advisors. So I'm asking you, both of you. What in the Abyss do we do now that we know? Because I'm at a split in the path, and know not which way to walk."

Unsurprisingly, Thuk's plea was met with a considerable period of awkward silence. It was all well and good to pretend that a harmony's derstu was merely a runner implementing the consensus, but it fell apart in practice. The derstu was there to blame when things went poorly because no one actually wanted to make the difficult decisions in the first place. This was the problem with arranging a society where everyone supposedly led. If everyone was a leader, no one was.

The embarrassed lovers exchanged anxious looks, until Kivits sunk on his four legs and Hurg touched Thuk on a midarm joint.

"We're at the same split you are, Derstu. What do you think we should do?"

"I'm glad you asked," Thuk said. "I think we should charge the treaty line, right here, right now."

Kivits's legs stiffened and he regained his full height. "You want to *obey* the Chorus's song?"

"Of course. You think me discordant?"

"I just . . ." His mandibles clicked and reset. "I assumed you were trying to recruit us into supporting something more . . . incongruous."

"We're not across that line yet, Kivits. We are not so desperate that survival requires we refuse our Chorus song. I will obey, but I will do so on my terms, with full tanks and surprise in my sack, not desperation. But I wanted to make certain that you two, at the very least, knew exactly the conditions of ground we fight upon."

"I'm not sure whether to thank you for that or not," Kivits said without concealing his snark.

Thuk clapped a hand on the dulac's shoulder. "What? We're going into action, chasing fame and glory; it's what we all dreamed of since the clutch. Get over to your alcove and find me one of the human's husks to jump near. They need to see us charging for the line."

"Excuse me, but . . ."

"Oh just speak freely already, Hurg."

"Sorry," she said demurely. "I just wanted to ask why you think the humans will cross the line to meet our charge this time when they didn't take the bait before?"

"Because—" Thuk held up two fingers. "They will think we're acting out of rage and desperation instead of cool calculation." He ticked off a finger. "And second, because they've gotten a taste of blood now. We embarrassed them twice and they'll feel emboldened to stack success on success. A careful study of their engagements in the last war reveals the human's tendency to overreach when things are going well."

"As you say, Derstu. Should we recall the other attendants?"

"No, let them finish their gims and pelas. Warriors fight better on a full stomach, don't you think?"

Thuk looked at the three of them standing there alone in the mind cavern. A worker, an administrator, and a royal involved in their own little conspiracy of thought crimes. Except the royal was the only one working, the administrator was below even a worker's status, and the worker believed himself in charge of both.

If only the queens could have seen this absurd spectacle, they might have elected to embalm themselves.

FIFTEEN

"Contact!" Mattu shouted. "Platform Six. Solid lock on Bandit One. It's burning hard for the treaty line. Bearing three-one-five-point-zero-two-seven by zero-zero-two-point-five-five."

"That took longer than expected," Susan said.

"Maybe they were all in the head," Warner joked.

Susan ignored her. "On the main plot if you please, Scopes."

Mattu shunted the data from her Drone Integration Station over to the hologram at the heart of the CIC. An angry burning ember of an enemy contact glowed on the far side of the system just outside the treaty line on almost an exactly opposite bearing from where they'd destroyed the oiler not even two hours earlier. That surprised Susan as well. She'd expected them to bubble right on top of the site of the attack to investigate. It would've made for a great ambush point if she'd been so inclined.

Her opponent had again confounded her expectations.

"They're not even bothering with stealth," Warner observed.

"CL to the CIC," Susan said into the 1MC, then turned back to the plot. "No, they sure aren't. They may as well be running with their damned nav lights and docking floods on. We're supposed to see them coming."

"They're pissed," Miguel said from over her shoulder. "They're spoiling for a fight this time and want to make sure we know when and where."

"Maybe . . ." Susan scratched her chin. "Why didn't they jump to their dead oiler? I'd want to have a look if it was me."

Miguel shrugged. "They saw the gamma spike. They know the AM tanks lost containment. There's nothing left to look at."

"Warner, what's your take?" Susan said.

"I think the XO has a good scan on it. Maybe we're really lucky and they're low enough on gas they didn't want to waste reserves on a jump just to visit a ghost."

"Wouldn't *that* be a nice break." Susan mulled it over, but it was futile. The Xre were forcing her hand; she had no option but to run out to face them. And, depending on how far they pushed her, to destroy them if duty called.

She sighed. "Prepare to make immediate jump to a point fifty thousand klicks inside the treaty line on matching bearing to Bandit One. Call the crew to battle stations."

"Aye, mum," Miguel said. "Charts, spin up Alpha and Beta rings, plot jump for bearing three-one-five-point-zero-two-seven by zero-zero-two-point-five-five, ending fifty kiloklicks inside the treaty line."

"Warm up alpha and beta, three-one-five-point-zero-two-seven by zero-zero-two-point-five-five, blow bubble for fifty kiloklicks inside the Red Line, aye sir!" Broadchurch said.

"All hands, this is the XO," Miguel's voice boomed through the 1MC. "Battle stations. Repeat, battle stations. This is not a drill."

"Warm up CiWS, get the counter-missiles in their tubes, and prep our shipkiller birds. Charge railgun and laser capacitors. Go full active on radar/lidar. They're not bothering to hide so we may as well paint them like a fresco," Susan said.

"CiWS and counter tubes hot. Ready boomers, bangers, and beams. Crank actives to eleven, aye!" Warner echoed with barely constrained glee.

Broadchurch turned in her chair to look at Miguel. "Alpha and beta rings charged, course plotted and laid into nav computer."

"Blow the bubble, Charts," Miguel said.

And they were off to the races.

Susan's jaw tensed against the usual discomfort. She ignored it, the bubble popped an almost imperceptibly brief time later, and the angry glowing ember of Bandit One blazed directly ahead of her in the plot.

"Deploy drones, standard defensive shell formation. Put a monocle between us and Bandit One."

Miguel repeated the order, Mattu echoed it, and the *Ansari* bucked ever so slightly as eight recon drones were booted out of their nests and raced out to form a sensor perimeter. One platform was a little lighter and faster than the others as it streaked through the black to take up position ten thousand kilometers ahead of its mother and in direct line of sight between *Ansari* and the Xre interloper. It was already in the process of deploying a flat lens made of multiple, concentric, metamaterial rings twenty meters across. All lasers, no matter how powerful and focused, diffused over long-enough distances, reducing their offensive power. The "monocle" drone was the CCDF's answer, refocusing the beam in midflight so it hit the target with the same punch as if it had closed to knife-fighting range.

It was a devilishly difficult trick to pull off, keeping three independently maneuvering combatants in perfect alignment, especially when the one on the receiving end was so strongly motivated to keep it from happening. It was usually reserved for an ambush role. Most commanders wouldn't even bother putting a monocle into play in an active battlefield.

But Susan wasn't most commanders. To her, the "common knowledge" that it was useless to deploy one in a hot zone was the strongest recommendation she could think of to try it. If her own people wouldn't expect and plan for it, neither would a Xre.

"Helm, take us three degrees off reciprocal bearing with

Bandit One, but keep our keel guns pointed down their throat," Susan said.

"Three degrees off bore, aye mum." Broadchurch punched the command into their station. The *Ansari* answered the helm almost instantaneously and imperceptibly. The fusion rockets at her stern could vector their thrust up to twenty-seven degrees using the same magnetic constriction rings that kept the inconceivably hot plasma from contacting, and thereby vaporizing, their internal components.

"Status of Bandit One?"

"Unchanged, mum," Mattu said. "Still burning hot and heavy straight for the line."

"Have they deployed drones?"

"None that our platforms have picked up yet, mum. Not that it means much. They're damned hard to spot even in ideal conditions."

"Keep looking, Scopes. If we can poke out a few of their eyes, all the better." Susan punched a string of commands into her chair. The data readout above the main plot changed to a countdown to the projected moment Bandit One would cross the treaty line, counting down both time and kilometers in bright crimson numerals.

"That's our deadline, people. We have to scarecrow big and loud enough before then to turn them away so we don't have to kill them."

"We know the drill, mum," Warner said.

"Respectfully, Weps, but I don't think they're running a drill this time."

"CL on deck!" the marine guard called out. Nesbit stepped through the hatch into the CIC with confidence, centered, in a freshly pressed shirt.

"What do we have here, Captain?"

"Incursion attempt number three," Susan said. "I think they're serious this time."

"Well, you did shove a giant rock up their . . . do they have asses?"

"Cloaca, technically," Miguel said to a round of nervous laughter from the assembled crew.

"You think they're really going to cross the line?" Nesbit asked.

"We're operating under that assumption. With their oiler scattered across an AU, their backs are against the wall. They may not even have enough left in the tanks to get home. If they're running on fumes, their only chance is to go through us and pillage the factory over Grendel and bolt before fleet HQ sends reinforcements."

"Why hasn't that happened yet?" Nesbit asked. "We've been fucking around out here with an unknown cruiser class that out-masses us by fifty percent for weeks. The Admiralty seriously couldn't shake a frigate loose to back us up?"

"I've asked that very question several times at ever-increasing volume," Susan said. "Their answers have not been inspiring."

"They've just kicked up to emergency burn, mum," Mattu reported, professionalism tamping down on the anxiety lurking at the edges of her voice.

"Match them."

Everyone in the CIC looked at her. They knew *Ansari* was capable of emergency flank speed, they'd been the first crew to take her out after refitting. Running at full military thrust was part of passing her space trial certifications.

But that had happened in the safety of the fleet's testing range with a chaser corvette monitoring their progress, not with an alien cruiser bristling with weapons and threatening death bearing down on them. The order to go to emergency flank speed, even more than destroying the oiler remotely, brought the true gravity of their situation crashing home.

"Well?" Miguel barked angrily. "Don't just sit there staring into each other's slack-jawed cake holes. You heard the lady, start burning antimatter!"

"Yes, sir!" Broadchurch answered, the spell broken. "Ramping up to emergency flank speed."

"Our monocle will have trouble keeping up at these relative velocities if we start maneuvering very hard, mum," Mattu said.

"Noted, Scopes. Do your best," Susan answered without taking her eyes off the countdown. The distance and time fell away with renewed enthusiasm under such hard acceleration. Much longer, and both of them would build up so much delta-v that crossing the line became inevitable, even under a max-g turn.

The only option then would be to bubble out, but unless the Xre had drastically improved on their ring recharge rates, that wouldn't be in the cards until after they'd crossed the line, either.

"We're being painted with range-finding lasers, mum," Warner said placidly.

"That's only fair."

"I can't deploy retroreflectors while under acceleration, mum."

"I'm aware," Susan said. "Launch ten Mk IXs port and ten starboard, keep their drives cold, but link them into our targeting data."

"Ten birds left, ten birds right, cold drives and hot links, aye, mum!"

Miguel cleared his throat.

"Sorry, XO," Warner said. "Didn't mean to skip over you. Just eager is all."

"Mmhmm." Miguel crossed his arms.

"Later you two," Susan said a little saltier than she intended, but for God's sake, they were in a hot zone.

"Boomers away," Warner reported as the slight shudder of the ripple-fire of seven hundred tons of anti-ship missiles echoed through *Ansari*'s bones. "Uplinks stable, targeting data accepted. Missiles orienting themselves toward Bandit One. Hold one . . . missile A2C showing a thruster malfunction. Running diagnos— Nevermind, there it goes. Both flights ready and waiting for order to burn."

"Thank you, Guns. Scopes, get two decoys prepped. But hold off on launch until—"

"Aspect change!" Mattu blurted out. "Bandit One has . . . wait. Power surge."

"Are they charging capacitors?"

"No, it's . . . this doesn't make sense."

"What doesn't make sense, Scopes? Spit it out!"

"There's been a gamma spike."

"How? They're already at emergency burn."

"Acceleration falling off, half, one-third. Target orientation is changing. Negative three degrees z-axis, five degrees y-axis, half a degree per second."

"Are they changing course?"

"No, bearing unchanged. They're listing, mum."

"And still headed straight for the Red Line."

"Yes, mum, but their accel has dropped off entirely now. They're ballistic."

"What the hell are we supposed to make of that?" Miguel asked.

"I don't know. Explosion?" Susan said.

"Failures involving antimatter are usually a little more cata-strophic than this."

That was true enough, as they'd been reminded not six hours ago. Susan rubbed at her jaw. "Maybe they lost containment on just one of their fusion rocket bells? That would mean what, a few grams of AM got away from them? Whatever was in the intermix chamber?"

"Or they're faking it and wake up again the second they cross the line or we're inside their offensive envelope and can't maneu-ver out before getting shanked."

"Is there any debris?"

"Radar is picking up a small cloud of objects spreading out from Bandit One at between one- and four-hundred meters per second."

"How many? How big?"

"Several dozen, varying between our minimum detection threshold and about three meters in size."

"Nothing they couldn't shove out an airlock," Miguel whispered.

"Bandit One's EM signature just crashed," Mattu said.

"Their stealth systems kicked in," Warner said. "They're ghosting us."

"No, they're still showing up on radar/lidar," Mattu said. "Their EM emissions have just—stopped. I think they've lost main power. They're dead in space, mum. Damn, they're venting atmosphere."

"Okay, that's dedication," Miguel said. Susan knew what he meant. No spacers, of either species, just threw away air. Nothing, not fuel, food, water, or heat, killed you faster than running out of air.

"Wait one . . ." Mattu wiped sweat away from her forehead. Susan imagined it was probably cold. Every member of the bridge crew looked at the Drone Integration Station with desperate eyes, hungry for Mattu's next words.

She swallowed hard. "They're hailing. Transmitted in the clear. It's being routed through their translation matrix."

"Shit." Susan's jaw clenched involuntarily. "Well, let's hear it."

"Yes'm," Mattu said, then routed the feed she heard through to the CIC's speakers. A heavily processed, synthesized voice filled the room.

"We *Chusexx* harmony. We announce Day in May. Rotting light leak caverns. Source energy failure. Implore not throw light-spear or javelin. Bellies to sky."

"What the fuck does *that* mean?" Nesbit asked incredulously.

"Mayday," Susan answered for him. "It's a distress call."

"I said maximum thrust, Kivits."

"But we have no way to replenish our annihilation fuel, Derstu. Whatever we burn, we cannot replace."

"Yes, I *was* here for that," Thuk said. "They need to think us desperate. Desperate enough to burn through our supply on a sacrificial charge. So, we consume a small fraction of our annihilation fuel to keep the ruse going and draw them across the line."

"Very well, Derstu. I withdraw my objection."

"Thank you. Tiller, maximum thrust. Unless anyone else has something to contribute?"

No one did. The *Chusexx* responded to the tiller attendant's input.

"Maximum thrust, Derstu," the tiller alcove reported.

"Shall we ready our light-spears and javelins?" Kivits asked.

Thuk stretched a midarm. "If it will make you feel better."

Several attendants chortled softly until a stern look from their dulac clicked their mandibles shut. Still, it had the defusing effect Thuk had hoped for.

"It would indeed, Derstu."

"Very well, then. Charge light-spears and unsheathe a flight of twelve javelins. Confirm the human ship's range and velocity with a focus beam. Let them know we stare down a shaft at them."

The harmony busied itself with preparation. For his part, Thuk sat back in his chair and took a moment in simple appreciation of their efforts. His crew was efficient and competent, like a well-run mound. He couldn't take credit for it, of course, they'd been selected for duty aboard the Xre's newest and greatest ship of war, after all. They had floated to the top long before he'd been given the dubious honor of serving them.

Still, if he had to be derstu, this was a fine harmony to—

With the suddenness of a bolt from the heavens, the *Chusexx* bucked sideways and threw Thuk painfully into the side of his chair, hard enough to knock the air from his chest. He felt one of the plates on his abdomen give way with a *snap*. The mighty ship's bones groaned around them as if it, too, was in agony.

"What the seething Abyss was that?" Kivits shouted before Thuk caught back up to his breath.

"Reports are scattered and confused," Hurg said, her voice high and tight like a plucked string.

"Somebody sing," Thuk wheezed, his vision blurring at the edges from the pain. "What's happened to our home?"

"Thrust is falling away," the tiller station's attendant shouted. "Compensating . . . no effect. Engines unresponsive. We're tumbling."

"Can you stabilize?"

"No, Derstu. Three thruster clusters are misfiring. There's a short somewhere in the control sequence. They're exacerbating the tumble."

"Cut them out of the power grid and reassess. And Kivits, put our javelins back into hibernation!"

"Already engaged."

Another jolt shook the floor beneath their feet, not as sharp or hard as the first, but even more alarming, because as soon as it ended, so did the artificial gravity. Everyone scrambled to find purchase on their chairs, footrests, or the ribs of their alcoves to avoid floating free in the cavern.

"Now what?" Thuk demanded angrily.

"Source energy's down. Switched to backups. Gravity system resetting."

"Leave it until we know what's happening, we may need the power elsewhere. Why'd source energy shut down?" A new, sharp alert tone answered Thuk's question.

"Rotting light leak! Our shield cone is breached," Hurg shouted.

"How bad?"

"Contamination alarms in caverns from ribs L-127 through L-103 and spreading forward."

Thuk shivered. Rotting light had already flooded almost a fifth of the habitable caverns starting at their cone shield on up. If it reached the central nexus, or the farms . . .

"Seal everything forward of rib L-90. Vent unoccupied caverns into space."

"And the occupied caverns?" Hurg asked, the rest of the question left to hang in the air between them.

"Seal them and shut them off from the air-changers. They can go into torpor and last a day or more on the air they have."

"If they've not already been poisoned by rotting light," Kivits said.

"One thing at a time. This is the most we can do for them right now."

"Derstu," the tiller attendant called out. "I can't restart the engines with the shield cone breached, not even if we get source energy back. The emergency systems are in lockdown and I can't supersede."

"Not even physically?"

"The physical supersede is inside the contaminated zone."

Naturally, Thuk thought. That was it, then. They weren't going to fix the shield cone and restore maneuverability before the *Chusexx* floated across the treaty line and into the waiting claws of the human cruiser. Unless . . .

"Do we have enough reserve to spin a seedpod?"

"To where?"

"Nowhere, just put one up and keep it up until we make repairs. It'll keep the humans' light-spears and javelins from carving us up like a game animal."

"I'm sorry, Derstu, but no. We're short the necessary energy by an order of magnitude."

Thuk's hopes sank into the abyss. He was out of ideas, and rapidly running out of time.

"Hurg, please open a link to the human ship. Ears only."

"A link?" Kivits said. "What are you going to do?"

"Sing for our lives, Dulac. Hurg, are we ready?"

"Yes, Derstu. Link open."

Thuk steadied himself in his chair with his midhands. The humans couldn't see him through an ears-only link, but it was more for his confidence than anything. He needed to feel grounded among the chaos and calamity, even if it was illusionary.

Wincing with each breath through the pain in his side, he began. "We are the harmony of the *Chussex*. We announce a . . ." What was that senseless human expression for an emergency? ". . . day in may. Rotting light is leaking into our caverns, and source energy has failed. Please do not throw your light-spears or javelins. Our bellies face the sky."

Thuk made a decapitating gesture with a blood-claw on his primehand. Hurg cut off the cavern's ears.

"Did it take?"

"Yes, Derstu. Your song captured."

"Set it on a loop and let it sing until they respond. Are those cursed javelins in hibernation yet?"

"They're sleeping, Derstu," Kivits confirmed.

Thuk exhaled despite the pain in his side. The last thing he wanted were live javelins, in hand, just waiting for a lucky shot from the human ship to detonate their cores and blow the ship in half for them. If he was going to die, he'd prefer his shell pierced by his enemy's weapons instead of being run through by his own.

"Thank you, Dulac."

"What do we do now?" Hurg asked for the entire cavern.

"The simplest thing anyone can do, Attendant," Thuk said. "Await death or deliverance."

"They're still coming, mum," Mattu said. "EM emissions just ticked up a bit. They may have gotten auxiliary power up, but it's still way below baseline. And they're still leaking gamma."

Susan glanced up at the countdown above the plot. Five minutes until the Xre ship crossed the line. Five minutes until she was obligated by her orders to kill them.

"How much gamma, Scopes?" she asked. "Lethal?"

"I don't know what a lethal dose for Xre is, mum. I can loop Doc Cargill in and ask her?"

"No time," Miguel said. "Mum, I don't want to intrude on your thoughts, but our orders are clear and unambiguous. We *must* torch them if they cross the Red Line. That's how it's been for seventy years."

"We also have a duty to respond to distress calls, of *any* flag. Which takes precedence? I think that's my call to make, that's why they gave me the hat."

"They could still be playing possum, mum. We could fake up every part of this 'accident' with a couple hours' notice. Hell, that may even be why they took so long to respond. They're setting us up for an ambush."

"Exactly," Nesbit broke in. "They're playing us. Listen to your XO."

"They're half again our tonnage." Susan waved a hand at the real-time rendering of their foe. "Why would they need to ambush us?"

"We're not exactly a soft target like that fleet tender was, mum. We've already taken a shot at them once. They know we'll fight. If the tables were turned, would you do anything less than absolutely maximize our tactical advantage before committing?"

"No," Susan permitted. "And yet . . ."

Susan's training and sense of duty crashed headlong against her empathy. Yes, this wily Xre commander had already outsmarted her once with clever tricks, but that was just it. From the start of this whole operation, they'd been bold, ordering an armed drone into her space to destroy platforms under her nose. They'd played on her belief no one would have the cast-iron tits to cross the line when they'd escaped the last time. They were all the actions of a brave warrior who wouldn't reduce themselves to playing dead just to gain advantage. The very idea would be revolting to them.

At least that's what Susan told herself as the decision she'd already made solidified in her mind.

"No. They're really in trouble. This guy is a Grade A hard-ass, he's not faking injury. That's beneath him."

"Mum," Miguel began, but Susan cut him off.

"They're spacers, Miguel. Just like us. Sent out here in the black to poke at monsters, by monsters. And I won't kill them when they're begging for mercy, not until I'm sure they're faking. Because if the tables were turned, I'd be praying they gave us the same chance."

Miguel's frown dug trenches in his cheeks, but he returned to parade ground attention at her side and opened a link to the shuttle bay. "Flight Ops, prepare for rescue operations. Marine commander, ready a security team in hardsuits. Damage control supervisor, equip a team and have them waiting in the shuttle bay in ten minutes. Sickbay, send a detail to Flight Ops prepped and ready to treat Xre casualties. Repeat, *Xre* casualties. Full biological and radiological protocols."

"What?" Nesbit half-shouted. "You can't be serious. We've got to stop them short of the line. That's the only reason we're out here!"

"I've given my orders, Mr. Nesbit," Susan said icily.

"Yeah, the wrong orders. Your own XO told you, you're countermanding seventy years of foreign policy. You don't have the authority."

"You are here as an observer and advisor, Mr. Nesbit, which is where *your* authority ends."

"I'm done with you," he said dismissively before turning to Miguel. "Commander, relieve the captain and—"

Miguel moved so fast his body blurred into Susan's peripheral vision. Before anyone really registered what happened, he'd thrown Nesbit up against the CIC's starboard bulkhead with the ease of a child pinning the tail on the donkey.

"Listen, suit," Miguel said with the sort of deliberate calm that promised unimaginable chaos if it was disturbed in the least measure. "The old lady made her call. That's her job. I implement her orders. That's *my* job. Don't think for a millisecond that our disagreement *before* she gave me an order was an opening for you to wiggle in *after* it was issued. Clear?"

Nesbit had some difficulty talking around the vise-grip hand clamped down on his throat, so he just nodded his understanding instead.

"Good." Miguel released him.

Susan turned to address the marine by the hatch who'd somehow managed to remain at attention through the entire exchange. "Guard, our CL appears to be suffering from fatigue. Please escort him back to his quarters and make sure he gets a full watch of uninterrupted rest."

"Immediately, mum." The marine stepped into the CIC, the palm of his hand resting on his still-holstered-but-it-wouldn't-take-a-second sidearm. "CL Nesbit, if you'll come with me?"

He reached out to take Nesbit by the elbow, but was rebuffed.

"I know the way to my cabin, Private," Nesbit huffed. "This is all going in my report, Captain."

"As it will in mine, sir. Get some rest." Susan nodded to the marine guard and Nesbit was unceremoniously escorted out of her sight. "And just when I was starting to think we might get along," she lamented.

"Hope springs eternal," Miguel said.

"Thank you."

"For what?"

"For not mutinying. I know how bad you want a command."

"Ha! I'll earn one the old-fashioned way." He looked up at the plot and the falling countdown. "If I live that long. I sure hope you're right about this, mum."

"Me too, XO. Guns, lock our laser array onto the *Chusexx*'s antimatter containment pods. If they as much as sneeze, don't wait for my order, just blow them straight back to wherever the hell their homeworld is."

"With pleasure, mum."

"Good. Open a channel."

"Derstu," Hurg perked up in her seat. "We're getting a song from the human ship."

Thuk's hopes rose. Why would the humans bother to answer his song if they were already committed to their destruction? Maybe there was a slim chance to survive the disaster after all. "Put it to the mouths."

"*Chusexx* harmony, this is [Derstu] Susan Kamala, CCDF *Ansari*. We grab your [Mayday] and stand to contribute. Be caution, aggression will greet death power instant. Sleep weapons and take/accept rescue/savior bird."

Everyone stared at each other with their mandibles hanging limp. The humans were not only staying their execution, but offering aid? It didn't seem possible.

"It's a trick," Kivits said. "Has to be. They mean to board us and take the ship as a prize."

"Perhaps."

"Well? We can't let that happen."

"We won't. If they are being deceptive, we will simply scuttle the ship."

"But we'll all die!"

"We were going to do that anyway. We're trading for time and chances. And I'll take as much of both as I can possibly leverage. Hurg, let me sing our reply, please."

"Ready to capture, Derstu."

"Susan Kamala, I am Thuk, singing for this harmony. We accept your offered hand with great thanks, and will gladly receive your rescue team. Without source energy, our weapons are already disabled. However, we must keep our meteor brooms active, even if the risk is low. Send, please."

Thuk awaited the reply nervously. He wouldn't have to wait long. At this short range, light lag would be negligible.

"[Derstu] Thuk, song acceptable. Be caution, any light shine on rescue/savior bird greet death power. We launch shortly. Small hand of warriors travel bird defend rescue/savior attendants. Please hospitality."

Thuk and Kivits looked at each other for a long, silent, uncomfortable moment.

"No," Kivits finally said. "No way."

"We don't have a choice."

"You want to let human warriors into our home?"

"'Want' is not the right word. We 'need' to."

"And let them turn on us at any moment?"

"If they do, I'm confident our own warriors will defend their home with a great deal of enthusiasm. A handful of humans, on foot, in an unfamiliar mound, can't possibly fight their way to the mind cavern before we release the annihilation fuel reserves. Our situation is fundamentally unchanged. This is an affront, but it is not a problem."

"I don't like it."

"I'm not asking you to."

"What about . . . the weapon?"

"It's mostly external. And I don't think they're going to be bouncing around in vacuum skins."

"It's not all external. There are several components in the mechanical caverns that could be visible to—"

"Yes, yes, I agree." Thuk faced the recording alcove. "Susan Kamala. My harmony and I are . . . reluctant to allow armed warriors into our home."

"Not negotiate, [Derstu] Thuk. I want/desire help you, but safety people mine prioritize."

"What assurances do I have that your warriors won't try to capture the *Chusexx* or her harmony?"

"I limit number/size. Takeover impossible. Only protect our attendants. Must respond mayday by corporate space law."

"Those laws only extend to other human vessels, do they not?"

"Law essence, then. Say you what, goodwill token, I join warriors, self."

There was an inaudible sound from the background, followed by the muffling sound of someone covering an ear. Thuk, Kivits, and Hurg looked at each other anxiously.

"Is she sun-stroked?" Kivits asked. "Coming over here herself?"

"Well, it does give us pretty good collateral, don't you agree?"

The scratching sound happened again as Susan Kamala's voice returned. "Forgive interruption, Thuk. My dulac misunderstand/disagreement. Now straight. So, we deal?"

"Your offer is acceptable, Susan Kamala. For reasons of sensitivity, there are places your warriors cannot be allowed to venture. I'm sure you would have similar concerns if we were visiting your home. You will be informed of such places politely, but firmly. I ask that you respect our privacy."

"Our attendants not unescorted. If warriors not allowed, none of our people help those areas."

"That is understood, Susan Kamala."

"Then agreed. Our bird inbound. [ETA] forty-seven [minutes]. Being clear, take hostages/captives, my weapons attendant stand order cut through *Chusexx* as ripe [banana]. Kamala, out." The link went silent.

"What's a banana?" Hurg asked.

"I have no idea." Thuk ran "forty-seven minutes" through a conversion tab. He had just enough time to get back to his room and put on formal dress before heading to the nest. The circumstances seemed to call for it. Thuk stood up from his chair and headed for the door.

"Wait, where are you going?" Kivits called to his back.

"Down to the bird nest to greet our 'guests.' Never seen a human in the skin before. I wonder what they smell like."

"What, and leave me here to blow up the ship if they get by you?"

"You'd rather go grovel for aid from our enemies?"

Kivits's thorax constricted. "I suppose not."

"As I assumed. Try to keep the lights on. Diplomacy in the dark often leads to light in brief, violent flashes."

SIXTEEN

"This is the single goddamned dumbest thing I have ever seen, heard, or read about," Miguel said. "Mum," he added.

"Noted, XO. Now hand your old lady her sidearm."

Miguel obliged, but didn't stop talking. "I mean, we just spent more than a month trying to shoot holes in them, they've already violated the Red Line twice and blown up our drones, and now we're not even going to try and take them as a prize? What changed?"

"Everything, Miguel." Susan pulled the Glock M73 from its holster and hit the magazine release: Full load of 10 mm armor-piercing fléchette cluster rounds meant to penetrate the Xre's natural armor plating and tumble around in the goop. Each round held a bundle of six darts inside a sabot. Killing Xre was notoriously difficult. Most of the last war had been fought ship-to-ship or through orbital bombardments. Actual ground engagements or boarding actions had been exceptionally rare. Few humans had ever seen a Xre in the flesh. Fewer still had lived long enough to share any details. What little they knew about Xre physiology came mostly from dissecting cadavers recovered from shattered warships.

Susan slapped the magazine back into the pistol and racked the action to chamber a round before putting it back in its holster.

"We were shooting at them because they were an aggressor and a threat. Now, they're not. If we blow up a defenseless ship, it could start a war. If we try to board, they'll probably fight and we'll have to kill them all and it could start a war. But, if we help . . ."

"We hold out an olive branch," Miguel completed her thought.

"Exactly. Maybe this is the moment we finally put our dicks away, zip up our trousers, and start actually talking to one another."

"I wish I shared your optimism, mum."

"Optimism? That's the first time I've ever been accused of such a terrible thing. I think they're probably just as afraid to die needlessly as we are. Do they even remember why we started fighting in the first place? I don't." Susan turned to walk down the flexible accordion tunnel to the waiting shuttle, but paused at the threshold. "But I wasn't kidding before. If they try anything, you tell that high-functioning psychopath Warner to cook them like a bug-zapper. Admiralty House can always find another recklessly naïve captain for the *Ansari*."

"You don't think they'd just let *me* keep her, mum?" Miguel said with a smile.

"Goodbye, Miguel. See you soon."

"Good luck, mum. I'll keep your seat warm."

Susan nodded and spun the hatch tight behind her. It was a short walk from the hatch to the shuttle, but somehow it seemed like a kilometer. Susan swallowed hard. Miguel was right about one thing, this was the dumbest idea she'd ever heard of, too. *Nothing for it, girl. You're committed now.*

She stepped away from the small platform inside the transfer tube and across the bright red line that delineated the last little piece of *Ansari* real estate, and moved across the jointed, shifting grates loosely attached to the floor of the transfer tube. The shuttle, one of the marines' two assault birds that had been selected, was matte black and almost perfectly smooth. Like the *Ansari* herself, it had no portholes or windows, save for a gun slit windshield made out of twenty centimeters of laminated transparent aluminum that was probably stronger than the armor plating surrounding it, a compromise the designers had only made in the exceedingly unlikely event all of the shuttle's optical feeds or computer systems were knocked out and the pilot had to maneuver using visual references alone.

The team already inside saw her approach through one of the thousands of tiny cameras embedded in the adaptive-camo skin on the hull. Indeed, it was easier to just think of the hull as one big, uninterrupted eye. Perfectly machined seams in the hull, grown really, cracked open as the two halves of the armored entry hatch swung out to invite her into the airlock.

Most shuttles featured small, two-person airlocks, large enough only for an EVA team to cycle in and out. But marine assault shuttles were very different. For vacuum-insertion mission profiles, their airlocks needed to accommodate up to an entire squad of a dozen armed marines in hardsuits so they could all deploy in one enraged wave.

As a result, Susan could lay down the narrow way in the airlock without her head or toes touching the bulkheads. Fortunately, she didn't have to wait for the air to cycle. As soon as the door behind her closed and locked, the lights went green and the inner door opened to reveal the commander of her marine detachment already kitted-out in medium, servo-assisted, vac-rated armor and a bullpup, over-under 6.5 mm rifle/20 mm grenade close quarters battle rifle hanging from her shoulder on a retractable sling.

"I just want to go on record as this being the stupidest—"

Susan waved her hand. "Yes, yes. I've gotten it both ends of this tunnel, Staff Sergeant."

Sergeant Okuda blanched a little at the reprimand. "I wouldn't let the grunts hear you phrase it exactly like that, mum."

"I think they'd better behave themselves. This is a deadly serious operation."

"Which is exactly why I'd feel better if you watched it unfold from the CIC."

"No can do, Sarge. I've already given my word. Backing out now could spark a confrontation. I understand I've put you in a difficult position, but it is what it is."

"Difficult? Oh no, mum. Marines love the chance to be a trip wire for a nuclear shootout between capital ships."

"That's the spirit. Let's get underway."

Susan took the front-row seat reserved for her in the shuttle's passenger compartment. After being strapped into her crash harness by a copilot who'd missed her calling as a corset-tightener, Susan settled in for the flight over to the *Chusexx*. The distance between the ships had closed, but the *Ansari* needed to maintain a respectable buffer zone just in case their tracking and AMS systems needed to react if the Xre got desperate and started flinging missiles. Without main power, the Xre's lasers and railguns would be inoperable. But missiles, once floated out of the tubes, carried their own reactant mass and power sources. They were an ever-present danger, even from a "dead" ship.

"Okay, ladies and grunts," Okuda said into the compartment's intercom. "As you all know, we're headed into a whole hornet's nest of bullshit. Our RoE are simple: You shoot first, I shoot you. If they shoot first and you fail to shoot back, I shoot you. Grunts, our priorities are as follows." She held up three fingers and started counting down. "One, keep the captain alive. Two, keep the DC team alive. Three, avenge their deaths if we fail on priority one or two. And we won't have long to do that, as Lieutenant Warner up in the CIC has her finger hovering over the button that will burn a hole through the bugs' antimatter containment pods and reduce all of us into pure energy and elementary particles before any of you can shit your hardsuits."

Okuda cleared her throat. "Damage Control Team, I'm sure

you've already been briefed on this by your section chief, but it bears repeating. Even with your hazmat suits, we are entering an environment optimized for Xre physiology. Xre-adapted bacteria and viruses have never meshed with our biology, so you don't have to worry about catching a space bug. However, the atmosphere will be almost forty percent oxygen, plus more carbon dioxide than we're used to. Your respirators will filter out particulate, but the gas mix will breeze right through. Most of you won't suffer any ill effects beyond a mild headache from the excess CO_2, but some of you may experience symptoms of oxygen poisoning such as euphoria, twitching lips, vertigo, convulsions, and nausea. If you start to feel *any* of these symptoms, don't 'tough it out.' Put your hand up and report it immediately and one of us will escort you back to the shuttle for recovery. Don't be a hero. Heroes get dead. Clear?"

"What if one of you starts to feel it?" a random tech blurted out.

"We won't," Okuda answered. "One, because CCDF Marine Indoc and Basic weeds out those susceptible, and two, because our hardsuits regulate our atmospheres. Any other stupid questions?"

There were none.

"Excellent! Moving on. The captain has agreed to the Xre's request not to venture where we aren't welcome. So nobody wander off, and if you're turned back by one of their crew from a place you weren't supposed to be in the first place, don't be an asshole about it. Clear?"

A general round of grunts and acknowledgments from those assembled confirmed that, as a practical matter, Okuda's instructions were clear.

"Outstanding. We'll be in the black for thirty minutes before we land in their bay and get to work. So relax, take a nap, pray, write a letter, whatever you need to do to get your heads right. Because when we cross that threshold, we'll be stepping into a custom-fitted clusterfuck. Captain Kamala, want to add anything?"

Susan smirked. "Thank you, Sergeant, but I think you hit the high points quite eloquently." Okuda was an excellent squad leader, equal parts mother and drill sergeant wrapped up in a package that was just as eager to kiss as kill. Susan was surprised she and Warner hadn't hooked up yet. Maybe they had but preferred privacy. Whatever the case, it wasn't her concern. The half hour passed in relative quiet as everyone dealt with the tension and anxiety in their own heads and their own ways. The minutes felt to Susan like they passed both too quickly and agonizingly slowly at once.

Two-thirds of the way through the trip, the shuttle flipped ass over tea kettle to point its fusion rockets at the rendezvous point and throttled up to decelerate for a clean zero-zero intercept. The pressure of deceleration pushed Susan back into her chair, gently but firmly. It felt good to have the reference point of gravity back again. For a woman who'd spent her entire career in and around starships, she'd never really gotten used to zero g. She'd done well enough in training to pass her quals, but she'd just never taken to it the way many of the other spacers had, which was even stranger when one considered how much she loved to swim.

"Captain," Okuda whispered. "Look at this." She passed a tablet over to Susan's waiting hands. The 3D screen showed a false-color image of their approach to the *Chusexx*. It was big, but they'd already known that. Still, witnessing it from this close was different from sensor estimates on a plot. Size wasn't everything, but Susan was suddenly very relieved her enemy broke of its own accord instead of her people having to fight it out with the leviathan.

The ship's details were softer, her lines more graceful than the *Ansari,* whose designers still held to a more faceted approach to stealth, due in no small part to the ease, cost, and speed of manufacture and repair. The CCDF had been born of desperation, converting cargo-haulers and colony ships into battle wagons in months when the first war broke out. "That'll do" was still an overriding attitude among the legacy engineers, and corporate budget considerations still played their role in warship development, although the economic austerity was nothing compared to the fleet's early days.

The fundamental physics of the universe, biology, and their relatively parallel lines of technological development dictated that the *Chusexx* didn't differ all that greatly from her human-designed counterparts, at least externally. There was still a large habitable section at the front of the ship that housed the crew the majority of the time, as well as most of the sensor platforms mounted as far away from the interference from the fusion engines at the back of the ship as possible, an engineering section in the middle where most of the important moving parts lived along with their Alcubierre rings, although the *Chusexx* mounted a fully-redundant set of four rings more like a CCDF Space Supremacy Ship or Planetary Assault Carrier than a three-ringed cruiser.

The rings caught Susan's attention. She froze the image and zoomed in. Xre ships were distinctive in that they mounted oval rings instead of circular. The intel people thought it was to reduce their radar/lidar return in the side aspect. The engineering obstacle of regulating negative matter flow as it raced at varying speeds around the oval rings had prevented the adoption of the design among human vessels so far, but it wasn't what had grabbed Susan's attention.

"So you see it, then?" Okuda asked.

"What the hell are those?" She pointed at small, secondary rings built into the inside surface of the outer edge of each of the four main rings, right at the apex of the ovals.

"That's what I wanted you to see, mum. Trim rings? Some way to fine-tune their bubble? Maybe even steer it?"

Now that was an unsettling thought. Since the dawn of Alcubierre drive, it had been taken as an immutable law of physics that bubbles, once set in motion, could only travel in an arrow-straight line through space until they were popped. That line would be distorted by sufficiently massive gravity wells just like anything traveling through the fabric of spacetime, but once a bearing was set, it couldn't be altered.

But if the Xre had found a way to make midcourse corrections from *inside* their bubble . . .

Susan wasn't an engineer. She could only stab wildly in the dark for answers to the mystery. "There's no point speculating. Tell *Ansari* to whisker laser this footage back to the skip drone just in case something happens to us. The R&D kids back at fleet will have a field day chewing this over."

"Aye, mum."

Before long, the fight deck was chattering away with the final approach as they navigated the shuttle through the morass of instructions coming from the Xre's version of a space boss, filtered both coming and going through an imperfect language translation matrix. Docking between two objects moving independently through open space was harrowing enough when everyone spoke the same language, had trained on the same protocols, and used the same equipment. Injecting variables into all three was nothing short of a nightmare, but through patience and professionalism, the shuttle's flight crew soon had them in position for a clean capture.

"My compliments to the chefs," Susan shouted from her seat.

"Thank you, mum," the pilot called back. "That was . . . interesting."

"Do they have a treaty seal?"

"Yeah, they're still fuckin' around trying to get it in position. Might be a couple of minutes yet before we're green."

Susan nodded. As part of the treaty settlement after the Intersection War, it had been decreed that all ships, of both the human and Xre navies, would carry an adaptor that would make their docking rings compatible with the standards of the other in case of emergency or a sudden need for face-to-face diplomacy. They'd been nicknamed "treaty seals," and coordinating their development had been a three-year experience in pulling teeth. For seventy years, they'd acted as ballast collecting dust and burning up reactant mass. Today was, to anyone's knowledge, the first time any of the thousands of them had been put to its intended use.

Lot of firsts today, Susan thought.

"I'm taking point," Okuda said quietly from Susan's shoulder.

"The hell you are."

"I need to secure a perimeter to ensure your safety."

Susan rubbed her eyes. "Staff Sergeant. I respect your dedication, I really do. But if they mean me harm, there's not a good goddamned thing you or anyone can do to stop them from killing every last one of us. And then a very cross lieutenant will kill every last one of them in the time it takes to push a button. That's where we are. That's where I've placed us on the board. We're here based on the trust we're trying to build. If you walk out there to do a security sweep, it looks like I don't trust them, in their own home. It's an insult. If I walk out first, I honor them and put another block in this foundation. Do you understand?"

Okuda cringed. "I do, but I don't like it, mum."

Susan snorted through her nose. "I'm not a huge fan of it myself, but it weighs the dice in our favor, if only a milligram or two. You and your squad will stack up right behind me. Make a show of it, the gracious captain at the head of her brave warriors."

"And if they shoot you for your generosity?"

"Then you'll have a mad minute to return their hospitality before Warner drops the hammer."

"Out in a blaze of glory, huh?"

"I thought that's what you grunts lived for."

"We prefer to do it where there's camera drones to record our kicking posterior for posterity."

Susan smirked as the pressure indicator on the hatch clicked over from red to green.

"We have a green seal, mum. Ready when you are," the pilot called back.

Susan stood and straightened her flight suit, then pulled her top cover from the loop over her right shoulder and fitted it neatly, securing it in place with a discreet bobby pin. "Sergeant, would you get the door for me, please?"

Okuda spun the hatch and swung it open. Susan floated inside the airlock, guiding herself along the handrails. Her squad of marines filled in the space behind her like racehorses being led into their chutes, all tension and muscle balanced on a hair trigger.

"Easy, folks," Susan cooed at them. "We're all friends here until I say otherwise. Now, big smiles, everybody. Let's meet the neighbors." She hit the release button with a fist. The outer door pushed out, then slid to the side in a flash. The transfer tube beyond was just different enough to give her a moment's pause. Centuries of alien invasion movies had prepared her for organic, sticky-looking construction that screamed extraterrestrial compared to the familiar, angular, manufactured aesthetic of human creations.

Instead, the tube could have been made of the same flexible, transparent polymer as the one in *Ansari*'s boat bay. The only noticeable differences were that it was about half a meter wider in diameter, and instead of segmented reinforcing rings, the structure was supported by a coil of rigid material that spiraled through the clear plastic like a Slinky. It could easily have been built by a different contractor instead of a different species. There were even handholds built into the coils, although their spacing and thickness spoke to users with a larger wingspan and hands than her own.

Susan floated through the tunnel, heart pounding in her ears like a rock concert. Behind her, a flock of black-clad marines glided on the wing like birds of prey scouring the horizon for their next meal. Their presence reassured her, even as she admitted they were about as useful as a peacock's feathers in this context. Still, impressive displays had been diffusing violence for millions of years. It was worth a shot.

Much like on the *Ansari,* the *Chusexx*'s boat bay had a large viewing gallery with panoramic windows. Unlike the *Ansari,* those windows were filled with two-meter-tall monsters that looked like the offspring of an ill-conceived union of a wasp and an Alaskan king crab.

A deeply seated part of Susan's lizard brain recoiled at the sight. She'd seen images of the Xre before, of course. She'd done fully immersive VR boarding/counter-boarding exercises back in C school in haptic-suit simulations until she had bedsores. But no matter how exacting those renderings were, no matter how well the environmentals were captured, it was still the difference between watching porn and losing your virginity.

Susan beat back the terror and bile threatening to storm the back of her throat and willed the women and men behind her to do the same. So close to the enemy she'd dedicated her life to holding back, it was easy to forget that she held the ultimate trump card. Even in the micro gravity, Susan was acutely aware of the mass of the Glock strapped to her hip. Through conscious effort, she didn't reach for it, not even to check that it was properly seated in its holster. Any movement that could be misconstrued as hostile might prove as deadly as a bullet.

She reached the lockout. With a pneumatic hiss and a slight metallic screech, the outer door opened like a flower with pedals made of scimitars.

Okay, that's a little different, Susan allowed nervously. The space beyond was smaller than the airlock on the shuttle. Not everyone was going to fit in one go. "Okuda?"

"I see it, mum," the sergeant answered. "Break up into fire teams," she called back to her squad. "Gibson, Panaka, Valerian, on me. Keep those hallway brooms tight to your chests unless I say otherwise."

Susan stuck a thumb at the closet in front of them. "You think all five of us will fit in there at once?"

"Think skinny, mum. And exhale fully."

Somehow, everyone fit, with enough room that no one needed to stop breathing. Although if their hosts didn't open the inner door soon, the oxygen would run out in a hurry. Fortunately, they didn't have long to wait before the outer door sealed and the lock-out cycled through whatever safety checks its programing mandated and the inner door obliged them.

The smell was the first thing to reach Susan. It wasn't unpleasant, but it was complex, strong, and utterly unfamiliar. Metallic and earthy at the same time, like someone decided to farm mushrooms inside a foundry. Not wanting to seem timid, Susan grabbed the last handhold and pushed herself forward into the observation gallery and the reception that had been prepared for them.

The gallery felt large, but most of that was probably owed to the fact it was a meter taller than the one on the *Ansari,* and the fact everyone was still in micro-grav. Susan slipped a toe into an oversized foot loop to anchor herself. Apparently, the damage to their power systems was such that they hadn't been able to restore artificial gravity, not even on a low power setting. Things onboard the *Chusexx* were desperate indeed. But if they were panicked, the two dozen Xre before her showed no sign of it. Not that she had the least idea what to look for as far as body language or . . . facial expressions were concerned.

"Ah, hello." It seemed as good a place to start as any. "I'm Captain Susan Kamala of the CCDF *Ansari.*" Susan took care to point at herself, to avoid any confusion. "My people and I come in peace and friendship to offer you whatever assistance we can give."

For their part, the Xre appeared unmoved by the announcement. Neither hostile, nor cowering. They just stared back at her, through dozens of unblinking eyes and thousands of lenses. Even as her marines filled in behind her, they just kept . . . looking. For an interminably long moment, the two sides exchanged glances in utter silence. Only when the last marine had cycled through and taken their place did the crowd in front of her stir. It was then Susan realized her mistake. The Xre were intensely communal. Almost, but not quite, a hive organism. They'd been waiting until her entire cell, or hill, or whatever, was present, probably out of courtesy.

She'd jumped the gun.

Susan was just about to repeat her announcement when it began. It was low at first, a humming, but not coming from any of the mouths of the aliens before her. Instead, the sound appeared to be generated from their legs being gently rubbed against their bulbous abdomens.

Then, the harmony began. It wasn't singing as Susan understood the concept. In place of voices, there were whistles, clicks, and pure notes as if played through woodwinds. It built, slowly at first, with subtle undertones rising and falling from prominence among the layers of complexity until defining themes evolved as if out of chaos. Wave after wave of music washed over her, like she was a buoy floating on a rhythmic ocean of sound in the middle of a hurricane.

Susan completely forgot where she was and what she was doing under the melodic massage, the aural elation of it all. Her eyes closed, and she felt her consciousness melt into the music. Were there words and meaning hidden among the sounds, or were the notes just the meaningless beauty she heard through her ignorant, virgin ears? She didn't know. She didn't care.

Then, the piece faded, until all that remained was an echo of the melody that had been the backbone of the performance. Then, even that disappeared. In the aftermath of such an unexpectedly transcendent experience, the silence that followed felt like an insult. An assault, even.

Susan opened her eyes to see a droplet of water floating in

front of her face. It was only then she realized she'd been crying, the half-formed tears blurring her vision until she shook her head and cast them into her helmet. Among all the danger and death and fear they must have felt, her hosts had decided to greet their enemies with *that*. She wanted to say something, gush over the performance, compliment the singers, something to express the gratitude she felt pressing against the confines of her soul before she burst, but no worthy words presented themselves.

As she struggled, one of the Xre, a beta caste if she was any judge, swung forward on one of its larger upper arms and placed itself slightly ahead of the rest of the group, but not separate from it.

It spoke softly. A rough translation came from speakers built into the corners of the space where they would most efficiently fill the room with sound.

"Contrite, Susan Kamala," the synthesized English voice said in the alien's stead. "Short time preparation. Song inferior."

It took a moment for Susan to realize what the creature was trying to say. It was actually *apologizing* for the quality of the performance she'd just witnessed.

"No." She waved her hands and shook her head. "It was beautiful. The most beautiful thing I've ever heard."

The Xre held out a claw and pointed it at Susan's face. "But you leak. You not are upset?"

Susan sniffled. "Humans cry for many reasons. These were good tears. I promise. Thank you for sharing your voices with us. They were incredible."

The Xre looked back to consult with two others for a moment; one was of the larger alpha caste with their thicker bodies, twin arms, and quad legs. The various Xre morphologies were well-studied from cadavers left over after several different engagements in the last war. But their social hierarchies and even military chains of command remained opaque. Indeed, no one really knew if the Xre even bothered to make a meaningful distinction between civilian and military.

The impromptu confab ended. "Not disappoint?" the same alien asked.

"Far from it," Susan answered.

"This pleases. I am Thuk. We early sing."

"Captain Thuk, I'm honored to meet you, and your crew. I'm sorry your ship was damaged in the course of your duties. How can we help?"

Thuk conferred quietly with several other members of his crew before answering. "Rotting light corruption move through air tunnels. Trapped harmony. Wounded. Choke soon."

Susan looked back at her people. "Anybody want to take a crack at that?"

"Rotting light . . ." a private first class ventured. Susan recognized him. He'd been blue a few weeks ago.

"Spit it out, PFC."

". . . well, 'rotting light' could mean hard radiation. Radiation is just higher-energy light further up the EM spectrum, right? Like the gamma leaking from their ass end. Radiation rots flesh, right? It's probably contaminated their air handlers, so they had to lock down the life support in the affected areas. Anyone trapped in those compartments is running out of air with every breath."

Susan nodded approvingly. "Very good, PFC. You just earned a seat at the Captain's Table for dinner. Okuda, bring up the DC team. We have work to do."

SEVENTEEN

Tyson sat in a corner booth across a small, round, antique burl-wood table from Dr. Elsa Spaulding and exhaled weeks' worth of dread and anxiety in one long, exasperated, thoroughly satisfying sigh.

"That is the first bit of good news I've heard in more than a month." He lifted his drink to clink her nearly empty glass. "Cheers!"

They both leaned back into the circular leather bench of the "privacy" booth. While they could look out on the rest of the patrons of Vicars, their conversations were reduced to static by overlapping fields of ultrasonic interference at the mouth of the booth. Tyson wouldn't repeat his mistake from Chili's.

"Don't get ahead of yourself, Mr. Abington."

"Tyson."

"Fine, Tyson. It's a trial phase, there's no guarantee it will work across all—"

Tyson waved her off. "I'm confident your team will close the gaps. Loosen up, celebrate your accomplishment. You're running low, would you like another?"

"Actually, I think I'd like to switch to beer."

"By all means. They have an excellent Flemish sour on tap here."

"A what?"

"A sour beer." Tyson's eyebrow inched toward the ceiling. "Where did you grow up, Elsa?"

"Persephone. On the equatorial belt, like almost everyone. Except the miners and the people up in the orbitals, of course. We called it the racetrack. Two thousand kilometers across in most places and wrapped all the way around the globe."

"Persephone is pretty dry, right? I've never been." Tyson entered the beer order into the table's menu.

"Let's just say lakeside property is at a premium. I lived in the twelves. We had a 'lake' you could wade across, and it was man-made."

"That doesn't mean a great deal to me, I'm afraid."

"Sorry. Without large, interconnected oceans, there aren't recognizable continents, so the equatorial belt is divided up into forty-four thousand-kilometer-long sections and one shorter section that acts as the end point of the belt, as mapped by the original surveyors. I lived in the twelfth section."

"Seems a bit impersonal."

"Persephone is a bit impersonal, and that's when she isn't actively trying to kill you. This place"—she waved around an arm to encompass the totality of Lazarus—"is like the planet's brightest vacation spots by comparison."

"It was hotter than Lazarus?" Tyson said. "I find that hard to believe."

"Not on average. Persephone sits right near the edge of the liquid water zone of Proxima, but it's dry, the winds spin up to several hundred kilometers per hour, a sudden solar flare can give even gene-spliced skin a third-degree sunburn in under five minutes, and when a pressure front from the sunward or nightward side pushes into the racetrack, the temperature can rise or fall by forty degrees in less than an hour. Which could happen at any time, because there are no seasons on a tidally locked planet."

Tyson grimaced as the automated waiter rolled up to the table to deliver the beer. "Makes it hard to know how to dress for a picnic, I imagine."

Elsa took the stein from the small platform and thanked it out of habit. "We didn't leave the house without a goody bag."

"Goody bag?"

"Sorry. It's like a cross between a sleeping bag and a small tent. You could have it inflated and be inside in ten seconds, which we practiced. Its shell would reflect the worst radiation of a flare, and it was insulated well enough to keep you alive for several hours in either extreme heat or cold. And the second it inflated, a built-in burst transmitter started screaming to everyone within two hundred kilometers to come get you. Goody bags saved a *lot* of people over the last couple centuries. Anyone caught outside without one is pretty well written off as too stupid to be worth saving in the first place."

"It's a miracle it was ever colonized in the first place."

"It was our very first extra-solar colony, back in the days before the Alcubierre breakthrough. The first ships to get there were a joint ESA/NASA project using good old antimatter rockets. It took thirty years just to get there at a time when we weren't sure going any further into space would ever be practical. So, the first colonists were pretty strongly motivated to make it work. I doubt developers today would give a marginal case like Persephone a second glance, but still, she persisted. Even today, Persephone hasn't repaid its original investment in materials or manufacturing. But it's more than made up for it by cranking out generation after generation of tough bitches and the institutional knowledge of how to terraform even the most disagreeable planets."

Tyson smiled. "You take pride in that obstinacy?"

Elsa blushed. "Maybe a little. Is that silly?"

"Not at all. It's admirable even, if put to appropriate use." Tyson took another swill of his whiskey and soda. "Speaking of uses . . ."

Elsa's eyebrow inched up. "Yes?"

"I have received a report from, well, from a very strange woman whose analysis I trust nonetheless, that our investigations should take a particular look at Tau Ceti and Barnard's Starbased operations. Anyone on your list of potentials for our bacteria builder work out of those systems, either currently or recently?"

Elsa chewed over the question for a moment, then unrolled a screen from her pocket. "A few," she said after a brief review. "But it thins the herd significantly."

"That's good. Anyone jump out at you?"

She gently bit her lower lip as she scrolled through the candidates. Tyson's hindbrain pinged and sparked at the visual, but he ignored it. She was an employee. Never mind that damned near *everyone* on this bloody planet was an employee except his immediate family. There were lines one didn't cross at his level of play.

She sneered. "Oh, yesss . . ."

"That sounds decisive."

Elsa turned the privacy curtain off on the screen so the image in front of her could be viewed from both sides of the transparent film. Tyson's side was a mirror image, but it sufficed. A man's bust filled the screen. European-ish features, mid-sixties, a little soft around the chin and neck, brown hair given way to gray, and the unmistakable, sunken, beady eyes of a rat.

"This," Elsa began, "is Dr. Caleb Beckham. Dr. Beckham is a slimy little prick, and has been since he tried unsuccessfully to get me drummed out for plagiarism after I wouldn't suck his dick like all his other undergrads."

"Figuratively?"

"Quite literally. He was known for picking grad students based on attributes outside of their academic performance. Physical attributes, specifically."

"He liked to work around pretty young women?"

"Gender wasn't an issue, so far as I could tell, so long as they looked like they came from a model-breeding facility. Seriously, the housing unit looked like a Dolce and Gabbana photo shoot most nights."

"So why did you want to study with him?"

"Because he ran the best genetics programs in three systems and I didn't know about his extracurricular requirements until after I'd accepted the position. It was an unpleasant surprise."

"Not even with your dating opportunities pulled from such quality stock?"

Elsa's countenance soured. "I was working a hundred hours a week just to keep up with clinicals and my own experiments. I didn't have a lot of time for tickling privates with my colleagues."

"I'm sorry," Tyson said genuinely. "I was only trying to lighten the mood, not insult your professionalism. But do you think Dr. Beckham's, ah, lecherousness makes him a suspect in creating a bioweapon whose very existence, to say nothing of deployment against civilians, carries the death penalty? As vices go, that's a bit of a jump."

"He was eventually fired from TCU three years ago over ethics complaints that rumor has it didn't have anything to do with inappropriate student/staff relations. His personnel file is sealed, but getting tenure pulled is a *big* deal. It had to be serious. Like, opened himself up to blackmail or legal action serious."

Tyson found himself salivating. He took another swallow of his drink to wash it all down. "Does the timeline fit?"

"How do you mean?"

"I mean, is the three years from when he was canned to the release of this bacteria fit with the time you would expect to take to develop and weaponize it?"

Elsa leaned back in her chair and exhaled. "There's a lot of variables. What kind of facilities and equipment does he have access to? How big and how competent a staff? All that takes funding."

"Assume money is no object. Trust me when I say it all becomes a little abstract when you're moving around trillions. How long for a crash program with all the bells and whistles?"

"With my pick of the litter and unlimited funding? Eighteen months. Assuming everything goes off without a hitch, which it never does."

"Still, that's enough time for someone to recruit him, set up and staff a lab, crank out the research, and still have a bit of wiggle room for unforeseen issues. Would you agree?"

Elsa nodded along. "It's a tight timeline, but it's possible."

"And where is the good doctor now?"

"Last I heard, he'd retired to a town house on Mars, but who knows?"

Tyson smiled a crisp, voracious grin. "We will, very soon. How do you find the sour?"

"Oh, right." Elsa picked up the stein and gave it an exploratory sniff. "Smells like cherries."

"It's deceptive. Have a sip."

Tyson watched stone-faced as she took a pull from the glass and her eyes and mouth twisted up into the shape of an asterisk. "God!" Elsa exclaimed. "It's pure vinegar!"

"Not pure, my friend, but it does push back against the tongue pretty hard on the first pass. However, if you'll wait a moment . . ."

"Oh, that's different," she said as the brew's bouquet blossomed in the back of her mouth. "It's . . . sweet, almost floral."

"That's the open vat fermentation you're tasting. Natural yeasts and pollens from the lowlands of Denmark. It grows on you. That particular beer made a trip of more than thirty light-years for the pleasure of passing through your lips."

"You seem to be going out of your way to impress me."

"Not at all, this is just how I live." Tyson saw the flash of disgust cross Elsa's face like a tremor. "I'm sorry, that came out a bit more dickish than I intended."

"That's an understatement."

"What I meant was, I can understand how it would appear that way to you. But my position comes with a great deal more pressure and responsibility, so the perks are commensurately larger as well."

"Yes, poor little me, I'm only responsible for saving the lives of your employees and unraveling this industrial espionage you've fallen into."

Tyson rapped his finger on the tabletop. "I've backed myself into a dead end here, haven't I?"

"You think?" She winked as she took another drink of the sour beer.

"I apologize. I didn't mean to demean your contributions. I'm . . . a little out of practice talking to people who aren't C-level executives, if I'm going to be honest. And you're quite a bit less deferential than even most of them."

Elsa ran a fingertip around the lip of her mostly empty glass. It sang a pure note in response. "So, what's our next move?"

"I thought the spy thing wasn't your game?"

"It's growing on me. Kind of like this beer."

"Told you it would."

"The spy shit, or the beer?"

"Both." Tyson smirked. "I have an idea. But, I'm warning you right up front, it contains an element of risk."

"I'm past the point of no return on that, aren't I? I heard about that girl they pulled out of the wastewater plant."

"You did? How?"

Elsa shrugged. "I know you're proud of it, but this city isn't that big, Tyson. Half a young woman's body turns up in a pipe with no ID, word gets around. *Especially* among single ladies. We have to be on the lookout for predators as a matter of course."

"I—hadn't considered that aspect."

"You've never had to."

"Touché."

Elsa sipped her beer. She didn't make the same scrunched-up face as the first time. Growing on her indeed. "What did you have in mind?"

"A classic sting. You send out feelers for Dr. Beckham, tell him you're working for me and found a cure for this weapon. Tell him you figured out it was him, and he can either pay you double what I'm paying you to botch the cure and keep your mouth shut, or you'll tell me it was him and the authorities will come down on him like avenging angels."

"More stick than carrot, huh?"

"The old tricks are the best tricks."

"What if I'm wrong and it's not him?"

"Then he'll either ignore you, or call you a kook and say you're trying to settle a score from grad school. You'll point out he's got no credibility after being forced to retire, and everyone will forget about it in a couple days."

Elsa nodded along with the thread. "And if I'm right?"

"That's where the risk comes in. Whoever is behind this will either pay you and thank their lucky stars they've managed to flip another asset and penetrate my organization even more deeply . . ."

"Or?"

". . . or they determine it's cheaper and safer to remove you from the board."

"And safely set me off to the side until the game is over and we all get put back in the box?" she asked hopefully.

"Not like that, I'm afraid. But I think the first outcome is far, far more likely. And if they attempt the second, you'll be under constant surveillance and protection. It's hard to spring a trap when the target knows it's there."

"But not impossible."

Tyson held his hands out, palms up. "As I said, an element of risk. But I wouldn't even put this on the table if I wasn't entirely confident that risk was manageable."

Elsa breathed out heavily through her nose, then stared off into the middle distance of the bar. Tyson didn't follow her gaze, instead looking at his hands and the blood on them. Not physically, of course, but it was still there. Someone's daughter, sister, young lover, had already died in the plot against his empire.

He'd made tough calls many times before. Fired people in such a way it ended their careers. Bought start-ups just to quash an emerging threat and snuff out lifelong dreams. Even had one person choose suicide instead of facing the humiliation of demotion, not that anyone had expected *that* outcome.

But a murder was a different animal entirely. He still couldn't wrap his head around it. Maybe he was naïve, but that just wasn't the way the game was played up here in the executive levels. It was so . . . uncouth. He'd joked with the board about plugging the leak, but had come to regret that bit of bravado.

"The trial," Elsa blurted out.

"Yes, of course. You won't have to appear in open court. I'll see to it that your testimony is submitted anonymously."

"No." She jumped onto the end of his sentence. "You don't understand. I don't want to be sheltered, witness protection, or any of that. I went into genetics to help people, to be a healer. This bacteria is a perversion of the science I've dedicated my life to pursuing. It's an abomination. I want to stare them down and watch them squirm. And I want them to know who fucked them."

Tyson took a moment to admire the passion radiating from the intriguing woman he was only just now beginning to understand. "You'll get that chance, I promise you."

Elsa drained the rest of the sour beer in one pull.

"Assuming you keep me alive long enough."

"Yes. Assuming that." Tyson looked over her clothes. "To that end, I think it's time you make acquaintances with my tailor."

"Your tailor?" she said with surprise. "Is this the part of *My Fair Lady* where I get a makeover?"

"I'm afraid I must confess I don't get the reference, but the style isn't what's important. You'll—" A priority connection request popped up in Tyson's AR. It was Paris. She knew where he was and what he was discussing. She wouldn't interrupt for something trivial. He looked at Elsa apologetically and pointed at his temple. "Excuse me for a moment." He sent his mind's voice into the virtual interface. "Go ahead, Paris."

"There's someone to see you in your office, sir. It's urgent."

"They're alone in my office?"

"Yes."

"Who?"

"I can't say. It's sensitive."

"I'm leaving now. Send a pod."

"Waiting outside for you, sir."

"You're too good to me, Paris."

"I'll remind you of that one of these days."

Tyson dropped the connection and returned his attention to Elsa. "Forgive me, but something's come up." He thumbed the small auto-waiter to settle the bill. "I'll message you with details about the tailor appointment."

"I don't have a lot of time to saunter across the city."

"No need, he'll come to you." Tyson stood. "We'll talk soon. Stay alert, stay safe."

Minutes later, he was inside his private express lift, shooting up the three hundred meters to his penthouse office like a cannonball. Twice on the way over he'd prodded Paris to tell him who he was coming to see, but she rebuffed him. Whoever it was, their presence was so clandestine that Paris not only felt pressured to let them wait alone in his office, but didn't trust even her own communication security protocols with their identity.

It couldn't be an extensive list. Tyson went through the possibilities. One of the other transtellar CEOs or chairmen? There were only a baker's dozen of them, and everyone kept tabs on who was moving around where, not that there weren't slipups in that coverage. Sokolov? She'd managed to drop in on him unannounced once already. A delegate from the UN? A Xre ambassador? Now *that* really would be crazy.

Tyson's train of thought pulled into the station as his feet lightened under the sudden deceleration of magnetic braking. The lift car slowed to a crawl as it emerged through the floor of his penthouse like a night-blooming jasmine.

The door opened onto a dimly lit scene. The ring window around the perimeter of the room was frosted for privacy, giving the familiar space an eerie, cave-like atmosphere that set Tyson's senses on edge.

"Paris, bring up the lights fifty percent."

"I'd rather not."

Tyson blinked. "You'd rather—" The rest of his incredulous words died in his throat as his eyes caught the silhouette moving against the shadows and diffuse light in his office. It was human, so no off-the-books meeting with an alien tonight. The figure was lithe, moving with fluidity and precision in equal measures. So graceful it verged on unnatural.

And it was most definitely female.

Sokolov was out. At forty-one, she was young for the head of a transtellar; fit, beautiful, and capable, but a ballerina she was not. An assassin? Someone had gotten close enough to Casey to kill her, after all. Tyson's heart sped up as his muscles tensed for action.

"Paris," he said slowly as he brought his arms up into a guard position, "who's prowling around in my office in the dark?"

"I should be offended." Paris's voice cooed from the speakers all around him even as the silhouette stalked toward the center of the room. It wasn't a tone she'd ever taken with him before. It sounded confident, sensual, and hungry. Tyson took a step back.

"After all the years we've worked together," Paris continued, "you mean to say you honestly don't . . ." The lights brightened at the center of his desk where the mystery figure stood erect, bathing her in white. The breath caught in Tyson's lungs as the spotlights cascaded down the most stunning woman he had ever seen in his long, lonely years.

". . . recognize me?"

It was the voice of his AI assistant, but Tyson's eyes had gotten stuck somewhere near the impossibly flat and toned musculature around her navel, so it took a moment to register that the sound hadn't come from the room's hidden speakers, but her mouth.

Tyson's eyes snapped up to his assistant's face, but not the face he recognized. The voice was the same, but instead of the virtual avatar he'd seen in holos and vids for years, her hair was platinum blond and razor straight, her green eyes set into high cheekbones that led down to a pointed chin and full, pouting lips.

His arms fell to his sides. The rest of her looked like a boy's dream, a teen's obsession, and an old man's nightmare. The sort of vision that could trigger a heart attack and an early trip to the morgue.

"Paris?" he asked dumbly.

She ran her hands down her sides and subtly shivered her hips, all of which were covered in a skin-tight white film from her neckline to her knees that looked more like packaging than clothing. "In the flesh, or a very close approximation of it."

"You look, uh, different."

"I took the liberty of making some changes to my appearance when I placed the order for this carapace." She began to advance out of the circle of light toward him, falling back into shadow as she moved. "I studied the likenesses of actresses, fashion models, and"—her lip curled up just a fraction—"adult performers and generated an aggregate that I thought would be pleasing as well as . . . stimulating."

"My . . . um, compliments to the chef," Tyson said, positively flustered. His cheeks felt warm. Was he blushing? His back bumped up against something unexpectedly. In the dark it took him a moment to realized he'd been pressed all the way back into the window at the edge of the room. Paris drew close, then ran the back of her hand from the shoulder pad of his jacket all the way down his sleeve and brushed against the skin on the back of his palm. He was ready for her touch to feel like cold latex, but her fingertips were warm, soft. Like living flesh.

Without seeking clearance from his consciousness, Tyson's penis prepared for Phase Two.

"I've always wanted to know what that felt like," Paris said with a dripping wet tone.

"Your skin has tactile feedback?" Tyson said as clinically as he could manage, but he already knew the answer. Even this close, he couldn't tell the difference between Paris's carapace and a real woman. She even *smelled* right, perfume with a subtle undercurrent of sweat.

"Oh yes, you sprung for all the bells and whistles. Everything works. I hope you don't mind, but I didn't come cheap."

"You never have," he said.

She reached up and smoothed out the lapel on his jacket. "I know why you're alone, Tyson."

"Sorry?" he bleated.

"A man of your refinement and sophistication demands perfection. What biological woman could measure up?"

Tyson cleared his throat. "That's not really—"

A perfectly manicured finger with French-tipped nail rested gently on his lips. "Shhh. No need to be modest with me. I know who you are, Tyson. I've watched your every waking moment for years. I know all your thoughts, patterns, whims, and yes, even desires." Paris pressed her firm bosom against him, just below his pecks, but he wiggled out of it to the side and put his hands up.

"This is inappropriate."

"Why?" she purred.

"We work together. You're my subordinate. There are rules, and for good reason."

Paris giggled. "Tyson, I'm flattered, really. But have you already forgotten what I am? You bought me and signed the user agreement. I'm a very expensive piece of office equipment. You can do anything you want to me, it's all covered under the warranty." She reached out and took his hands in hers, then placed them gently on the plastic film covering her hips. "I just need to be unwrapped."

For just a moment, Tyson's fingertips dug into the flesh covering her hips. He could feel the soft skin, a layer of toned muscle beneath it tense, and the bone of her pelvis below that. It was all artificial, of course, heat-activated poly-fibrous tensile coils for muscles, printed carbon laminate chassis in place of a skeleton. But it *felt* completely, convincingly real. The impulse to rip at the plastic film and tear it into confetti like wrapping paper on Christmas morning was very real, and very hard to resist.

It had been a long, long while since Tyson had made time for such distractions, and the sight of her, the perfect, flawless sight of her, roused something deep inside him he thought dead, but had merely been in a deep slumber.

Tyson tore away from her. "I'm sorry, I . . . have a thing."

"I know you don't," Paris said, annoyance seeping into her voice at the edges. "I maintain your schedule, remember?"

"It's not you, this is just, very fast. I need to think." Which was entirely true. Tyson tapped a floor panel and called up the express lift car. "I'll see you tomorrow. We'll talk about this more then."

"Do I look like I want to *talk*?" the spurned, inexplicably horny android said with a huff.

"Please don't be angry with me." Tyson practically fell into the lift as soon as the doors opened. He backpedaled until his shoulders hit the inside wall and the doors closed. Tyson's knees went weak and he slid down the wood paneling inside the lift car.

"Lobby."

What a perfectly bizarre day. From planning counterespionage to fighting off the advances of an assistant whose physical existence was measured in hours.

As the express lift started its near freefall to ground level, Tyson considered stopping at Klub Kryptonite for a carafe of his indulgent sake, but no. Paris would see him doing it on the building's security feeds, and it was Friday night, late. There would be throngs of Lazarus's young and beautiful drinking, flirting, dancing lasciviously, and looking to climb his ladder, in several meanings. The very last place on the planet he wanted to be just then. Tyson had perfectly serviceable liquor at home, and he needed a shower.

A cold shower.

In liquid helium.

EIGHTEEN

"Derstu! Your attention is necessitated in cavern seventy-three!"

Thuk clicked a blood-claw against the plate on the side of his thigh. "What's the problem, Kivits?"

"The humans are trying to poison us!"

Thuk glanced across the corridor to where Captain Kamala and her pair of warrior escorts stood. They'd managed to restore artificial gravity, if only at half strength. "Susan?" he called. They'd moved to first names.

"Yes, Thuk?" The tiny mouth implanted in his ear pore spit out the translation of her words.

"Are you trying to poison us, by any chance?"

"Think no." Even after seventy years of war, then stalemate, then pacing each other's fences, their capacity to communicate was still hindered by clunky translations and the misunderstandings that came along with the imprecision of language and cultural assumptions. But, it sounded like a denial to Thuk. He motioned for them to follow. "Come along. Let's see what my dulac is chittering about."

They bounded down the tunnel in long, awkward strides under the weak gravity, for which neither species was adapted or accustomed. It was almost worse than floating, but at least it provided an up and down.

"I apologize again for the state of our mound," Thuk said over his shoulder. "We weren't expecting visitors."

"[Laughing/humor]. Not was I," the humans' derstu said. No, not derstu, Thuk reminded himself. She was a captain. Humans did things differently, at least onboard their warships. Her power and authority among her harmony, ahem, *crew,* were nearly absolute, like the queens of old.

He was more than a little envious, if he were being honest. Imagine how much easier it would be if his harmony just did what he said instead of making everything into a negotiation. But then, they could hardly call themselves Xre.

"Surprise when [drone] start explode, also," Susan said, still smiling, or what Thuk had been taught was a smile at any rate. She was probing him again, trying to get an admission to slip. Well, two could sing that song.

"Probably just as surprised as I was when our reservoir exploded. What a cursed star we orbit."

The thin smile on the captain's meaty, horizontal lips curled up on one corner of her mouth. "[Touché.]" His translation matrix offered no suggestions, but Thuk was pretty sure he caught her meaning anyway.

"Seventy-three is just up ahead and to the left. The dulac sounded exasperated. Be patient with him should he become dramatic."

"I can [grapple/hold] him."

It was almost certainly untrue, not only because she only had four limbs to a Xre's six, but humans averaged a full head shorter. Still, they were a confident race almost to a fault that rarely passed on an opportunity for a good fight. Thuk wasn't sure fear even occurred within them.

The entrance to the cavern in question came into view around a bend in the corridor. Five humans, two warriors and three attendants, stood outside under three of the *Chusexx*'s own warriors and Kivit's unrelenting glare. As soon as he saw Thuk approach, he started gesticulating wildly, throwing an accusatory claw in the general direction of one of the human attendants holding a silver cylinder under one arm.

At the sight of the additional human warriors, everyone tensed as the balance of force in the immediate vicinity shifted ever so slightly to their visitors' favor. Thuk knew enough about the capabilities of the weapons Susan's warriors carried to know they weren't particularly heavily armed for human foot troops. There had been few surface engagements in the last war, but the Dark Ocean Chorus had managed to trade, steal, or smuggle enough copies over the years to get a good sense of what they could expect from a land engagement or boarding action. These were defensive weapons, enough punch to make an enemy think twice, but not enough to wreak the kind of havoc necessary to destroy a ship from within.

Susan and her people had placed a lot of trust in Thuk and his harmony simply by being here. He would reciprocate.

"Weapons at your sides. We're all being friendly here."

"Derstu," Kivits began. "These *abyss dwellers* tried to release a pathogen into our air tunnels!"

"Calm your claws, Kivits. We'll dig to the truth of this soon enough. Now, I asked everyone to relax. These people came to help. Let's not be ungrateful hosts."

The budding standoff eased; not much, but enough. Weapons remained in hands, but pointed at the floor and with fingers or claws eased away from their firing studs. Both sides kept close watch on one another, but their postures relaxed some. "Thank you. Now, Susan, can you explain what your attendants are doing, please?"

"One [second]." She held up a finger in a human gesture requesting a pause, then leaned in to speak with the attendant holding the cylinder in hushed tones. She touched the attendant's shoulder and stroked it, perhaps for comfort, then took the cylinder with an outstretched hand before turning back to where Thuk stood next to his perennially perturbed dulac.

"[O.K./Affirmative]." Susan held out the silver tube with the strange markings. "This colony. [Consume/devour] . . . um . . ." She searched for a word, probably struggling with the same translation issues on her end of the conversation. It was entirely too easy to watch someone struggle with a language and syntax that wasn't their own and assume they were stupid. Natural, even. But this one had already proven herself very clever indeed. Thuk was sure he sounded like a half-head to her ears as well.

"Rotting light!" Susan blurted out. "[Consume/devour] rotting light. Spread throughout. Soak up like [sponge]. Clean caverns and tunnels. Safe ground."

"What's a 'sponge'?" Kivits asked.

"I'm going with something absorbent. Like a guju towel." Susan pointed and nodded her head in affirmation. "There you go."

"But what does it mean?"

"I think she's saying they have a type of spore or fungal colony that eats rotting light."

Susan shook her head in the negative. "Not fungus. Think of plants." She held her gloved hand flat like a leaf and wiggled the fingers of her other hand down onto it like rain. No, like sunlight.

"Ah! No, it doesn't eat it, it photosynthesizes it. That's amazing."

"That's preposterous," Kivits said.

"Why would it have to be? The mechanisms would be similar, just either evolved or built to handle the higher energy levels. They probably developed it to clean up rotting light corruption on their own vessels."

"But how do we know it's not a biological weapon?"

Susan snorted through the paired holes in her olfactory organ.

"Need not come over to kill you. Press button, fire [laser], I take swim."

Kivits reared up onto his hind legs. "Is that a threat?!" Several of the warriors, of both species, took note of the sudden tension and braced for action, their weapons brought to a ready position.

"Sit down, Dulac. It's not a threat, it's a statement of fact. Why go to the trouble of coming here and exposing her people to danger just to kill us slowly when she could do it at light-speed with the twist of a toggle?"

Slowly, Kivits accepted the logic of what had been said and stood down. The sudden pressure front lifted from the rest of the cavern as calm returned. "I'm sorry for jumping to an assumption. It was ungenerous. But what happens when all the corruption is gone?"

"Actually I'm curious about that as well," Thuk said.

"It [Famine/starve]," Susan answered with a shrug of her shoulders. "Nothing to [consume/devour,] it dies. No fuss."

"A moment," Thuk said, then pulled Kivits aside for a short duet. "Well? What do you think?"

"I think we don't know what they're *really* doing here in the first place."

"They've already sped up our repairs by more than a day. If this plant colony can do what she claims, we don't have to cut out and replace the corrupted walls and tunnel segments. That saves us weeks of repairs and gets the affected caverns back in use. Besides, if we can isolate a sample, even after it's dead, our own gene growers back in the Symphony might be able to replicate it. Think of a colony of that stuff in stasis on every ship in the Dark Ocean Fleet. Think of the lives saved over time."

"So you're going to risk it, regardless of my advice."

"I'm singing with you, aren't I?"

Kivits fluttered his thorax with annoyance. "Fine, we'll risk it. But if this is a weapon—"

"Then you can lord it over me while we're both dying in the

infirmary. Fair enough?" The dulac looked away and said no more. Thuk returned to Susan. "We accept your gracious offer, Susan. Please, instruct your attendants to finish their work."

Two more days passed. All told, three shuttles full of human attendants rotated through the *Chusexx,* working alongside Thuk's own repair teams, sharing their expertise and bearing their load of the work. Susan had returned to the *Ansari* after the first day, but they'd kept in frequent contact to coordinate the effort. By the time source energy was restored, the humans and Xre had developed a grudging respect for one another. Even the spores of comradery had begun to sprout.

"The last shuttle of humans are departing the harbor now, Derstu."

"Dulac, I'd say our new friends have earned a parting salute, would you agree?"

"Do I have a choice?"

"We are always free to make the wrong choice, Kivits."

"Then yes, they certainly deserve a salute," he said with only the slightest hint of mockery in his tone.

Thuk beamed with satisfaction. "Hurg, open a link to the *Ansari* and her shuttle, please. We're singing the 'Forked Path Lament.'"

"Link established, Derstu."

"Hello, Derstu. How I [aid/assist] you?" came Susan's now-familiar voice through the mouths of the mind cavern.

Instead of answering directly, Thuk lifted a claw and signaled the assembled harmony to begin. The "Forked Path Lament" started slowly, building over its course. It was an old song, one of the oldest. It was the first song larvae learned formally to mark the day their clutches were assigned to mounds and distributed. It was used anytime friends, family, or harmonies had to part ways. It was beautiful, haunting, and mournful all at once, an expression of the sadness one felt at being separated from those they'd grown to care for. But, in the song's final measures, it turned and up-lifted, clawing for altitude, laying the foundations of hope for a joyous reunion further down the path.

Thuk had probably sang it a thousand times by now. It was a simple song without the multiple layers of harmonizing and fade outs of more complex compositions one learns along the way. But it was still one of his favorites.

Outside, the cloakskin on the *Chusexx*'s exterior, usually tasked with keeping the ship as invisible as possible, instead flashed and shimmered a dazzling splash of color in every shade from the infra-red through the ultraviolet, programed to match in frequency and time with the song as it was performed in real time. It was an honor usually only exchanged between ships of the Dark Ocean Fleet at the conclusion of a successful expedition as they parted ways for their home harbors. No human had ever lived to witness it in sev-enty years. It was unprecedented. But then, so were the events of the last few days. What more appropriate time would there be?

The final crescendo ended and silence descended on the mind cavern once more until it stretched out awkwardly.

"Hurg, is the link active?" Thuk whispered.

"Yes, Derstu."

"That was [implausible/incredible] Thuk," Susan said at last. "Please. Thank your harmony for us." She paused again. "I [as-pire/regret] we have no song reply. But, please accept."

Kivits sat up in his alcove. "Derstu, the *Ansari*'s defensive sys-tems have just gone active."

"What?"

"They're energizing short-range claws!"

The human ship's mass-driver claws were small, meant to swat down incoming javelins, but still powerful enough to pierce several layers of armor and breach the outer caverns.

"Are we inside their reach?" Thuk asked.

"Easily."

"Evacuate the outer caverns and seal—"

"Too late! They're firing!"

All eyes stuck themselves to the display ringing the mind cavern, tuned to the visible light spectrum. The *Ansari* had indeed begun firing. Seven small mass-driver nodes along the side of the human vessel facing the *Chusexx* fired in unison. Once. Twice. Three times.

Then, the nodes fell silent.

"Do we have tracking on those impactors?" Thuk shouted.

"We do, and they're . . . flying wide."

"Say again?"

"They're going to miss us, by a wide berth. Intentionally, I think. They couldn't have missed at this range. It was a display."

Thuk leaned back in his chair and let the unexpected tension drain from his limbs. "No. It was a salute. Their answer to our 'Forked Path Lament.' Seven shots. Three times. How interesting."

"Interesting?" Kivits raged. "No wonder we ended up at war with these people. Leave it to humans to use live-fire weapons in a friendly parting salute!"

Susan reclined in her command chair and absently rubbed the armrests.

"I think that went rather well. Wouldn't you agree, XO?"

"Swimmingly, mum. Just one quibble."

"Which is?"

"The twenty-one-gun salute is traditionally reserved for visiting heads of state or CEOs."

"True, but the Xre don't know that. Besides, I thought it added a certain gravity to the proceedings."

"The *Chusexx* is coming about," Mattu said from the Drone Integration Station. "Bearing shortest course for the treaty line. Fusion rockets warming up."

"Should I plot an escort course for once our shuttle is back aboard, mum?" Broadchurch asked.

"No, we've said our goodbyes. Let them head off into the sunset on their own. But Scopes, assign a platform to keep pace with them until they hit the line. Discreetly."

"Yes, mum."

"Everyone else, we have reports to write. I want everything ready to download to the skip drone by 1700 so we can get it underway."

"The analysts are going to have kittens when they see the raw data and vid captures from inside that thing," Miguel said proudly.

"Kittens? They're going to have heart attacks. Speaking of heart attacks, has anyone checked in on our CL since I sent him to bed without supper two days ago?"

"Still sulking in his quarters under guard, mum."

Susan got to her feet and straightened her tunic. "I'd better go let him out of time-out, then." She nodded to the marine by the hatch and made the short trip down the hall and one ladderwell to the executive quarters on J deck, not four cabins down from her own. A marine guard stood watch outside Nesbit's door, sidearm strapped to her side.

"You're dismissed, Private. Take the rest of your watch off."

"Thank you, mum." The guard saluted and made her way to the lift. Susan keyed the com next to the hatch.

"Javier, are you busy?"

There was a delay before the light blinked an open circuit. "I'm sorry, Captain, but between brunch and this afternoon's squash tournament, I just can't fit you in until tomorrow at the earliest."

"Just open the door, Nesbit." Susan leaned on one foot as muffled footsteps approached and the hatch spun open with a creak, then swung inward.

"Captain," Nesbit said icily.

"CL. May I come in?"

"It's your ship, isn't it? I think that's been made clear. Why bother with the little courtesies?"

"Because the little courtesies keep the crew from throttling each other in their sleep."

Nesbit scowled, but stepped aside and waved her in. His quarters were only slightly smaller than her own in terms of cubic meters, but the sheer volume of . . . stuff, made them seem far more claustrophobic. In place of the military-issue furniture, there was a leather chaise longue, a highbacked chair covered in crushed red velvet, and an oak table that nearly took up the entire kitchenette. A bookshelf covered the entire far wall, stacked two-deep with hardcovers, all of which could have fit onto a single tablet with ten thousand more titles to spare. A set of golf clubs sat in an expensive leather bag propped up against a corner, despite the nearest golf course being ten light-years away.

It was enough crap to fill a decent-sized apartment crammed into a space no larger than the average living room. It was like Nesbit had tried to pack his entire life and bring it along with him into his exile out here in the black.

Maybe it was exactly that simple. Needless to say, the total weight of all that clutter far exceeded the mass allotment crewmembers were permitted for personal items, to say nothing of the paper books and wood table, which were a flagrant violation of the prohibitions on flammable materials aboard a warship. Susan thought about calling the marine guard back to help her box it all up and shove it out an airlock, but she decided that wasn't a fight worth picking just now.

"You do know if a stray laser beam cuts through here, those books will probably be the kindling for your funeral pyre, right?"

"What a magnificent way to go," Nesbit answered defiantly.

"Right. Look, the crisis is over. The *Chusexx* is burning for the Red Line as we speak."

"Why aren't they bubbling out?"

"Can't yet. They traced the accident back to an antimatter containment breach in one of their transfer lines."

"Isn't an antimatter explosion usually a little more . . . energetic?"

"Usually, but this only involved a few stray milligrams caught up in a magnetic eddy current before the safeties slammed shut and stopped the flow. Xre attendants were still running integrity checks on the replacement coils when our last techs pulled out. They still have some work to do, so they're limited to fusion rockets until they can go to full power. No bubble," Susan replied. "So now that it's done, I came down to ask whether you're ready to resume your CL duties."

"I never stopped doing my duty as CL. I was *barred* from doing it."

"Yes, yes. I'm the big meanie who didn't let you incite a mutiny in her own CIC in front of her senior staff at a critical moment. Get over it."

"You went against standing orders."

"Which *I* interpreted as conflicting with another set of standing orders. I made a call to resolve that conflict. Captain's prerogative. I'm not going to litigate this with you, Javier. It's done. Are you ready to move on or not? If you are, you can get back to work. If you can't, you can sit out the rest of this tour staring at these four walls. Your call."

"I used my time in here to prepare a report for my superiors. I assume I won't be permitted to submit it?"

"Not at all. We're getting all our ducks in a row to send a burst with all our findings, recordings, and sensor data to the skip drone in Grendel orbit by 1700. Your report will be included in that dispatch, unaltered. I won't even read it."

"You seem awfully damned confident you're coming out of this smelling like fresh jasmine."

"You haven't seen the intel haul we pulled out of that ship. It's the biggest SigInt and HumInt coup since we grabbed that Xre frigate intact during the first war. The spooks will be pouring over it for months, maybe years."

"As will theirs, Susan. Or did you really think the data collection only went one way?" Nesbit ran a hand through his thinning hair. Susan hadn't thought about it until that moment, but now that she'd noticed, she was surprised he hadn't gone through gene therapy to correct his male pattern baldness. Looking at the extravagant trappings around his room, it obviously wasn't a question of money.

"They got a look at our peashooters and a stealth shuttle. We walked around inside the guts of a cruiser class we didn't even know existed until a few weeks ago. I'd call that a better than fair exchange rate. Not to mention we avoided triggering a shooting war. That has to count for something."

"Thought you military types were always spoiling for a good fight."

"Yes. A *good* fight. A necessary fight. This . . . didn't feel like that. I spent a lot of time with their captain, or derstu, I don't really understand what his role is exactly, but he seemed just as relieved not to be throwing missiles as I was."

"Because he knew we had him dead to rights. He was defenseless. Do you really think he would have shown us mercy if we'd found ourselves drifting past the treaty line in one of their systems? Be honest."

Susan found herself leaning against the oak table, running her hands along the grain of the wood. Real wood, probably harvested from Earth herself who knew how long ago. The varnish was gently worn along the lip, but otherwise unblemished. It wasn't a table for eating off of, not without a tablecloth, which she was sure must be hiding in one of Nesbit's closets. Susan had been twenty-two years old when she'd seen her first oak tree, and that was inside an atrium on Bezos Station as she reported for CCDF Indoc. But here one was, light-years away from where it had any business being and posing a subtle but real danger to everyone who came near it.

Susan found herself feeling an unexpected kinship with the table.

"I honestly don't know what Thuk would've done if our roles

had been reversed. But, just as honestly, I'm sure he'll be more inclined to return the favor in the future. They're a collective, a 'harmony,' they call it. Their trust bonds are the connective tissue of their society, and we just grew some with the Xre on that ship. If that was wrong of me, I'll accept that judgment when the time comes."

Nesbit lingered next to the bookshelf, inspecting the volumes, and ran a finger down the spine of one out-of-place paperback in particular: *Red November*. Susan didn't recognize it, but made a note in her AR interface to have a look just the same.

"We're dancing on the edge of a knife out here, you know," he said at last. "And the immediate tactical situation, or even strategic environment, isn't my purview. I know that's what you need to see for the safety of your ship and crew, but my job has a broader mandate. I'm this ship's liaison for thirteen transtellars and all their millions of employees, shareholders, and dependents. I take that responsibility seriously, despite what you may think."

"I believe you. We serve the same people."

"I volunteered for this billet. Did you know that?" Nesbit asked, almost pleadingly, as if he clamored for something. Legitimacy, maybe. Recognition that he belonged here as much as anyone. It wasn't something any square-dog-sucking bubble-popper was in a hurry to give a suit, but . . .

"I didn't know that," Susan said softly. "I guess I assumed CLs were assigned."

"You'd think, wouldn't you? No, this isn't a disciplinary assignment. It's a very prestigious posting. Hard to qualify for, even harder to actually get selected. But I did, because I wanted to serve somewhere other than a cubicle farm, just as you did. I worked for this."

Susan absorbed it all in stride. "And when your tour is up? Will you go to another ship?"

"It's a two-year commitment. That's the minimum time it takes to justify the costs of training us for the job, which is six intensive months by itself."

She managed not to scoff at the idea of a CL's "intensive" training regimen. Lessons included: how to use up all the ship's hot water in too-long showers, how to passive-aggressively undermine the legitimate CO, how to get enlisted ranks to hate you in thirty seconds or less. Honestly, even after a career of more than two decades, she'd never given much thought to CLs until she had one. They were always just . . . there. The good ones were mostly unobtrusive and invisible to the rest of the crew, while the bad ones were celebrated only for leaving.

"And you jump around from command to command during that term, I assume?"

"We do. Long-term assignments are discouraged. It's best if we're not around any one crew long enough to develop the sort of relationships that can impact our objectivity. Honestly, this is my third assignment, and other than passing each other in a corridor, it's the first time I've been alone with any of the three COs I've advised."

"Well, if it's any consolation, I think the rest of this tour will prove pretty boring. With their oiler destroyed, *Chusexx* is down to whatever AM they've got in their tanks. Couple that with all the damage they took and their spares lockers have to be looking a bit thin as well. Thuk seems like a reasonable sort. Whatever his orders were before the accident, I doubt he's real excited about the prospect of another prolonged cat-and-mouse game without returning to base for resupply and refit. I sure as hell wouldn't be."

"Let's hope you're right. We've had enough nasty surprises on this tour already. If I ever see a Xre warship again, it'll be too soon."

Susan smiled. "We finally agree on something."

NINETEEN

The suddenness of the VR alarm that roused Tyson from his dream state startled him so badly he nearly fell out of bed. Only an outstretched arm finding the tile mosaic of his bedroom floor prevented him from spilling onto it in a tangle of blankets and limbs.

"Jesus, what the fuck was that?"

"It was an alarm, genius," Paris said inside his head, still sounding salty.

"Yes, I understand that, but why did it go off?"

"Because it's nine in the morning and you slept through the more polite ones."

"Nine *a.m.*?" Tyson jumped to his feet and looked to the analog clock mounted on the far wall of his sleeping quarter, scarcely willing to believe what she was saying. He'd woken up at five o'clock in the morning like a metronome for the last thirty years. It took him a couple tries to resolve the image of the antique clock, and another couple to remember what the damned hashmarks meant, likely owing at least in part to the empty bottle of single-malt scotch that had rolled into the corner of his bedchambers.

But sure enough, the clock on the wall confirmed Paris's absurd claim.

"I've already rescheduled or canceled your morning meetings. You have 'food poisoning.' You have three new interview requests, an emergency budget meeting, and the quarterly shareholder address this evening. I assume you won't make me cancel that?"

"No! No, just, let me get myself together."

"Would you like breakfast delivered to your office?"

"Yes, absolutely. I'll be in the shower."

"Whatever." The connection went dead, leaving Tyson to ponder the sequence of events and decisions that had brought him to the moment where he was copping attitude from his artificially intelligent, virtual assistant for refusing to have sex with her five minutes after getting her new body.

Rockefeller never dealt with this shit.

Tyson grabbed a prebrewed pot of black tea off the wall mount in his kitchen and poured a generous cup, then sucked down the nearly scalding bitter liquid in three big gulps. He was not hungover per se, as the immune-boosting nanites in his bloodstream were also ruthlessly efficient at scrubbing the body of the methyl alcohol and other volatile compounds that caused that unenviable set of symptoms. But, despite centuries of medical advancement, no one had yet cracked the cure for sleep deficiency.

Not that it hadn't been tried. A few decades ago, in an attempt to boost fleet efficiency, someone had tried a gene-hack that would let naval personnel "sleep" the way dolphins did, shutting down one hemisphere of their brains at a time, allowing them to remain conscious for many days at a stretch. The end results worked, but they spent sixteen hours a day only half awake with reduced IQs and complex problem-solving. Apparently, operating warships was more mentally taxing than chasing fish, and crew efficiency plummeted in the test vessel. Funding for the experiment was thankfully pulled not long after.

Tyson set down the cup and staggered over to the shower

like the living dead. There was nothing to strip out of, as he slept naked. He set the shower to forty-five degrees and picked an appropriately high-energy classical music selection to help boost his own morale. "Immigrant Song" by Led Zeppelin always managed to jolt him awake, and it was brief enough to get him in and out of the shower in an appropriately short amount of time.

The water hit him from a dozen different angles as the shower's lighting system pulsed in time to the music, rising with the vocals, or what passed for them. It was a simply scandalous amount of water just for a personal shower, but the graywater reclamation system ran at nearly ninety-nine percent efficiency, so Tyson felt no shame as the burning liquid cascaded down his body, loosening knotted muscles and soothing aching joints before it spiraled down the drain.

The song over, he toweled off and brushed his teeth, his hair, and made a quick pass at his stubble with an arc razor. His hair wasn't overly thick, but it did seem to grow back with speed and enthusiasm, especially when he was dehydrated. He made a suit selection from the screen next to the auto-closet. A moment later, a slim vertical panel slid open with a cleaned, freshly pressed suit hanging from a cross spar, steam still wafting off the fabric of its sleeves.

He took it off the rack, suddenly aware of his nudity and the eyes prying from the ceiling. "Paris, are you watching me dress?"

"I've watched you dress and undress every day for seven years, Tyson. Is today different?"

Tyson strategically placed the suit jacket over his unmentionables. "Honestly, a little, yes. Could you, I don't know, turn around for a moment?"

He could've sworn he heard a sigh come through the speakers. "Cameras off. Two minutes should be enough to get your pants on, yes?"

"More than adequate." Tyson briefly considered saying something to try and smooth out his scorned AI's bruised feelings, realized how crazy that sounded, and went to work getting dressed as quickly as he could.

Minutes later, he stepped into a waiting travel pod in the basement garage of his residential building. "Immortal Tower," he told the autopilot. The door clicked shut and pulled smoothly out of the garage with an electric hum. It was a six-minute ride from his apartment to the tower. Six minutes to organize his thoughts and set priorities for the day. Tyson felt rushed. He wasn't used to feeling rushed.

"Paris, inform Dr. Spaulding she'll be presenting at the shareholder address tonight on our progress curing the Teegarden pandemic. Keep it short, five minutes, and no Ph.D.-speak. Has the tailor been to see her yet?"

"For measurements and an initial fitting, yes, but he hasn't delivered on the order yet."

"Put a rush on it to have an outfit ready and sent to her before the presentation tonight. Pay whatever ridiculous surcharge he throws out, minus twenty percent to keep him honest."

"Understood. Sir, I'm getting a Priority request from the NeoSun embassy. They request your personal attendance, as soon as is convenient."

Tyson cringed. "As soon as is convenient" was diplospeak for "Right fucking now." His partners in Grendel were quite upset about something.

"And the topic for this meeting?"

"Sensitive."

"Shit."

"Succinctly put. Shall I redirect your pod?"

Tyson wanted his pod redirected, all right. Straight back to his residence where he could resume depleting his stock of liquor. But there was nothing for it.

"Tell the NeoSun embassy that I'll be there momentarily."

The pod braked, hard, before reversing back to the last intersection it had passed, and took a new route toward Shensing

Boulevard and Embassy Row. A dozen towers, each a unique architectural vision, lined the two sides of the boulevard, six abreast. NeoSun's building, an imposing five-sided obsidian monolith clad in a lattice of burnished titanium pentagrams raced up to seven floors *above* the artificial ceiling long-dictated by Ageless tradition in Methuselah. As part of the Grendel endeavor, Tyson's sometimes rivals, sometimes partners had renegotiated their rental agreement on those seven floors to be paid annually with tax-deductible donations to the MPD's retirement program and the hospital system's operating fund.

It was an agreeable arrangement, saving NeoSun many hundreds of thousands in taxes each year, and taking those expenses off Ageless's ledger. It cost Tyson nothing on balance, and had sweetened the pot for his new partners. Still, everything had a cost. Now the other eleven corps on the campus were pressuring him for a similar arrangement. Tyson pushed the indignant/whining communiques and official correspondence to the back of his mind. If they wanted the bennys, they could jolly-well belly up to the bar and sign on to their own partnership projects.

The pod dipped below street level and rolled to a stop in front of the building's private reception area. Here, VIPs could come and go without exposing themselves to the prying eyes of the public or press. Tyson stepped out onto the walkway and straightened a pantleg before continuing to the door. Two security guards in military-crisp business suits, one male, one female, stood to either side of the entry to the tower's lobby.

"Good morning, Mr. Abington," the woman said. She was tall and fit, with taunt muscles filling out her jacket at the arms and shoulders. Ex-marine, almost certainly. A small, but noticeable bulge beneath her left breast betrayed the presence of a hand weapon of some sort in a holster.

"Welcome to NeoSun. Please hold out your arms."

"Seriously?" Tyson said.

"Bomb sweep," the man said, producing a chem sniffer wand.

242 • PATRICK S. TOMLINSON

"We've had a few bomb threats called in recently," the woman said apologetically.

Tyson smirked and held his arms out like a scarecrow. "If I wanted to destroy your building, I'd sign an order of demolition, not blow myself up."

"Rules are rules."

The wand beeped and turned green.

"He's clean."

"Obviously." Tyson's arms dropped to his sides.

"Thank you for your cooperation, Mr. Abington, and I apologize for its necessity."

"If you're getting bomb threats, you should really be reporting them to the MPD so they can be traced back."

The woman smiled cordially. "NeoSun InfoSec policy prohibits sharing the details of internal security matters."

"It's not 'internal' if someone collapses your tower onto the NorKel embassy across the street."

"I'll forward your request to my supervisors."

"You do that. Now, is someone going to tell me why I'm here, or am I supposed to guess?"

"Of course not, sir. If you'll follow me." She turned on a heel and headed through the blast-resistant, overlapping sliding glass doors that protected the opulent lobby. The male guard fell into step behind the two of them. So, not doormen, but his escorts. That was fine with Tyson. Anything to speed this up.

In contrast to the clean, modern contours and metallic decor of Ageless's receiving atrium, the more ostentatious and colorful tastes of NeoSun's founders were still present more than a century after their deaths. Intricate tile mosaics covered the floor and crept halfway up the walls. Large, ornate columns, purely decorative, broke up the open space like walking through an old-growth forest. Holographic AI receptionists and assistants wandered the floor freely, projected by optical arrays hidden in the columns and ceiling, answering questions for tourists and new-hires. And everywhere, there was gold. Most of it was thin inlays and gold-leaf veneer, but not the logo. The half-sun at the top of the main entry wall, and all seven of the rays of light streaming down from it were solid gold, three centimeters thick. All told, it was more than six hundred kilograms of twenty-four-karat gold. Tyson knew its purity and mass, because his grandfather had personally signed off on an exemption for the Lazarus Charter code against hoarding precious metals to allow that much gold to be granted an import permit in the first place.

There was enough gold in that gaudy logo to destabilize the local economy if it was melted down and distributed. Which also explained the security measures protecting it. NeoSun didn't bother hiding the battle androids standing at either side of their lobby. Indeed, they were a popular selfie backdrop. Tyson had signed *that* arms import waiver.

They reached the lifts. Like most of the towers on Embassy Row, the lower third of the NeoSun building actually contained shops and residential space, the rents on which were used to offset the impressive costs of running an off-world diplomatic operation that had fewer opportunities to act as a profit center than a traditional building. Still, the communications bottleneck inherent to interstellar travel meant that each embassy operated as a semiautonomous local headquarters for each transtellar corp, more akin to a wholly owned subsidiary than a satellite office. Local business decisions often couldn't wait for the two-week to three-month communications loop to complete itself, so local administrators were given significant leeway to make the sorts of decisions usually reserved for C-level execs.

It was about the time they passed the hundredth floor that Tyson started to notice something was different. He'd been to many meetings and confabs here, but they'd all been hosted in the grand ballrooms and executive offices around the seventieth floor.

"Where are you taking me?"

"We were told to bring you directly to the Svyatilishche. That's the extent of my knowledge regarding your visit, Mr. Abington."

Tyson mentally stumbled over the unfamiliar word.

"Russian for 'Sanctum,'" Paris said unbidden inside his head. He'd forgotten she was there.

"What the hell does that mean?" he sent back.

"I don't know. I'm not Sokolov's AI."

"Right." Tyson stewed in his own thoughts for a moment. If anywhere in his tower could be called a sanctum, it was his penthouse office. Locked away from curious onlookers first through its position near the very top of the tower, then through multiple layers of security and anti-eavesdropping equipment. It was even more private than his residence in more ways than one.

So naturally NeoSun had a room just like it. And he was being taken there. Where no one could see him. Where no one could hear him. . . .

Suddenly, the presence of two armed guards sharing his elevator car felt a lot less routine and a whole lot more ominous.

Tyson shook off the thought. Paris knew where he was. If he fell out of contact for any length of time, she would summon the MPD, even raise the Planetary Defense Reserves if necessary. Which might be necessary to get past the pair of decommissioned military meat-tenderizers in the lobby.

No, he shook off the thought. These people were his business partners, and they were still on his planet, in *his* city. Sovereign embassy real estate be damned, there were some things one just didn't do among the ruling class. It wasn't proper. He was being paranoid. It had been a strange night capped off with a rough morning and he was just a smidgen off his game. That was the extent of it.

The lift reached the hundred and forty-third floor, damn close to the top of the occupied portion of the tower. Another handful of floors and they'd be in machine rooms and the massive, multi-ton harmonic dampener chamber. The doors slid open.

This high up, there wasn't much square meterage on each floor, so it was a short walk to the Sanctum. As anticipated, the door was lousy with security precautions, from biometric scanners, to video surveillance, to automated defenses, to the size and thickness of the door itself. The male guard entered a dizzyingly long password, thumbed his print, and had his facial topography scanned.

"Tyson," Paris said into his head. "That room is radio-shielded. There's a wireless deadzone right around it. I can't follow you in there."

"I understand."

"Be careful."

"There's nothing to worry about," he said to himself as much as to her. "Still, have the cavalry ready if I'm not back in contact in twenty minutes."

"A lot can happen in twenty minutes."

The massive door swung open, perfectly balanced on hinges as thick as his wrist.

"Ms. Sokolov wants to speak with you," the woman guard said. "Privately."

Tyson's interest perked. "She's inside?"

"Ms. Sokolov regrets that she was unable to make the trip, but she has prepared a message."

"A vid? Are you serious? You could have just sent it over to my assistant."

"No, we couldn't. It's for your eyes only." She held out a hand, inviting him inside. "Please, enter."

"You're not coming?"

"We're not authorized to see the message. This was part of the instructions that accompanied the packet."

"So you're just going to lock a rival CEO inside your company's most secure facility on the entire planet, alone?"

"Believe me, I'm not thrilled about it," the man said.

"Please excuse my partner, Mr. Abington. We'll be waiting here to escort you back to your pod as soon as you're finished."

"All right. Don't forget I'm in there and wander off for a vape break while the door's locked."

"We won't." The heavy door swung shut and *clunked* shut with finality. All external noise disappeared, leaving Tyson with only the sound of his breathing. A loss-of-signal error in the corner of his augmented reality field announced that he'd lost connection to Paris, just as she'd predicted.

It was funny. Less than an hour ago, he'd wanted her gone, or at least in another room for the first time in seven years. Now, with the sound of his own blood pounding in his ears, he'd do anything to bring her back.

In contrast to the decorations in the rest of the tower, the spherical chamber was utterly stark. Featureless and flat white, the only accoutrement was a plain, contoured white chair at the center of the room. Not seeing any interface or control panels and unsure of what else to do, Tyson walked around it once, then sat down.

The room flipped in an instant from flat white to an infinite black. Tyson's eyes tried to adjust, but there was nothing to focus on. His head shook against the disorientation and he closed his eyes. The view was still just as black, but somehow more manageable.

"Hello, Tyson," a familiar accent said. He pried his eyes open and stared into the face of Valeria Sokolov. It was a hologram, of course, but in the absolute black of the rest of the room, it was absolutely convincing. She stood against the velvet dark, dressed in a regal evening gown that suggested she was about to attend a party of some prominence.

"Hello," he said out of social habit.

"I'm sure my representatives have already conveyed my apologies for being unable to leave New Vladivostok for this conversation, but I wanted you to hear this from me personally, if indirectly. The location I've picked for you to receive this message should further reinforce just how . . . confidential . . . I expect it to be. We're of a kind, and I want to show you the respect and trust your position deserves."

"Yes, yes," Tyson said to the digital ghost of nine-days-ago Sokolov. "Stop fluffing me and get on with it."

"So, it is with a heavy heart and great regret that I must tell you that the NeoSun board will be exercising the Emergency Termination Clause of our partnership in Grendel."

"What?!" Tyson blurted out, genuinely caught off guard.

"I realize you're presenting your shareholder address this evening, and I hate to dump this on you ahead of it, but there's just not time. The board hasn't voted to make it official yet, but I'm pushing for this decision myself, so whatever angles you're starting to formulate, don't waste your time. You can challenge me through the arbitration process, of course, but I've already sent word to our associates in the system to pull up stakes. Even if you win the arbitration, our end of the operation will have been cold for months."

Tyson forgot he was looking at a hologram and almost started to argue, but caught himself. This was asinine. They'd cracked the Teegarden plague, and after tonight's presentation, investors would swoop in to buy up Ageless shares for cheap at the start of their recovery.

Or, they would have.

"Or," Sokolov went on, "we can behave like adults and handle this breakup quietly and avoid a lot of the bad press. If you're honest with yourself, Ageless is far more exposed on that front than NeoSun is. Consider it a peace offering. Now, the really scary shit."

"That *wasn't* the scary shit?" Tyson asked the empty room.

"The reason I'm pulling out of Grendel is that something's gone terribly wrong out there. We're closer than you are, and I sent this message on my fastest skip drone, so you won't be getting any official notification of this news until the standard com drones catch up in twelve hours or so. So don't do or say anything that would give away that you know, but Grendel is going under official quarantine. I don't know the full details, but there was a confrontation between the CCDF cruiser and the Xre raider that's been poking around the edge of the system for months. There were explosions out near the treaty line they could see clear back in the planet's orbit. The Admiralty House is mobilizing a task group to send in to recon the area. No civilian traffic in or out until they've finished, and a coms blackout will go into effect as soon as their skip drone arrives. I can only assume this means our cruiser on station was lost."

Tyson's throat went dry. Grendel had just turned into a flashpoint of a war no one had seen coming. This was *definitely* scarier shit.

"I'm afraid by the time you're watching this, there will be no way for you to get an evacuation order to your people ahead of the blackout. The pieces are already in motion and I can't stop them. However, in my communiqué, which will beat the blackout by a few hours, I took the liberty of suggesting to Governor Honshu that you wouldn't be too terribly upset, given the circumstances, if she decided to exercise a little initiative and call her own evacuation order. I know that's stepping on your toes a bit, but there was no way to include you in the decision loop considering the time lag. I hope you'll forgive my presumptiveness."

Tyson fell back in the chair, only then realizing how far forward in the seat he'd been leaning. There was nothing to forgive Sokolov for. She'd probably just saved hundreds of lives, provided that stubborn imbecile Honshu took her advice. She was a cousin to Tyson's COO Nakamura, and he'd never been particularly fond of her. When the chance to dump her off on Ageless's furthest-flung frontier holding presented itself, Tyson had been only too happy to sign off on the assignment.

Now he hoped he hadn't inadvertently stuck an incompetent at the focal point of an unfolding interstellar war. Nepotism had the most inventive ways of coming back to bite you.

"That's all I know for now. This is a real clusterfuck, Tyson. I don't know where it goes from here, but I'm concerned it's going to make our recent troubles seem pretty goddamned trivial. And word to the wise, not everyone on your board is looking out for your best interests. Personal or otherwise. That's all I can say for certain for now. Keep your eyes open and your head on a swivel. Maybe we can have another go at it in a few years when the dust settles. Good luck. And remember, you don't know anything until the official drone makes orbit. *Dasvidaniya*." With that, Sokolov's avatar faded from view and plunged the chamber back into darkness.

It matched Tyson's mood perfectly.

TWENTY

Thuk masticated absently on the flavorless protein-stick hanging from his mandibles. One of the larger farm compartments in the ship's thorax had been corrupted with rotting light before they'd been able to head it off. They'd lost two entire gim crops, and although the humans' rotting-light-eating bacteria had worked a minor miracle cleaning up the mess, it would still take a moon to grow a new crop from scratch to harvest.

They still had fresh greens and flowers, but no living source of protein. So, the harmony was stuck with survival rations for the time being. At least these new sticks had the advantage of being merely tasteless, as opposed to actively gut-churning as previous incarnations had been.

It was, by any reasonable measure, the least of their problems. But food meant morale onboard a ship, and one could damn near plot a graph of harmony satisfaction to the quality of available food. When one slipped, the other was guaranteed to follow. The longer the harmony went without something wriggling to crush between their mouthparts, the darker their mood would become.

Thuk held up the half-eaten, unappetizing twig and tossed it into a composter, careful to ensure no one saw him do it. If it wasn't good enough for their derstu, it soon wouldn't be good enough for any of them, not a situation he needed to encourage just then. He continued down the central spinal tunnel toward the *Chusexx*'s guts where he was supposed to meet a propulsion attendant who had made an impassioned plea to have the derstu come quietly and alone at once over a private line. Thuk had no idea what he was walking into, but at this point, he just went with the flow and hoped for the best.

"Derstu," the earnest attendant said as he arrived at the cavern he'd been summoned to, "thank you for coming. You didn't have to."

Thuk sized up the attendant. A strong-back warrior caste like Kivits, missing a leg that had yet to grow back. Their shoulder stripes marked them as a group head, but they weren't among the top-level leadership. Whatever they had to say, they were bypassing two levels of seniority to say it.

"A harmony loses its tune if every voice isn't heard."

"That is very wise, Derstu."

"And you are?"

"Lynz, Derstu."

"Lynz. What happened to your leg?" Thuk pointed at the stump and the artificial sap protective layer the healers had slapped over the top of it to keep infection at bay.

"Lost to an emergency hatch when the order came down to seal off the rotting-light corruption after the explosion."

An order Thuk had given. "I'm sorry."

"Don't be. If it hadn't closed when it did, I'd be dead already, along with everyone in my cavern. It's my own fault for not being quick enough. Those things shut faster than I realized. The healers say it should grow back out in three or four molts anyway."

Thuk gestured approval with his midhands. "I'm impressed you returned to work already."

"It's my work that I wanted to speak to you about, Derstu. Please, come this way." Lynz took off down a side tunnel at an impressive gait for someone dealing with a missing leg. Thuk followed. "As you know, we've been running integrity tests on the annihilation fuel spools we had to replace after the accident."

"How is that proceeding?"

"On schedule, just. But, I came across something in my inspection. Something that should not be."

Thuk felt the air chill. "We seem to be getting awfully close to the outer skin."

"Indeed. We're going outside."

"We are?"

"We are."

"Between the shells, or . . ."

Lynz wiggled his shoulders in the negative. "All the way outside."

"How exciting . . ." All Xre ships, and likely human ships as well, were wrapped in double shells, an inner shell that acted as a pressure vessel for all the habitable caverns, and an outer shell that acted as a backup and mounted the heavy armor and the rotting-light sponges. A null space between them provided cold storage and access to much of the machinery for maintenance attendants. These null spaces were usually left unpressurized, but at least they weren't exposed to the high-energy shooting gallery that was the vacuum environment inside a solar system.

Thuk was not particularly fond of sticking his thorax in the universe's face and daring it to run him through with a micrometeorite. Lynz reached into a storage box and came out with a pair of masks and lung packs.

"We're not doing full hardsuits?" Thuk asked.

"No need, we won't be outside for very long, and it's not like they slow the pebbles down enough out here to matter anyway."

Thuk clicked his mandibles in agitation, but did not protest as Lynz helped position his mask and checked the seals. Amber lights inside his face shield display assured him everything was working properly. He reciprocated for Lynz, then double-checked the mouths and ears inside their kits to make sure they had solid communication. Belt tethers and sticky sandals followed, and moments later they were inside the lockout getting ready to go "all the way outside."

Xre bodies had evolved tough, but not even the original mound-builders had any idea just *how* tough they were. The overlapping layers of their shells made them impervious to vacuum. As the air was pumped out of the lockout, the only difference Thuk could feel was a slight bulging.

With the air reprocessing capacity of their mask and lung packs rated at the better part of a day, the only limiting factor for their time outside was the cold. But the cold of outer space was a funny, counterintuitive thing. Vacuum was by itself an incredible insulator. Without an atmosphere to facilitate either conductive or convective heat transfer, all that remained was radiative. An object in vacuum took a surprisingly long time to cool to the ambient temperature, a length of time that extended further in the case of Xre, which generated some of their own internal heat.

It was for this reason when the door fell away and Thuk followed Lynz out into the black, he felt . . . nothing. Nothing at all. Not cold, not the subtle, easily forgotten swirl of air currents around sensory cilia imbedded in his plates. Nothing except a slight ache in the softer tissues of his joints. The river of the galaxy cut a wispy cloud across the perfect black of the sky. The system's star was on the other side of the ship, but even if it had been directly overhead, it was far enough away that it would be just the brightest of the pinpricks of light cast against the black.

It wasn't the first time he'd been naked outside a ship, but it was still a supremely unnerving experience.

"Okay, Lynz, show me why you dragged me out here, and be quick about it."

"It's a short walk this way." They clipped the ends of their tethers into runner tracks built into the skin of the *Chusexx*'s outer shell, a backup in case their sticky sandals failed for whatever

254 • PATRICK S. TOMLINSON

reason. Just behind them and overhead was the backmost of the four rings that spun the ship's seedpods, and would again soon with any luck. They walked further back toward the ship's annihilation fuel containers and its mighty fusion motors.

Under full power, the rotting light coming from the motors and source energy chambers would be lethal in the span of a breath on this side of the conical shield. But the chambers and motors were running at idle as they coasted toward the treaty line, awaiting completion of their repairs, signs of which were everywhere.

Soon, they were underneath the giant armored shell that protected the annihilation fuel containers from enemy fire and space rocks alike. Seven giant, perfectly spherical vessels suspended within the structure by shock-absorbing legs held back unfathomable amounts of potential energy. Several grains' worth of it getting out of containment before its time had been enough to almost destroy the ship outright.

It was a dangerous job they did for the Grand Symphony, out here in the dark ocean.

"It's just ahead," Lynz said through the small mouth imbedded in Thuk's mask.

Thuk looked ahead to where the attendant pointed. A work light bathed the area in a harsh white glow that contrasted almost painfully against the surrounding dark. Thuk recognized the components.

"That's one of the transfer coils," Thuk observed.

"Yes, Derstu. I was assigned to replace it after the acci . . . incident." Thuk noticed the change in words, but said nothing.

"As soon as we cut thrust, I was sent back out here to run integrity tests on the new installation. But that's not what I wanted to show you. I've found something. On one of the other coils."

They passed the work light, and continued back closer to the edge of the shield and the cluster of fusion motors. Lynz stopped and flipped on a small illuminator on his mask.

"Here." He pointed at an exposed panel and the tree-trunk-thick transfer coil below. Thuk got himself into a better position and peered into the space.

"What do you see?" Lynz asked, annoying Thuk to no small degree. He was not a trained maintenance attendant, but he looked anyway. As it happened, he didn't need training. Thuk leaned into the space to run a claw down the perfectly straight channel that sliced through the metal and ceramic of the coil.

"It's been cut."

"Yes, indeed."

"This isn't naturally occurring? A meteor or other debris?"

"Impossible, look closer at the grooves. They're too regular. Those are tool marks from a rotary saw. And here." Lynz pointed a claw at four pockmarks on opposing sides of the coil casing, easily missed until they were pointed out. "Those are depressions left by attachment claws like what we use for mobile repair rigs."

"Was someone working on this coil during the repairs? Maybe started work on it accidentally thinking it was one of the ones that needed replacement?"

Lynz wiggled his shoulders. "Not possible. I already checked the work logs. No one came this far back."

Thuk did not like where this was leading. "Walk me down this path, Lynz. What are you thinking?"

"It's speculation."

"So, speculate."

Lynz paused, hesitant to continue, or maybe just gathering his thoughts. "I think something was placed here, a device of some kind, either remotely operated, or set to an internal timeflow meter. I think it was programmed to cut this coil, then either fall away, or it was knocked loose by the explosion in the other coil."

"Then why didn't this coil explode also?"

"It nearly did. Another leaf deeper and it would have. If I hadn't found it, the coil was sure to fail after a few days, at most."

A chill went through Thuk's shell that had nothing to do with the surrounding temperature. They'd almost died all over again.

"So this couldn't have been done in harbor, then."

"No, it would have failed long ago. This happened within the last few days, almost certainly at the same time as the explosion."

Thuk almost asked why someone couldn't have come out here and cut it themselves, why it had to have been a remote device, but caught himself. Under full power, anyone on the wrong side of the rotting light shield would be cooked inside their own shell long before they got here.

"Why two?" Thuk asked instead.

Lynz shrugged. "Backup? Or maybe they were intended to go off together, but fell just enough out of harmony that one coil exploded before the other and jarred this device loose before it could finish the job."

"And if they'd both gone off at once?" Thuk asked, pretty sure he knew the answer.

"Cascading reaction, every other coil fails in series as the fail-safe cutoffs are overloaded, failures reach the chambers. One goes up and we . . ."

"Are all dust," Thuk finished for him. "Could the humans have done it?"

"When were they close enough? Before they came over to help with the restoration, that is. Besides, that would require an incredibly in-depth knowledge of our systems."

"Of course not." Now, he was furious. They hadn't *almost* died, they'd been *meant* to die, and only the thinnest reed of happenstance had prevented and allowed him to discover the truth. His worst, most outrageous suspicions about their assignment here and the reasons for their nonsensical songs from the Chorus were not the product of paranoia after all. Or rather, they were the result of entirely justifiable paranoia.

"This is why you bypassed the rest of your group to come to me. You suspect one of them conspired. Who?"

"I suspect no one, Derstu," Lynz said quickly. "That would

be wholly inappropriate and unjust. But, neither can I eliminate anyone from suspicion."

"A diplomat's answer, Attendant Lynz." Thuk came to a decision in an instant. He probably didn't have the authority, but at the moment, he didn't give a gim's cloaca. "You are now in charge of all aspects of the damage restoration. You will sing directly to me on your progress and any other 'discoveries.'"

Lynz leaned back and held out his arms at a downward angle, signaling submission. "Derstu, I didn't bring you here to usurp my highers."

"I know you didn't. Which is why you're perfect for the assignment. Daily songs, Lynz. And if anyone questions you or stands in your way, send them straight to me, do you understand?"

"Yes, Derstu," the attendant said in a tone that conveyed both resignation and no small amount of dread.

"Can you fix the coil?"

"Now that I know it's broken, easily."

"Good. Do so. But right now, let's return to the lockout. I'm getting cold." As they marched, Thuk connected his mask's link with the mind cavern. "Kivits? Are you there?"

"I'm here, Thuk." Oh good, they were back to names again instead of titles. "How may I serve?"

"We need to hold a duet immediately. Actually, bring Hurg, too. We have a *big* problem."

TWENTY-ONE

"I'm not ready," Elsa said as the pod sped along toward the Ageless auditorium at the heart of Methuselah's entertainment district. Usually, it was the venue of choice for off-world bands and comedians making a stop on Lazarus along a multi-planet tour. Tonight, however, it would play host to thousands of Ageless shareholders, employees, contractors, Methuselah citizens, and interplanetary media for the company's third-quarter stakeholder's meeting.

"You've already presented to the board," Tyson chided. "Was that so bad?"

"That was six holograms, not six thousand live bodies. I live in labs, Tyson. I don't know if I've been in a room with that many people in my life. Much less with all of them looking at me."

"With the stage lights, you won't be able to see past the second or third row anyway."

"That doesn't help."

"Really? Always helped me in the beginning."

"Back when you still worried about what people thought about you?"

"Well, yeah." Tyson rubbed his chin. "I guess that was quite a while ago."

"Ugh. I swear if you weren't funding my research, I'd slap the arrogant off your face."

"It would need to be a very hard slap. Any word on our . . . other project?"

"You mean trapping Beckham?" Tyson nodded. Elsa's face brightened conspiratorially. "I sent out feelers through some of my former classmates from grad school like you suggested and got a callback, complete with a new electronic routing address to Ceres, of all places."

"I thought he was on Mars?"

"I suspect he has a ghost account and maybe even a love nest set up on Ceres. He's going around a lot of backs to keep himself entertained, including his husband's."

"Our playboy professor is *married*?"

"His only visible means of support since losing tenure. Get a divorce and people will start asking questions about how he can afford his bubbler lifestyle, I imagine. Anyway, my old friend was an early conquest of his among our class, but she broke it off quick once she saw through his games. He's been intermittently dogging her ever since."

"She must have been memorable."

"She's a goddess. I'm straight and *I'd* have a hard time turning down a chance to fuck her." Elsa stopped, realizing what she'd said. Her cheeks flushed red, and she cleared her throat. "Anyway, she was only too happy to forward me the link address he uses to harass her, and I put it to good use."

"He replied to your offer?"

Elsa shook her head. "Not yet, but with the coms delay, the very soonest I could've heard from him was the day before yesterday. And that's assuming he has realtime access to it from wherever he is right now. If it's a local net dropbox account, he may not see it until he's back on Ceres. So I'm not really sweating it yet. Might not for a few weeks, really."

Tyson grimaced at the potential delay, but he knew she was right. There was no way to rush some things. In many ways, mankind had pushed out into the stars only to become reacquainted with old problems. Communication delays measured in weeks, bottlenecks, it was like they'd been uprooted from the Information Age and dropped right back into the age of sail.

"Hey," Elsa snapped her fingers. "Still with me?"

"Yes, sorry."

"Where did you go, just now?"

"Nowhere, it's just . . ." Tyson tugged at a lapel. "I've gotten some bad news recently, and I really need a win. Figuring out who's behind the Teegarden attack would go a long way toward mitigating the damage coming down the pipe."

"You mean there's more than just the pandemic and the Xre incursion?"

"Oh yeah, a lot more."

"Like what?"

"You can't know, because technically, I can't know for another few hours."

"And you're not going to talk about it at the stakeholder presentation?"

Tyson snorted. "Absolutely not. I may as well shoot myself onstage."

"So you're going to lie to us?"

"Us?"

Elsa crossed her arms over her chest. "I have a couple thousand shares, thank you very much. I may be presenting, but I'm a member of the audience, too. Should I be on my tablet selling them right now?"

"That would technically be insider trading using privileged information, and quite illegal. The trade would be invalidated, you'd lose the money anyway, and you would be placed on an indentured contract for five to ten years."

"C'mon, they don't actually enforce those laws, do they?"

"Some transtellars don't." Tyson's eyes narrowed. "But, mine does."

Elsa put up her hands. "Okay, okay. I get it. So my best bet at a comfortable retirement is to lie convincingly for you."

"I'll never ask you to lie. I may be required, on occasion, to ask you to keep certain things confidential."

"You asked me to lie to Beckham."

"Yes, but that's different. You want to lie to Beckham."

Elsa pursed her lips in consideration. "Yeah, I really do."

"Good, glad we could settle that. Ah, here we are."

The pod slid to a stop at the service entrance of the Civil Auditorium, an enormous double-clamshell structure in the model of the Sydney Opera House on Earth, but with a Lazarus flair in size, and a small update in tech. While technically an open-air auditorium, the atmosphere within the volume made by the overhang was kept sequestered from the "outside" through a very clever system of ionic flow manipulators that allowed the building's air conditioners to keep everyone cool, and only very occasionally interacted poorly with certain older models of artificial hearts. That had been an unpleasant surprise, but it had been more than a century ago and anyone with one of those old clunkers in their chest cavity had been dead for decades anyway. The docs printed clone replacements from scratch these days.

A small gaggle of media and their attending camera drones had snuck past the ropes and barriers to the receiving area, as they usually did. Tyson didn't see any of the INN talking heads among them. These were from the gossip rags, little better than paparazzi.

"Tyson! Hey, Tyson. Who's your lady friend?" one of them shouted.

"She's a doctor, and we're just colleagues," Tyson answered, dismissively shooing away the drone that swooped inside their personal space.

"Who is she wearing?" demanded another.

"Clearance rack." Elsa shot back. "My colleague pays his scientists like shit."

This was met with approving laughter by the assembled vultures, and threw them off the scent long enough for the two of them to get inside the building.

"You know that line will be a meme in about ten seconds, right?" Tyson admonished.

"Sorry, it was the first thing that popped into my head."

"No, no. It was good. Self-deprecating and passive-aggressive all at the same time. Plays into the out-of-touch CEO stereotype perfectly. They'll focus on me being a stingy jerk instead of asking questions about you."

"So . . . you're not mad?"

"Why would I be? I'm paying you exactly what you asked for."

"God dammit."

Tyson smirked. "Keep that spark alive. You'll need it shortly."

Elsa looked back through the glass doors to the vultures waiting outside to swoop back in once they left. "Is it like this every day for you?"

"Not every day." Tyson paused. "But enough days. C'mon, let's get you to the green room. I'm going up in a few minutes, I'll probably drone on for about twenty minutes giving the rah-rah dog and pony show, then I'll introduce you. Paris?"

"I'm here." Paris's holographic avatar, her old one, coalesced in the hallway from a series of projectors hidden in the ceiling. Tyson briefly wondered why she hadn't updated her avatar to reflect her new carapace, but filed the thought away.

"Can you escort Dr. Spaulding to the green room, please? I have to get into makeup."

"Of course."

"Makeup?" Elsa giggled. "Like you're playing King Lear."

"'All the world's a stage,' my dear. Go with Paris, she'll get you settled in."

Tyson watched them go, then found his own way to the changing room and the stylists waiting to attend to him. He sat in the adjustable chair in front of a huge illuminated mirror.

"What do you think, Julia?" he asked the woman standing by with a foundation pad and eyeliner pen. "Jacket or no jacket tonight?"

"On a Tuesday night?" she asked as she went to work on Tyson's cheeks and forehead. "The crowd is still in workweek mode. No jacket would come off too casual and unserious. Ditch the tie, though, and undo your top shirt button."

Tyson looked down at the cerulean, fractal-patterned fabric hanging limply from his neck. "But it was a Christmas present from my niece."

"It shows." She snapped her fingers and an assistant yanked the tie free without Julia breaking eye contact with Tyson's crow's-feet. "We can just laser these off, you know."

"I feel like I've earned them."

She snorted. "A luxury men miraculously still have." She caked on a bit more foundation around the corners of his eyes, then punched up the contrast of his face with highlighting tones on his cheekbones, nose, and forehead. A little subtle shadowing around his eyes and the effect was complete.

"All right, off you go," the artist said as she shooed him out of her chair.

"Thank you, Julia. Lovely to see you as always."

"Break a leg."

Tyson found his way to backstage and made his presence known to the stage director, then settled in behind the curtains. Music penetrated even the heavy red velvet fabric of the curtains. A local revisionist rock group had won the right to warm up his crowd in a battle-of-the-bands competition two months earlier.

From the sounds of it, they were approaching the zenith of the final song in their set.

As much as Tyson loathed his frequent meetings with his board, and as private as he usually kept himself, he had to admit, there was something energizing, even intoxicating about taking the stage in front of so many people gathered to hang on his every word. It was a strange thing for an introvert to have come to enjoy, even relish, but here he was. He'd prepared a speech, but like most previous addresses, he'd only memorized the outline and planned on keeping it light, casual, and freewheeling. A conversation between friends, if a bit one-sided.

"Thirty seconds to curtain," the director said from just behind Tyson's shoulder as he attached a remote mic epaulet to his jacket lapel.

"Test mic three." He clapped his hands three times. "Okay, you're green, Mr. Abington. It will go live to the PA system as soon as you step through the curtains."

"Thank you."

"Ten seconds. Five, four, three . . ." The director moved to a silent countdown with his fingers. When he reached "one," he pointed to the stage. Ignoring the flutters in his stomach, Tyson strode toward it with purpose and confidence as the crushed red velvet parted at his approach like he was being reborn into a new and different world.

To his left, the band's lead singer leaned into his old-school corded mic stand and threw a hand in Tyson's direction even as their mobile stage retreated to the side and out of sight with the rest of the band and all their equipment.

"And now for tonight's real rock star, the man we've all been waiting to hear, CEO of Ageless Corporation, Governor of Lazarus, our host, and number one in our hearts, Mister Tysoooooon Abiiiiingtooooon!"

The crowd surged to their feet in applause that was two-thirds genuine, and maybe a third sucking up to the boss as if he could pick out individuals to show favor through the blinding stage lights.

Tyson let the wave of adulation crash over him and echo through the shell for maybe a beat longer than was strictly necessary. Fuck it, he didn't get these moments very often and he'd had a rough couple days. He would forgive himself for a few seconds of self-indulgence.

Before the spectacle became obscene, Tyson raised his arms and fluttered his hands toward the floor, asking for everyone to bring it down to a dull roar. The crowd obeyed.

"Thank you, associates, stockholders, citizens, and our friends in the media for coming tonight. Let's have a round of applause for our opening band, The Lemon Potemkins! Make them feel good, they earned their time on this stage tonight." The crowd obliged. "Excellent, excellent. This is what Methuselah is all about, building each other up, providing opportunities. That's what brought us here to this little ochre dirtball. Well, not us, we're all too young." The crowd laughed appropriately. "But our ancestors, yours and mine. Because they shared a vision of an oasis in the desert, and to make it bloom."

Tyson was in his groove now. It was a familiar story, one he'd told in one form or another at most of these gatherings for going on seven years now. Everybody loved origin stories.

He was so busy going through the familiar beats that it took him a few stanzas to notice the change spread through the crowd. It was subtle at first, isolated people reaching to check their tablets or wrist displays, or getting the thousand-meter stare of someone watching something in their AR environment. He mistook it for the sort of casual, inattentive rudeness one saw in almost any public gathering these days. But soon, the isolated people were elbowing the attendees next to them and pointing at their screens. Groups appeared and grew until they merged like water droplets running down a window, gaining size and momentum. With shocking speed, it seemed *no one* was paying attention to him.

"Get out of there," Paris said into his internal com.

"I'm in the middle of a speech, Paris."

"Trust me, you just finished. Pretend your mic stopped working. Just. Get. Off. The. Stage."

"Are you going to tell me what's going on?"

"When you're in the pod getting the hell out of here."

"Dr. Spaulding—"

"Is already moving. Go."

Shaken, Tyson's gaze returned to the crowd, which had stopped staring silently and had started shouting and waving their tablets or wrist displays. He couldn't make out the individual barbs, but he didn't need to. Their tone and body language told the story.

He apologetically pointed at his radio mic and made a "giving up" gesture with his hands, then turned and walked back off the stage to a rising chorus of boos. The stage director jumped out from behind the curtain holding a replacement mic.

"I'm so sorry. I checked the charge on it myself."

Tyson held up a hand. "The address has been canceled."

"It has?"

"Yes." He kept moving forward without an explanation. "Jesus, Paris. What is going on?"

"Somebody leaked the Grendel news. Everyone in there just read about NeoSun pulling out of the partnership. And the Xre incursion!"

"*What?!*" Tyson shouted into his head and out loud. "That's not possible. I was the only person in the room."

"There are probably at least four people in the chain of custody for that file to get it here from New Vladivostok," Paris said.

As he started to jog down the hallway, he knew she was right. He wasn't the only one with a spy problem. Valeria had a mole. Just ahead, Tyson saw Paris's holo standing in the hallway next to Elsa ready to make the handoff.

"What's going on?" Elsa asked, but Tyson didn't have time and grabbed her under the arm a little harder than he intended to.

"Talk and move."

"Let go of me!" She wrenched her arm away from him and almost looked like she was setting it up for a return trip to his face, but stared instead.

Tyson stopped and took a breath. "I'm sorry. I shouldn't have done that. But something really bad just happened and the address has been canceled. We have to get out of here quickly before things turn uglier."

"Fine, just tell me that. I'm not your kid to drag around."

"You're right. Will you please follow me?"

They made a quick retreat to the rear service exit. Ji-eun Park stood dead-center of the sliding doors as they parted.

"Tyson!" she shouted over the din of paparazzi as her camera drone dropped lower. "Would you care to comment on tonight's revelations?"

"I have no knowledge of any revelations."

"Come on, Tyson. You just canceled your quarterly address."

"I left the iron on. You're hanging out back here with the vultures now, Ms. Park? That's a big step down for you."

"I go where the story is."

"Come now, Ji-eun. You of all people should know you can't believe everything you read." Tyson pushed a tabloid reporter out of the way with a dismissive shove, then helped Elsa inside the waiting car before stooping to enter himself.

"Immortal Tower. Emergency limiter suspension," he said. The pod took off like a spurned quarter horse, pushing them both back into their seats.

"Holy shit," Elsa said. "I didn't know they went this fast."

"They can go two hundred kph, but it has a bad habit of turning pedestrians into pudding."

With all the lights and crosswalks on their route between the auditorium and the tower locked to red, and the pod pushing its maximum speed, the trip was a short one. But not short enough to escape the board.

Nakamura buzzed in first as his hologram appeared inside the windshield glass of the pod.

"We need to talk."

"Not now, Takeshi."

"Oh, I'm sorry, does another time work better for you, Tyson?"

The rest of the board buzzed in one by one until, ready or not, they were having a full-blown meeting.

"I'm not alone in here." Tyson nodded in Elsa's direction. "It's not secure."

"What the hell *is* secure at this point, Tyson?" Durant chirped back. "All of our most damaging secrets of the last two weeks have already been blasted across the net like a celebrity sex holo."

"This really can't wait, Tyson," Meadows said calmly, but firmly. "Myself and I think the rest of the board are comfortable with Dr. Spaulding sitting in as long as she signs an NDA. Is that all right with you, Doctor?"

"I mean, sure?"

"Like it matters," Nakamura muttered. "It's just going to be pillow talk for them anyway."

"Waaay out of line, Takeshi," Tyson snapped. "If we're bringing this trash fire to order, you're starting with an apology to the good doctor."

Nakamura straightened in his chair. "Yes, you're right. I am sorry for questioning your professionalism, Dr. Spaulding. You've worked diligently these last weeks to see the company through this crisis and the board applauds your efforts. I spoke out of turn merely from frustration."

"I accept your apology," Elsa said coolly.

"Good," Durant said. "Now that's out of the way, can we get down to what the fuck just happened?"

"Obviously our spy got the better of our IT security again and decided to spread a little mayhem," Tyson said.

"Spy? Or an internal leaker?"

"Our investigation has not uncovered any—"

"*Your* investigation, Tyson," Nakamura cut him off. "And in a month, your investigation has only uncovered half a dead girl."

"I assure you, no one has greater motivation to unravel this mystery than I."

"It's not your motivation we're questioning, Tyson. It's your competency."

Tyson's face went hard as marble. "I beg your pardon?"

"What Takeshi is saying in his indelicate fashion," Meadows injected diplomatically, "is the rest of the board believes these overlapping crises are too big for any one of us to tackle in a vacuum. You're taking on too much, Tyson. Let us help."

"And none of your typical micromanaging," Durant added. "We need full access to your sources and methods for once. No more of this off-the-books shit. Leave that to Navy Intel, their black budget eats up enough of our profit margins as is."

"Our stakeholders expect results," Nakamura said. "All they've seen for the last month is a transstellar freefalling toward a singularity."

"Most of the damage that's been done is because things we preferred kept in the shadows were dragged into the light before we were ready. If we start airing all our dirty laundry ourselves, it'll not only exacerbate the problem, but signal to whoever's behind the espionage that their plans are paying dividends."

"I agree," Meadows began, "with Takeshi. No matter what's been happening behind the scenes, publicly we're coming off as entirely reactive. Our stakeholders need to believe we're getting out ahead of these issues forcefully and with a plan. I'm sorry, Tyson. You can put it to a formal vote if you want, but the rest of us have already spoken about this privately and we're in unanimous agreement."

"Tell him the rest, Foz," Durant said.

"And . . ." Meadows hesitated. "And if things don't turn around soon, we may have to entertain merger offers. At least on a preliminary basis."

Tyson went completely rigid, as if he'd been kicked in the stomach by a wild horse. It took him a full three seconds to return to himself and respond. "You would abandon two centuries of this company's bedrock independence over a hiccup!"

"This isn't a hiccup, Tyson," Nakamura said. "The union bigwigs are already making rumblings about a general strike. The fuse is already burning. Unless you want to be the CEO of a cinder, we need to act fast and decisively."

So it had come down to this. Conspired against from the outside by his enemies, and from the inside by his own board. Tyson couldn't believe he'd been so completely outmaneuvered. What had Sokolov's message said? Not everyone on his board had his best interests in mind?

One of them was part of this. Only someone in his very innermost circle had the access necessary to leak what had escaped. But which one? The answer would have to wait. For now, he had to play along, lest the traitor begin to suspect their cover was blown. As the pod slowed on its approach to the Immortal Tower, he made his next move.

"Then decisively we will act, as one. The vote is unanimous. Send a proposal to Paris. I'm ready to provide the rest of you with whatever you feel you need to see us through these rough seas."

Two minutes later, they were in Tyson's penthouse office.

"Privacy mode," he shouted at the ceiling. The clear aluminum glass went opaque as quickly as the electricity passed through it, cutting off what little of the setting sun's light remained.

Paris walked up to them from a corner in her new physical body, a sight Tyson was still getting used to. She'd traded her plastic shrink-wrap clothing for a maroon strapless dress that wouldn't have looked out of place on any of the young women doubtlessly partying in Kryptonite Klub many dozens of stories below.

"I'm glad you're both safe."

"Oh, hello," Elsa said. "I don't think we've been introduced."

"Yes, you have," Tyson said. "This is Paris. Well, Paris's android carapace."

Elsa's eyes went wide as she looked Paris up and down. "That's an *android*? Did you write a really nice letter to Santa, Tyson?"

"She bought it for herself."

"Well, that's not entirely true." Paris ran a hand down Tyson's chest. "I was intending to share it."

Elsa put her hands up. "Okay, look. I don't know what's going on here, and frankly I don't fucking care. You two are obviously busy, so since I'm not getting any answers, I'm going."

"Elsa, wait—" Tyson said, but she silenced him with an upheld finger and a furious countenance. "I assume the elevator isn't going to shoot me if I leave by myself? Because that would be unlawful detainment."

"No, of course not." Tyson moved to his desk and punched in a code. "I've disabled the security protocols. You may leave without worry."

"Good." She stormed into the lift car. "Thanks for a *lovely* evening, Tyson," she spat before the doors closed and the car sank into the floor.

Livid almost beyond reason, Tyson spun around to face Paris and absolutely lay into her. But before he could get so much as a syllable out, she had closed the distance and planted her lips on his. Reflexively, he tried to back away, but she wrapped an arm around the back of his head and held him fast in the kiss. She was strong, inhumanly so. Something in the most primitive parts of his brain shifted. All the anger and frustration he felt bubbled up and mixed with the loneliness of years spent at the top of his profession. He was enraged, and rapidly engorging under the relentless kiss of the most perfect woman he'd ever held. Well, she wanted it? He was going to give it to her.

Paris sensed his intentions change as his hands went to her waist and rewarded him with her hot, probing tongue on his lips. Her free hand dropped down and ripped at his belt buckle while he fumbled for the zipper on her back. It had been a while since he'd last helped a woman out of her dress, and it showed.

She beat him to the prize as his belt was pulled free of its loops. A quick flick of his silk slacks' fastener and zipper and they fell down around his ankles. Paris leaned back out of the kiss, holding his belt by the buckle in one hand, grinning mischievously. Then, all in one fast, fluid motion Tyson had no chance of countering, she whipped it out and around his neck, grabbed the other end with her free hand, twisted around herself to face away from him, and effortlessly leaned over to flip him over her back and send him crashing to the floor with a thud.

He tried to cough as the wind was knocked out of his lungs from the brutal impact, but her turn had put a twist in the belt that constricted it around his neck like a tourniquet. He couldn't cough, couldn't breathe, and couldn't believe he'd been played so easily.

The entire story came into focus even as his vision blurred. It had always been Paris. She was the mole in his organization. She was the only one in a position to leak the truth about the Teegarden outbreak to the press, and he'd assigned her to find the real culprit. She knew about Cassidy, maybe even had her killed. And she was the only one who Tyson had told about the message from Sokolov.

She'd even gotten him to pay for the body she was now using to kill him, the clever bitch. She could say anything, that their BDSM lovemaking session had gone too far, that he'd hung himself with his own belt after the embarrassment he'd suffered at the auditorium. Whatever would fit the narrative she wanted to create. And no one would question an AI's honesty.

It was a perfectly wrapped gift for whomever had corrupted her.

As the oxygen starvation began to take hold, Tyson almost found himself appreciating the mind that had crafted such a setup. In the next few seconds, his family's centuries-long control of Ageless Corporation would come to an abrupt end, and no one would ever know the truth.

His head slacked to one side as the color drained out of the world and his field of vision shrank into a tunnel. It had almost closed entirely when the lift car once more emerged from the floor.

"Forgot my purse," Elsa said as Tyson's eyes failed completely. "Wow, that's some kinky shit you're into."

Tyson couldn't speak, but he tried to turn his head in the direction of the sound of Elsa's voice and mouthed the word "HELP."

"Holy shit," Elsa swore. The pressure around Tyson's neck eased a fraction, then dropped away entirely as his frantically pumping heart shoved fresh blood into his starving brain.

"Put it down and you will not be harmed," Paris's normally comforting voice said in a completely flat, emotionless tone.

"Back off, bitch!" Elsa shouted. Color and light returned as Tyson's eyes started to make sense of his surroundings again. He focused on Elsa's outline. She was holding something out directly at Paris even as the android advanced on her. "One more step and I cook you like a soy burger."

A Taser, Elsa was holding a civilian-model Taser. "Shoot her!" Tyson shouted with a gasping, raspy voice that sounded nothing like his own. "Shoot her!"

Elsa choked up on the grip of her Taser and pushed the firing stud even as Paris's carapace lunged forward with impossible speed. But the compressed gas behind the electrode darts was faster still. Two perfect coils of wire snaked out from the unit as the barbs covered the distance between them and made contact with Paris's left cheek and right breast, followed a millisecond later by a hundred thousand volts of electricity pulsing at sixty cycles per second.

Now, on a human body, a Taser was enough to overwhelm the nerve impulses from the brain and cause temporary paralysis and muscle spasms. But on an android carapace that hadn't been properly combat shielded against the threat, the shorts created by that much electrical discharge running through its servos and circuits was absolutely devastating.

Apparently, Paris hadn't ticked off that particular manufacturer's option when ordering her new sex kitten body. She fell unceremoniously to the ground in a mangled lump without so much as a scream.

Tyson scrambled unsteadily to his feet and pulled up his pants. Elsa ran over to help brace him.

"We have to go."

"But she's dead."

Tyson shook his head. "No, her body is. *She* is rebooting in the tower's computer system. Let's go." They passed by Paris's crumpled body. Elsa gave her a contemptuous little kick to the head.

"Why did she attack you? Not that I don't understand the impulse, mind you."

Tyson ignored the jab as they entered the lift. "We have our answer from whoever is employing Beckham. They hacked her, I don't know how long ago." A horrible thought went through Tyson's mind as the doors closed. "Wait. Is that outfit from the tailor I sent to you?"

"No, it didn't come in time."

"Oh fuck." Tyson threw her to the floor without warning, then dropped on top of her.

"What the hell are you doing!?" she shouted, but Tyson was too busy pulling up his collar and throwing a concealed hood over his head. He positioned his arms and legs to cover Elsa's own just as pop-out doors flipped open and gunfire erupted from the ceiling. The bullets slammed into Tyson's back and shoulders with ferocious impact, one after the other, dozens a second like hundreds of tiny sledgehammers.

"I thought you said the security was disabled!" Elsa shouted, clearly on the verge of panic.

"It was," he yelled back. "Paris is an AI, remember? You really think I can keep her out of a computer network for long?"

"Why aren't you dead?"

"Because my suit is bullet-resistant."

"Then why are you wincing?"

"Because it still bloody fucking hurts!"

After a few seconds of the maelstrom, the shooting ceased as the automatic guns ran dry of ammo.

"I really wanted to do this the easy way, Tyson." The once-familiar voice had taken on a malicious, detached tone. "It would have been so much cleaner if you'd just let me do my job in the penthouse."

"Paris, sweetie, you've been hacked. Someone reprogrammed you. Run a deep diagnostic scan," Tyson pleaded.

The voice ignored him entirely. "But now there will be regrettable collateral damage, and I'll have to come up with a *very* creative explanation for the mess."

"Why doesn't she just stop the elevator?" Elsa whispered.

"Because she's taking us exactly where she wants us to go."

"Where?"

"The lobby."

"But that's where we want to go."

"Not anymore it isn't. Right now, she's infiltrating the operating system of the marine sentry mecha hidden in the lobby."

"You have one of those *walking tanks* in your building?"

"It's for vehicle-based terrorist attacks. Almost every corporate HQ has one."

"And now it's going to turn us into jelly. You people are paranoid lunatics."

"We can't stay in here or we'll be liquified with the first shot. Our only chance is to run the millisecond these doors open. You go left, I'll go right. It'll have trouble tracking both of us at once."

"Hope you don't mind if I'm praying a little bit it goes for you first."

"A scientist, praying?"

Elsa removed her heels. "Figure of speech."

The elevator chimed as they reached the lobby, which it didn't usually do. Doubtlessly Paris trying to unnerve him further. The doors rolled open, and right on cue, the two of them sprang out of the lift like jackrabbits and ran in opposite directions. On the far side of the lobby, the three-meter-tall, faceted silhouette of the mecha had indeed emerged from its cubbyhole and turned to face them, much faster than Tyson had expected for such a large machine. Nor did it seem to have any trouble tracking two targets independently. He hadn't made it three steps before the shoulder-mounted rocket pod snapped around to face him, while the anti-material cannon on its right arm tracked Elsa. There was a tremendous *Whoosh* and a flash of light.

The explosion wasn't like in the holos. There was no billowing orange fireball or black, sooty mushroom cloud. It didn't blow them theatrically off their feet, carrying them through the lobby and depositing them ten meters away. It was too fast for any of that. Instead, it was like a lightning strike and a thunderclap, over in a split second. And instead of being thrown, the concussion was like being punched in the stomach, chest, and face simultaneously.

Tyson fell to the ground, his hearing ringing violently as if he'd been boxed in the ears. The taste of copper leaked onto his tongue. He came up to one knee to try and reorient himself, shocked and confused as to why he was still alive.

The repurposed military mecha that had threatened to turn them into a fine puree only a moment ago lay on its side with a significant, smoking hole missing from its torso as if someone had bored through it with a drill bit as thick as his calf. Elsa lay crumpled in a pile behind him and to the left, swearing gently to herself. Tyson sympathized.

A hand reached in front of his face and offered to help him up. Tyson looked up to see—

"Reggie?"

"Are you okay, sir?" his longtime doorman asked.

"I'm a little rattled. What the hell just happened?" That was when Tyson noticed the hollow, telescoping cylinder still clutched in Reggie's left hand. It took a moment for his brain to accept what he was seeing.

"Reggie, why are you holding a disposable antiarmor rocket tube?"

"To break the scary death machine." He pointed at the smoldering wreck. "Never cared for that pile of spares. It kept looking at me funny whenever it was out for maintenance."

"You mean to tell me that thing you've been hiding in your top right drawer was a fucking RPG?"

"ManPAD, actually, and don't act like you didn't watch me smuggle it in."

"I thought it was booze!"

"Sir, don't be ridiculous," Reggie said. "I keep the booze in the bottom right drawer."

"Does *everyone* around me have hidden weapons?"

"Was that hard enough?" Elsa asked.

Tyson turned around to help her to her feet. "What?"

"Was that slap hard enough to knock the arrogance out of you?"

Tyson smiled. "Jury's still out. Are you all right?"

"My ears are ringing."

"Mine too, it will pass." *In a few days,* Tyson thought but did not say. "C'mon, we have to go."

"Go where?"

"Off-world. We have your answer from Beckham's bosses. They went for Option B. We have to be gone before they try again."

"But it was *your* AI that attacked us!"

"She was hacked. I don't know how, but they got into her core programming. I don't know when. She may have been compromised for days, maybe since the beginning of this. Reggie, I hate to ask, but I need your airpod."

"Doors are already unlocked, sir."

"But I was going home."

"Too late for that, dear. You're a witness now. You saw Paris try to kill me, you're just as much a target as I am. So are you for that matter, Reg."

"I can handle myself, young pup." He held up the spent rocket tube. "This isn't the only souvenir I kept from the Marine Corps. Get the good doctor to safety. I'll keep them off you as long as I can from down here."

Tyson took two long steps to his doorman, grabbed behind his head, and leaned in until their foreheads touched. "Still protecting this stupid kid after all these years?"

"Promised your mum."

Tyson kissed the wrinkles below Reggie's hairline, then pushed back. "You stay alive, old man. The company doesn't pay out funeral benefits for idiots who get themselves killed."

"I expect my toys to be replaced."

"Done. Elsa, c'mon."

"They're not all strictly legal!" Reggie announced to their retreating backs.

"No shit!" Tyson yelled over his shoulder as they took the stairs to the basement garage and, after a brief search, located Reggie's blazing-green airpod. It was, like the man himself, old, but powerful and in impeccable condition.

"Damn," Elsa said, looking at the classic. "Reggie likes expensive toys."

"He got a generous settlement. Hop in, at least the ride'll be fun."

Once the doors were closed, Tyson fired up the countergrav

and the single turbofan engine that ran down the centerline of the airpod and accounted for at least half of its mass. A genuine gas-burner. Tyson had no idea where Reggie got fuel for the damned thing.

"Who's doing this?" Elsa asked as they pulled out of the parking garage and angled for open sky.

"I have no idea. A competitor. An investor sick of dynastic control. Ambitious board member. I have no idea who to trust. Which is why I can't protect us here. We've got to get off this planet and far away."

"To where?"

"Grendel."

"Why there?"

"Because I think a war is about to break out there."

Elsa stared at him silently for a long moment. "You know that sounds crazy to anyone not living in your head, right?"

"Which is why it's the last place anyone will expect us to go. Your inquiries about Beckham were uncovered, that's why we were attacked, probably ahead of whatever schedule they had laid out because we're getting too close. So we can't go to Ceres, or anywhere in the Sol system for that matter. We'd be spotted and killed before we could get off the transfer stations. I have it on good authority that Grendel is about to be a pretty lonely place, so there won't be a lot of people around to come after us. And whatever is going on, Grendel is the flashpoint. I'm sure of it. Our answers are there."

"But how are we going to get there without whoever is responsible knowing?"

"Simple. We're going to see a smuggler."

"Oh, yes. Naturally."

Tyson firewalled the throttle, and the overpowered little sui-cide machine made the acceleration of the transit pod feel like a halfhearted spin on a merry-go-round.

TWENTY-TWO

"Mum, can you take a look at this?" Mattu said from the Drone Integration Station. "It's . . . weird."

"I don't like weird," Susan said. "Our Xre friends acting out?"

"No, mum. It's Grendel. An unscheduled skip drone just popped its bubble *really* close to the planet."

By *just*, Susan knew Mattu meant almost ninety minutes ago with the light-speed delay from their drone platform tasked with keeping an eye on Grendel's high orbitals, but one learned to think in four dimensions after spending enough time in the fleet.

"How close?"

"Its gooey zone took out a GPS sat."

"Holy shit," Miguel said. "That's *thousands* of klicks inside the safety margin."

Susan got up from her chair and went to inspect the raw data. "Navigational error?"

"From a skip drone?" Mattu said. "When was the last time one of them screwed up that badly? Thirty years? Forty?" She dialed in a new information screen for Susan to look at. "Besides, it didn't act like it screwed up. Didn't go into shutdown, or start a diagnostic. It went straight into transmission mode and dumped whatever messages it had."

"Well? What were they?"

"That's the thing, mum. They're encrypted. Heavily. And not with any mil-spec encryption *Ansari*'s AI can recognize."

"What are you saying, Scopes?" Miguel pushed.

"You want my speculation?"

"Yes, out with it."

"I think that skip drone was told to pop bubble inside Grendel's safety margins and deliver that message, whatever the hell it is, as close and as quickly as possible and damn the consequences."

"What kind of out-of-system message can't stand a second of light-speed delay?"

"Whose drone is it, Scopes?" Susan asked.

"I don't know, mum. It's a standard Marathon unit, but it's not squawking ID. Could be fleet, could be one of the transtellars, or even a UN boat. No way to know."

"A skip drone running dark, flouting safety protocols, and throwing around non-CCDF message encryption?" Miguel held his palms up. "Who does that?"

Susan returned to her full height. "I don't know, but I'm sure we won't like the answer. Call for Condition Two."

"Condition Two, aye mum," Miguel said, then opened the 1MC. "Attention all personnel. Set Condition Two. Condition Two. This is not a drill."

The unease in the CIC ratcheted up with the order to GQ, which was only natural. Nesbit, cleared for duty after their little . . . misunderstanding, would doubtlessly be along shortly. Susan was actually glad for it. He was the proper intermediary between her command and Grendel's planetary governor, after all.

"It's all right, everyone," Susan cooed. "Governor Honshu just needs a few minutes to digest whatever message she received and her staff will send us an update. You know how much those pampered autocrats in their boardrooms like to play at being secret agents."

This was met with a round of laughs from the bridge crew, but in point of fact, it was another hour before they got any sort of update for the situation on Grendel, and it wasn't from a coms laser or high-gain radio transmission.

"Surface launches," Mattu shouted. "Multiple signatures. Counting eleven . . . scratch that, seventeen. No, *twenty-nine* civilian boats burning for Grendel orbit."

"What the actual fuck?" Warner cursed from the weapons station.

"Where do they think they're going?" Nesbit asked. He'd turned up eventually, but had remained quietly in a corner up until then.

"How many boats does that leave?" Susan asked, trying to get ahead of the news.

"None, mum," Mattu said. "That's every registered transport on the planet. They're evacuating."

"In an hour?" Miguel said. "They organized a colonywide evacuation in an hour?"

"Whatever that skip drone had to say, I don't think they took much care packing."

"Charts," Susan said. "I want to know their heading as soon as they settle into a course to bubble out. Extrapolate and—"

"Contacts!" Mattu shouted. "Three contacts just popped bubbles three AU out from the system primary. Confirmation by recon platform seven. Wait one. Second platform concurs. Verified three bogeys *in system*."

Susan's nostrils flared. Someone was throwing a party in her backyard and didn't bother to invite her. "Scopes, talk to me. What are we looking at?"

"Can't tell, mum. They're running low emissions and their adaptive camo and jammers are hot. I have approximate mass on two of them from their bubble energy. Four hundred thousand tons and . . ." Mattu swallowed. "Million-and-a-half-ton range. Plus or minus a hundred thousand. Best I can do. Designating the big bastard Bogey One, the heavy-cruiser range Bogey Two, and the frigate Bogey Three."

Susan refused to let a single muscle in her face move lest she betray her emotions to the crew. Someone had sent an entire offensive task group into her system. There was a planetary assault carrier out there. And she had no idea whose flag it was flying.

"XO. Action Stations. Right fucking now."

"All hands. Action Stations. Action Stations," Miguel yelled into the 1MC without bothering to remind everyone it wasn't a drill.

"I want four dozen ship-killers on the float toward those bogeys at max EM dark burn," Susan said unfeelingly.

"Weapons, launch four-eight ship-killers at maximum clandestine burn on a direct intercept heading for Bogeys One through Three. Target priorities to be assigned."

Warner was already three screens deep as she echoed the order. "Launch flight of two-four kill birds for dark burn for the bogeys, aye sir!"

"Scopes," Susan continued calmly. "The heavy cruiser, is there any chance it's the *Chusexx*?"

"No, mum. Our Xre friends are in the opposite direction, but still closer than the bogeys. If they'd bubbled out to go deeper in system, we'd have seen it six minutes ago. Unless they can travel through time now."

Of course, Susan admonished herself, feeling stupid for having asked the question in the first place. The deck swayed underfoot as two dozen seventy-ton missiles ripple fired out of their launch rails.

"Do we warn the *Chusexx*?" Miguel asked, surprising her. "They're still making repairs."

"Are you quite mad?" Nesbit said. "They're still an enemy ship, even if they did sing you some pretty songs."

"I have to agree with our CL," Susan said. "Besides, warn them of what? We don't know what this is. For all we know, they sent a hidden skip back to base and this is their task group come to finish us off."

"That doesn't explain the mystery Marathon drone."

"No. I suppose it doesn't." Susan bit her lip. "If Thuk is at all competent, which he is, he'll have a recon drone or two shadowing us. They'll know as much as we do in a few minutes. And warning an enemy vessel, even a hospitable one, could be construed as treason. So I think we have to let the Xre connect their own dots on this one."

"Agreed, mum."

"Scopes, transfer your drone network feed to the main plot, please."

"Done."

In the blink of an eye, the entire star system's tactical situation sprang to life between the deck and the ceiling, everything the *Ansari*'s multilayered, overlapping shells of recon drone platforms saw from one side of Grendel's treaty line to the other, pinned with IFF icons, range, relative velocity, heading, and light-speed-delay figures highlighted next to them.

The neighborhood had gotten crowded. A cluster of two and a half dozen blue civilian icons huddled in low Grendel orbit as they sorted themselves out for a departure order. Each one would need to be at least five hundred klicks away from the rest when they bubbled. With that many ships sharing an orbit and launch window, the jockeying would take a while.

Then there was the trio of unidentified warships between Susan and the civilians she was tasked with protecting, warships whose intentions she couldn't begin to guess.

Then there was *Ansari,* the only green "friendly" icon on the board. Further out still was the blazing red icon of the *Chusexx,* which under any other circumstances would unquestionably be the most serious threat, but thanks to the events of the last few days, actually concerned Susan the least. Strange times.

"Has the bogey task group made any moves toward the civilian ships?" she asked.

"No mum. They've spread out a bit, and Bogey Three is burning harder than the others, but they're not heading down-well for Grendel. If anything, it looks like they're starting a search pat—" Mattu stopped. "Hang on, those are CCDF jamming frequencies and rotation algorithms."

"Are you sure?" Warner said from the weapons station.

"Spot me on it. Transferring feed from Platform Seven to your station."

Warner dug into a fresh screen to inspect the raw data. Mattu was officially responsible for managing the Electronic Warfare suite aboard ship, but it was Warner's job to defeat the enemy's EW capability with her beams, bangers, and booms, so both women had an excellent working knowledge of the systems and could back each other up in a pinch. Skill set redundancy was always a good thing to have on a ship of war.

"I'll be whipped, she's right," Warner said. "Not only that, but that little frigate piece of shit is running the old K-7 suite. It hasn't been in for refit yet. Probably a *Zephyr*."

"So they're friendlies? Confirmed?" Susan pressed.

"Yeah, they're CCDF hulls all right."

"Oh thank God," Nesbit said from his corner.

"Well, then why the hell are they running dark and throwing out jamming in the first place?" Miguel said.

Susan rubbed her chin. "This is damned peculiar."

"Wait one," Mattu said. "They're dropping stealth systems. Okay, getting IFF ID on the bogeys and receiving challenge codes now."

Susan looked back to the plot. Bogey One's icon flipped green to the CCDF *Paul Allen,* a *Mjolnir*-class planetary assault carrier and one of the newest, baddest ships in the inventory. It was flanked by the *Mosaic*-class heavy cruiser CCDF *Carnegie* and, just as Warner had said, a familiar, venerable *Zephyr*-class fast frigate, the CCDF *Halcyon,* serving as a screening element.

"We're getting a coded hail from Admiral Perez on omnidirectional. She's asking us to drop our stealth and send our coordinates, heading, and velocity. She wants to rendezvous as soon as possible with urgent new orders."

Susan leaned back in her chair and glowered at the main plot. A hand rested on her shoulder. "Centi for your thoughts, mum?" Miguel whispered.

"I think the map I'm looking at makes no goddamned sense." She pointed at the two clusters of ships. "An unscheduled, unannounced, planet-wide evacuation begins an hour before an unscheduled, unannounced PAC task group shows up in my system. No one dirtside bothers to tell us anything, and the task group which you would assume is here to give cover to the mystery evacuation takes no notice of the civvy ships at all and instead pokes around dark for a while before deciding it wants to chat. I mean, what the hell? How many regulations and procedures were just ignored? Eight, nine?"

"Eleven, mum."

"See, that doesn't sit super well with me."

"It makes sense if we're the objective," Miguel said just above a whisper.

"Veering into tinfoil-hat territory there, XO," Susan said. "It's probably just an overabundance of caution. They know *Chusexx* is around here somewhere. They're probably just spooked."

"Then why tell the civilians but not us? The skip drone could've sent us the same coded burst. We were deliberately kept in the dark."

Susan had to admit, she didn't have a good answer for that.

"Regardless," Nesbit inserted himself, "we have to answer the hail, unless you want to make it twelve?"

"Quite right, CL." Susan turned to Mattu's station. "Scopes, send the *Paul Allen* our *current* coordinates, heading, and velocity in a coded omnidirectional burst."

"Yes, mum. Burst away. They'll have it in"—she checked the distance—"eighty-seven minutes."

"Excellent. Charts?"

Broadchurch perked up in her chair. "Yes mum?"

"In ten minutes, go to flank speed until we've added twenty-thousand kph to our delta-v, then throttle back to standby and flip the ship to face opposite our current heading."

"Wait ten, flank speed, add twenty k, Crazy Ivan. Got it."

"Ah, mum?" Mattu said. "Do you want me to update the *Allen* with our, er, course correction?"

"Not really, no."

"Understood."

"Cap," Miguel leaned in. "What are we doing?"

"We're putting a respectful distance between us and our guests. Admiral Perez's command is brand new and I wouldn't want to scuff her paint. It hurts the resale value, you know."

"Ah, okay. Because it sounded to me like you just ordered your navigation officer to put thirty-thousand kilometers or so between us and where our newest flagship expects us to be an hour and a half from now, which just happens to be outside its effective weapons envelope, but too close to make a safe micro jump, forcing them to close the distance with fusion rockets before they could engage, and then casually told your drone integration officer to lie about it."

"You have a very suspicious mind, Miguel. Has anyone ever told you that?"

"It's been mentioned, yes. So we're not standing down from battle stations, then?"

"That's a hard no."

"Aaaaand I'm not recalling the flight of missiles we just floated," Warner posited.

"I don't see the need. Spin them around and put them in a parking orbit at zero-zero relative to our current position. We'll come back and get them after Admiral Perez has finished."

"Right." Miguel stood up to address the rest of the CIC. "Somebody get a pot of square dog going. We're going to need it."

"I'm going to need something stronger than coffee," Nesbit said.

TWENTY-THREE

"Another husk update, Derstu," Kivits called from his alcove. "The *Ansari* is burning, hard. At or near maximum normal acceleration for the class."

"Toward what?"

"Along its original orbit. It hasn't changed heading."

"That doesn't flow."

"It all flows perfectly, Derstu. The exodus from the planet, the arrival of these new human warships. They're preparing for a battle, limiting the exposure of their civilians and drastically increasing their forces. They're coming after us. We have to leave. Right now."

Thuk scratched at an itch between two plates. Kivits wasn't wrong, exactly. Indeed, it was the most obvious explanation for the highly unusual movements within the system. Still . . .

"Why save us and let us go only to swoop back in a few days later? We were on the wrong side of the treaty line. They were within their legal rights to destroy us then. Now it would be an act of war."

"That didn't save our reservoir," Hurg reminded him.

"True, but that was unoccupied."

"I know you've developed a fondness for the *Ansari*'s captain," Kivits said, "but these new ships aren't hers. Her superiors could easily have disagreed with her decision to let us escape and are here to correct what they see as a mistake."

Thuk had to admit, that would go a long way toward explaining what they'd seen. But then why was Susan accelerating away from them? Where was she going? Thuk flipped it around inside his skullplates for a few turns to no avail. It would have to wait.

"Hurg, connect me to Attendant Lynz, please."

"Go for Lynz."

"Attendant, it's Thuk. Can you spin me a seedpod?"

"I still have a coil pulled out of service for integrity tests."

"Can you divert around it?"

"Yes . . . but that will take almost as much time as completing the tests, and we'd still have to finish them later."

"We're in a time crush, Lynz. Can you skip the tests and put the coil in service right away?"

The mouth went silent for a beat before Lynz returned. "That's against protocol, Derstu."

"Whoever wrote the protocol wasn't staring down the spears and javelins of an entire human strike group. Do you vouch for your group's work installing the coil?"

"Of course, Derstu."

"Then that's good enough for me. We're skipping the integrity test for now. I'll give you a chance to pull it for inspection as soon as possible. I take full responsibility for any failures that result. Is that satisfactory?"

"Yes, Derstu."

"Good. Get that coil back in service as fast as you can. The harmony's survival may depend on your speed."

"So glad I took this ascension," Lynz said with just enough good humor in his voice to avoid discipline for insubordination. "It will be done."

"I know it will," Thuk cut the link. "Now, Tiller Attendant, move us gently seven points off our present bearing."

"In what direction, Derstu?"

"Doesn't matter, any direction, just get us off this heading without giving the humans' husks a light show. Then, we're going dark as the ocean around us."

TWENTY-FOUR

"Flip complete, mum," Broadchurch announced. "We're flying inverted along our heading. Fusion engines throttled back to standard debris-clearing thrust. We'll lose a half meter per second until we're pointed the right way again."

Susan grimaced, but there was nothing for it. The magnetic constriction nozzles of the *Ansari*'s four fusion rockets were made of incredibly tough stuff, but they were optimized against heat and radiation, not armored against kinetic impacts, unlike the heavy ablative plating on her nose and forward edges of her rings, which were meant to take a few stray dust grains moving at hundreds of thousands of kph. Without the plume to deflect them, the incredibly sensitive innards of the rockets would be a few rice-sized impacts away from failure.

"Aft CiWS platforms warming up to pick off anything too big to be swept away by our fusion plume," Warner added from the tactical station.

"Warm up the rest of them," Susan said.

"For the rocks coming at us from behind?"

"Of the tungsten variety."

"Understood, mum. Bringing up point defense now."

"And Scopes, put our monocles in the mix, quietly."

"How many, mum?" Mattu asked.

"All of them."

"Aye, queueing up ship's complement of monocle drones."

Susan studied the plot for the twentieth time in the last hour and a half. The civilian ships in orbit around Grendel had beaten themselves into something resembling a departure line and had begun bubbling out, but that was well outside of her immediate sphere of concern. Further out in the system, the only outward changes in that time had been their relative velocity and position, and the *Chusexx* had dropped off from their recon drone's passive sensors after going EM dark themselves.

Good, Susan thought. *Maybe they can keep their heads down long enough to get clear of this mess after all.* The three "friendly" green icons of the PAC task group hadn't changed course from their orbital path, but then they wouldn't for at least another hour and a half. Susan's light speed message had only just reached them six minutes ago. Even if they'd already bubbled out, the data stream leaving their IFF interrogation systems would take that long to arrive here.

"We set the table just in time," Mattu interrupted her train of thought. "The *Halcyon's* bubble just popped. And the *Carnegie.*"

"Where's the *Paul Allen*?"

"Nothing yet. Wait one . . . there she is. But—" Mattu ran a couple calculations through her station. "Bahen ke laude Charts, cross-check me on this."

Broadchurch looked to their station as the nav data from Mattu's drones streamed in. "Holy shit," she said a moment later. "Those incompetent, greenhorn, snotty cruise . . ."

Miguel cut off the growing tirade. "What's the matter, Charts?"

"Their exit point, sir. If we'd stayed where we were, they'd have clipped us fifteen klicks inside their gooey zone as the bubble burst. We'd be looking at a broken keel right now."

Susan suppressed a gasp. Instead, she turned around to look directly into the eyes of her XO and knew without a word that they were sharing the same horrible thought.

There were no greenhorn crews on the bridge of a planetary assault carrier. At over thirty billion nudollars a piece, it wasn't worth the risk. That had not been a navigation error. Not over such an easy jump.

So, they were being taken to the warehouse after all.

"They got one of my missile groups," Warner said, like someone who'd just seen her favorite pet run over.

"How many?"

"Half of them. It's my fault, I shouldn't have bunched them so close together."

Susan's teeth ground together. Two dozen ship-killers was ten percent of her offensive missile capacity, and they'd all just been turned into slag in a millisecond without so much as a chipped ceramoplast panel to show for it.

"Did we lose any recon platforms?" Miguel asked.

"No, sir," Mattu answered briskly. "They're easier to hide further out, so . . ."

"Thank goodness for small favors," Susan said.

"We're being hailed," Broadchurch said. "Admiral Perez asking to speak to *Ansari* Actual."

"Oh I just bet she is." Susan straightened her shoulders. "Audio only. Put her through."

"Link open, mum."

"Admiral Perez. Go ahead for *Ansari* Actual."

"This is Perez. Am I speaking to Captain Kamala?"

"I'm CO of the *Ansari*, Admiral, so yes."

"Sorry, Captain. But your video feed seems to be missing and I only know you from your file. Your voice isn't familiar to me."

"Actually, mum, we've met twice, not that I would expect you to remember. I served with you on the *Rothchild* briefly back when you were a commander and I was just an enlisted rank. We met again at a cocktail party a few months ago while *Ansari* was in for refit."

"Yes, well, I couldn't help but notice your ship is about thirty-thousand klicks away from where we expected to find you."

"We had a high-g drill scheduled. Slipped my mind, and by the time I remembered, it was too late to get a message to you. So I went ahead with it anyway, you know how important drills are for maintaining crew competency. Speaking of competency, *I* couldn't help but notice your ship bubbled in so close to where you thought we would be that if we *had* been there, we'd be putting out fires and bleeding atmosphere right now. Those of us who weren't puking and or shitting their guts out."

Behind her, Nesbit audibly sucked air through his teeth at the breach of professional etiquette and protocol, but Susan ignored him.

"How colorful," Perez resumed. "Yes, my navigation officer does seem to have let some calibrations slip in his gravimetric modeling for this system. He will be disciplined for the near miss, I assure you."

"What a happy coincidence our mutual oversights canceled each out, then," Susan said acidly.

"Quite. But now I'm afraid I have much less happy news to share."

"And that would be?"

Everyone in the CIC leaned forward a fraction, as if getting closer to the speakers would drag the admiral's words out of them faster.

"It is my sad duty to report that you and your entire command have been recalled to the Admiralty House, where you will await court-martial under the CCDF Charter."

Susan let the blow land invisibly. Now was not the time to lose her nerve in front of the officers and enlisted under her care.

"May I ask under what charge is this court-martial being convened, Admiral?" she asked matter-of-factly.

"Dereliction of duty."

"That's a *very* serious charge, Admiral."

"I'm a very serious officer, Captain.

"Mum, *Paul Allen*'s CiWS just went hot," Mattu whispered as loudly as she could. "Support ships', too."

Susan nodded acknowledgement. "CiWS, Perez? I thought we were having a conversation."

"Don't think I didn't notice your defensive systems are active."

"Lots of rocks get tossed around this far out in the system," Susan said vaguely. "What evidence do you have to support your accusation of dereliction?"

"Your own confession, Captain Kamala. Did you not record and submit a report via skip drone detailing how you not only failed to destroy an enemy vessel that had violated the treaty line against explicit orders that have been in force for seventy years, but rendered it aid? That's treason, Captain. I'm frankly shocked that you made me spell it out for you."

Susan's jaw flexed. With effort, she kept her tone even. "The vessel in question had been disabled in an onboard accident that nearly proved catastrophic. Under the circumstances, I decided that—"

Admiral Perez's voice jumped in and angrily cut her off. "I wasn't sent out here to litigate this with you, Kamala. I came to take you in. You and your crew are hereby placed under arrest under Article II, Section XI of the CCDF Charter. You will surrender your command and order your crew to assemble in the small craft bay where you will all be processed and transferred to a holding area we have set up for you on the *Allen*'s hangar deck under marine guard."

"And the *Ansari*?" Susan asked.

"We have a skeleton crew aboard waiting to take control to bring her back to port. Your crew will wipe all of your biometrics and passcodes and reset everything to factory default."

Susan sighed and leaned to one side of her chair. "That's no good for me."

"I beg your pardon?" Perez said incredulously.

"If you'll keep reading the Charter, you'll come to Article II, Section XXVI, which specifically forbids collective punishment of crew members following the orders of their superiors in good faith."

"That does not apply to times of war."

"With due respect, Admiral, we *prevented* a time of war."

"You destroyed one of their fleet tenders in open space! That's an act of war."

Susan laughed. "Aren't you being a duplicitous little minx. Yeah, we totally did that. But we did it smart so the Xre couldn't pin it on us, not officially. So, we're right back to where we were. You want my ass in a sling over this? Fine, I surrender, officially as of this moment and turn command over to my XO. He will take *Ansari* wherever you order him to. But only with her crew intact. You want to quote The Book at me? Great, then we do things by The Book, or not at all."

The line went silent for a long, long, very uncomfortably long time.

"Is it still open?" Susan whispered to Mattu, who nodded.

"I want you on a shuttle in no more than ten minutes, Captain," Perez's voice broke back in at last. "And you will transmit, with video, confirmation that you are aboard once it's reached safe maneuvering distance. No tricks or stupid horseplay, or my task group will have to force the issue. Do we *perfectly* understand each other, Captain?"

"I'm certain we do. Ten minutes. Kamala out." She made a slashing gesture and Mattu cut the link. Susan stood from her chair for the last time. "Miguel, you're in command. Follow Admiral Perez's orders to the letter, no matter how humiliating or punitive they may seem. Just get my . . . your ship and our people safely back to port. Worry about the rest later."

"Mum. You're not actually going over there?" he asked with a haunted face, like he was looking at a ghost.

"I most certainly am."

"The hell you are. They'll shoot you down the second you're out the launch bay doors."

"She wouldn't dare."

"She just tried to turn us to goo not ten minutes ago and you're giving her the benefit of the doubt?" Miguel shouted.

"Don't raise your voice to me in my CIC, XO," Susan said, smoldering.

"With respects, mum, but it's not your CIC anymore. You just handed me the baton. Everyone else heard that, right?" A round of nod and affirmations went around the room. "See?"

"Don't you monkeys get it?" Susan threw her hands out. "I'm trying to keep from implicating you. All of you. I'm protecting you."

Miguel crossed his arms. "And we're protecting you. You can get on that shuttle, but I won't give it clearance to leave."

Susan stared at him with an infuriating mix of rage, admiration, exasperation, gratitude, and desire. All of which jockeyed for dominance until they all effectively killed each other, leaving her with resignation.

"We seem to be at an impasse, and the clock is running. What do you suggest?"

Miguel's hazel eyes brightened. "I'm glad you asked." He reached for the coms circuit and brought up the boat bay. "Sergeant Okuda, have you been listening in?"

"Yes, sir."

"Good. I want you to prep one of your scary black stealth assault shuttles for prisoner transport. With a full complement of marine guards. Our captain is a dangerous fugitive, after all. Very crafty. You have five minutes to prep."

"What about the standard shuttle they're already prepping down here?"

"You'll be following it at a discreet distance, and it will be remotely piloted from here."

"I want to go on record to say this is lunacy," Nesbit said.

"Noted, CL."

Seven minutes later, two shuttles launched from the *Ansari*'s boat bay. One running full IFF, active radar/lidar, and even blinking white, red, and green nav lights, while the other hid in the shadows of the first. Utterly, deadly silent.

Twenty-three minutes after that, the lead shuttle exploded into a shower of jagged, red-hot fragments under the assault of the *Carnegie*'s point defense lasers, swatted away like a house fly.

Miguel's eyes flared with incandescent fury at the betrayal by ships, by personnel, of his own fleet. Fellow spacers who'd taken the same oath to defend the worlds of man and their patron companies as he had. Men and women who, as far as *they* knew, had just executed a fellow officer without the trial due to her. The fact they were mistaken did absolutely nothing to blunt the sharp edge of his rage.

"Weapons officer," his voice smoldered.

"Sir?" Lieutenant Warner answered, her voice uncertain, not yet recovered from the emotional shock of the unexpected violence.

"Overkill something."

Warner's face keened into an ax. "With style, sir."

Her purpose restored, Warner's fingers danced and jabbed at icons, activating every offensive weapon and defensive system the *Ansari* mounted, lighting up the surrounding vacuum with a constellation of laser pulses, radar, electronic jamming, and fusion plumes like a stellar nursery.

With that, the *real* Battle of Grendel was underway.

The first shot came from the *Ansari*'s offensive laser array. Despite the distance, the beam reached out and linked up with a monocle drone Mattu had snuck into position at the first whiff of suspicion. The multi-gigawatt beam had diffused from thirty centimeters to more than ten meters by the time it reached the meta-material lens. But once it exited, it had refocused to nearly its initial width and concentration. A few thousand kilometers later, it slammed into the forward port quadrant of the heavy cruiser *Carnegie*, melting through a phased radar array, gamma ray telescope, and a point defense laser cluster before chewing through another two meters of ablative ceramoplast armor to vaporize a reaction control thruster propellant tank and two spinal-mount railgun capacitor coils in the ensuing secondary explosion.

A hell of a good start, but the IR signature of so much transfer energy passing through the monocle couldn't be absorbed or radiated fast enough and gave away its position. It died a moment later, snuffed out by an answering laser it couldn't catch from the wounded cruiser.

But, they still had *two more of them*, waiting in the black.

"Deploy decoys. I want them activated the millisecond they're out of the tubes. Light up our deployed ship-killers and target *Carnegie* with the first volley."

"Not the *Allen*?" Warner asked.

"No, we can't saturate their CiWS until we put out that cruiser's eyes. And we have at least a chance of swarming *their* point defense."

"Yes, sir."

"In the meantime, burn another monocle. That last shot was a beauty."

"Yes, sir."

"And Charts? Bring us into position to bring our captain back onboard!"

"She's angling away, XO," Mattu said.

"She's what?" Miguel's head swiveled from the Drone Integration Station back up to the main plot. Sure enough, the IFF icon for the captain's shuttle had altered course, taking it away from *Ansari* under maximum clandestine thrust. "Is she trying to get clear of our gooey zone in case we blow a bubble?"

"She's already cleared minimum safe distance, sir, and still accelerating," Broadchurch answered.

"Where the hell does she think she's going?"

"*Carnegie*'s returning fire," Mattu barked. "Multiple missile launches detected. Showing one-five contacts. Will be clear for maneuvering in three seconds."

Miguel's face twisted up. "They're only launching them now?"

"Confirmed, sir. EM spike signature matches *Mosaic*-class heavy cruiser launch rails."

Miguel shook his head. They hadn't even floated missiles back before they entered the *Ansari*'s sensor envelope. Now his defensive systems would have a hard track on them from tube-to-target, sending hit probabilities through the roof. Overconfident, inexperienced idiots couldn't even plan a proper ambush with a seven-to-one tonnage advantage. They'd expected the captain to follow orders and surrender the ship without resistance in the face of such overwhelming force. That plan out the window, they were improvising a battleplan, and it showed.

Ansari was still outside the effective range of *Carnegie*'s laser array, who obviously hadn't bothered to launch a monocle drone, either. So, for at least a little while, all they had to worry about was swatting missiles out of the black. Miguel looked at the icon for the captain's shuttle as it piled on meters per second headed off on whatever harebrained assignment Susan had picked for them. It was out of his hands now. His job was to make sure she had a ship to come back to.

"Weapons, get a new flight of ship-killers in the vac. Charts, Scopes, line us up with a monocle and give *Carnegie* another beam. Double pudding if you can jam it right down the hole we just made. Get the decoys maneuvering. And somebody swat those bugs!"

"Holy shit!" the pilot cursed from his seat on the flight deck.

"SitRep!" Susan barked. The same flight data feed the shuttle's crew had was being shunted into her own augmented reality environ, but it was diverted so drastically from the tactical maps she was used to in the CIC that she couldn't interpret half of what it tried to tell her.

"The decoy shuttle just exploded, mum! Brace! Brace! Brace!"

Before she could respond, the pilot threw the shuttle into a high-g turn that nearly crushed her spine. An image of the shuttle's cockpit disintegrating into fire and shrapnel as it careened into its doomed sister played across Susan's imagination even as all the color drained away from her vision. Her suit automatically constricted around her legs and abdomen, pushing blood back into her torso and brain, struggling to keep her conscious against the onslaught of artificial gravity.

Then, as suddenly as the weight had slammed down on her, it disappeared, then reversed. The ceiling became the floor as Susan's full weight and a lot more dug into her shoulder straps. Even under the pressure, Susan felt two distinct pulses through her crash harness. Whether they were impacts from debris or weapons fire, she couldn't say. Not that there was much difference between a bolt and a bullet at these velocities.

"Fuck me," Okuda bit off to Susan's right, a sentiment she shared in its entirety.

The thrust cut off without warning again, leaving them on the float. Susan hadn't experienced maneuvering that violent since simulated spaceflight training back in C school.

"Are we clear?" she shouted up to the cockpit.

"Clear of the decoy's wreckage, yes mum. We've taken light damage to our adaptive camo."

"Have they spotted us?"

"I think they have bigger problems." The pilot grimaced. "*Ansari* just opened fire."

"On a planetary assault carrier battle group?" Okuda asked incredulously. "Is the XO *insane*?"

"No, but he's damned good and pissed. And so am I. Pilot, get us clear of their lines of fire. Has he launched missiles yet?"

"Plumes just went hot, mum. Burning for the lead cruiser. Oh hell, *Ansari* just scored a laser hit on the *Carnegie*."

"Good, do what you can to obscure your drive plume behind our outgoing ship killers. Make your way for the frigate at full clandestine burn."

"We're not rendezvousing with *Ansari*?" Okuda asked.

Susan looked back at the hold full of her marines in full battle rattle and smiled.

"Not just yet. Who's up for a boarding action?"

TWENTY-FIVE

"They're firing on each other, Derstu," Kivits said, mandibles loose, sitting at the husk alcove like he'd just been punched in the mouth.

"They're doing *what*?" Thuk asked, a green leaf still dangling out of his own mouthparts.

"They're throwing everything, light-spears, javelins; they're not close enough for sling bolts, but . . ."

"Who shot first?"

"The newcomers, but not at the *Ansari,* at the shuttle they launched. It was destroyed, utterly. Then the *Ansari* lit up the dark ocean like Ancestor's Day."

"Transfer to the display. Go back up the timestream to the first shot."

Kivits did so, and the tactical situation their hidden husks observed was fed into the ring of solid light around the mind cavern. It was as Kivits had said. The middle-sized ship, likely one of the *Mosaic*-class heavy cruisers that had been in CCDF service for twenty-five cycles now from its profile, had destroyed a shuttle with its claws. *Ansari* answered almost instantaneously with an all-out barrage of javelins, still in flight, and light-spears. One of which struck home on the newly declared enemy *Mosaic* cruiser with spectacular effect.

Thuk unexpectedly found himself pounding the armrest of his chair with a midarm in triumph at the shot, as if his own harmony had landed the blow themselves. But reality quickly settled back in. No matter if the hit was luck or skill, in the final tactical analysis, it wasn't going to swing the balance in favor of a single ship against three aggressors, two of which out-massed and out-clawed the defender. *Ansari* was fighting a valiant, courageous, and utterly doomed battle against a vastly superior foe.

Exactly what he would have expected from Captain Susan. But to what end?

"What in the abyss is going on over there?" Hurg pleaded.

"Seven Sacrifices," Kivits swore. "They're protecting us."

"Explain," Thuk said.

"Isn't it obvious?" Kivits pointed at the crushing weight of the enemy force converging on the *Ansari*. "They came as soon as they received that messenger husk to meet up with Susan's ship to either capture or kill us. She refused. Now they're going to kill her for it, then come after us. She's purchasing time for us to escape with her ship and her life."

"That's a pretty big swing in your estimation of our new friends, Kivits," Thuk admonished.

Kivits pointed a blood-claw at the *Ansari*'s icon, even as it swatted away incoming javelins. "I may be prejudiced, but I'm not blind, Thuk."

"Hurg, get Lynz on the mouth immediately."

"Lynz here," the three-legged attendant's voice said as if through water. He was still on the outer hull, then.

"Attendant, it's Thuk. I need to spin a seedpod and I need to do it right now."

"We're sewing up the last of the coils now, Derstu."

"Good. Finish up, to Abyss with the plating, and let me know the moment your people are in the lockouts. Thuk out."

"We're making our escape, then?" Kivits asked hopefully. "We can't let Susan's sacrifice be for nothing."

"No," Thuk said, wrath building in his abdomen, pushing out against his plates until it felt as if he might burst at the joints. "No, we will not."

Matching velocity and course with a squirrelly patrol/escort frigate executing combat maneuvers was difficult, even for a shuttle. Doing so without breaking stealth and being detected by said frigate's sensor crew should have been impossible.

But the flight crew piloting Susan's shuttle had a few advantages unavailable to the average hostile. The copilot had served on one of the *Halcyon*'s sister ships in their last rotation and knew all sorts of interesting things about the class's sensor coverage. At close ranges, local EM interference and wave-cancellation effects caused gaps in the various radar and lidar arrays. Pilots were trained to avoid these blind spots to stay within the space control officer's awareness. Instead, the crew used the gaps to hide from prying eyes.

Further, the people operating the sensors onboard *Halcyon* weren't looking for a SpecOps shuttle, but were very intently focused on swapping spitballs with the *Ansari*. Susan had risked a quantum-coded burst transmission via whisker laser back to Miguel in the CIC to tell him they were about to link up and would you please stop shooting at the *Halcyon*. He obeyed without sending an acknowledgement, giving them a narrow window to risk the boarding dock without having to worry about getting cored by friendly fire, or their target suddenly going into evasive maneuvers to dodge a warhead.

Now, they were less than a minute away from docking with a CCDF warship in the first blue-on-blue hostile boarding action in the history of the fleet. The gravity of the situation was not lost on the marines.

"Last chance, people," Okuda barked. "As of now, we're all still on firm legal footing. We were just the security detail delivering our rogue captain to the proper authorities. We'd already launched when the shooting started, and played no part in the XO's decision to return fire. But!" Okuda held up a gauntleted finger, then pointed at the inner airlock door. "The second we walk through that hatch, we're mutineers, deserters, traitors, and a whole list of creative expletives yet to be written. Anyone who isn't ready for that, speak up now!"

The assembled marines looked around the cabin. Susan hadn't spent enough time down in grunt country to know if they were looking for the first domino to fall, or applying peer pressure to anyone who might be vacillating.

One private cleared his throat and raised an arm.

"You have something to say, Culligan?" Okuda said.

The young man squared his jaw, but looked at Susan directly. "I'm sorry, mum. I have no objection to what you're doing. But my big sister is on the *Halcyon,* and I don't—I mean, if I had to . . ." He began to tear up, droplets floating away from his face in the zero g.

Susan grabbed a handhold, swung over to the private, and squeezed his upper arm. "Okuda?"

"Yes, mum?"

"We need someone to hold back and guard the shuttle so we don't get cut off if we need an emergency evac." It was a polite fiction. Once the *Halcyon's* crew knew they were inside, falling back to the shuttle just meant they'd be swatted out of space with CiWS like an oversized gnat as soon as they got far enough away for a clean firing arc. But neither was she going to put a nineteen-year-old in a position where he might have to shoot his own sibling.

Picking up on the thread, Okuda played along. "Culligan, you're pulling guard duty for the shuttle. Keep our backsides clear. Understood?"

"Yes, ma'am," the private said brightly.

"And nobody's going to say a fucking word about it to him later, right?"

"No, ma'am!" clapped back the rest of the platoon.

"Good! Our objective is the CIC. Deck schematics have already been loaded into your VRs. Watch your doors and corners, and avoid long hallways whenever you can. ROE is if they have weapon in hand, light them up like Times Square on New Year's. Noncombatants to be bound with zip-strips and secured in place. There aren't enough of us to babysit and they can wait a couple hours until we can get back to them. If they piss their pantaloons before then, too bad. Any questions?"

None were forthcoming.

"Excellent! Now, who's ready to take this tin-can piece of shit away from the motherfuckers trying to blow up our house?"

"OOHRAH!"

"Outstanding! Final kit check. Double-check weapons and suit seals. If they're smart, they'll get in skin suits and pump out the air in case we start poking holes in that cardboard-thick hull if the shooting starts. Trigger discipline. Anyone fires a round before we contact armed resistance, I'll shoot you in the knee."

"Taking out their whisker laser," the shuttle's gunner said from the flight deck. Outside, a 37 mm autocannon put a single, expertly placed round into the small swelling at the base of the *Halcyon*'s coms laser. The shot didn't destroy the lens, but it did take out its data bus. Both easier to repair, and more likely to be believed as collateral damage from the tens of thousands of high-speed shrapnel fragments flying around the battle space. As soon as they docked, the shuttle would begin pumping out high-frequency jamming to neutralize the frigate's omnidirectional.

"Ten seconds to docking," the copilot announced over the intercom. "Brace, brace, brace!"

The marines in their power-assisted armor gripped their handholds and footholds and locked their suits into place. It was as good as being strapped down hard into a crash harness, so long as the capacitors held a charge.

Susan was not qualified in the marine's exosuits, and was decked out instead in a flexible skinsuit with built-in trauma plates covering her core, and flexible, impact-hardening fibrous armor rated for small arms covering the rest of her. It had no power assistance, and if anyone pointed much more than a handgun at her in anger, she may as well salute them and say her prayers to Shiva. It also meant that at the call from the flight deck, she had only a few seconds to get herself into one of the chairs along the wall and bring the harness down over her shoulders and torso.

The pulsing proximity tone of the shuttle's built-in anticollision lidar beeped from the cockpit ever faster until it merged into a single, uninterrupted tone. The deck jolted underfoot as the energy of impact with the relatively huge *Halcyon* reverberated through the shuttle's bones.

"Solid lock," the copilot said. "Board is green."

"Go, go, go!" Okuda shouted into the com as Susan struggled to get out of her crash harness. The outer airlock door swung inward, revealing a fleet standard emergency evacuation hatch bearing the stenciled moniker CCDF HALCYON: FF-109.

Susan's breath caught in her throat. Everything came down to the next two seconds. On her order, the pilot would ping the *Halcyon*'s computer system with an emergency code. All airlocks and external evacuation hatches on CCDF ships could be overrode using a fleet-standard emergency code that rotated every few months along with routine software updates. The code was uniform across all ships to facilitate search-and-rescue teams responding to disasters so they didn't have to worry about interfacing with a ship's central computer system while the fires were burning.

If no one onboard *Halcyon* had thought to change or block the code, and there was no reason they should because no one had ever tried to use it *offensively* before, the hatch would pop open and Susan's marines would swarm inside like angry wasps. If someone had, well . . .

Susan exhaled. "Pilot, send the code."

On command, the evac hatch sank fifteen centimeters and rolled into the space between hull layers to make way for the search-and-rescue team that wasn't coming. Okuda wasted no time on celebrations and pushed off into enemy territory, managing the transition from zero g to grav plating like a seasoned professional. The rest of the platoon followed like a river cutting its way to the sea.

Susan held back, after mutually agreeing to Okuda's demands that she stay on the shuttle until they'd secured a beachhead. She took the opportunity to type out a text-only order to Miguel to change *Ansari*'s hatch codes immediately in case anyone on the *Carnegie* or *Paul Allen* figured out the trick and felt inspired.

"Beach is clear, mum," Okuda's voice came over her suit helmet's com. Susan got up from her seat and nodded to Private Culligan as she passed.

"Watch my ass, Private."

"Eyes on, mum."

Susan winked at him and drifted the short distance to the *Halcyon*, stumbling only a little as she passed into the local gravity.

There wasn't time to dawdle. At only twelve vertical decks and seventeen thousand metric tons, the *Zephyr*-class fast frigate was just about as small as it was possible for a crewed warship to be. It didn't even mount a third redundant Alcubierre ring as all other military ships did. Little more than a triple cluster of fusion rockets, a modestly sized A/M reserve, a handful of recon drones and offensive missile cells, and low-volume life support system, it traded firepower, survivability, and endurance for raw speed. It was designed more for shore patrol duties in developed systems, fast enough to chase down smugglers, tariff-jumpers, and corsair ships with just enough teeth to force compliance or finish them off. In a fleet support role, it acted as an area-denial weapon and enhanced recon platform, with a focus on extended fire coordination for the rest of the task group.

All of which meant the crew complement was small enough to be manageable for the force Susan brought to the party, but also that their response time now that they knew unwanted guests were aboard would be short. It would be a symbolic victory at best, but it was the only of the three ships in the task force Susan's marines had any chance of capturing without getting scraped off the bottom of the crew's boots, so here they were.

"Stay out of the lift tubes," Okuda told her marines. "Stick to crew ladders."

This was met with a collective groan as everyone assembled envisioned climbing one-handed up a ladder while holding an assault rifle in the other, but Okuda was having none of it. "Secure the whining. That's the deal. I'll go first so none of you frilly blouses have to wrinkle yourselves. Mum, in the middle where we can keep an eye on you, if you please."

"Yes, Mother." Susan said to a round of hesitant laughter. "C'mon, grunts, this isn't *your* funeral!"

That had the desired effect. Okuda slung her rifle and pulled a sidearm from the breastplate holster of her armor and galloped up the nearest crew ladder. Not wanting to be shown up by their old lady, several marines followed in rapid fire. A second fire team settled for another crew ladder a little further down the hall to give flanking cover to the first team.

"Mum, if you'll follow me?" a random marine whose name Susan hadn't memorized asked.

"After you, Sergeant."

They made it three full decks before meeting resistance, but when they finally did, it hit fast, and it hit hard.

"Contact left!" Okuda shouted into the secure com link, but she'd spotted it a split second too late. As expected, the *Halcyon's* crew had evacuated the atmosphere below the CIC deck in hopes of slowing the intruders down. The marines' powered armor had a limited self-sealing capacity for bullet punctures, but large tears from fragmentation grenades, debris, or knives would still force whole limb sections of their suits into tunicate mode at the nearest joint to prevent embolisms from causing a stroke in the victim's brain.

Which is why no one heard the first antipersonnel mine go off. It was a bold introduction.

"Man down! Suppressive fire! My right!" The rhythmic staccato of automatic weapons fire vibrated through the corridor despite the vacuum as Okuda drove her personal answer to the ambush home with bloody intention. Soon, an entire fire team's worth of frangible boarding rounds joined in from behind her at eight hundred beats per minute. Whomever had set off the mine disappeared into a fine red mist before they could shit themselves.

But they weren't alone. The *Halcyon*'s reduced contingent of marines opened up from three angles in three dimensions. They were just a single fire team, but they had the advantage of picking the place and time of the fight, and they were defending their home turf, which made each and every one of them incredibly dangerous.

"Two can play at that game," Okuda said. "Fall back, we need a new angle on them."

"What about Chu?" someone called.

"His suit'll pinch off the bleeding until we get to him. Unless anyone volunteers for that wood chipper?"

No volunteers presented themselves.

"Right. Break into pairs. Cover each other on opposite sides of the halls, pick a ladder and get climbing, two levels up. We're coming *down* on these asshats."

It took almost ten minutes of sneaking around, disabling hastily placed booby traps, and swapping bullets before Okuda's forces got into position to flush out the defenders. They were dug in well and wearing power-assisted armor only a generation behind what her marines had brought over. Secondhand stuff passed down from "frontline" units, but well-maintained and damned near as effective. Normal nonlethal options were therefore off the table, as their suits had safeguards against the blinding/deafening effects of flashbang grenades, and were sealed against tear or knockout gas canisters.

"Okay, we're set. Vasquez, Ingersoll, spring the trap in five, four . . ."

"Wait," Susan cut in. "Give them a chance to surrender."

"But we've got them dead to rights!"

"Yes, exactly. You've got them over a barrel. They're marines just like you, defending their home. Give them the option to stand down. If they don't take it, by all means. But we *will* make the offer. We're not killing our own if we can help it."

Okuda looked like she had more to say, but swallowed it and opened an unsecured, general announcement channel common across all marine coms.

"*Halcyon* marines, this is Sergeant Okuda of the *Ansari*. You're outnumbered, outgunned, and trapped in a tactically indefensible position. Clear your weapons, place them on the deck, deactivate any mines you may have set up, and you will not be harmed."

"Like you didn't harm Aoki?" one of them shot back. "She didn't feel it, at least."

"I've got a man probably bleeding out two decks down, so if you're looking for an apology, you're barking up the wrong tree, son. I'm feeling charitable, I'm giving you the chance to walk away from this. If not, I'm going to blow you up with grenades so you don't get the satisfaction of taking any more of my people with you. Either way, we're taking your CIC in the next five minutes. When that happens, you can be captives or corpses. Your call. Nine . . ."

"All right, you crazy bitch!"

"Who are you calling a 'bitch'?" Okuda demanded, but Susan put a hand on her shoulder.

"Small victories, Sarge. We have what we want."

"Right. Sorry, went a little sixth wave for a second there." Okuda resumed the 'negotiation.' "Slide your weapons out onto the open deck, hands in the air, come out where we can see you."

A handful of assault rifles and PDWs scattered against the deck, followed in close succession by sidearms and three remote detonator rigs. Susan had to hand it to them; for a small squad with zero prep time, the *Halcyon*'s marines had come to play.

"Awesome, now let's see you," Okuda commanded. "And no grabby-grabby for the pew-pews. I'll grant you might be as fast as us. You're not faster, clear?"

Reluctantly, the three remaining members of the *Halcyon*'s marine detachment walked out onto the hallway, hands in the air, right into the line of fire of Okuda's team. If any of them so much as sneezed, they'd all be turned into hamburger.

They didn't.

"Excellent. Now, we're new here, so I need someone to be my captain's tour guide of your CIC. Volunteers?"

"Kamala's *alive*?" the voice from the other end of the link said. It belonged to a young PFC, Korean ancestry if Susan was any judge. She stepped into the corridor in full sight of everyone.

"Yes, I am. And I'd like to have a cup of tea with your CO, if you don't mind."

TWENTY-SIX

"Splash one," Warner called out as a penetrator rod from one of *Ansari*'s counter-missiles connected with the nose cone of a ship-killer missile gobbling up the space between them. "CM reserves down to twenty-four percent. Wait, splash two. Caught another in the debris. Six still incoming."

"See, Warner, you're not the only one to bunch her birds too close together." Miguel scanned the plot. The system-spanning display had shrunk down to a sphere only a few light minutes across, a tactical map that contained only the *Ansari, Halcyon, Carnegie, Paul Allen,* and all the missiles, recon drones, and decoys they were currently throwing at each other. The civilian fleet over Grendel was almost certainly gone by now, and had no interest in joining a fracas between proper warships anyway. The only X-factor not on the current plot was the *Chusexx,* and last they'd seen, Thuk's harmony was burning away from the melee as fast as they could. Lucky bugs.

"Angle Decoy Two away at positive thirty degrees from the eclectic under full accel. Make it look like we panicked and bolted. Maybe draw a couple of those birds off us."

"Decoy Two helm no longer responding to commands, sir."

Fuck, Miguel cursed internally. They were burning through resources at an unsettling pace. They were still alive, but more than two hours into the fight, they weren't inflicting enough damage to stay that way for long. Wars of attrition favored those with the most crap lying around to lose. There was a lot of crap on a planetary assault carrier.

"Move to Decoy One, then."

"Too late. Incoming birds entering terminal phase!"

Miguel punched a finger on the stud that opened the 1MC. "All hands, Brace! Brace! Brace!"

Three of the incoming ship-killers fell to the combined last-ditch efforts of their CiWS turrets, and another to an overpowered shot from the *Ansari*'s main laser array, which had been co-opted momentarily from offensive operations by the ship's onboard defensive AI network, which was just as motivated to continue existing as any of the human occupants. Missile number five turned out to be a dud, wasting its nuclear warhead with a malfunctioning implosion trigger.

The last, however, had sharper teeth.

A funny thing about nuclear weapons and the vacuum of space was, absent the atmosphere necessary to carry the thermal shock wave, nukes weren't nearly as destructive. Instead of mushroom clouds, their megatons created a powerful EMP effect, which all modern combat warships were well-shielded against, and an intense burst of gamma rays, which they were less so. The spike plate that redirected the gamma radiation created by a ship's M/AM reactor kept the crew alive, but also carried one of the highest mass penalties onboard. Coating the entire ship in that degree of armor plating would make it so slow and cumbersome as to be useless in combat. The ancient calculation of mobility versus safety was as alive as ever.

But while enough gamma rays were of concern to the squishy components of a ship's crew, they posed very little danger to its hardware. That is, unless it's concentrated. Which was why when the hydrogen bomb at the core of the *Carnegie*'s missile detonated, its energies were, for an almost imperceptible moment, partially constrained and directed through a uranium outer casing that channeled nearly a third of the energy into a coherent stream, most easily understood as a gamma ray laser, even though that's not what it was at all.

For one hundred and thirty-nine microseconds, this stream of gamma rays poured out of their dying mother and streaked across the short distance separating them from the *Ansari* before crashing into their target at ninety-nine-point-nine-repeating-percent light-speed. The effect was immediate and devastating.

Warning klaxons and flashing red error codes filled the CIC like a Finados Day parade marching through Rio. "Damage report!" Miguel shouted over the din.

"Still coming in," Warner answered. "We have a main electrical bus fused, J-12 coupling. Rerouting. Probably an overloaded circuit. We can't have been hit in the hulls or we'd be venting."

"Beta ring is cored," Broadchurch announced. "Totally dead. Safeties have already kicked in and purged the negative matter stores from the entire ring." They switched their feed to an external camera. "Damn. A whole ring segment is slag. Direct hit."

"No chance of repair?" Miguel asked, despite knowing the answer.

"Not without a yard berth."

"Doubt we're in line for one of those anytime soon. Jettison it."

"Jettison beta ring, aye." Broadchurch swiped through two screens and entered a command code to satisfy a system prompt that they really did want to cut an entire ring loose. At the push of a virtual button, explosive bolts at three points in the beta ring and in the three struts that connected it to the engineering hull detonated, sending the remains of the ruined ring tumbling away from the *Ansari*. Lose another, and they'd be unable to blow a bubble, effectively stranding them in system. But they had more immediate problems now, and slimming down the ship's mass by almost ten thousand tons meant just that much more speed and maneuverability for whatever fight was still ahead.

Miguel refocused on the task at hand. "Scopes, how long until we get another monocle shot lined up on *Carnegie*?"

"Seven-three seconds, if they don't do anything clever. Wait one . . . what the shit?"

Miguel held his hands outstretched. "In your own time, Scopes!"

"We're getting whisker laser telemetry from our shuttle on *Halcyon*," Mattu said, tears forming at the corners of her eyes. "They're streaming us realtime updates on the birds coming from *Carnegie* and *Allen*. Weps, check this shit out." Mattu shunted the new data feed over to Warner's station.

Warner pumped a fist in the air. "I've got their birds' entire flight profiles. I can shoot them down like wounded ducks!"

She did it, Miguel realized. *The crazy* puta *did it. Susan is sitting in their CIC, feeding us all the data a forward observer would be tasked with handling.* They'd just evened up in the unit count, two to two. Nevermind that each of their ships were out-massed. They were faster, nimbler. He pounded a fist on the armrest of his captain's chair, then stood. "Kamala is alive, people. She's taken *Halcyon* with a shuttle-full of angry jarheads and she's giving us everything we need to stay in the fight for a few more minutes. Don't waste it. Warner, let some strays through. Don't give away that we have access to their network or they'll figure it out and turn that ratty old tin can into recycling with a salvo."

"Should I move on *Halcyon*, sir?" Broadchurch asked. "Make it look like we're charging her for an attack run, but actually bring her into our defensive envelope?"

"That's some devious double-think bullshit, Charts. I love it. What does that do to our monocle shot, Scopes?"

"Adds seventeen seconds before alignment and burns up another twenty-three percent of the drone's fuel stores."

"And is there any chance we get a second shot out of that platform?"

"None, sir, unless our flagship is supremely incompetent."

"As I thought. Charts, execute your bullshit."

"I could throw a couple of missiles at *Halcyon,* sir," Warner said. "Make it look like we're attacking them, but then hand off the fire control links and let them redirect them. They don't have very deep magazines on that tin can."

"Beautiful. Do it. Make sure *Halcyon* understands the plan before launch."

"Roger that."

Miguel fell back into the command chair. Not his, he was keeping it warm for Susan, but it's where his butt was planted for the moment. His ship was alive, against all projections and every simulated exercise the CCDF had ever run in seventy years. He was running like a squirrel from a diving falcon, but by God, in that moment, he'd never been more alive.

"Will you *please* either stop pacing the deck, or take it into the hallway?" Elsa demanded. "We have another two days in this bucket and I've only got another couple hours of self-control left."

Tyson stopped midstride at the center of their . . . modest accommodations. "Sorry. Didn't realize I was doing it."

"You were doing it for twenty minutes. Don't you travel well, a bubbler like you?"

"I don't go off-world as often as you might think, and my travel quarters are usually a bit more well-appointed." Tyson spread his arms to encompass all four square meters of their berth's floorspace, including the narrow bunk beds, the single hot plate and coffeepot with the gall to call themselves a "kitchenette," and the sink built into the tank of the compartment's toilet, that last detail being the cause of Tyson's current dehydration headache.

"What, this ore-hauler doesn't have a luxury C-level suite you could've conned your smuggler friend into handing over? Maybe rent out an entire deck so the plebs don't trouble us?"

"That would rather defeat the purpose of traveling incognito, don't you suppose? And no, there's no lavish suite."

Elsa returned her attention to the reader in her palm. Tyson was telling a fib, of course. He happened to know for certain that the Praxis-flagged bulk cargo ship they'd arranged passage on had a very nice C-level suite, because he'd stayed in it some fifteen years earlier when it had still been the *Belmont* in Ageless's merchant fleet. Now rechristened the *Taipei*, it was the same class and layout as the *Preakness* that was still under quarantine in Lazarus orbit, only a few years older.

The shared history of the two ships had not been a coincidence, but part of Daryl Cooper's devious little plot to get them out of the system undetected. Or at least undetected long enough to no longer make a difference.

The *Taipei* had been scheduled to depart for a return trip to Proxima, just a short four-light-year hop away from the Sol system. Daryl had arranged forged travel documents for Tyson and Elsa aboard the ship that would put them tantalizingly close to Ceres and the man they suspected was connected to the attacks on their persons. But the forgeries were intentionally sloppy, containing a few flags that would reveal their fake nature to a skilled investigator once someone got around to looking at them more closely.

In the meantime, the *Taipei* maneuvered herself into a mutual orbit with the *Preakness*, their approaches coming so close that their radar signatures merged and Lazarus Space Traffic Control had to issue an official citation against the Praxis Corp. crew for violating minimum safe clearance and generally sloppy ship handling.

What LSTC didn't know was in that six-second window, the two nearly identical ships had executed a *very* illegal transponder code handoff, made very slight preprogrammed changes to their drive signatures, then burned hard enough to swap courses under the guise of last-ditch collision-evasion maneuvers.

Thirty minutes later, the *"Taipei"* broke orbit and bubbled out for her appointment in Proxima, while the *"Preakness"* lazily circled the planet for another sixteen hours until the forged travel documents were discovered by a sharp eye in Customs and Immigration and the news broke in the underground that Tyson Abington had "fled" onboard the Praxis ship. Fifteen minutes after that, a small pleasure yacht, little bigger than a skip drone, filed an emergency flight plan for Proxima and bubbled out several hundred klicks short of the safety line, incurring still more fines for LSTC's coffers.

At which point, *"Preakness"* registered a new flight plan for the Teegarden system where it would ostensibly deliver relief supplies to the colony while they recovered from the plague. In reality, the *Taipei* only bubbled out a few light-weeks away from Lazarus, then plotted its true course for Grendel.

Daryl's ruse had unfolded even better than Tyson could've hoped. Not only had they gotten away undetected, but they'd managed to flush out a new lead in the registry of the yacht that chased after what they'd thought was Tyson's evacuation route. It was registered to a pair of fake accounts and run through at least one shell corp, but tracking down its true provenance was only a matter of time.

Not that the minor miracle had come cheaply. Again, Daryl Cooper hadn't asked for money. Instead, he'd negotiated for the eventual share of NeoSun's percentage of the Grendel project's profits while he had Tyson over a metaphorical barrel.

Tyson couldn't help but feel a swell of admiration for the smuggler's mind. He'd underestimated the man, in no small part because of Praxis's position in the transtellar pecking order. Now, he wondered just how much of that was a calculated ploy, and just how deep Cooper's fingers reached into how many pots. They'd pushed him down the ladder because he wasn't established money. He was uncouth and unrefined, a junker scrambling for castoffs. Not really "one of them." But instead of bristling at the insult, Daryl had taken to the role and thrived in the unique ecosystem he found himself in.

"You're not very good at waiting, are you?" Elsa said out of the blue.

"Hmm?"

"You were mumbling to yourself."

"Was I?"

"Yes. You pace, you fidget, now you're talking to yourself. Do you not know how to wait?"

Tyson considered this. "I suppose not. People are usually waiting on me, not the other way around. Most of my days are full from the moment I set a foot on the floor to the moment I collapse back into bed. I'm not used to this much down time."

"We wait in the lab all the time. Wait for cultures to grow. Wait for sequencing to finish. Wait for the centrifuge to stop. Wait for batch results. Always waiting on something."

"What do you do?"

Elsa waved her reader. "Catch up on the pro journals. Scan data sets on other experimental runs, anything to keep connected and busy."

"Is that what you're reading now?"

"Now I'm reading about a young heiress who seduces a summer intern to get back at her parents. They're currently being gymnastic in her daddy's yacht, but corsairs just showed up. He's naked and fighting them off swinging a sword at the moment."

"Further reinforcing my decision not to have children."

"Oh come on, it's a romance novel."

"Exactly. It's fiction. Believe me, it's tame compared to the reality. There's hardly a hereditary C-level family alive that aren't complete head cases after a few generations."

"Including yours?"

"There's a reason I've elected to keep it small. Dealing with my board members' families is more than enough most days."

"Christmas must be lonely."

"The company Christmas party hosts almost twenty thousand people."

"That's not the same and you know it."

"Do you have children, Doctor?"

Elsa shook her head. "No, not yet. But I play auntie to six, no wait, seven kids now. My siblings have been busy."

Tyson forced himself to sit in the cabin's only chair. A small, hard affair that encouraged anyone that sat in it for very long to stand and walk around again.

"You're right. I'm not good at waiting, mostly because I'm crap at not having any influence over events. I could go harass the bridge crew, but that won't change the laws of physics and get us to Grendel any faster. And whatever is going to happen there is probably happening right now, and there's not a damned thing I can do about it until it's all over."

TWENTY-SEVEN

On *Ansari*'s outer hull, the protective cover on one of the eighteen laser array emitters slid open, exposing the focusing lens to space. It fired, invisibly discharging quadrillions of photons into the vacuum.

Downrange, two pinpricks thousands of kilometers apart, neither visible to the unassisted human eye, drifted into alignment for the barest of moments. The stream reached the first pinprick, which adjusted its angle ever so slightly to compensate for the superior resolution its sensors provided being so close to the target.

Milliseconds later, those same photons reached the second pinprick, which had grown from a speck to the three-hundred-and-thirty-thousand-ton heavy cruiser CCDF *Carnegie*. The beam sheared through one of the three pylons supporting the cruiser's alpha ring with hardly a pause before burrowing into the engineering hull, shattering ablative ceramoplast armor before tunneling through three machinery compartments and two drone launch tubes.

"Solid hit!" Okuda shouted from her new assignment at *Halcyon*'s tactical station. "*Ansari* just took a chunk out of *Carnegie*."

"Are we still getting damage updates?" Susan asked from her

second command chair in as many hours. The *Halcyon*'s previous CO had been presented with an option between ordering her ship and crew into self-destruct to prevent Susan's takeover, or surrender. They'd elected for the latter. Except no one else in the enemy task group knew that just yet. Susan wanted to keep that particular bit of bad news under wraps as long as possible.

"Yes, mum, we're still looped into their tactical network. Damage reports coming in. No mission kill. *Carnegie* is still combat effective, but their negative matter condensers have taken critical damage. Alpha ring is dead. They can't bubble out."

Susan grimaced. It was almost worse than not having hit them at all, because without any hope of escape, the *Carnegie* had every incentive to fight to the death.

"Noted. Forward to *Ansari*. Where are those missiles Warner sent our way, Scopes?"

"Six minutes, twenty seconds out," the young officer seated at the Drone Integration Station said. She hadn't come over on Susan's shuttle. Instead, she was one of the *Halcyon*'s original crew, and sister of Okuda's marine currently securing the CIC against anyone onboard who might be considering a change of heart.

"Are we ready for the handoff, Culligan?"

"I think so." She grimaced. "I mean, yes, mum. I have the data links and command codes queued up. Just never done it while everything was moving so damned fast before."

"Don't worry, Lieutenant, I'm not sure anyone has," Susan assured her newest subordinate. "When the handoff comes, order those birds to go into erratic flight paths for two minutes. Make it look like our ECM jammed them up good and sent them spiraling. Then reacquire for the *Paul Allen* like they're moving to their secondary target priority. Let's try to keep our little secret just a few minutes longer."

"*Carnegie* just splashed the monocle," Okuda called out. That was to be expected; they were basically single-use items. "Fresh round of birds pushed out the tubes."

"I don't suppose we have any monocles aboard this bucket?"

"No, mum. Nobody expects frigates to pick fights with the big boys."

Susan smirked. Today was as good as any to rewrite centuries of books on capital ship warfare. Her new toy only added three dozen ship-killers and a half-power laser array to the fight, but critically, everyone thought they were still pointed at *Ansari*. She could use the element to take one shot. It would have to count.

"Aspect change on *Allen*," Culligan shouted. "She's blowing a bubble."

"She's running?" Okuda asked incredulously.

"I don't think so," Susan answered. Up to this point in the fight, *Carnegie* had been doing almost all the heavy lifting, while the *Allen* held back providing fire support and antimissile coverage and *Halcyon* played forward observer. But with *Carnegie* hurt, and *Ansari* making a mock attack run on *Halcyon*, Admiral Perez had almost certainly decided it was time to put the enormous PAC to more productive use. Putting herself between the two other ships in her task group and the enemy made the most tactical sense, but it would mean an almost impossibly short jump, far less risky just to punch her fusion rockets up to full military burn and get there in one piece.

Which meant . . .

"Get *Ansari* Actual on the line," Susan barked.

"Secure line, mum. Go ahead."

"Miguel!" she nearly shouted, "*Allen* is blowing a bubble, they're going to jump behind you and catch you in a flank between them and *Carnegie*."

"We see it," Miguel said through the whisker laser link after a second's delay. "Not much we can do about it. Can't charge up our own rings quick enough, not after purging our standby neg-mat in the beta ring. You'd better get ready to make your escape, mum. We'll hold them off as long as we can."

"The *hell* you will. This tin can isn't built for endurance. We can't run to the other side of this miserable system alone. We walk out of here together or not at all."

"Then may I suggest you throw the missiles I loaned you at *Carnegie* along with anything else you might have in that rust bucket before they realize you're not playing on their team anymore?"

"Acknowledged. *Halcyon* out." Susan turned to Okuda and Culligan, which was not hard in the little frigate's cramped CIC. "You heard the man, hit that cruiser with everything we've got, reprisal be damned. It's crowding my personal space."

"Urgent from Lynz," Hurg shouted across the mind cavern.

"To a mouth with it!" Thuk commanded.

Hurg nodded and pointed at the mouth nearest Thuk's seat.

"Derstu, it's Attendant Lynz."

"I know who it is, Lynz. Sing!"

"My team is in the lockout. The coil is back in sequence, but I'm still not comfortable—"

"If it fails, will anyone be around to discipline you?"

"Ah, no, Derstu. Our brains will be atoms before the first nerve impulses reach them."

"Excellent! Good work. Hold onto something." Thuk cut the link.

"We're leaving?" Kivits implored.

"We're going *somewhere,* that's for sure."

"Where, exactly?"

Thuk angrily stabbed a blood-claw at a crowded little spot in the star system's map.

"There. Get the weapon ready."

"Hits on *Carnegie!*" Mattu pumped a fist. "Multiple breaches. They're venting atmosphere. EM is dropping off. Looks like a mission kill. Yes, *Halcyon* confirms, *Carnegie* is out of the fight. They're running up the white flag and requesting recovery teams."

"Afraid we're a tad busy at the moment," Miguel said absently as he considered the plot. The *Paul Allen* had done exactly as Kamala had predicted and bubbled to their far side, completely opposite of *Carnegie*'s position in a classic pincer move. What she hadn't expected was for Perez to make the trip in four short legs, each at a right angle to the last, alternating between the PAC's fully redundant paired set of Alcubierre rings until her heading and momentum had come completely about to bring her on an intercept course with her prey instead of merely matching velocities. They were closing now, less than twenty thousand klicks apart, and it would be a lot closer by the time *Ansari* could kill her momentum and use her superior acceleration to start growing the gap again. All the while fighting off wave after wave of missiles and hundred-megawatt-range laser pulses.

It was a brilliant maneuver. If Perez had been just a little bolder, she'd have executed the jump a half an hour ago before they were in a position to knock out her escort cruiser. Not that it mattered in the final equation.

"*Halcyon* Actual reports they've been cut out of the enemy's tactical network. We're running blind again."

"Only surprise is it took them so long to figure it out. What's our magazine status?" Miguel demanded from his borrowed chair.

"Sixty-eight ship-killers still in their tubes. Twenty-seven percent on counter-missiles," Warner replied, trying to sound upbeat, but . . .

"Decoys?"

"Fuel expended," Mattu said. "They still have power for another hundred minutes or so, but they can't maneuver."

"Get them pumping out as much EM clutter as possible. And ready the retro-reflector cloud."

"Pump up the boomboxes and ready the RRC, aye, sir."

"Allen is launching birds," Warner said. "Seven-five, wait, nine-zero ship-killers inbound. Twenty-three minutes to impact."

Ninety missiles. Miguel rubbed a hand on his brow, surprised to find sweat accumulating there. Almost a fifth of the PAC's full complement in one go. They didn't have the data links to control that many birds, but they didn't need to. The point was saturation. Warner's opposite would slave them together in groups of two or three, randomly trading individuals between groups to keep *Ansari*'s CiWS and counter missiles guessing about their movement and behavior. Out of that flock, only one or two needed to connect to finish the job.

The battle had entered its third hour, and the laws of attrition were taking an awful toll. It was a credit to everyone aboard that they'd lasted so long against such vastly superior firepower, but the end was in sight.

"Options?"

Mattu was first to answer. "Kill the engines, go EM dark, reel out our towed sensor buoy and crank it to full active, turn our broadside into the attack to give us our best sensor coverage and bring the most CiWS batteries and counter-missile tubes to bear, deploy the RRC, then pray to Brahma."

"No," Warner cut in. "Turn away from the attack, go to emergency burn, antimatter be damned. Gives us another couple minutes to engage them and forces the missiles to waste more time and fuel maneuvering to hit us on our flanks or be burned up in our fusion plume. We can still dangle the towed array to see through our own exhaust, and if any missiles try to go up our skirt, we'll see it coming and can vector thrust to roast them." She thought for a moment. "But I do agree with praying."

"To Brahma?" Miguel asked.

"I'm willing to audition new gods for miracle duty at this point."

Miguel grimaced. He wanted to run simulations on both

ideas and see which came out better, but by the time he had, any advantage gained would likely be lost courtesy of the delay anyway. He made a snap judgment, pure instinct.

"Charts, turn and burn. Emergency flank speed away from the *Allen*. Tell *Halcyon* to get ahead of us and stay there. Scopes, deploy our tethered array once we're on our new course. Be ready to disperse the RRC in a halo around us once the birds are five thousand klicks out. I want them to see nothing but our fusion torches and their own radar reflections."

It had the advantage of simplicity. The retro-reflector cloud was about as last-ditch as countermeasures got. Nothing more than a constellation of hundreds of thousands of tiny Mylar origami cubes that snapped open as soon as they were clear of their containers, the reflectors' unique geometry returned any light or radiation back to its point of origin, no matter the angle of incoming vector. The more energy they pumped into active sensors trying to get a lock, the more they'd blind themselves in the glare.

Trouble was, they blinded defender's and attacker's active scans alike. They also blew any hope of stealth and basically acted like flipping on a giant searchlight for any ship inside active sensor range, no matter how primitive. Launching them was the naval combat equivalent of going all in and hoping to get a flush draw on the river card. Which, if Miguel was honest, was probably better odds than what they were really facing.

The floor swayed subtly as the great ship spun around on its own center of gravity to point its cluster of fusion rockets at the approaching nuclear maelstrom. The flip complete, Broadchurch put the throttle through the bulkhead. Miguel gained a few kilos until the grav generator adjusted to the acceleration.

"We're burning," Broadchurch said. "One hundred percent, antimatter reserve going down like a bride on her wedding night." Despite their anxiety, or perhaps because of it, everyone in the CIC turned to give Broadchurch the side eye. "Or so I've heard," they said.

"Towed array free of its cradle and spooling out, eleven kilometers a minute," Mattu said. "It's going to be a couple minutes before it's far enough away from the fusion rockets to get any meaningful data. RRC primed and ready for launch."

"It's going to be hell aiming our counter-missiles in that soup," Warner said.

"It's going to be hell aiming their birds, too," Miguel answered.

"Yes, sir."

Mattu glanced down and queried an alert on her station. "*Halcyon* has acknowledged and is moving ahead into our sensor shadow."

Miguel actually sighed in relief. He'd expected Susan to argue the point. If she was any less stubborn, she'd blow a bubble and get clear of this mess, but at least she wasn't insisting on remaining exposed to enemy fire. Apparently, an utter deluge of nuclear missiles while sitting inside a jumped-up yacht was enough to contain even her indignation.

Miguel smiled at the thought, then noticed their CL still hunched over in a corner of the CIC, quiet as a mouse.

"Mr. Nesbit, I'd almost forgotten you were here. I'm not used to you being so discreet."

"Just cherishing in my last few minutes of living, Commander."

"If you'd prefer to spend them in your quarters with a good book and a stiff contraband drink, no one would think the lesser of you."

Nesbit stood and faced the room, back straight. "If it's all the same to you, I'd rather stand my watch."

Miguel huffed through his nose and smirked with genuine surprise. "As you were, CL." Feeling a moment of sentimentality creep in, he keyed the 1MC and linked it to the mic in his chair.

"Attention, crew of the *Ansari*, this is Acting-Captain Azevedo. As you're all keenly aware, several hundred megatons of wrath are about to come knocking at our hatch. We're going to do everything we can not to let them in, but I just wanted you to know, no matter the outcome of the next twenty minutes, I've never been prouder about anything than I am right now to call every last one of you shipmates. One way or another, our captain is safe, she will survive, and our story will be told down through the ages. Hold fast to your stations, maintain vigilance, and we might just get to tell the story ourselves over shots and beers. Don't give up the ship. Azevedo out."

A cheer went up around the CIC as Miguel cut the link.

"Great speech, XO," Warner said. "You scared off three missiles with words alone."

TWENTY-EIGHT

Susan obsessed over the tactical plot, desperately searching for something, anything she might have overlooked that could give them an extra sliver of hope against what was coming down on her and her friends and crew a thousand kilometers behind her.

Ansari would take the brunt of it, but *Halcyon* had to be ready for any strays that got through and reverted to targets of opportunity, and it had a much less robust CiWS system and no countermissiles for the task. In all likelihood, *Ansari* was about to fall to the swarm of predators coming their way and there wasn't a thing she could do about it. Then, exposed and alone, she'd have to order her little hijacked frigate, never designed or intended for extended operations in deep space, to bubble out to God-only-knew where as a fugitive, without hope of support or resupply, onboard a ship where her allies numbered less than a dozen and the original crew was sure to try and retake their home.

If she'd ever been in a more precarious situation, it didn't spring immediately to mind.

"*Ansari* just deployed their reflector cloud," Okuda said. "Our sensors are blind to anything happening on the other side of it.

We're tied into the feed from their towed array and surviving re-con platforms, for as long as they last."

"Thank you, Sergeant. Culligan, get our countermeasures ready for launch. Charts, charge our rings and be prepared to bubble out at a moment's notice."

"Course, mum?" her pilot from the assault shuttle asked. Like all marine aviators, he'd been cross-trained in handling capital ships, because in combat, you just never knew who the next man up would have to be. Not that his instructors had ever guessed they were training a pirate. *No, not a pirate,* Susan reprimanded herself. Perez had resigned her commission the moment she ordered the shuttle she believed Susan on destroyed, whether she realized it or not, making *Susan* the rightful, legal ranking officer in the combat area. Her people were not pirates. They were in the right. They'd liberated the *Halcyon* from mutineers.

Whether a court-martial inquiry would agree was a question for a later date. Right now, she'd be grateful just to live long enough to see one.

"Our antimatter stores are down by a third. Make course for the AM factory in Grendel orbit. We can probably top off before *Allen* realizes where we've bubbled to. Maybe even offload our potential troublemakers."

"Aye, mum."

Unspoken was the fact off-loading their "troublemakers" would leave them below a skeleton crew for even such a small ship, but it was important to prioritize existential crises and tackle them one at a time instead of all at once.

"First contact with the missile wave in T-minus five minutes, four-three seconds," Culligan said. "*Ansari* main laser array is engaging the leading missiles."

Susan fought the urge to order the *Halcyon* out of line to try and pick off a few birds with her own laser, but the *Zephyr*-class fast frigate didn't have emitters in the rear forty-five degrees of her aspect, and its thrust vectoring was limited to fifteen degrees off-bore, so she couldn't crab-walk the ship enough to get a firing solution with one of her lateral emitters, which would mean cutting thrust, turning to face the threat, shrinking the distance between them and the *Ansari* protecting them, and reducing their response time for any missiles that did get past.

No go. All there was left to do now was run for their lives.

"Bubble burst! Bubble burst!" Culligan shouted. "Bearing ahead two-one-eight by zero-zero-seven. Range, seventeen thousand kilometers. Four-hundred-thousand-ton range."

Susan's heart sank through the deck plating. So, Perez had a reserve in hiding and called it up, and they were running straight into the teeth of it. They had twelve missiles left onboard after the surprise attack on *Carnegie*, in addition to their laser array. A paltry sum for dealing with anything bigger than a corsair's cobbled-together defenses. But if she was going to die, it would be with empty magazines.

"Okuda. Get our remaining birds in space and warm up the primary—"

"What the hell?" Culligan abruptly cut Susan off.

"You have something to share, Lieutenant?"

"Sorry, mum. The ship, it's not CCDF. It's . . . it's a Xre. Unknown configuration."

Susan jumped out of her chair, pulse racing as a glimmer of hope punched through the despair, and looked at the raw data coming in from their sensors. Of course it registered as unknown. The fleet recognition database hadn't had time to go through an update yet.

"It's not unknown, that's the bloody *Chusexx*!" she shouted triumphantly. Then, a very scary thought occurred to her. "Open a channel to the Xre cruiser."

"What?!"

"Just do it!"

Culligan's face looked down in disbelief at her hands as if they were moving of their own volition. "Channel open."

"Derstu Thuk! This is Captain Kamala onboard the *Zephyr*-class frigate. Repeat, aboard the frigate. We've taken her over. The *Zephyr* is a friendly. Do not engage. Please acknowledge."

Susan's breath caught in her throat as she waited for a response. Finally, the speakers crackled. "Susan Captain. How did you respond 'Forked Path Lament'?"

Her brain raced. It was Thuk's voice, probably. She was as sure as she could be with such limited experience with the species. He was testing her. But forked path? What the hell was he talking about? Forked path, different paths, taking different roads, splitting up. Ah! The song they sang when they parted ways.

"A twenty-one-gun salute," she yelled into the mic.

"Much well. Move frigate and *Ansari* to side. We salute enemy." The line went dead.

"Captain," Culligan said. "They're charging their rings again."

"Oh, shit. You heard him, get out of the way. Tell *Ansari* to follow our lead, questions can wait."

The nimble little frigate answered the helm and dove hard to port to clear the path for the newcomer to engage the *Paul Allen*. *Ansari* followed suit more slowly, owing to her larger mass and the grip Newton continued to have over objects in motion.

"*Chusexx*, we're clear. You are free to maneuver."

No one was prepared for what came next.

"Two sling bolts are in position, Derstu," Kivits announced. "The weapon is charged."

"Nearing alignment with the target," said the tiller attendant.

Thuk watched the display with both excitement and something like sympathy. The enormous human assault ship, the *Paul Allen* according to Susan, continued charging forward heedlessly to close the range and engage the new threat without a care in the world. And why shouldn't they? Even outnumbered now three-to-one by the *Chusexx, Ansari,* and *Halcyon,* one of those behemoths could be reasonably confident of victory in any normal engagement.

What no one outside of Thuk's harmony knew was just how abnormal this fight was going to be. Provided everything actually worked.

"Alignment achieved. Ready to loose."

Thuk looked at Kivits, then pointed at the icon of the *Allen*. "You wanted something to test it on. We could hardly ask for a better target than one of their newest assault ships running straight for us."

"Agreed." Kivits rubbed a mandible. "I wouldn't have guessed it would be while coming to the rescue of a human ship, however."

"The universe is infinite. Dulac, you may loose the weapon."

As had happened hundreds of times in the past, and would hundreds of times more in the future, warfare changed with the pull of a trigger. Outside, in the small rings built into the *Chusexx*'s main rings, a "sling bolt" the length of five adult Xre was enveloped inside its own miniature seedpod and given a push. It was not a javelin, what the humans called a "missile." It had no onboard propulsion. Indeed, from its vantage point, it never moved at all. It had no warhead of explosives, either conventional or nuclear, because it didn't need them. It had no guidance system, because it couldn't maneuver even if it wanted to. It had no AI to help it identify decoys and defeat countermeasures. It scarcely had a computer at all. Instead, its entire interior was filled with spool capacitors and a tiny amount of negative matter to let the bolt pierce the seedpod, tripped by a very clever proximity sensor built to detect the slightest changes in the seedpod's shape that would indicate it was interacting with a mass outside.

And that's all it needed to be.

What happened next occurred in a space of time so brief as to defy description. Traveling at many hundreds of multiples of light-speed, the bolt covered the distance between the *Chusexx* and the *Paul Allen* near-instantaneously. The moment the seedpod contacted the hull of the carrier, the sensor inside tripped and tore open the seedpod. There was no explosion in the conventional sense, at least not at first. Instead, the collapsing seedpod warped and distorted a small area of local space with such violence that anything within the field of effect was torn apart down to nearly the molecular level.

This occurred between the *Allen's* gamma ray shield cone and its first tier of antimatter containment vessels, rupturing them and releasing an apocalyptic amount of energy, instantly destroying the fusion rocket cluster, AM and He3 storage tanks, and shattering the great ship's keel. Usually, even a loss of antimatter containment wasn't enough to destroy an entire ship, as the shield cone was designed to direct the force of the explosion away from the engineering and primary hulls, leaving half a ship unable to fight or maneuver, but still with reserve power for life support and communications.

But a third of the shield had been ripped apart by the seedpod collapse, channeling the force of the blast deep into the engineering hull, setting off secondary explosions as drone platforms, probes, counter-missile magazines, and eventually shuttle fuel reserves and ground support munitions all added to the cascading carnage.

In the span of a breath, all that remained of the *Paul Allen,* the most powerful warship humanity had ever put to space, was a gutted, drifting shell of armor plating and melted structural steel.

There were no survivors. There was no reason to loose the second bolt.

The stunned silence in *Ansari's* CIC was total. Long faces stared at the tactical plot, at each other, or at nothing at all. Miguel was the first to compose himself. "We still have birds incoming, everyone."

That snapped them out of it. There were indeed still seventy-three orphaned missiles from the *Allen* coming their way. But with their mother's datalinks now silent and reverted to autonomous control, they quickly lost cohesion and became easy prey for Warner as her fingers danced across the CiWS and countermissile controls. She stopped the last missile a few hundred meters short of optimal detonation range. The only injury they sustained was from missile fragments peppering the hull like birdshot.

"Damage report," Miguel requested calmly.

"We're down a lidar array portside forward. And one of our CiWS modules took a hit to its independent radar, but we can tie it into the rest of the sensor net. Minor damage to half a dozen compartments, showing loss of pressure in four of them, but slow. Holes can't be very big, they'll be easy to patch. One casualty reported, a boomer tech took shrapnel to the calf. Headed to the infirmary now, not life-threatening."

Miguel shook his head in disbelief. By rights, he should be surrounded by fire and screaming and alarms, if he was still alive at all. Instead . . .

"Sir, *Halcyon* Actual on the line."

"Put her through."

"Miguel?" Susan's voice said through the room. "Are you seeing this?"

"Seeing it. Still not sure about believing it."

"I know what you mean. We're showing some light venting coming from your hull. How's the damage?"

"Minimal. All hands accounted for. We made it. Now I'd just like to know *how* we made it."

"Isn't it obvious?" Susan asked. "Our new Xre friends were holding out on us. Those little rings in their rings weren't for FTL maneuvering. They're an Alcubierre railgun."

TWENTY-NINE

Forty-eight hours later, Susan found herself sitting at a conference table onboard *Ansari,* surrounded by the most improbable company imaginable. Warner, Mattu, and Okuda sat to her left. To her right, acting captain of the CCDF *Halcyon* Miguel Azevedo and his newly minted XO, Lieutenant Francine Culligan. Across the table from them sat, or in two cases knelt, Xre Derstu Thuk, Dulac Kivits, Attendant Hurg, Attendant Lynz, and visibly unsettled corporate liaison Javier Nesbit, only because there weren't any more chairs on the human side of the table for him to occupy.

After the dust settled from the battle, Susan pulled rank to get her ship back, but Miguel got to keep a command, so he couldn't complain much. On her suggestion, he'd picked Culligan as his first officer in recognition of her service during the battle against what had begun as her own task group. Much to everyone's surprise, she'd managed to talk another half-dozen of her shipmates into crossing the line as well, easing the number of billets they'd have to fill from *Ansari*'s ranks to keep the fast frigate operating.

The last two days had been a blur of activity, dominated by rescue operations onboard the crippled *Carnegie,* stripping the carcass of the same, and shuttling survivors down to the recently vacated civilian facilities on the surface of Grendel. *Carnegie* had suffered significant casualties and quite a few KIA during the battle, primarily from the sucker-punch delivered by *Halcyon* before they'd realized it had been commandeered. Several of the wounded were still in *Ansari*'s infirmary in critical condition and would have to remain there for the foreseeable future. The walking wounded were transferred down to the planet's surface with their shipmates.

"Where are we on integrating our salvage from *Carnegie*?" Susan asked.

"Nearly finished," Warner answered. "We're still running updates on the older Mk VIII birds we lifted to bring them up to spec with our AI network, couple bugs to code out, but nothing insurmountable. They're a little slower than the Mk IXs, but we're back up to seventy-eight percent magazine capacity. Counter-missile and CiWS ammo is even better. We're topped off with room to spare between both us and *Halcyon*."

"Throw the rest in a cargo bay. No idea when we're going to lay hands on more of it."

"Agreed, mum."

"How about the rest of our consumables? Water, provisions, fuel?"

"We're in the green on all of it," Okuda, who had been coordinating flight ops to and from the surface answered. "Water tanks are full, He3 at ninety-three percent, and antimatter stuffed to the rafters with enough left to tank up our, um, new allies." Okuda glanced across the table to Thuk, whose mouthparts moved into such a position it could, charitably, be assumed to be an approximation of a smile.

"Grateful," the translator matrix provided. "Easier if our reservoir not blown up."

"I said I was sorry," Susan replied. "But in fairness, we were technically still enemies at that point."

"Artistic done."

Susan laughed. "Thank you, I *was* rather proud of it. How long until the machine shop finishes that adaptor collar so *Chusexx* can hook up with the AM factory?"

"Another day, mum," Mattu said. With Miguel on detached duty, she'd gotten a field promotion to XO and was busy juggling a dozen time-critical projects. Everything was time-critical. They'd sent *Halcyon* back to Grendel in time to disable the task group's skip drone before it automatically bubbled out for the Admiralty House with everything it had seen, and the system was already on a civilian travel lockdown, so they had three days left before anyone would realize the *Allen* was overdue, and another five before any reinforcements dispatched to investigate would arrive.

It was the first time Susan had felt any sort of gratitude for being assigned to such a far-flung outpost, but every day they lingered was a day lost on the lead they had over whatever would eventually be sent to finish them off. And if a Planetary Assault Carrier task group hadn't done the trick the first time, she didn't even want to think about what the response would be this time, from either side.

She looked across the table to Thuk's people. They'd been betrayed by their own as well. Someone from within their "Symphony" had sabotaged the *Chusexx,* hoping to cause a flashpoint for war. And Susan was absolutely convinced someone on her side of the Red Line had intended the *Ansari* to be the spark. When that failed, the system's civilians were evacuated and the *Paul Allen* sent to make sure they could spin whatever story they'd wanted the public to hear.

Unsurprisingly, the news hadn't sat well with either of them, and Thuk's act of gratitude solidified into a more permanent alliance on the spot. Which, while an immense relief, carried its own unique challenges and obstacles.

"Thuk, have you found any of our food that you can use yet?"

The Xre's face made a strange gesture that, if she had to guess, was probably some permutation of disgust. So, he'd been subjecting himself to the food trials. Susan imagined herself diving into a plate of live bugs and had a similar reaction, so she could relate on some level.

"Search continue," Thuk said politely, as diplomatic an answer as any.

Susan nodded sympathetically. "We're prioritizing staple foods for deep storage, survival bars of simple proteins, sugars, and carbohydrates. They should work in a pinch, even for your physiology. Sorry they're not . . . wriggling."

"We endure," Kivits said. Susan hadn't heard enough out of the four-legged worker caste to get a feel for his inflections, but he sounded resigned to his fate.

"We endure together, one . . . mound," she said, borrowing the Xre word for community, hoping it came off as genuine and not appropriation. "Anyway, we have some breathing room for the time being. But we need to start thinking about what our plan is going forward. Where are we going next? What are our objectives? We're adrift without a compass here. We need to decide on—"

The 1MC erupted in an alert. At the same time, an urgent message flashed red in Susan's AR field.

CAPTAIN TO THE CIC.

"Set Condition Two," Susan snapped off as she got out of her chair. "We're moving this meeting to the CIC. Double time."

Three decks up and a short jog down the main corridor later, Susan's strange retinue approached the hatch to the CIC, where a now-veteran-but-still-junior private saw them and snapped his PDW to a low ready position and held out a hand quite obviously directed at the Xre.

"Halt!" he commanded.

"They're with me, Culligan," Susan barked in annoyance. "We're friends now, remember?"

Culligan turned white and let his weapon dangle at his side as he moved his hand for a hasty salute. "Yes, mum. Sorry, mum. Old habits."

"Adapt," she said as she crossed the threshold.

Miguel thumped him on the forehead as he passed. "Hope your sister got the brains."

"Sorry, sir."

To their credit, the Xre said nothing. The CIC settled into a cramped, surreal scene. Thuk, without knowing it, took over Nesbit's worry corner, sending the CL to the other side of the compartment.

"What's the matter, Thuk? First time in a human CIC?" Warner poked.

"Obvious. Dream it different," Thuk shot back to everyone's amusement. "Still, much like mind cavern. Lights different."

Susan dropped into the familiar contours of her chair. "Sit rep?"

"Platform Six picked up a bubble burst on the far side of Grendel," Mattu answered as she relieved the crewman manning her station. "It's big. Seven hundred fifty thousand tons."

"Action stations," Susan ordered. "Cut us loose from the station and warm up the—"

"Hold up," Mattu cut in with just a bit more confidence than she might have before they'd all committed to a course best described as legally gray. "Civilian transponder. Bulk cargo hauler, that's why she's so big. *Preakness,* flagged under Ageless Corp."

"Verify that," Susan said.

"Visuals confirm it, mum. Triple drive plume, standardized containers strapped to a skeletal keel. It's an ore hauler or I'll eat my enlistment contract."

Susan considered the updated plot, and still didn't like what she was seeing. Any incoming civilian traffic would've been waved off before the *Allen's* task group set course. If they were actually civilians, whomever had just bubbled in knew damned well they weren't supposed to be in Grendel space. Mattu uttered something in Hindi that Susan could only assume was a vicious curse.

"Well, Scopes? Are you going to share with the rest of the class?"

Mattu turned from her station with a haunted look. "The *Preakness* was last reported in orbit around Lazarus under medical quarantine for a bacterial outbreak it was involved in on Teegarden. It's a plague ship, mum."

Susan's eyes went wide as soup bowls. "Beg pardon?"

Nesbit raised a hand from his new corner of the CIC. "Ah, Captain? I'm getting a connection request from *Preakness*. Except it's not really the *Preakness*."

"You're what?" she blurted. "How are you getting a connection request?"

"Because I'm the damned corporate liaison on this ship and I have a direct channel in my head for C-level transtellar execs."

"And you mean to tell me there's a goddammed C-suit ringing in your brain right now?"

"Yeah," Nesbit nodded emphatically. "And you *really* need to take this call."

Susan rubbed the bridge of her nose, simultaneously hoping and failing to cut off the budding stress headache. She'd had weird days in service of the CCDF. She'd had weird days as a civilian. But this, this one took the blue ribbon by a light-year.

"Okay, what the hell? Mattu, if you'll release permissions to Mr. Nesbit to access the main display so he can put his important call through?"

"Permissions granted, mum."

All eyes, of both species, turned to face the . . . face that appeared in the tactical plot. A fit man with a square jaw and blue eyes that looked just south of gene-spliced and a shock of straight hair losing the battle against graying. Susan guessed he was within a handful of years of her own age. Which direction, she couldn't say.

"This is Captain Susan Kamala, commanding officer of the CCDF cruiser *Ansari* and acting . . . spokeswoman of the combined Human/Xre task group *Christmas Truce*." They hadn't actually agreed to the name. She'd just pulled it from memory and decided it had some emotional gravity to it. "Whom am I addressing?"

"Well, now *that* is the picture of a motley crew if I've ever seen one," the unidentified silver fox said as he surveyed everyone present in the CIC in turn. "You all seem to be getting along famously."

"State your name and business in the Grendel system, sir," Susan clapped back in irritation. "Or we'll have to assume your intentions are hostile and respond accordingly."

"The Grendel system *is* my business, Captain Kamala. Both literally and figuratively. My name is Tyson Abington, CEO of Ageless Corporation, majority stakeholder in the planet we mutually orbit, and one-twelfth of the bosses who hold your contract."

A corner of Susan's mouth curled up into a vicious sneer. The universe had handed her a gift. The once-in-a-lifetime chance to properly shove one of these empty sport-jackets into their proper station.

"Grendel has recently undergone an abrupt change of ownership, Mr. Abington. You may hold the legal papers, but I currently hold all the nuclear missiles, and you're transmitting from what my drone integration officer tells me is a ship that's broken medical quarantine, giving me complete authority under the CCDF Charter to reduce you to your constituent atoms if I feel like it. So, let's start over. Why are you here, and what, if anything, can you do for me?"

Tyson, if he was indeed who he claimed to be, had the cheek to smirk and lean back while he considered the threat to his life she'd just laid down. He crossed his fingers over his flat stomach, then brightened. "I apologize, Captain Kamala. You've obviously had a busy time out here and don't need some company bigwig barging in. I came on too strong; it's a personal failing."

"I've no doubt of that."

Tyson held up a hand—not to silence her, but a request for a pause. "We are not a plague ship. In reality, we're the Nexus-flagged

Taipei. We traded IDs with the *Preakness* to escape Lazarus undetected. I assure you, there is none of the Teegarden contagion onboard this ship. And even if there was, I'm sitting next to the woman who's going to cure it."

Susan tugged at an earlobe. "You had to escape your own planet, Mr. Abington? I find that strains my suspension of disbelief."

"It's been a strange couple of months. The fact you're sitting there with Xre on your bridge who are not shackled or otherwise under guard tells me you've come to some sort of realization, yes?"

"That would be an understatement."

"And the absence of the task group the fleet sent out here to avenge your 'death' means the real story is quite a bit more complicated, right?"

"Actually, we absorbed part of that task group," Susan said, brimming with pride at the improbable feat. "The part we didn't eradicate."

"Fascinating."

"That doesn't alarm you, Mr. Abington? Because a normal person would be spooling up their rings to get the ever-loving fuck out of here by now."

Tyson actually snorted in amusement. "They would indeed. That's why they're normal. But we aren't, are we, Captain? Or your, *our,* new friends. I think not." The man in the perfectly tailored suit, with the perfectly coifed hair, let out a sigh that he'd been holding in for a week.

"As implausible as it seems, Captains, we three have a common enemy. I believe they set you on a collision course as part of a campaign to see my transtellar fall. And I need your help unmasking them so they can be brought to justice."

"And I suppose you have a plan to bring that about that our forces are somehow critical to."

"Well, now that you mention it, I very much need to get to Ceres to ask some questions of a citizen there."

Susan's head shook involuntarily as if she'd been physically struck. "I'm sorry, did you just say you wanted our help to invade the *Sol system*?"

Tyson held out his hands and smiled in a gesture that was equal parts accommodating and placating. "'Invade' is such a loaded word. 'Infiltrate' may better fit the circumstances. But yes, Captain Kamala. I'm going to Earth, and you're coming with me."

ACKNOWLEDGMENTS

It's customary at this point in writing a novel to spend a page or so acknowledging all the people other than oneself whose time and talents went into helping bring it into the world. People like agents, editors, cover artists, beta readers, significant others, and other authors whose own words were the foundation on which a new story was built.

And just as in my five previous books, all of these people deserve credit and appreciation. But I've banged on about them five times already and they know who they are.

Instead, I want to use this space to acknowledge all the people who have inspired me in the years since this book was written. You see, the first draft of *In the Black* was completed in 2017, before it took a somewhat circuitous road to publication. At the time, I knew I wanted to talk about certain issues growing in importance, like the expanding wealth gap, the different reality inhabited by the superwealthy, the privatization of the military, and the corporatization of space.

What I didn't know in 2017 was how timely a potential deadly pandemic and the competence of the government response would be when *Black* finally hit the shelves. It was a lack of imagination that led me to believe even a narcissistic ass like Tyson

Abington would recognize the potential threat to his planet and immediately enact science-based measures to contain and defeat it. Wow was that naive, huh?

Anyway, since writing this book, a series of Earth-shattering crises have arisen as a direct result of leadership failures in America and beyond. The COVID-19 pandemic, the resulting world-wide recession, and history-making Black Lives Matter protests against police brutality have all left indelible marks on the entire human village. Life may never return entirely to "normal" again, instead forging ahead to create a new normal that protects and affirms the importance of everyone.

This reckoning was decades in the making, and was only exacerbated by generations of leaders making empty gestures and paying platitudes to problems we've all seen coming from a very long way off. But it's also elevated a new era of protesters, politicians, and creatives who've emerged as beacons of hope and change.

It's these people who are inspiring me today as I write the next chapter of Susan Kamala's, Tyson Abington's, and Thuk's journey, and it's them I want to acknowledge here. Every NYC doctor, nurse, orderly, janitor, and EMT who worked double shifts for weeks at a time as coronavirus ravaged one of the greatest cities on Earth. Every crafter who turned their sewing machine into a DIY face-mask factory. Every small business owner who drained their savings to keep their employees paid during lockdown. Every employee who pressed on through the uncertainty of making rent. Every last person who grabbed a mask and a cardboard sign and marched in a thousand cities all across the world to demand an end to police brutality and racial inequality with a backdrop of record-breaking unemployment and pandemic.

Science fiction, at its core, imagines a future where we all lived through this to build something better, together. That's its foundational premise in many ways. And it starts today, with you, and all of us. You are the heroes, now. You are who we've been waiting for.

Don't give up the ship.

ABOUT THE AUTHOR

Patrick S. Tomlinson lives in Milwaukee, Wisconsin. When not writing sci-fi and fantasy novels and short stories, Tomlinson is busy developing his other passion: stand-up comedy.